THE
BRIDES

THE BRIDES

Charlotte Cross

NIGHTFIRE

First published 2026 by Tor Nightfire
an imprint of Pan Macmillan
The Smithson, 6 Briset Street, London EC1M 5NR
EU representative: Macmillan Publishers Ireland Ltd, 1st Floor,
The Liffey Trust Centre, 117–126 Sheriff Street Upper,
Dublin 1 D01 YC43
Associated companies throughout the world

ISBN 978-1-0350-5926-3 HB
ISBN 978-1-0350-5927-0 TPB

Copyright © Charlotte Cross 2026

The right of Charlotte Cross to be identified as the
author of this work has been asserted in accordance with
the Copyright, Designs and Patents Act 1988.

All rights reserved. No part of this publication may be reproduced, stored in
a retrieval system, or transmitted, in any form, or by any means (including,
without limitation, electronic, mechanical, photocopying, recording or
otherwise) without the prior written permission of the publisher.

Pan Macmillan does not have any control over, or any responsibility for,
any author or third-party websites (including, without limitation, URLs,
emails and QR codes) referred to in or on this book.

1 3 5 7 9 8 6 4 2

A CIP catalogue record for this book is available from the British Library.

Typeset in Adobe Caslon Pro by Six Red Marbles UK, Thetford, Norfolk
Printed and bound in the UK using 100% Renewable Electricity by CPI Group (UK) Ltd

This book is sold subject to the condition that it shall not, by way of
trade or otherwise, be lent, hired out, or otherwise circulated without
the publisher's prior consent in any form of binding or cover other than
that in which it is published and without a similar condition including this
condition being imposed on the subsequent purchaser. The publisher does not
authorize the use or reproduction of any part of this book in any manner
for the purpose of training artificial intelligence technologies or systems.
The publisher expressly reserves this book from the Text and Data Mining
exception in accordance with Article 4(3) of the European Union
Digital Single Market Directive 2019/790.

Visit **www.panmacmillan.com** to read more about
all our books and to buy them.

For Trev

THE
BRIDES

PROLOGUE

It is my beloved and yet not. It is some creature, wrong, twisted inside, made vile in a manner for which I do not have words. Her smile is not of warmth but of some species of malice, of cruelty, of hunger. The green dress she wears, made for a woman long dead in an era long past, fits her like snakeskin.

'Come here, my love,' she whispers in her siren's voice. 'Come to me and kiss me, and we will be together for ever.' She moves closer, holding out her cold white hand. 'Is this not what you have always wanted? Come to me, and be mine for eternity.'

PART ONE

Sir John Seward's personal diary
Monday, 5th January 1903
Littlemore Hospital, Oxfordshire

Sitting in the train, I gazed out of the window and allowed my mind to wander. The hills rolled by, gentle raindrops ran down the glass, and the rhythm of the wheels lulled me into a half-doze.

Slowly, from nowhere at all, I began to feel a prickling of unease. It was of a kind which would have been familiar to our distant ancestors, those poor brutes who in such early days were still prey to beasts more vicious than themselves. The feeling grew and grew until I was almost nauseous with it. Gradually, so gradually, a mist appeared on the very edge of my field of vision. I felt I sensed rather than saw it coalescing. From the corner of my eye, I caught a glimpse of a familiar long, pale face. My heart began to pound, my head turned of its own volition, and at last I saw him, fixing me with his cold red stare through the glass of the compartment door. A hideous smile stretched to breaking point across his ghastly visage, flashing those brilliant sharp white teeth. Carefully, deliberately, never taking his eyes from mine, he reached for the door handle.

I awoke with a start at the sound of the guard announcing my stop. I hurried on my Ulster coat and my new bowler hat, still a little too tight, and tried to shake off the nightmare which has dogged me in various guises for almost a decade. As ever, I had little success.

It was cold and damp when I stepped off the train at Littlemore railway station. I was the only passenger to alight. I wondered for the thousandth time if I had made the right choice in accepting this post, but I couldn't stay in Essex with my memories forever. I crossed over the footbridge to the lodge carrying only my valise, my trunks having been sent on ahead. Before me, the asylum buildings seemed to vanish away into the mist. Their butter-coloured Cotswold stone and overhanging eaves were no longer so pleasing to the eye as they had been on my previous visit in the warm autumn glow of late September.

I presented my letters of introduction to the guard at the gatehouse. He signed me in with a 'Welcome, guv'nor,' and handed me off to a stout orderly to show me to my new home.

The orderly, Burton, informed me that he had orders to take me to meet Deputy Director Knight at my earliest convenience. There being no time like the present, I declined the opportunity to deposit my valise with my new housekeeper and followed Burton across to the main building. After quite a climb to the top floor, during which I rather regretted my decision to keep hold of my valise, Burton shepherded me down a long corridor before stopping suddenly outside a door bearing the legend 'Deputy Director'. I briefly wondered where my own office might be, but Burton was already propelling me through the door before I could catch my breath to ask.

The room beyond was bright and airy. Tall windows looked out to the north, showing the university's dreaming spires poking upwards out of the mist. Only three miles separate the asylum from Oxford's hallowed halls of learning but it might as well be three hundred. Floor-to-ceiling bookshelves lined the walls, excepting where a new-fangled filing cabinet squatted in a corner next to an empty hatstand.

My deputy was seated behind a grand mahogany desk, studying a patient's file.

'Sir John,' she said, laying her reading material aside and getting up to shake me by the hand. 'We're so glad to have you join us here. Would you care for a drink?'

At almost my height, she came closer to six feet tall than any woman I have yet met. Her practical attire marked her out as what my dear departed wife Kate would approvingly call a New Woman – entirely appropriate for our profession, naturally. Her hair was flaming red and her skin significantly freckled, I imagine as a result of her having been several years in India before coming to Littlemore.

'Yes, thank you.'

'You're very welcome.' She poured from a decanter set on one of the bookshelves. It was Scotch, and rather good Scotch at that. 'Please do sit down.'

I sat in one of two chairs opposite the desk. Instead of resuming her place behind it, Dr Knight took the seat next to me and turned it so that we almost faced each other.

'I am glad to meet you in person at last,' I began.

'Likewise, Sir John, likewise. I'm a great admirer of yours.' She took a sip from her glass, wincing only a little at the burn. 'In Bombay I used to await my copies of *Nature* and *The Lancet* with great impatience, in case you'd published a new paper.'

I have never been much good at receiving compliments.

'Goodness, I mean, thank you very much,' I stuttered.

'I don't mean to flatter. I'm truly glad to be working with you.'

I hoped that the blush I felt threatening my cheeks was only in my imagination.

'So,' Dr Knight continued, 'I believe this is a rather different sort of establishment than you're used to?'

She leaned on the arm of her chair and rested her chin between thumb and forefinger in an attitude of great concentration.

'Yes. My private asylum, Carfax, was a great deal smaller. Your own experience with hospitals of this size will compensate for the deficiency in mine, I'm sure.'

'I hope the same regarding my lack of experience in scientific publication. I'm very keen to publish any research that we do here, so I hope I can look to you to share your greater knowledge.'

'I would be delighted. I'm sure we'll make an excellent team.'

She swirled the Scotch in her glass, and took another sip.

'I hope so, Sir John. I certainly hope so.'

Was there some more subtle meaning to her words, I wonder? I suspect that in the past Dr Knight will have worked with those who did not respect her opinion merely by reason of her being a woman. I would almost expect it from some members of our profession. I admit that I once held to ideas of the inferiority of the female sex, but in my life I have been fortunate enough to know such excellent women as must put thoroughly paid to such nonsense. My friend Jonathan Harker's wife Mina, for one, and my own dear Kate for another. Ah, Kate. I have finally done as she bid me, and begun to rebuild my life without her. She would chide me for how long it has taken, but I hope she would be proud that I have made a start.

'Well, now that we are a little acquainted,' Dr Knight said, returning my wandering mind to the present moment, 'we must turn to business. I assumed you'd rather not address the staff until the morning, given how fatiguing travel can be. I've arranged a briefing in the Assembly Hall for nine o'clock tomorrow. Afterwards, I'll take you on a tour of the premises. Will that suit?'

'Yes, thank you. I appreciate your forethought.'

'Not at all. It's my pleasure.'

I wondered if this was my cue to leave and almost began to rise from my chair, but Dr Knight raised a hand to stop me.

'I do realize you must be keen to get settled in but there's one other matter I'd like to bring to your attention before you go, if you'll permit.'

'Yes, of course.'

'I've agreed to a patient referral from a private institution in Yorkshire, concerning zoophagy. The patient's family asked for you specifically, given your expertise on the subject.'

I wish I could have told Dr Knight how much I would give never to have learned of zoophagy, never to have been forced to make the unnatural consumption of animals a subject of detailed study.

'I see. When do we expect him?'

'Her. The patient is a woman. A lady, in fact.'

I shook my head, confused.

'I'd understood that here we don't—'

'No, our patients are generally not of the upper classes. The lady's relatives understand this but were most insistent she be treated by you, being the foremost specialist in the condition.'

'Is zoophagy her only symptom?'

'You can see for yourself,' she said, indicating the open file on her desk. 'I've only just begun, but it makes for grim reading. She's been in a medical establishment of one sort or another for years, and was cared for at home for some time before that.'

'So I see,' I replied, standing to look through the pages. 'Recurring nightmares, fits of uncontrollable weeping, insomnia, hallucinations, physical symptoms including dizziness, sick headaches, decreased immune function . . . This is quite the list. Ah, the zoophagy is recent.'

'Yes, the onset was only a few months ago.'

'It's odd that she developed this so recently when all her other symptoms have been present for much longer. I wonder if there was a trigger of some sort.'

'I thought the same. We might be able to ask her, when she's in a lucid state. If you look at Dr Raxworthy's referral notes he writes that she has sustained periods of lucidity, although he found no pattern in when those manifested.'

'We'll learn something from her response, rational or otherwise.' I thought for a moment. 'Excepting the zoophagy I believe I've seen such symptoms appearing together before, in soldiers returning from the battlefield. I had occasion to treat several veterans in my previous institution, and I wonder if she was exposed to warfare. Does this Raxworthy say anything about that?'

'No, I don't believe so.'

'Perhaps some deep emotional injury, then. Does she have children?'

'Yes, two. Why?'

'I wondered if she had lost a child, or perhaps suffered greatly beyond the usual measure in childbirth.'

Dr Knight fell silent as she squinted through the notes in Dr Raxworthy's terrible scrawl.

'No lost children as far as I can see. Looking back to the late eighties, before she became unwell, I see that her family doctor, a Dr Williamson, attended the births of both her children. They seem to have been very straightforward, though I could be in error; his handwriting is even worse than Dr Raxworthy's.'

She handed me the relevant papers, somewhat yellowed with age. The writing was barely legible. I found myself running my finger underneath every word and sounding out each one under my breath like a schoolboy.

'Do we have photographs of the patient?' I asked, when I had waded through the dense scrawl of this long-ago colleague. While the usefulness of psychiatric photography continues to be debated, I have found it helpful on occasion.

'One moment.'

Dr Knight got to her feet and dug through the reams of paper for quite a lot longer than one moment, eventually unearthing three rather battered photographs dated just after onset in 1893, and a fourth dated 1900.

I studied them carefully, taking my time. The first set depicted a beautiful young woman with an unfocused gaze and a somewhat sleepy countenance, a look I have seen before on those who have dissociated from their surroundings. In the pictures, she wore a long white nightdress with her hair braided down over her shoulder, a veritable study in early matronhood. The fourth image, however, showed her as she was three years ago – blurred, gnashing her teeth, and struggling against the orderly restraining her. The sight moved me so deeply that I didn't notice Dr Knight attempting to get my attention.

'Sir John! I might have something significant. Sir John?'

'My apologies. What is it?'

'It could be the emotional injury you hypothesized. Look at this letter.' She held out an aging piece of paper, covered in some kind of German copperplate. 'It seems to have been kept in with the family doctor's records, from late August of 1884.'

'1884? So much earlier?'

'Indeed. The patient was holidaying on the Continent when she witnessed the deaths of several fellow travellers. It seems their carriage fell down a ravine. She survived, but was left stranded in the countryside overnight during a severe rainstorm. She was treated in the Queen Elisabeth hospital in Buda-Pesth for possible pneumonia, and a Dr Arminius there wrote to Dr Williamson. For a young lady living a sheltered and respectable life, such an incident could have been very damaging.'

'I agree, but why then did her mental illness not develop until a full, what, nine years after the fact?'

Dr Knight sighed. 'I don't know.'

'Neither do I, yet. I'll give it some thought.'

'As will I. Thank you, Sir John. I appreciate your giving me so much of your time when you've only just arrived.'

'Not at all.'

We shook hands again, and our interview was over. I found myself a little sorry for it.

Burton had waited for me and he escorted me to the superintendent's house, or rather, my house, back the way we had come. I found the place to be well-appointed and neatly furnished, though of a size to accommodate a family rather than a widower. After a brief tidying of my person and a light dinner, I retired to my study to write these notes. I cannot seem to give the habit up, and it serves me better than the phonograph recordings I used to make even if it takes rather longer. Now I find my eyes growing heavy, and as tomorrow will likely be an exhausting day, I am headed for bed. I'm sure I will sleep badly as everyone does at first in new surroundings, and that is even more reason for an early night. I hope that my sleep might be dreamless, but as always I will steel myself in case it is not. The human mind's capacity to hold on to long-past fears seems to be, unfortunately, infinite.

Letter: Alice Smith to Mary and Sarah Smith
Wednesday, 2nd April 1884
Whitby, Yorkshire, England

Dear Mam and Sarah,

I'm sorry I've not written sooner. I had to wait until my afternoon off to find the time. So far, I love living in Whitby. Today I walked all the way up the 199 steps to take in the view of the harbour.

When we went to church on Sunday we were hustled along so quickly there was no time to enjoy it. The Abbey ruin is almost right next door, and looks very majestic. Please don't be angry about me going to the Anglican church, Mam. Mrs Cartwright let me go to the early Mass at St Hilda's as long as I didn't make a to-do about it, but she did ask I go to St Mary's with the rest of the household for appearances' sake. This is how it's going to have to be, but I promise not to get swayed.

Mrs Cartwright is a much kinder lady than I'd ever hoped to serve. Her Christian name is Eliza, isn't that pretty? She's quite particular but always very clear in her instructions, which I've been writing down just so in my commonplace book. I always keep it in my pocket with a bright-yellow pencil so that every time something new comes up, I'm ready to make a note of it. The only times she's been at all stern are when she was talking about the importance of cleanliness for good health, and about followers not being allowed. I heard from Cook that the previous holder of my position got into trouble, so I see why my new mistress was so firm on that score. Cook says that Mrs Cartwright sent the girl off to Portsmouth with two months' pay in her purse, there to marry her Navy beau. What a thing! I could hardly believe it. Of course, you know I've no intention of any of that sort of nonsense.

There aren't many staff, only three housemaids, Cook and her kitchen maid Annie, and Morton the valet-cum-footman-cum-butler. Don't fret, Mam, he's too long in the tooth to be a threat to anyone's virtue. There's also old Nanny Roberts who takes care of Miss Elsbeth, called Beth. She's my mistress's sister, not daughter as I first thought, who she took in after their parents' deaths. It's very sad, but at least the little girl will be too young to remember any of it.

Look after yourselves, and remember to get to the butcher's as early as you can on Tuesdays. I send you all my love.

Alice

P.S. Sarah, don't read this out to Mam. May God forgive me for taking advantage of her blindness in this way, but I'd never want to make her worry.

I found the packet of lemon beebrush that you stashed in my trunk. Thank you! The last thing I need while I get settled is for the dreams to ruin my sleep. I know Nana, may she rest in peace, said that they're from God but they can be so terrible that I just don't always have the guts to face them. I still think of that nice old man at Bluebell Cottage, where they found the bodies of all those little children buried in the garden.

Please pray for me.

Lucy North's journal
Thursday, 3rd April 1884
Lowell House, Kensington, London, England

I have decided upon a career as a lady writer. Now that I am of age, I must prepare to earn my crust in the world and supplement my small income. No matter how often my Mafalda tells me she will take care of me, I do have a little pride. I would rather starve than take a post as a governess, and I have not the stomach to nurse. I might like to teach, but only if I could set up a school like the one I attended, long since closed, where we were taught a curriculum more expansive than just music and dancing and embroidery. Sadly, I do not have the necessary funds, or not yet. What I do have is this beautiful notebook which my dear friend Eliza sent from Whitby, and this elegant pen which Mafalda bought for me at Stanford's as my just-passed birthday gift. I feel like an ancient poetess rather than a modern lady of letters, but I am glad to begin my career with such marvellous tools. I vow to set down everything that happens to me as well as I can, and to hold nothing back.

At present it is evening, and Mafalda and I are sitting at home in the salon that connects our two bedrooms. There is no access from the hallway to this private space, so we are sure not to be disturbed. Mafalda is seated very upright at her bureau. She is writing a letter to her distant relative and our friend, Joseph, who has just returned to the country and who treated us to many delightful excursions and entertainments while he was in town. His birthday gift to me was a visit to Kew Gardens, which I enjoyed a great deal. I must ask Mafalda to reiterate my thanks in her letter.

From my position on the chaise, I see my darling in profile. I mark her high aquiline nose which some say is a sign of noble birth, her dark hair curling thickly down her back, her skin glowing golden in the candlelight, her black brows frowning slightly as she reads over what she has written. The cast of her face is beautiful, yet clearly of some other place than England. Her mother's Székely blood shows in her so strongly it is as if her father had barely anything to do with the matter, save for her eyes which are green rather than black. I ought to train myself to be a newspaperwoman, that would be most practical, but looking at Mafalda moves my soul to lyricism. I swear I could look at her for a lifetime and never tire of it.

I met her at school, when I was not quite thirteen. Mafalda was ushered into the classroom by the headmistress, partway through the autumn term. Her hair was plaited in one long snake that hung down over her left shoulder, and somehow the ugly school pinafore seemed the height of glamour on her tall and slender frame. Her face, startling in its uncommon beauty even then, was the very picture of fury. Mafalda was placed at the empty desk beside me and sat fuming throughout the rest of the lesson. I could barely concentrate for curiosity.

After the morning's classes were over and we filed out towards the dining hall, the headmistress appeared and drew Mafalda and I aside.

'Miss Lowell, as you have not attended school before and are unfamiliar with our rules and regulations, I am assigning Miss North to introduce you to how we do things. We want to ensure there are no more misunderstandings, don't we? Miss North, you will ensure that Miss Lowell settles in as quickly as possible.'

What misunderstandings had there been? I wondered, as the headmistress swept out and left us by ourselves in the empty corridor.

'The dining hall is this way,' I said, pointing.

'I'm not coming. I'm going home, and if that woman won't send me then I'll just have to get there myself.'

'You want to run away?' I didn't understand. The only home I had to return to was full of silences and hostility and everyone's private miseries.

'I don't see that it's any of your business.'

'The headmistress told me to take care of you.'

Mafalda scoffed. 'To be my jailer, perhaps.'

I didn't see what I could do other than physically restrain her, or go and tell tales. This was hugely frowned upon in our school, and even my own fear of rule-breaking could not induce me to earn the reputation of a tale-teller.

'What did she mean by "misunderstanding"?' I asked.

'Nothing.'

I waited, hoping my silence would encourage her to say more – a little trick that still works, by the way.

'When I was brought here, I tried to leave. The misunderstanding was that I would be permitted to do so. But as I said, I'm none of your concern.'

'But—'

Mafalda had already started marching away. I scurried after her but she scowled at me and told me to go and boil my head. She was so fierce that I slowed my pace and allowed her to disappear down the corridor leading to the east wing, where pupils were forbidden to go. My courage permitted me neither to follow her nor to tell any of the adults where she had gone, so I went to the dining hall alone. I was chastised for being late by the prefect and was not given the chance to explain where I had been. There would be no hot food for me, just bread, cheese and an apple. I knew of other girls who had tried to run away and remembering them, I slipped the bread and cheese into the pocket of my pinafore.

That night, when Mafalda was dragged up to the attic dormitory by the two games mistresses, she was covered in mud and her face was red from crying. She was deposited unceremoniously on an empty bed by the door, where a trunk with her name on it was already waiting. It was late and most of the other girls were asleep or nearly so, but I had also been waiting. I retrieved the bread and cheese from lunch, and padded in my thick socks over to where Mafalda lay face down, not moving.

'I knew you'd be hungry so I saved you this,' I whispered. 'I'm afraid the bread might be a little stale.'

Mafalda lifted her head and I caught a glimpse of the fear and the loneliness in her eyes, the first and last time I ever saw either there. Sitting up, she took the food from my outstretched hands and wolfed it down as fast as she could. When she had licked up the very last crumb, she turned to me.

'How did you know?'

'Do you think you're the first girl to try to run away?'
'You? Really?'
'Never. Other girls. Do you have a nightgown?'
'I've no idea. In there, I suppose?'

She nodded towards the trunk. I opened it as quietly as I could and after some careful rummaging, I located a thing of beautiful white cloth finer than anything I expected to own in my life.

'Here you are.'

'I need to bathe first,' she said, indicating her mud-covered limbs.

I found a towel and a cloth in Mafalda's trunk, and led her out of the dormitory and across the landing to the washing room. I wrestled the lid off the not-quite-empty water tub while she stood by, looking utterly defeated. I filled the jug and set it back on the washstand.

'Go ahead. I'll wait outside.'
'Stay there until I call.'

I stood on the landing, shivering. I realized I had spent almost the entire day waiting for Mafalda, of whose existence I had been completely unaware until that morning. I knew even then that something fundamental had occurred. When I heard her soft sobbing begin, my heart broke for her. It seemed to go on and on, and I lost all sense of time. Eventually, she called my name. I had not even realized she knew it.

'Lucy?'
'Yes?' I said, putting my head around the door.
'I'm finished.'

She stood in her nightdress, streaks of mud still visible on her shins and down towards her feet. Her expression was firm, determined, as if she had reached the very depths and was prepared to sink not one inch further. Her hair was loose and wild as a dryad's and I wanted nothing more than to wrap my hands in it and be held prisoner there, as close to her as I could be. I did not yet understand what this feeling meant, nor that it set me apart from the majority of women. I know now what I am, what *we* are, though no kind word exists for us or none that I have yet found. I—

Ah, Mafalda calls to me and wants to know what I am scribbling! Shall I show her? Perhaps not yet.

Mafalda remembers that first night differently. She remembers her sense of exile and the terrible chill of the cold water, and my attentions doing little to alleviate either. Little, that is, until I curled up next to her in her narrow bed and held her until she warmed enough to fall asleep.

Mafalda is most insistent that I go and distract her. How might I do that, I wonder? Perhaps I shall ask her if she is cold...

Letter: Maria Lowell to Réka Jacobinus
Thursday, 3rd April 1884
Lowell House, Kensington, London, England

[Editor's Note: Translated from the original Hungarian. Maria Lowell wrote frequently to her sister, Réka Jacobinus, often to discuss her concerns regarding her daughter, Mafalda Lowell. However, only this particular letter was pertinent to the matter at hand.]

My dear sister,

It has finally come to pass! Mafalda is at last to receive the proposal that her father and I have hoped for! We are, of course, utterly delighted, but the situation remains most delicate. Mafalda could quite possibly take it into her head to cut off her nose to spite her face, as the English say. I certainly do not want to push my only child into a marriage not of her choosing but then – oh, Réka, please forgive me. In my present state of tension I find that I have started in the middle. I will begin again, at the beginning.

I do not believe you ever met my husband's cousin, who was at one time the heir to his baronetcy. That is your good fortune; he was a man of immoderate habits and was generally very unpleasant. Drink carried him off a number of summers ago, and that was when his son Joseph became my dear Sir Gerald's heir. You have met Joseph once or twice, I think, while he was living with us after his father died? He is a very sensible young man, who, fortunately, inherited his late mother's calm temperament rather than his late father's more volatile one. When he came of age, my husband decided to give him charge of the Lowell family estate. After several years of labour, Joseph has done wonderfully well. Beechwood is performing excellently, the gardens are flourishing, and the tenants are happy. There is only one thing missing from this idyll – a wife!

Of course, my husband gave his permission as soon as Joseph came to ask. It's such an excellent match! While Mafalda will inherit Sir Gerald's business concerns, even in these enlightened times she cannot inherit either his baronetcy or Beechwood. That can only be Joseph's lot.

I can confidently say that Joseph is a steady young man who would never knowingly make a wife unhappy. He is just the kind of solid person any mother would choose for her daughter. I told him to take some time to court Mafalda rather than proposing at once, and indeed he has been doing so, but what else do you think Sir Gerald and I can do to smooth our daughter's path to making the right choice? Help me, sister, as I fear I am rather at a loss. I hope she will come to desire the match on her own given a little time and, perhaps, the generous wisdom of a devoted and favoured aunt? You know we only want her to be safe and well cared for, with a husband who would be understanding of her particular disposition and her forthright ways.

    I remain, as always, your most loving sister,
        Maria

Letter: Réka Jacobinus to Maria Lowell
Thursday, 10th April 1884
Buda-Pesth, Austro-Hungarian Empire

[Editor's Note: Also translated from the Hungarian.]

Dearest Maria,
Firstly, I am very surprised that Mafalda has not had more proposals by now. What is the current tally – only four? She has all the excellent looks of our family, and even without the consideration of her fortune she should have a vast number of suitors annoying her at every possible opportunity. Secondly, with all the respect due to you as my elder sister, I must refuse your request. I won't encourage Mafalda to marry any man, however decent and suitable, simply because you and Sir Gerald approve of him and he comes with Beechwood attached. Mafalda does not need to marry for a parcel of English dirt! I could get her a far more dashing husband in an evening here, and with a *proper* title already his own!

    I remember that which you seem to have forgotten. When Sir Gerald proposed to you in the garden at the Embassy ball, you were overjoyed! He picked you up and twirled you around and kissed you under the stars, and as soon as you came home, you practically sprinted upstairs to tell me all about it! I was sitting up late for you, desperately jealous that you were old enough for such glorious romance, and yearning for the day that it would be my turn. As one whose marriage was arranged, whilst my darling Gabor and I are wonderfully happy *now*, it was not an easy beginning. You say you have no wish to force this match on Mafalda. Well then!

I will set myself to finding her a handsome *noble* husband, with whom she will certainly fall madly in love, and she can come and live here where she belongs. Sir Gerald should abandon all his foolish notions of her taking over his businesses when he passes on. A woman ought not to be involved in such things. No, send her here! We have more than enough nobility to go around among our own kind.

I miss you, you know. I do so hope that we can see each other soon. At Baden-Baden, perhaps? It depends, of course. I may yet have some *particular* good news to share which will mean I cannot travel. Please pray for me.

Do give my love to Mafalda, and to dear sweet Lucy.

Always your most affectionate sister,
Jacobinus Gaborné Székely Réka

Lucy North's journal
Monday, 14th April 1884
Lowell House, Kensington, London, England

[Editor's Note: You may be wondering what this all has to do with the matter at hand. I ask you to have patience. Without the context given here, the later communications will be at best unhelpful and at worst meaningless.]

It has been a quiet few days, so my promise to write all that happens must operate within some limits. We visited the dressmaker on Friday and the milliner on Saturday, and that is all.

I have been reading and practising my languages while listening to Mafalda play the piano. She does not play like a proper young lady but like a *maestro*, with true passion and great feeling. Lady Maria often seems unsettled by it, but sighs and says nothing.

It occurs to me that I ought perhaps to lay out how I came to live with the Lowells. It is a sad and simple tale, which might have had a far more unfortunate ending.

I was unwanted at home. My father was not interested in me, and my stepmother even less so. Fortunately, my father's pride would not allow him to shirk his eldest child's education, however unwelcome that child might be. And so, I was sent to the well-regarded and conveniently far-away Medhurst School for Young Ladies. Founded by Lord Lyttelton, that famous advocate of female learning, pupils at Medhurst received a well-rounded education. We learned drawing and dancing and playing the piano, certainly, but also geography, the classics, French, German, history and mathematics. An older girl was assigned as housemother to each new pupil, and mine, Eliza, gave me the first fussing familial love I had ever received. I made friends. I enjoyed my lessons. I was, by any standards, extremely lucky.

Things were different for Mafalda. She was, and is, a much-loved only child, her equally well-loved infant siblings being now in God's care. Having no living son, Sir Gerald was adamant that Mafalda be educated properly to equip her for the City and for business. Mafalda did not agree at the time, and saw off many a tutor before Sir Gerald despaired and sent her to Medhurst. I would like to note that she has since come around to her father's plan. It pleases her rebellious streak to follow a profession, rather than adorning a drawing room.

When Mafalda and I first became friends, I told her all about my family. I never visited them for the holidays, and they never visited me. We rarely corresponded. On learning this Mafalda was appalled, and the Christmas after we met Mafalda informed me I was to come home with her for the duration. There was no question asked, no formal invitation issued. From then on, I spent each and every holiday with the Lowells. In fact, the first time Mafalda ever kissed me was a Christmas Eve.

I had loved her first, with no hope that she might return that love in the same measure. I was contented with her friendship, or almost contented. Though we had spent that one night curled around each other, for two long years she showed me no more physical affection than any other pair of friends might show each other. Her arm through mine when we walked the grounds with the other girls, the occasional cheerful and momentary embrace, the braiding of hair, the tying of stays. Until that night, with snow falling softly past the window, and the salon which we would one day share lit gold by the haze of the dying fire. Mafalda had fallen asleep on the chaise, and I found myself gazing at her for far longer than ordinary good manners could ever allow. When her green eyes flicked open, she caught me and I could not look away. She smiled her knowing half-smile, and came to kneel beside me on the hearthrug. She laid her warm hand against my cheek, and kissed me with a soft tenderness that surprises me still when I think of it.

By the time Mafalda and I finished our schooling we had been attached for several years. That summer, I went with the family to their estate at Beechwood and spent the long sunny days with Mafalda and Joseph just as usual. When autumn came, we returned to Lowell House and I simply never left. No one ever so much as mentioned my leaving, not even when Joseph came of age and removed permanently to Beechwood and the question might have naturally arisen. I suspect Sir Gerald had some correspondence with my father on the subject, but I cannot imagine it amounting to very much. I'm sure he was happy to forget me in favour of my stepmother and my two young half-brothers. A daughter by an unfortunate previous wife who had despised him for his intemperate habits, and whose money was tied up in clever legal ways so that after her death he could not access it to finance his foolish schemes – why, such a daughter is no use at all. I bless my half-remembered mother for putting what little she had in trust for me. I pray she has found the peace in Heaven that she never had in life.

I read a great deal during my unloved and unloving childhood, and with only indifferent nurses to superintend me I wandered where I wished in my father's library. I came time and time again upon tales of ancient goddesses spinning or weaving the fates of men, and might there not be a truth in an image found in so very many cultures? I believe my fate was woven with my beloved's into one tapestry, and that it has always been so and could be no other way. For that, I am more grateful to those spinning, weaving ancient ones than I can possibly express.

Telegram: Réka Jacobinus to Maria Lowell
Friday, 18th April 1884
Buda-Pesth to London

[Editor's Note: Translated from the Hungarian.]

MARIA, COME AT ONCE. STOP. GABOR KILLED IN DUEL. STOP. I NEED YOU. STOP. RÉKA.

Letter: Eliza Cartwright to Lucy North
Monday, 21st April 1884
Whitby, Yorkshire, England

Dear Lucy,

I was so happy to receive your letter, even if it does come under such tragic circumstances. Please give my condolences to Lady Maria on the loss of her brother-in-law. I hope that she and Mafalda will be a comfort to her sister at this difficult time, and that their journey to Buda-Pesth will be both swift and safe. It must be hard for her to leave Sir Gerald when his health is not good, but I don't doubt that the best London doctors are engaged to attend him whenever necessary. I find an onion poultice is always excellent for chest problems, if his medical advisors have no objection.

Of course you must come and stay with us while her ladyship and Mafalda are away. It is no imposition at all! How can you even think such a thing? We would be delighted to have you. I can hardly believe that the last time I saw you was over a year ago. It has been far, far too long.

My husband the Colonel is quite well, thank you for asking. He sends his regards to Sir Gerald, and hopes they might meet again to trade war stories. The sea air keeps him very healthy, and frequent salt-water bathing means his old injury doesn't plague him nearly so much. My pride and joy, little Elsbeth, loves the silver rattle that you were so kind as to send for her birthday. My husband quite dotes on her. His army career kept him so busy when my stepsons were small that he hardly knew them until they were men. He is thrilled to now have the time to spend with such a sweet child. Not every man would be happy to take in his wife's orphaned sister, and I thank God every day that he is as he is. We recently engaged a photographer to take her picture, a copy of which I enclose for you.

We will have a delightful time, I promise. There's no end of things to do here during the summer months, the air is wonderfully healthful, and you may earn your keep by telling me tales of your glamorous London life! Our carriage will meet you and Mr Joseph Lowell at the station. It is very good of him to escort you. Is he quite sure he must return to London the very next day? He would be welcome to remain longer, if he wishes.

I can hardly wait to see you.
Your friend,
　　Eliza Cartwright

Letter: Alice Smith to Mary and Sarah Smith
Wednesday, 23rd April 1884
Whitby, Yorkshire, England

Dear Mam and Sarah,
Some exciting news – Mrs Cartwright is having a guest come to stay, a young lady from London! She'll arrive tomorrow night, and I'm to wait on her as well as Mrs Cartwright. Imagine, me a lady's maid to a proper London miss! We've all been pitching in to make things ready, and it's been quite the whirl.

Do you think Mr Saunders might lend you his carriage one Wednesday next, so you could come up and see me? All the servants here will still have their afternoons off, guest or no. Mrs Cartwright has been very clear about that, God bless her. I can write and ask Mr Saunders if you'd rather not? At any rate, please give him and Mrs Saunders my regards. I owe Mrs Saunders so much for training me up, and now for recommending me to Mrs Cartwright. I hope I am a credit to her, and to you.

Mam, before I forget, on Sunday Father Anthony told me he's been praying for your trouble with your wrist. He says you should light a candle and pray to St Alphonsus every night for seven nights. Sarah will help you with mixing up a ginger poultice.

I send you all my love and prayers.

Alice

P.S. Sarah, I beg you, don't pray for the Sight. You don't know what you're asking. You see Mam reading futures for the village girls and you think how quiet and easy it looks. You were so little, you don't remember when Nana screamed in her sleep for a month, until Da went round to old Mrs Crocker's house with the justice of the peace and unlocked the attic. Even with the lemon beebrush, sometimes the nightmares still break through. Do you know what I dreamed the night before I left home? I dreamed of some poor soul being chased through a forest by wolves. Wolves, Sarah. I felt all their fear, and all their desperation. I wouldn't wish this on anyone, let alone someone I love as much as you.

Please pray for me, as I will pray for you.

Lucy North's journal
Wednesday, 23rd April 1884
Lowell House, Kensington, London, England

A fine writer I am! I've not opened this book in an age, but I am beginning again with more commitment. Tomorrow I am to leave for Whitby to stay with Eliza. My trunk is packed and waiting in the hall, and my bedroom is assuming that heartless air of impersonality so common to places about to be abandoned.

Despite her kind words assuring me that it's no trouble, I feel ashamed to burden my first friend. For years after leaving school at Medhurst, Eliza's life was nothing but caring for others. She tended not only her youngest siblings in their schooldays, but also her mother during frequent bouts of ill health and then a late-in-life childbed. Eliza had barely a moment to herself, excepting, so she told me, when family friend Colonel Cartwright would visit. He would always make sure to sit down with her, and offer both practical assistance and a listening ear. He asked for her hand knowing that his new wife would need to give all her time to her old family. Eliza accepted, as while he may have been a widower twice her age, she had already seen that the Colonel's good nature would not be found wanting during trying times. When Eliza lost both her parents in quick succession – her mother from a heart complaint, and her father from grief – he stood steadfast. With none of her brothers married at the time and no other appropriate relation available, Eliza had to take in her infant sister, and her new husband opened his home to little Elsbeth without question. The girl is quite the cherub still, judging by the photograph Eliza enclosed with her letter. I suppose it is a mercy that she is too young to remember such dreadful loss.

The sad truth of it is that I have no other place where I would be happily received. My father and stepmother might take me in for form's sake, but personally I would rather spend the night in the Clerkenwell workhouse. The welcome would certainly be warmer.

While it wouldn't be exactly improper for me to stay here alone with Sir Gerald, it wouldn't be quite proper either. I also can't travel such a great distance by myself, so someone must be inconvenienced to accompany me and Joseph volunteered for the cause. I suppose propriety wouldn't exactly agree with that either, but no one will know us on the train.

Lucy North's journal
Thursday, 24th April 1884
Whitby, Yorkshire, England

As pleasant a person as Joseph is, I had thought that conversation would necessarily stall on such a long journey northward. I had assumed, more fool I, that I would be bored. How I wish it had been so! I have been made a confidante to the most awful secret: Joseph intends to propose to Mafalda. This is why he took us on all those excursions when he visited last month. He was courting her, and I was the unwitting chaperone!

I must be calm. I must lay it all out as it happened.

This morning, Joseph called for me in a hansom which bore us all the way to King's Cross station. One porter loaded my trunk onto a trolley and spirited it away to the guard's van, while another saw us to an empty compartment. The scent of tobacco lingered, evidence of a former occupant who had neglected to open the window while indulging in his habit. My giant of an escort chivalrously stowed my carpet bag neatly on the rack above my head, while I set my picnic basket down on an empty seat. Cook had prepared it for me against my protestations, clearly thinking we might starve on the way to Yorkshire. When the whistle blew and the train began to chuff its way out of the station, I served us each a jam puff.

After some little while our light conversation came to a natural pause. I had him bring down my carpet bag so I could read my book, while he took up a newspaper. I was quite lost in the story until I realized he was trying to speak to me.

'. . . if you might give me some advice?'

I put the book in my lap and folded my lace-gloved hands atop it, a habit left over from school.

'Sorry, I was quite immersed. What were you saying?'

'I was asking if I might seek your advice, as a young lady. It's on a rather delicate matter.' He looked at me rather intensely, which I think now was to see if I had any inkling as to what was coming. 'It concerns Mafalda.'

'Mafalda?'

'You see, the thing is . . .' He took a deep breath. 'I've asked Sir Gerald for permission to propose marriage to Mafalda, and he has granted it. Her ladyship has also given her blessing.'

For a split second I did not understand. Propose marriage to Mafalda? My Mafalda?

'I would like to ask, as you are Mafalda's dearest friend, if I ought to propose by letter or if I should wait until she returns from Buda-Pesth. I'm torn as to the right and proper thing to do, especially as she is in mourning for her uncle.'

Anger rose like bile in my throat, the vilest hatred and loathing I have ever experienced threatening to overtake me. My heart beat wildly, and I grew hot and then cold and then dizzy in quick succession. What should I do? What could I do?

I took a deep, slow breath, trying to quiet my rising nausea.

'Thank you for confiding in me,' I said, holding my hands firmly in my lap so that he might not see them shaking. 'I am deeply honoured by your trust, and will give you my honest answer.' He leaned forward, an eager puppy. 'Give up your suit. Mafalda does not see you as a potential husband.'

'Oh. I see.' He looked downcast for a moment, before recovering his usual good humour. 'Well then, I must hope to change her mind.'

My skin prickled with creeping gooseflesh.

'Do you feel you have reason for such hope?'

My tone was not as soft as it could have been but he took no notice.

'Some, I think. She seems to enjoy both my letters and my company.'

What a fool! When Joseph came to stay, he took us all over London to lunches and dinners and museums and river-boating and even to see Mr Irving's latest scandalous play at the Lyceum. Mafalda would have smiled and expressed her enjoyment if she had been on the arm of Ivan the Terrible himself!

'I suppose both courses of action have their merits. You must choose for yourself.'

I made to hide in my novel but Joseph leaned forward and placed his vast hand over mine.

'Will you speak in my favour, Lucy? Will you tell her how happy I will make her? How much I will care for her?'

'I can tell her that that is what you intend,' I said, forcing a tight smile.

This seemed to satisfy him, and he sat back in his seat.

How can this be? Joseph is good and temperate and until today I liked him a great deal, but now I swear I would rip him limb from limb if I were able. To think mine and my beloved's life together could all be swept away on a man's whim! As I took up my book again, I saw that I had gripped my left hand so hard with my right that four perfect bloody semicircles had stained the torn white lace of my glove.

The remainder of the journey was less awkward than might be imagined, as Joseph clearly thought that nothing was amiss. My world might be in turmoil but he had not been diverted from his purpose. I shared some of our picnic with a respectable widowed lady whom we met after changing trains at York, and her garrulousness saved us from having to make further conversation with each other for some time.

After she disembarked, other passengers came and went while I feigned sleep in the corner. Despite my roiling mind, the deception gave way to the reality and I did not wake until we reached Whitby. Eliza had sent a carriage which whisked us up to the West Cliff, jolting over the cobbles. It was almost dark so I gained little sense of the town as we headed upwards, excepting the sound of the waves and the taste of salt in the air.

The journey was mercifully brief though it felt otherwise, as Joseph talked passionately of nothing but carriages and coachmanship for the duration. Mafalda would have pushed him out onto the cobbles for being a dull companion.

Eliza's home is quite lovely. The house forms the end of a terrace that is perhaps a hundred years old, and has all the character of that period. As Joseph handed me out of the much-discussed carriage, he chose to cheerfully remark upon the building's excellent condition even given the rigours of the sea air. How can a man be so enthused by absolutely everything?

An aged butler greeted us, and showed us straight through to the drawing room where Eliza sat waiting. She is much changed since I saw her last, and for the better. She is out of mourning, and slowly filling out again after the hardships of grief. Her blonde hair holds its enviable natural curl unencumbered by black crepe, her eyes that she always disparagingly calls 'winter sky' once again sparkle with good humour, and her skin is no longer grey-pale but is as clear and pink-and-white as when we were girls.

'Lucy,' she greeted me, kissing my cheek, 'how was your journey?'

'Very easy,' I lied smoothly. 'All the trains were on time and we were most comfortable. May I present Mr Joseph Lowell, who has been kind enough to accompany me.'

Eliza shook his hand. 'Thank you for seeing Lucy here safely.'

'It was an honour, Mrs Cartwright. Thank you for offering me your hospitality.'

'It's my great pleasure. Now, I thought you would be exhausted so baths are being drawn for you at this very moment. A supper has been prepared; just ring and it will be brought straight up. My husband sends his apologies. He is accustomed to retiring quite early, but he will host you at breakfast.'

I could have wept with relief that we were not to be subjected to a formal dinner and late hours. Bless Eliza, who assumes everyone is as unwilling to endure dust and grime as she is herself.

'Thank you, how thoughtful.'

'I want you both to feel welcome in our home, and not that you must stand on ceremony when you're travel-weary. Lucy, I'll send my maid to you shortly. Mr Lowell, Morton will attend you if you wish.'

'No thank you, Mrs Cartwright, although I appreciate the offer. I'm a plain sort of fellow. I can shift for myself.'

'Gentlemen manage rather better without attendants than us ladies do, I think,' Eliza said in her customary polite manner. It is a relief to see that returned. 'Please, follow Morton and he'll show you up to your rooms.'

Eliza has put me in the Blue Room, a large chamber at the front of the house and across the hall from her own. A restful and homely scene met my exhausted eyes. My nightgown was laid out on the counterpane, a bath screen had been set up on the hearthrug with the bath – one of two, it seems! – waiting behind it, and an unseasonal fire burned in the grate. My luggage awaited me at the foot of a grand four-poster bed, which looked so comfortable that if Eliza's maid had not been present I might have fallen face down onto it and not risen again until morning.

The frizzy-haired girl bobbed a curtsey and wished me good evening in the local accent.

'Madam had a fire lit for you, miss,' she informed me as she began the laborious process of peeling off my travel clothes. 'She feared you might feel the cold, coming from t'south.'

'I dare say she's right. What is your name?' I asked as we removed garment after garment from my person.

'Alice Smith, miss. Madam calls me Alice.'

'Then I will also call you Alice, if that's alright.'

'As you please, miss.'

Evidently Eliza has become one of those modern ladies who prefer not to call their maids by their surnames, and as her guest I felt it polite to follow suit.

Alice sat me down at the dressing table and unpinned my hair, brushing it out carefully. I watched her flat, clear face in the mirror, stoic and absolutely absorbed in her task.

'How would you like your hair, miss?'

'Please twist it up.'

'Yes, miss. Like this?'

'Yes, thank you.'

'My pleasure, miss. I'll take your things down to launder, and you can ring when you need me.'

She left with a veritable mountain of my clothing in her arms, towering so high she could hardly see over the top. Once she was gone, I threw off my chemise and sank into the bathtub. I felt the dirt of travel lifting from my skin, along with the tension I had held in my muscles since Joseph's announcement.

Mafalda will refuse him, I told myself over and over. Of course she will refuse him, no matter what her parents might say. I know I could never marry while she lives and breathes, and when has she ever given me cause to suppose her heart less faithful than mine? Much of my bitterness comes from my envy that Joseph can offer her a life I never could, with social position and approbation and all the benefits that go along with linking oneself to a man. What do I have to offer? Nothing at all but myself. Is it enough? Am I enough?

I remained in the bath with such unhelpful and unhappy thoughts, until the water was almost cold and my fingers had wrinkled. Alice had left a towel to warm so I dried off and put on my nightgown. I rang for my tray, which turned out to be cold cuts along with tea and biscuits. As always, Eliza plans ahead very well.

Alice has just turned down the lamp, leaving me with only candlelight. I will curl up and think of Mafalda and hope that I dream of her. A cold comfort, but better than none.

PART TWO

Sir John Seward's personal diary
Tuesday, 6th January 1903
Littlemore Hospital, Oxfordshire

This morning's briefing went very well, as did my individual meetings with various members of my staff. I found the doctors to be both highly competent and familiar with modern methods, the nurses and orderlies to know their work well, and the institution as a whole to be fully embracing the new century. Dr Knight was kind enough to give me a tour of the entire premises and it turns out that my office is opposite hers, which is most convenient. It has a southern aspect and enjoys a view of the countryside, which I'm sure will be charming come spring.

The hospital itself is built in the usual mid-century two- and three-storey double-cruciform style of such places. One wing for the women, one for the men, and a central block given over to the many other functions necessary to support a hospital of this size. My house is positioned between the chapel and the women's wing. It is more newly built than the rest of the complex, the former apartments for the overseer having been broken up into committee rooms and staff quarters. Dr Knight has her own set of rooms there, which she says is most convenient.

After the tour, Dr Knight and I lunched together in my over-furnished dining room. Earlier I'd taken the opportunity to reread her curriculum vitae, as they call it nowadays, and her career speaks for itself. A graduate of the London School of Medicine for

Women, she worked under Dr Hyslop at Bedlam for several years before going out to India to set up the Bombay Women's Asylum. I wondered briefly if Hyslop's more questionable views – of which he has many – had given her pause, but I could hardly ask at this early stage of our acquaintance.

'I realize I haven't congratulated you on your recent honour, Sir John,' she said as we set about our meal. 'It's very well-deserved, if I may say so.'

I might have coloured a touch, yet again.

'I'm not yet used to it. When someone calls for "Sir John", I can't quite believe they're addressing me and not someone far more illustrious.'

Dr Knight smiled at this, a true smile that reached all the way to her pale grey eyes.

'Modesty indeed! I'll make sure that the staff knows to assist you by calling you "Sir John" as frequently as possible.'

I smiled in return, enjoying her style of humour. 'I'm sure that would be very helpful.'

I split a bread roll, and cheerfully began to pile it high with butter.

'I've been thinking about our incoming patient,' Dr Knight said, changing the subject, 'and as familiar as I am with your published work, I don't believe I've ever read of your very first forays into the study of zoophagy. How did you come to be interested in it?'

All my good cheer vanished in an instant. I had guarded this part of my professional history for many years, and with good reason. As I searched for how to respond, I seemed to be back at Carfax, the asylum that had been both my workplace and my home for so long, facing down the patient whose desire to consume as many lives as possible and absorb them into himself foretold the coming of the one he called his Master, the infernal being who had stolen the lives of countless men and women across the centuries, who—

'Sir John? Is all quite well?'

My mind had apparently absented itself during my downward spiral, leaving my body halted with butter knife aloft. Across the table, Dr Knight's face was a picture of friendly yet professional concern.

'Yes, yes, quite well.' I set down both knife and roll, and consciously brought myself back to the present time and place. 'I'm afraid it's rather too unpleasant a subject to discuss over a meal.'

My colleague seemed to accept this, and turned the conversation instead to her time in India, a fascinating topic in its own right. Nevertheless, if I were a gambling man I would bet a sizeable sum that my 'discovery' of zoophagy will loom large in my nightmares tonight.

Letter: Alice Smith to Mary and Sarah Smith
Monday, 28th April 1884
Whitby, Yorkshire, England

[Editor's Note: You are asked to excuse the informal style of these letters, and to bear in mind the young writer's lack of quality education. The spelling has been amended where appropriate in this typescript. The original is included for the sake of completeness.]

Dear Mam and Sarah,

Thank you for coming up to see me today. It made my heart glad to lay eyes on you both, even if for such a short visit. An hour is no time at all! You see how kind Mrs Cartwright is, letting me swap my afternoon? I said you didn't need to worry about me!

Mam, I'll take good care of your silver crucifix. I'm wearing it now on a long chain tucked into my dress. Please thank Mr and Mrs Saunders again for getting you up here, and tell them I'll keep remembering them in my prayers for all their kindness to us since Da died.

I hardly got to tell you about the antics of the sweet baby of the house, little Miss Beth, or about Miss North just come up from London. Miss Beth has taken quite a shine to me lately, and toddles after me whenever she can. Don't worry, Mam, I'm not spoiling her, just keeping a bit of an eye on her when Nanny Roberts has her afternoon out. The Colonel is quite a fatherly figure, which you'd hardly think of such a gruff military man, and seeing the young miss's fondness for me he's content to let me entertain her when it doesn't take away from my duties. She's a sweetheart, all blonde curls and chuckles, and easily amused. She can even say a few words, which my mistress is convinced is a sign that she'll be a very intelligent girl when she is grown.

Miss North is a good lady. I've learned a lot from her about the new fashionable hairstyles, and I've made a great deal of notes in my commonplace book. Miss North likes to chat while I dress her, in a way that makes me think that she might be a bit unhappy here. Certainly, she misses the friend whose family she lives with down south, who's had to go abroad to visit a newly-widowed aunt, who isn't very well. I hope I give her some comfort with my care of her person, as well as a listening ear. So far, it seems this is as much a part of a lady's maid's job as mixing pomade!

I send you my love, and some of my wages. I know you said not to, but no arguing. I have more than I need.

Your Alice

P.S. Sarah, something happened. The other day, Nanny Roberts was on her afternoon out. The ladies were resting and didn't need me so I was helping with the young miss, sitting in the family's parlour playing patty-cake. The Colonel sat in an armchair nearby, half reading the paper and half smiling over his half-moon spectacles at the girl's laughter. He asked me to bring her to him so I did, holding the little one's hand carefully and guiding her shaky steps. The Colonel reached out for her and I put Miss Beth's hand into the Colonel's. His hand brushed mine, and that's when it happened.

I saw the poor man sat in that same chair but late at night with a fire in the grate, holding a photograph. It was of a group sitting, I think, but I couldn't see it properly. The Colonel held the picture tightly, weeping with a depth of such grief in his soul as I pray I never feel again. The seeing only lasted a moment and then it vanished, and I came back to myself. The Colonel had Miss Beth on his lap and was asking if I was alright as I had come over quite pale.

'Yes, sir,' I stuttered, 'just a bit dizzy all of a sudden.'

'Oh dear. Get some fresh air, girl, and I'm sure you'll be right as rain. Missy and I will do quite well.'

With that he turned his full attention to Miss Beth, bouncing her on his knee. I thanked him and staggered out through the French doors into the garden. I tried to breathe deeply and not to panic, but, Sarah, I don't understand! It wasn't like Mam when she reads futures, little flashes of something and nothing that go as quick as they come. It felt just as if one of my nightmares had leaked into my waking life! Who is it to be this time? Who was it in the photograph?

Send more of the lemon beebrush as soon as you can. If I have some in the morning as well as at night, maybe it will make this stop.

Letter: Mafalda Lowell to Lucy North
Monday, 28th April 1884
Buda-Pesth, Austro-Hungarian Empire

Dearest Lucy,

I cannot tell you how awful today has been. It rained all day, and the grey dampness only added to the general sense of tragedy. The funeral was at the basilica, and was less a memorial for Uncle Gabor than an event on Buda-Pesth's social calendar. I swear that nine out of every ten attendees were only there because of the scandal. Aunt Réka was stone-faced through the entire service, maintaining a completely rigid posture and never taking her eyes from the priest. Some rows behind us there was a woman hidden by an opaque veil, who sobbed and sobbed throughout so that it was all but impossible to hear the liturgy. When I asked Mama later who she was, assuming it was some near relation who was so vocally bereft, Mama grimaced.

'That was Baroness Tolvay, the cause of all this trouble.'

'Really? Are you sure?'

'I am. We were girls together. I knew her very well at one time. She was so virtuous; I can't imagine how she came to disgrace herself so.'

I can't imagine how she had the gall to appear in public at all, let alone at her lover's funeral! Everyone knows her husband fled the country after the duel and abandoned her to humiliation. If I was her, I'd have thrown myself in the Danube for the shame.

How Aunt Réka survived today I hardly know. Mama was surprised she managed to keep her composure during the various ceremonials. Over a hundred guests came to the house after the service, shuffling around the ballroom offering condolences with insincere faces. The women gossiped in clusters under the black-covered chandelier, and the men buzzed around my aunt dripping faux-sympathy and inappropriate flattery, hoping they might be the next husband in line. As Aunt Réka is left so rich, they seem to be prepared to overlook her new notoriety in order to secure her hand. And Uncle Gabor hardly cold! I may not have known him well, but the disrespect still makes my blood boil. Vile creatures.

When all the gawkers had finally left, and the very last would-be suitor had been ushered out – really, one Major Oberleitner had to be practically kicked into the street – Aunt Réka retired to her rooms. Mama and I changed and went to sit in Mama's private sitting room from where we could, if we so wished, enjoy a view of Buda Castle. A maid brought coffee, and we sipped it carefully as Partridge let down first Mama's hair, then mine. I miss your light touch with a brush. No one else has such a gentleness yet thoroughness as you, and certainly not Partridge. I'm surprised I have any hair left on my head.

'It is a shame that Réka wants to shut herself away,' Mama said, her accent coming out more strongly here than it ever has in England. 'She says she refuses to appear in society as an object of horrified fascination, and yet she will not leave the city.'

'Could you not persuade her to come back with us to London?'

'I doubt she would agree, but I could try. She ought not to be alone.'

'Perhaps we should offer to stay here with her, in that case. Just for a little while.' I was not at all keen to do so but I felt I ought to offer.

'Actually—' Mama began, but she got no further.

The maid reappeared, asking for Mama to come at once to Aunt Réka. As she opened the door, I could hear an unearthly wailing sound. All day long Aunt Réka had been as composed as Patience on her monument, but once she was alone the facade cracked. I pity her. She loved my uncle, and not only did he betray her but he died in defending the supposed honour of his mistress. Cruelty upon cruelty.

I miss you, my love. It has been such a day and now I have to sleep alone and uncomforted. I would give anything to have you here with me.

Your own,
Mafalda

Letter: Mafalda Lowell to Lucy North
Wednesday, 30th April 1884
Buda-Pesth, Austro-Hungarian Empire

My dearest Lucy,
You won't have received my last yet, but I find my pen scratching away on another letter to you just the same.

All Aunt Réka's stoicism is gone. She is so prostrate with grief as to be quite ill. She is silent and eats little, only rising from her grand green-damask-covered bed in her darkened bedchamber to sit at her dressing table and stare at her own face in the mirror. She shivers constantly, so the ceramic stove must be kept alight day and night. She does not often sleep, though when she does she sleepwalks and so must be watched constantly. The doctor came and prescribed complete rest for the moment; that and a tincture of morphia. On his recommendation Mama has ordered a professional nurse from Vienna to take on the burden of care, but until she arrives we must shift for my aunt ourselves. The foolish maidservants help a little, but Aunt Réka's staff are not of the kind to be truly trusted with seeing their mistress in this state – gossips, all of them. With that in mind, I did ask several if they knew how Uncle Gabor's duel had come about, how the Baron had found out about his wife's infidelity, but oddly for such loose-lipped women they either knew nothing or wouldn't tell me.

I am writing to you now from my aunt's sickroom, squinting in the dim light at the letter pad on my lap. I have been sitting here so long that I feel myself becoming one with the spindly Rococo bedside chair. Aunt Réka lies staring at the ceiling while I chatter to her of this and that, mainly of you and your travels. When you write to me, mark portions of your letters that I may read aloud to her. I read to her all the livelong day. Poetry, folk tales, everything she loves, but she barely seems able to hear me. Her friends write to her daily and I read her their letters, hoping she might be comforted. I do not know if my efforts have any effect.

At present I'm alone in my watching, as Mama and the steward have gone to meet with Uncle Gabor's land agent, Mr Török, and a prospective buyer for one of my uncle's properties. Some time ago my aunt met a count from the Transylvanian Carpathians at one of her nationalist events, and they formed quite the bond based on their shared heritage. This elderly gentleman has shown a great deal of interest in one of my uncle's properties, a ruined manor and some farmland, and wanted to see the place in person. I would like to have gone too, as I am always amused by how frightened Mr Török is of Mama. He called yesterday to arrange the meeting, and the poor man practically twitches with nerves whenever he sees her. Even Mama is a little entertained by it, and she needs to find laughter where she can. Between worry for Aunt Réka here and for Papa back in London, she is becoming quite pinched.

I too, my love, must find my enjoyments where I may. I miss you more and more. I do not know when I will be able to return home and that makes it all the worse. My birthday approaches but it can hardly be marked with things as they are. Besides, any celebration without you would be no celebration at all. The Romantic in me likes to think of you walking with Eliza, gazing out over the cliff-tops of Whitby with the wind in your hair, yearning for me like a Navy wife waiting for her husband to return from some foreign war. I ought to say that I hope you are not missing me too much, but you know I could not. I want you to be as sad in my absence as I am in yours, and I know that you will forgive me for such dreadful selfishness.

 Your ever-loving
 Mafalda

Letter: Mafalda Lowell to Lucy North
Friday, 2nd May 1884
Buda-Pesth, Austro-Hungarian Empire

Dear Lucy,
You must have written to me by now. I wonder where the letter is? I know I cannot expect it for some days yet, but I think of it wending its way across half a continent to reach me and I imagine the sentiments it might contain. I hope it is full of your agony at my absence, and of deep and terrible distress and misery. I hope you tell me how much you yearn for my return, counting the days as they go by and cursing each sad and empty one.

 This time I am writing to you from my uncle's study, where I now spend much of each day. I have been released from the sickroom, at least for a time, as Mama has rather struggled in attempting to put my uncle's affairs in order and has decided I must take over. She told me I ought to put to use 'all that mathematics your father insisted on you learning', and so I have. It is wonderfully quiet in here, as it looks down onto the courtyard rather than the street. It smells delightfully of leather, and of the old books that line the walls. What a pleasure to be able to throw the curtains wide and let the light in! There is even a door onto a covered balcony-cum-walkway, from which I may enjoy the sunshine even more. Who cares a whit for a freckle or two?

Not that I spend my days sunning myself. The work is a challenge, and I find that my mind relishes it. My uncle has no heir but Aunt Réka, and she has charged us with disposing of the majority of his property portfolio, which is vast and widespread. Well, I say 'charged', but when Mama asked her what she wanted done, she said only 'Get rid of it, all of it' and turned her face to the wall. The steward, young Mátyás, has been helping me work through Uncle Gabor's papers to ensure this divesting can occur with ease. Things are in relatively good order, and we have fortunately not discovered any debts or financial indiscretions that would cause problems. Vast amounts of nationalist literature which Mama is nervous to have in the house, yes, but no swindling at least! Mama has had me checking all Mátyás's work, which is not at all necessary but which rightly affirms her trust in me. She says Mátyás is so new to the job he cannot be entirely relied upon. His father, my uncle's previous steward, retired not long ago and apparently could not be enticed to bestir himself from his armchair and return. He told Mama most forcefully that his son was perfectly capable of any task that she chose to set him, which appears to be true so far. We have mostly completed an inventory of Uncle Gabor's holdings in-country, which means there is a now a long list of tasks to attend to. Reliable or not, Mama has had to turn to Mátyás to complete all of those which require a man's signature, which seems to be most of them. I must grit my teeth as he signs this, that, and the other document, knowing that I am as competent or more so than he. Mama seems not to mind, but I chafe under this repeated disenfranchisement. I worry that this will be my life when Papa 'goes to his reward' as they say, my own intelligence and business acumen meaning nothing, a man's legal permission meaning everything.

While Mátyás traipses about from bank to broker to agent to 'business associate', I have begun on the household's own accounts as I should be able to manage these without too many complications. I could tell you about them but I worry I will bore you, so suffice it to say I sit crumpled and ink-covered chasing incomings and outgoings up and down columns for hours on end, missing you every moment.

I wait for your letter each day, my love. Give my regards to Eliza.

Mafalda

Letter: Mafalda Lowell to Lucy North
Monday, 5th May 1884
Buda-Pesth, Austro-Hungarian Empire

Dearest Lucy,

With every day that passes, I find it more and more uncomfortable to look at Aunt Réka. You know my aunt and I were always so very alike that to see her face has always been to see myself ten or so years hence, but the ravages of her grief have left their mark. To look at her now is like looking into the very bleakest vision of my own future. Her dark hair is streaked with new grey, and in the fortnight since my uncle's death she has lost so much weight that her skin seems stretched over her bones. Her so lovingly cared-for hands are now dried-up claws. Lines have appeared on her face where there were none before, and she has no trace left of her previous lustre. It is as if all that was Aunt Réka has been bled out, leaving only a husk.

Still, despite my distaste, I do what I must. Early in the

evening yesterday, Mama summoned me from my work in Uncle Gabor's study to take my turn sitting with the invalid. She sat propped up on her pillows while I read to her, peering at the text in the half-light. I became aware of her studying my features as I wrapped my tongue around the Magyar poetry, assessing me, perhaps with my same thoughts of our lost resemblance. I squirmed under the unrelenting black gaze.

'Is there anything else that I can get for you, Aunt?' I asked as I reached the end of a stanza. 'Do you need more morphia?'

That appraising stare continued.

'You are a beautiful girl, Mafalda. You remind me of myself, before my marriage.' Her speech came slowly at first and somewhat thickly, as if the words needed to rise from some long-forgotten place.

I did not know quite what to say.

'Thank you, Aunt. Shall I continue?'

'Why . . .' She took a deep and struggling breath. 'Why are you not yet married?'

'Papa is strongly against girls marrying too early.'

'Ah! Your papa. Does he not know the troubles that befall girls who marry late?'

'Twenty is hardly late, Aunt.'

'I was younger than you. Much younger.'

She sighed a long, rattling sigh. I proffered the most polite response I could think of.

'You have always told me to marry for love, and there *is* no man that I love.'

It is true, though a little disingenuous.

'Love? Oh, Mafalda.' Aunt Réka made a coughing noise that might have been laughter. 'Let me tell you of *love*.'

'I beg you not to distress yourself. Let me fetch Mama, she will give you a tonic.'

'No, niece, you will listen and you will learn.'

I should have stopped her, I should have fetched her medicine, I should have insisted that she rest. I am tormented with guilt and shame that I allowed my curiosity to get the better of me – no, it is worse than that; I know that I *ought* to be tormented and I am not. The tale she told me explains so much!

Slowly and painfully, Aunt Réka pulled herself further upright.

'My mother, your grandmother, came into my rooms one morning and told me that Jacobinus Gabor – the Magyar people must not bow to the naming conventions of our Austrian occupiers, Mafalda, do not forget that – had been to ask for my hand. I barely knew him but he was wealthy, he was of our own stock's blood on his mother's side, he had the proper feelings about our nation, and he was handsome even though he was nearing forty. Due to bad investments, my father had joined the tragic class of lower nobility that must sell its daughters to rich untitled men, or risk ruin. Did you know that?'

'No, I had no idea.'

'Your mother was lucky; she was long run away and married by then. Maria came of age in better times. I was my parents' only hope for material rescue. Your father helped the family as best he could, but your grandfather's pride was such that he could not stand taking money from a foreigner, and a heretic Protestant at that. What was I to do? Your grandmama told me that your grandfather had agreed to the match, and that Gabor would come and I would give him my assent. I had no choice. I only considered myself lucky that I wasn't disgusted by the man. Five weeks later we were married.'

Aunt Réka slumped down against her pillows, worn out by this lengthy speech.

'But you did fall in love,' I said gently, hoping to soothe her.

'Oh yes. Yes, I loved him. In the end.'

She began to weep, growing more and more agitated with each gasping breath. Then that noise; that howling, shrieking, anguished noise that had rent the house on the night of the funeral rose up from her throat. She gripped my forearm with her claw-like hand and I was pinned there, watching in horror as her screaming sobs racked her withered body as if it could not contain its own sorrow and would rip itself apart. She slumped to the side and curled up, still clutching me as she wailed, powerfully strong in her mania. I tried to reach the bell-pull but the sounds had already summoned a nearby housemaid, whom I sent at once for Mama. I tried to hush her, to calm her, but she clutched all the harder.

Mama arrived at a run, and released me from Aunt Réka's grip by sheer force. My arm was already bruising purple where she had held it so tightly. Mama took one look at my face, and ordered me out.

'Ring for a brandy, then go to bed.'

I did as she said, and here I have lain ever since, chasing sleep with the sting of the brandy still in my throat.

I wish that you were here with me. You always tend to me so well.

Love always,
    Your Mafalda

Letter: Mafalda Lowell to Lucy North
Friday, 9th May 1884
Buda-Pesth, Austro-Hungarian Empire

My dearest Lucy,

I will hurry past my thanks for your birthday wishes. You will forgive me when you hear what I have to say.

This afternoon, Mama and Mátyás went out to complete the land purchase. Quite against my will I was stuck behind the French ledgers, which I had hoped to leave with Mátyás but of course, a man's signature was needed on the bill of sale. No gadding about the countryside for me!

When my hand began to ache and cramp, I decided I might as well grit my teeth and go to see Aunt Réka. She is calmer, but I would not say she is any better. She asked me to read to her, as always, so I selected a book from the perfectly height-organized little shelf by her bed. I chose at random, my aunt watching me all the while.

'Would you like to hear a translation of Petrarch?'

'Why not? It's as good as any other.'

I did my best, choking through the purple verbiage. I read for an age, my throat becoming more and more hoarse, until at last Aunt Réka slipped into sleep. It was when I was reshelving the book of sonnets that I saw something odd. A small red volume of fairy tales was out of place. I picked it up, meaning to return it to its proper home, but it rather piqued my interest. Thinking it would do well as a distraction when I next suffer from insomnia, I slipped it into the pocket of my dress. I whispered a goodbye to my sleeping aunt, and crept away as quietly as I could.

After that, between the French ledgers and various household duties, I did not have a minute to myself until the evening. Mama herself returned just before dinner. She was in a wonderful mood, thrilled that the farmland has finally been sold and convinced that her presence meant that the buyer, the elderly Transylvanian count I have mentioned to you, paid more for it.

'He remarked upon my resemblance to his late mother,' Mama told me, while I did my best to pretend to pay attention. 'Apparently it is most significant. The colouring, he said, and the high-bridged nose. I chose to take it as a compliment.'

I could not have cared less. 'Is that so?'

'Indeed. It is not so surprising; all the great families of the old days were connected somehow or other. I must say though, some of his views on the Empire were very outspoken, and wouldn't be out of place in one of your aunt's nationalist pamphlets.'

I responded dutifully and went to bed as early as I could, pleading a headache from all that reading in dim light. Partridge even came up and rubbed lavender oil on my temples. She does not have your skill at the task, and I missed you more than ever.

When sleep duly refused to come I took out the red volume from my pocket and examined it. It was a book of old Magyar folk tales, unsurprising as Aunt Réka has many such. It had been well thumbed in the forty years since its printing. It was sheer luck that I began my reading with the very last tale – 'The Witch of Drachenwald'. When I closed the book, I saw its back cover was bulkier than it ought to have been. On closer inspection, I found that a slit had been made between the lining and the leather of the cover itself. Something crinkled thickly within. With the aid of my letter opener, I encouraged the contents out onto my writing desk. Several letters, made slender and yellow with age and handling, slid out. They were all addressed to my late uncle in a flowing and feminine hand that was definitely not my aunt's.

I opened the topmost, and began to read. I have stayed up until almost dawn to translate them into English that I might send them to you. Be warned, my love. They are shocking. What should I do with them? And why does my aunt have them tucked away on her bookshelf? Tell me, for I am at a loss.

Write to me as soon as you have read all.

Love always,

    Your Mafalda

Letter: Piroska Tolvay to Gabor Jacobinus
Saturday, 25th April 1874
Őriszentanna, Transylvania, Austro-Hungarian Empire

[Editor's Note: The translation made by ML was good but to-the-letter, and some terms and idioms lost their intended sense. I have tidied this up where possible so the English reader will better understand the content. Also for the English reader, I have noted names in standard English name order with the family name placed second, except where absolutely necessary.]

Dearest Gabor,
I, or rather, we, arrived safely on Thursday evening. You were right that this place would not be what I am used to, but needs must. Nurse Erzsébet has made me very welcome. I believe she secretly disapproves, but for love of you and of your unborn child she is willing to accept me and treat me kindly. Her house is not at all as rustic as I had feared. It is a quaint building in the local style, somewhat larger than her neighbours' but with the same long, sloping tiled roof and prettily carved shutters as it had in my imagination. It certainly has its own charm, which I'm sure I will grow to love during my stay.

So far I have been largely left to my own devices during the daytime, when Nurse Erzsébet attends to the women of the surrounding villages. I am glad I brought a good supply of books. In the evenings we sit and sew, or read, or talk. Tomorrow I will join her and the rest of the household in attending the village church, which she visits at least once every day. I have warned Giselle in the strongest terms that she is not to give us away with any of her airs and graces. Speaking of Giselle, she has made a friend of both Nurse Erzsébet's maid Janka and the cook, Csilla, and together they are all conspiring to feed me up. Paprika hendl is to be served at least four times a week, I am told. I am not sure if this is a promise or a warning. At least Giselle has found some occupation other than gazing worriedly at me. She was not pleased to leave the city. You were right that a French maid would not be thrilled by a remove to the Transylvanian countryside but she is a good and loyal girl for all her grand ways and I know I am fortunate to have her. I wish I could have brought more servants but I have been obedient to your orders. There is, as they say, a first time for everything.

My greatest wish of all is that I could have stayed in Buda-Pesth with you. I know what you will say and you are wise to say it – it is better I am hidden away and taken care of by those you trust until after the birth. I have not heard from the Baron since he refused my request for a divorce. I left him an address at an inn in Kolozsvár, and have arranged that any letters for me that arrive there will be sent on here. As I say though, so far, nothing. When I present him with our child he cannot but give us the freedom we desire. I can hardly wait to spend the rest of my life with you at some quiet country villa, with only our little family to concern us. The baby moves with greater strength every day, keen to be out in the world to meet his papa. Not so very long now, little one! I am quite sure he is a boy. I hope he has your character and all your virtues.

Nurse Erzsébet has come to tell me I must go to bed at once. Apparently I must have as much sleep as possible and not overexcite myself. If only I could sleep! My body feels lethargic and yet my mind is alive with the hope and joy of our future together.

With all the love in the world,
    Your Piri

Letter: Piroska Tolvay to Gabor Jacobinus
Wednesday, 29th April 1874
Őriszentanna, Transylvania, Austro-Hungarian Empire

Dearest Gabor,

Thank you for your letter. I am glad to know that arrangements for our departure are progressing so well. It makes me so happy whenever I hear from you.

Nurse Erzsébet continues to take very good care of me. She likes to tell me stories about your mischief when you were a boy. So far my favourite is the one about the frog, which made me cry with laughter. One day I hope to tell such tales of our son, although I would be quite happy to have him go his entire life without granting a frog its liberty on the dining table during a formal banquet.

I had feared that at church on Sunday I might attract undue attention but in the end it was no more than any other new face might. Everyone knows and trusts Nurse Erzsébet given her position in the community, so they simply accept it when she tells them I am a distant relation of her late husband. We walked home with a few of the more genteel local women and it was pleasant to listen to their gossip. Apparently the son of the butcher has run away from home and it is the source of much discussion. Had he been mistreated? The butcher is known to be quick to anger. Perhaps he is simply disobedient? Perhaps; boys will be boys. Did he wander into the forest and meet with some accident? It could be so, it could be so. Could he have been attacked by an animal? Unlikely, but possible, always possible. Redheads are said to be unlucky and he has the reddest hair anyone in the village has ever seen. None of the women were overly anxious, merely entertaining themselves before the return to their domestic duties. The consensus was that the boy would probably turn up somewhere soon.

By Monday it was entirely forgotten because a party of Szgany came to the market and caused quite the distraction. Giselle was absolutely beside herself, buying lace and ribbons and trinkets and carved wooden birds and all sorts of things. I let her do as she pleased as she has had so little enjoyment of late. An old Szgany woman with a face like a wrinkled apple offered to tell my fortune but I pushed Giselle forwards instead. The woman squinted at Giselle's palm for some while before telling her that she is to meet a charming stranger who will change her life, and very soon too. At least, I think that's what she said as her accent was extremely strong and the words came out mumbled from her toothless mouth. I bought some pretty lace myself from the next stall, kept by a young woman who was truly vast with child. She looked at my belly and smiled rather shyly, before giving me a much better price than she had Giselle.

'Does he kick you a great deal in the evening?' she asked. I was a little shocked to be addressed by such a person, though I suppose the normal standards are relaxed out here in the provinces and of course she would have no idea of my true rank.

'Sometimes,' I told her as I handed her the money, 'but I go outside after dinner and stroll around for a while and then he quietens down. And you?'

'Oh yes, my little one kicks hard, but I would take a tisane for it. I would not go outside! You ought not to either, madam.'

'Why not?'

Before she could answer, the old fortune-teller appeared at her elbow and whispered to her in their strange undulating language.

'Please excuse me, madam, my mother tells me that I should not have spoken to you so.' She shot a glance at the old woman and stared down at her feet, or such of them as she was able to see.

'The night air is not healthy for you in your condition. The spirits might come for the baby,' the old woman told me firmly in her mumbling manner.

'I thank you for your concern,' I told them, and moved quickly on before I could be drawn into any further conversation. What odd people, and what peculiar superstitions they have in this part of the world!

Your son seems to know I have written this, as he is now moving about with quite some force. I might go and walk a little now in the hope that he will spare me when I am trying to sleep. I will summon Giselle to accompany me. I am sure she would scare away any wandering spirits with her chatter, or at the very least bore them into submission.

Later

It seems the old woman might have spoken truly, or so Giselle insists. Not about the spirits, but about her fortune. It was just turning from sunset to twilight as she and I were taking a turn around the garden. We were saluted over the low wall that separates the herb garden from the street by a tall man dressed entirely in black, clean-shaven but for a long grey moustache, and with a courtly air about him. I returned his salutation and, politeness being satisfied, he made to continue but Giselle quite dragged me down to the gate.

'Good evening, madam, miss,' he greeted us both. 'A lovely evening for a walk, is it not?'

Giselle hung upon this pronouncement as if it were great philosophy.

'Indeed,' she replied, moonstruck.

'Indeed so, sir,' I added, 'but we ought to be getting back to the house.'

'I can tell from your voice that you are from Buda-Pesth – surely there they keep later hours than this?'

'My mistress is in a delicate state of health, sir, and becomes tired very easily,' Giselle interjected.

The gentleman was clearly sensible of the impropriety of her remark but had the breeding not to dwell upon it.

'In this part of the world most people go to sleep not very long after the sunset. Peasants are always afraid of the dark.' He smiled, revealing sharp white teeth. I could not say why, but I shuddered. Giselle giggled, clearly not of my mind.

'Are you from nearby, sir?'

'Yes, my family has been here for many centuries. Yours, I think, come from the great French metropolis, am I correct?'

'Quite correct, sir.'

'The City of Light, they call it. Perhaps Parisians are also afraid of the dark?'

I could not bear it. The entire exchange was not at all appropriate.

'I have heard today that if I remain out of doors after nightfall I shall have trouble with spirits, so I must insist on going inside. Come, Giselle.'

'Ah, more peasant superstitions. I assure you, you are quite safe, madam. There are not so many monsters abroad as they might have you believe.'

'I appreciate your reassurance,' I said, turning away.

'You are quite welcome. I beg that you forgive my rudeness; I have not asked your name.'

Of course I did not wish to give it, so I did as we agreed I would, and claimed Nurse Erzsébet's married name as my own.

'I am Madam Lakatos. And you?'

'I am Count Dracula.' He bowed. 'I must be on my way. I bid you both goodnight. Perhaps we will meet again when I next pass.'

With that he continued on down the road, leaving Giselle practically whimpering as he drew further and further away. I scolded her all the way back to the house for speaking to a man unknown to us and not introduced. She merely whined that he *must* be the man the ancient Szgany woman had spoken of, and then sulked when I pointed out that he was well over forty and therefore far too old for her. She is not usually so ridiculous; I cannot think what has got into her. Perhaps it is the isolation here, and lack of proper society? I sent her to bed as soon as I could.

What would you advise me to do with her? You are so wise in such matters, and I envy you your reliable attendants. It is a shame that Nurse Erzsébet did not have a daughter to serve me as her son serves you. Perhaps I will have a better idea of the right course of action in the morning. Your own son seems to have gone to sleep so his mother will follow his fine example.

I love you always, my darling.
　　Your Piri

Letter: Piroska Tolvay to Gabor Jacobinus
Thursday, 30th April 1874
Óriszentanna, Transylvania, Austro-Hungarian Empire

Dearest Gabor,
Oh how bitterly I regret my words of yesterday! This morning, Giselle did not appear to awaken me. Nurse Erzsébet came herself, bringing a vial containing one of her tonics which she insisted I drink right away.

'Baroness,' she began as soon as I had swallowed the last drops, 'I am deeply grieved to have to tell you that early this morning the night-watchman saw Giselle fall from her bedroom window. She did not survive. I am so terribly sorry.'

I do not think I truly heard her, or understood.

'She fell? How could she fall?' My hands shook as they shake now, and Nurse Erzsébet took the glass bottle from me.

'The night-watchman said that he saw some dark shape at her window, a bird or a large bat. Giselle was leaning from the window, perhaps attempting to shoo it away. She leaned too far and, well, there was nothing anyone could have done.'

My poor, poor girl! Nurse Erzsébet held me close while I wept, as she must have held you as a child when some sorrow befell you. Giselle has been with me for years now, and her sweetness and her silliness have charmed and exasperated me in equal measure. She served me so faithfully for all her faults, and now she must remain here, out in the wilderness! Nurse Erzsébet would not let me see her lest the shock do me some damage, or harm the child. She tells me I should rest abed today, and she will send her own Janka to attend me. I must write to the Dupont family and send them a lock of Giselle's hair. I know her parents depended in part on her income so I must make some provision for them. Will you see to it, while I am here so far from civilization? I need to rest now; I will write more later.

Later

Janka is a sturdy and hard-working girl, but she comes from the village and is full of the fears and superstitions of her people. She was clearly under orders not to distress me but after an hour of her reading aloud from the Gospels I could bear it no more, and pressed her to tell me if she knew anything else beyond what I had already been told.

'I may not speak of it, madam. My mistress says you must rest and be calm.'

'I am the more upset from not knowing. You would not want that.'

'But my mistress has said—'

'Please. I must know.'

Janka sighed. She closed her Bible, clutching it tightly across her chest as if she would hide behind it.

'My room is next door to – was next door to . . .' She halted, unable to force out the words, but I was too impatient to allow for her stuttering.

'Yes?'

'It's like this, madam,' she began hesitantly. 'Giselle slept in the attic room next to mine. I was sitting at my window stitching a hem which I had not had time to do the day before. The window was locked, of course. We don't open our windows at night here. Giselle though, she laughed at that and would do as she pleased. I was focused on my work when I heard a noise, a sort of scrabbling next door. I thought nothing of it and now I wish I'd gone to check! Though if I had . . .' Janka shuddered. 'I carried on with my stitching and heard nothing more until . . . until she fell. I heard it, madam, and I won't forget it until my dying day. I heard poor Giselle's body hit the ground!'

She began to sob. I felt guilty for pushing her, but I did not stop. Please do not think badly of me, my love. I was in my own grief and desperate to know how my poor companion had met her end. The strangeness of it drove me on. Giselle was graceful and deft in her movements, and certainly not clumsy enough to fall out of a window while shooing away a bird.

'Then what happened, Janka? What did you do?'

'I looked out of the window, and saw her there, sp . . . sp . . . sprawled out. The night-watchman came running round the corner, and I dashed out and down the stairs as fast as I could. We were too late. But,' she said, leaning over the counterpane and grasping my hand, 'I did not hear her scream! If she had screamed as she fell I certainly would have heard it, and who would not scream as they took such a fall? And, madam, she had marks on her neck like puncture wounds—' Here she could bear it no more and fled from the room, and has since refused to speak to me again.

What does it mean? Oh, my darling, I wish you were here to comfort me! Write soon.

Yours ever,
Piri

Letter: Piroska Tolvay to Gabor Jacobinus
Monday, 4th May 1874
Őriszentanna, Transylvania, Austro-Hungarian Empire

My darling,
I am so very frightened. Fear is contagious and everyone here is afraid, even Nurse Erzsébet, though she does her best to conceal it from me. She attends me herself and tries to calm me but how can I be calm? It is some day of local superstition here, when the peasants believe evil walks abroad, so the entire house has been sprinkled with holy water by the priest. All day he has gone door to door, sprinkling and sprinkling. I pray desperately that it helps.

We buried Giselle this morning. It rained all throughout. Nurse Erzsébet did not want me to go to the funeral but I insisted. I felt I owed Giselle that at least. If only I had not brought her here! The service in the little church was short and cold. As we followed the coffin into the churchyard, I seemed to feel Giselle there with me, tormented at being left so very far from her home and from the life she had known. My knees weakened. Janka and Nurse Erzsébet had to support me, one on either side. I did not want to leave Giselle in the ground all alone, and I confess I became quite agitated.

But worse, much worse, was to come. As we stood at the edge of the grave, the gravediggers in their earth-stained clothes came forward to roll away the canvas covering laid over the dark hole that was the fruit of their labours. The priest began to speak the holy words as they did so, but he had barely got out half a sentence before he stopped with a strangled gasp. I followed his wide-eyed gaze down, and there, in the bottom of the fresh grave, was the mangled body of the red-headed butcher's boy. His limbs were flung out at odd angles and his neck was bent in such a way as to show it must be broken. His face was caught in a rictus of terror that I will not forget for the rest of my life. In my last moments of consciousness before I fainted, I saw that on his neck were two red wounds like puncture marks.

I was insensible for hours. I awoke later in my bed, with Nurse Erzsébet sitting by me. She gave me another tonic and told me that a rider has gone to Bistritz to send a telegram to you. She wants you to come at once, with as short a delay as possible. She is not keen that I be moved but, she says, to be at the scene of so much tragedy will not be good for me or for our son so you must take me away. I know that writing this letter is ridiculous given that I will soon see you, but it soothes me a little to imagine that I am speaking to you and telling you all these troubles. I comfort myself knowing that you will be here shortly to take over that duty in person. If we are fortunate, you might even be here by morning. I will sleep now that it might come all the sooner. Nurse Erzsébet has left me another tonic which I will take now. I pray to God that He grant me a dreamless night.

Your Piri

Letter: Piroska Tolvay to Gabor Jacobinus
Wednesday, 1st July 1874
Buda-Pesth, Austro-Hungarian Empire

Dear Gabor,

How can you ask me if I still love you? I will love you until the day I die. That is part of my punishment. I have told you and told you again that I cannot see your face without seeing our son's in my memory, cold and blue and still. How can you be so unfeeling? How can you want this for me for the rest of my life? You say we will have other children, as if this one were not his own unique soul, as if this loss will not haunt me all the days that are left to me. You say I am ungrateful. No, I feel the truest gratitude to you for all that you did in removing me home and in engaging doctors to oversee my recovery, but that does not mean I owe you my very self!

I know you do not believe what I have told you about the night our son died. I know you say it is a brain fever but you are wrong. I know that I saw the night-watchman from my window by the light of the just-past-full moon as I paced, unable to sleep. I know that I saw a dark shape swoop down upon him, I know that I heard his cry cut short. And I know that when I doubted myself and peered out to see better, a stark demonic face looked up from its feeding with the night-watchman's blood running down its chin. I know that it grinned to see my terror. I know that I turned, I know that I tried to run, I know that I slipped and fell hard on the wooden floor, and I know that I was racked by the cramping that heralded the too-early coming of our child. I know that I heard mocking, hellish laughter as I cried out in heartache and pain. And I know that I saw the devil outside my window, hoping for entry.

You cannot imagine that night. Nurse Erzsébet did all she

could but had to admit defeat and send for the priest. I see God's hand in the fact that he survived the journey, while that thing stalked outside. Nurse Erzsébet paid the man handsomely to baptize our son and to believe, contrary to the evidence of his own eyes, that the little one had lived just long enough for that not to be blasphemy. I held our son in my arms and my tears fell on his face so that it seemed he mourned his own passing. He looked so like you.

And now? Now, I beg Our Lord for His forgiveness and His protection. Now I have given myself back to my husband. He does not know the name of the man who tried to seduce his wife away, and I have certainly not told him about our child. I trust that you will keep these secrets. I told him that I had an attack of conscience when it came to the point of true betrayal, and he loves me enough to believe me. He even blames himself for leaving me alone and lonely so much of the time. Now, when he travels, I will go with him. It may be that we are hardly in Buda-Pesth at all in the future. I will try to be a good wife to him even while loving you. It will be my penance. I bid you marry and forget me. Find some cheerful young woman who has known no grief and no horror and no fear, and have those other children you wished for us to have together.

Do not write to me again. Do not come to the house. If we see each other in society we will smile and talk lightly, as if all this were only a sad dream.

Goodbye, my love,
    Piri

PART THREE

Sir John Seward's personal diary
Friday, 9th January 1903
Littlemore Hospital, Oxfordshire

With all the business of such a large establishment to wrangle I had expected to find myself exhausted, but it is not the case. I feel invigorated, even exhilarated. I eat well, I sleep well, and my nightmares have not returned for several days.

Our newest patient arrived this afternoon, accompanied by her husband and an attendant. Dr Knight was busy elsewhere so I interviewed the husband alone. I took him into my office while the nurses saw to his wife. He is one of the tallest men I have ever beheld, and with the build of a bull to boot. I imagine in his youth he must have been impressive, though he seems to be ageing rather prematurely. I doubt he is much over forty, but he has the careworn face of a man a decade older than that.

He sagged in the chair on the other side of my desk with the look of despondency I have seen on many over the years. When I was younger, I was rather more affected by seeing such emotions. Now, whilst I would never wish to be unfeeling, I know it is of far more service to the patient to expend less effort on comforting their relatives and more on my medical assessment.

I assumed my most business-like manner in the hope that he might find it reassuring, as men of the upper classes often do.

'I'd like to begin by asking you some questions, if you'll permit. You may have been asked them before by others but I want to make sure I have a correct and complete understanding of your wife's case.'

He passed a tired hand across his tired eyes.

'Doctor, my wife has taken to eating ants. I would do anything you asked of me if it might help her.'

'I'm certainly glad to hear that,' I said briskly. 'Let's begin by talking about that consumption of ants. Your wife's records state that it began approximately six months ago. Is that correct?'

'Yes, that's correct.'

'Did anything unusual or out of the ordinary routine occur around that time which might have particularly upset your wife?'

'I really couldn't say.'

I made a note.

'In your opinion, has your wife so far received any treatment that has led to any material improvement of her affliction?'

'No, I don't believe so. Rotation therapy rendered her silent and withdrawn for months. Warm-water hydrotherapy had no long-term effect although I was told that she seemed to enjoy it, and was quite calm for a handful of hours afterwards. She has since undergone this regularly. *Cold*-water hydrotherapy gave her a chill, and bleeding did nothing at all. She does experience periods of tranquillity and lucidity at times, often when Mrs Lakatos is with her.'

'Mrs Lakatos?'

'Yes. You might have seen her; she came with us here.'

This must be the attendant I'd glimpsed in passing.

'Ah, yes. I believe I did.'

'She has a gift of soothing my wife which I do not possess. I've always supposed it to be a feminine ability of some sort. That's one of the reasons my wife has been in Yorkshire. Mrs Lakatos resides there.'

'Is it not a great deal more inconvenient for you to visit her?'

'I . . . Well, to tell you the truth, doctor, I don't like to visit often. It breaks my heart to see her so ill and to know that I can do nothing to alleviate her suffering.'

I had wondered, privately, if the husband might be the source of his wife's trauma. Now with him here before me, I could hardly credit it. His eyes began to fill with tears, and I made as if regarding my notes very intently while he blotted them away with his handkerchief.

'Has Mrs Lakatos been in your employ for a long time?' I asked when he was once again master of himself.

'She isn't in my employ. She's a close friend of my wife's, and has been for perhaps twenty years. They were quite devoted to each other before my wife became ill, and her devotion continues still.'

'In that case, I ought to speak with Mrs Lakatos as well.'

'Of course.'

I made another note to set up an appointment.

'Now, the next few questions may be difficult for you to answer but it's of the utmost importance that you do so as fully as you can.'

'Very well.'

'Thank you. The onset of your wife's illness was in 1893, I believe?'

'Yes, that's correct.'

'Please can you tell me about that? What symptoms did you notice first?'

I expected him to have need of his handkerchief again. I did not expect his mirthless laughter.

'Symptoms? There were no symptoms!'

I forced down my repulsion to his reaction, reminding myself of how sustained stress may affect even the best of men.

'What do you mean?'

'She had no symptoms, no gradual decline of any sort. One day she was perfectly normal, the next she was mad!'

The medical record had contained the words 'sudden onset' but I had not imagined anything quite so dramatic as this.

'Tell me, if you would, what happened on that last day before she became ill.'

'We were staying at our London home. I had taken my wife shopping, for hats or gloves or some such. I used to like to buy her gifts. She'd receive them with such good cheer that it was a true pleasure.' He paused for a moment, lost in the recollection. 'I remember this next as if it were yesterday; I've been over it so often in my mind. We were leaving Giuliano's boutique on Piccadilly. My wife had been waiting outside in our carriage, and I came out and brought her her purchases, all wrapped up. She looked up and smiled at me and then suddenly her expression changed. The memory of it is burned into my brain – such abject terror! I turned to see what had prompted it and saw nothing of note, really nothing at all to give her such a reaction as that. She fainted dead away and I had her brought home as quickly as possible. The next morning I found her on the terrace, deathly pale and in a sustained swoon from which she was unable to be awakened. When she finally did wake much later in the day it was as if she were sleepwalking.'

'Sleepwalking?'

'Yes, she was almost not present in herself. She continued this way for several days, wandering the house and gardens, growing weaker and weaker, until our family doctor, Dr Williamson, recommended removing her to the countryside. We went to our estate, and there my wife did eventually return to full consciousness, but ever since it has been nothing but hallucinations, nightmares, physical infirmities, shaking, and now this vile consumption of ants of all things!'

He seemed poised to continue, but I interjected.

'Do you know the approximate date of this swooning?'

'The date?'

'Yes. It may be important.'

'Why?'

'Various reasons,' I hedged, not wanting to admit that I asked at the prompting of some sparking in my brain whose origin I couldn't quite identify. 'Do you recall?'

'I will never forget it. It was September of 1893.'

I wrote it down carefully.

'Doctor, there was a period of time when she could not even recognize our children. This illness has destroyed our family. I beg you to help her in any way that you can.'

'I will do my utmost, I promise you,' I said, with all the reassurance I could muster. 'This is a new century, and advances in medical science mean that we have a greater understanding of the mind than ever before. I will employ every modern scientific method to help your wife.'

'Thank you, doctor. Thank you. Will you examine her today?'

'No, I'll give her time to recover from her journey. Nurses will attend her and make sure that she is quite comfortable. I will see her tomorrow, possibly with my colleague Dr Knight on hand as well. Are you staying in the city?'

'Yes at Christ Church, my old college. The Master is a good friend of mine. Mrs Lakatos is lodging with his mother in Iffley, and will be available to speak with you whenever you wish.'

'Thank you, Sir Joseph. I will keep you informed.'

Poor fellow. He pressed my hand hard, like a man who has felt a flicker of determined hope for the first time in a long time. For his sake as well as for my patient's, I want very much to justify it.

Lucy North's journal
Sunday, 4th May 1884
Whitby, Yorkshire, England

[Editor's Note: For reasons of the reader's comprehension, documents are not always presented in strict chronological order.]

I wondered why Eliza was so insistent that we allow time for a rest after attending church, and now the mystery is solved. The famous hundred and ninety-nine steps up to St Mary's, of which I had never heard, are quite a challenge to the constitution. Still, I am pleased to have a moment to myself with this journal as the last few days have been too busy to allow it. I have managed to write to Mafalda, of course, between engagements, but otherwise it has been quite the social whirl. Eliza has taken it upon herself to introduce me to all of her friends, of which there are an adoring myriad. We have taken tea with various dowagers, picked flowers with their daughters, given basket after basket to the poor of the town, and brought medicines beyond number to the sick – the less contagious sick, of course. Eliza is Eliza, after all.

My dear friend has been very good to me but I surmise that she thinks by keeping me busy I will miss Mafalda less. All and sundry have come to dinner to this end, including the most handsome vicar in the history of the world. At first I could hardly look him in the eye. Really, such looks are inappropriate for one with a religious vocation. I had a very interesting discussion with him on the nature of the Trinity, and on how it may be best explained to those in far-away lands who have never heard the doctrine. I am not sure he agreed with my opinions, or indeed agreed with a lady holding any opinions at all, and has become less attractive as a result. Today in the box pews there were several well-dressed misses attempting to catch his attention while he delivered the sermon, so this seems not to be a barrier to his desirability for most.

Let me see, where did I leave off my tale before?

Joseph left Whitby the morning after our arrival, as planned. He and I breakfasted downstairs with the Colonel presiding, while Eliza enjoyed her married privilege and ate in her room. Colonel Cartwright has a most military air, and anyone would pick him out as an army man without him speaking a word. I still find it a little shocking that he is almost the same age as Mafalda's father, Sir Gerald. They served together in India, before Sir Gerald's brother died and he inherited the baronetcy and had to return home. I longed to ask about his time on the subcontinent but on discovering that the Colonel had once visited Beechwood, Joseph rather dominated the conversation. The Colonel was a good host and humoured him graciously even as Joseph kept on about cattle and crops and improvements to the gardens until almost the very last moment. Certainly no one could ever accuse Joseph of being less than dedicated to his life's work!

Eliza came down just as Joseph was about to leave, to shake his hand and wish him safe travels. When my turn came to bid him farewell, he did not shake my hand but bowed over it and kissed it.

'You have stood a good friend to me, Lucy. I will trust in your discretion in the matter we spoke of.'

'Of course. Goodbye, Joseph; I wish you the very best.'

What else could I say? He put on his hat and hopped into the waiting carriage, waving jauntily as he left.

'Whatever did he mean by that?' Eliza asked as we went back into the house.

'I wish I could tell you, but I'm afraid I'm not at liberty to say.'

'Really?' she said, with a smile creeping across her face. 'Are you and he—'

'No! No, it isn't like that.'

'Forgive me, I didn't mean to offend.'

'It's nothing, really. Joseph asked for my advice on certain personal matters, and I did my best to give it. That's all.'

'Well then,' she said with the grace that wins her such affection from so many, 'I'm sure he feels all the better for your help. Now, shall I send Alice up to help you into a visiting dress?'

And so began the whirl of the last few days, bringing me here to the writing desk in the Blue Room, with aching limbs from the climb to church.

The question that now occupies me is this: should I tell Mafalda what Joseph intends? He asked me to speak favourably of him to her, and I'm unsure now if he meant before his proposal or afterwards. I hardly think I can do either and keep faith with myself. I can't tell my beloved to marry a man just because he wishes it! I hope she sends him away utterly stung. I hope he marries a country woman and breeds an army of tall, well-built children who run wild at Beechwood and scare all his precious cattle. No, no, I don't mean it, or at least I hope I don't. I only want him to forget that he ever thought of Mafalda in such a way.

The clock is chiming and it is time for luncheon. Alice will be here to dress me at any moment, and her attentions always seem to soothe me. She is a wonderful listener. Not that I am gabbling my innermost thoughts to my borrowed maid, but she is such a steady creature that when I talk to her I feel her steadying me in turn. A truly valuable gift.

*

Night

Oh God, what if Joseph decided to ask by letter? His proposal might already be speeding across the Continent. What if she says yes? I shouldn't think it. I mustn't think it. But, what if?

Lucy North's journal
Thursday, 8th May 1884
Whitby, Yorkshire, England

Today is Mafalda's birthday. It is the first time since we met that we have not spent it together, and it pains me beyond the expected measure. I miss her almost as much as she wishes me to. I was relieved to find not one but two letters from Buda-Pesth awaiting me at breakfast, which I have tucked into these pages. Mafalda makes no mention of any communication with Joseph, thank goodness. Though, as I think about it, he would have had to send a telegram to get his proposal to her fast enough for her to write of it so quickly.

I ought to be ashamed of myself, being so caught up in my own troubles. Aunt Réka sounds dreadfully and frighteningly ill, and I will make a note to remember her in my prayers.

After breakfast, Eliza and I went out to the telegraph office to send a telegram to Mafalda to convey our birthday greetings. We had a pleasant walk around the town afterwards, taking in the view of the sea from the promenade despite there being a rather strong breeze. We walked as far up to the lighthouse as is permitted before turning back. It is a most beautiful vista, with the houses of the old town climbing all over each other in such a jumble of rooftops as one might see in pictures of medieval German cities. Eliza enjoyed the promised 'healthful' fresh air and remarked upon it several times, though to my London-accustomed senses it all smelled a bit too much of fish.

There were hardly any other people walking on such a windy day so we had the place to ourselves. When we had almost reached the town, Eliza stopped and turned to me with a most penetrating look upon her face. I had been about to suggest we brave a walk all the way up to the Abbey which broods from its hilltop and which I have not yet visited, but seeing her expression I changed my mind.

'Lucy, will you tell me a truth if I ask it?'

'Yes, of course.'

'Even on a sensitive matter?'

I paused before answering.

'I'd rather hear the question before making such a promise.'

'And I would rather have your promise first.'

Eliza has never been a dramatic sort of person and my curiosity was piqued. Rashly, I promised. Eliza took a deep breath. Her words, when they came, were exceedingly cautious.

'Do you ever intend to marry? Or are you . . . do you not . . . is it not for you?'

'Why do you ask?' I responded, cautious now.

'Reverend Baker has asked me if he might come to call on you.'

I was convinced that I had misheard her, supposing that the wind had snatched some crucial words away.

'What did you say?'

'Reverend Baker wishes to call on you. He was quite taken with you after you sat next to each other at dinner the other week, and he wrote asking if you might welcome deepening your acquaintance with him.'

I was stunned into silence. I knew as well as Eliza what this meant. I have never, not even once, considered myself to be an object of male attention or desire in any way. Why should I? My looks are unremarkable, I have no real sense of style other than what Mafalda has imparted, I have but a very little fortune, and I am no more intelligent than any other young lady who has received such education as I have. Why, I thought, would any man ever look at my mouse-brown hair, muddy eyes and plain face and want to 'deepen his acquaintance' with me?

Seeing I had no answer, Eliza ploughed on.

'I have known him for all the time I have lived here, and the Colonel has been acquainted with him even longer. He is intelligent and sober enough, though not so much as to be dull. He has a wit and, of course, those glorious looks! You would make such a charming couple.'

It seems strange now as I record this, that for the blink of an eye I seemed to see an alternate future laid out before me. I could say yes, and Reverend Baker would pay me a call. He would come and sit in Eliza's drawing room and we would sip tea and speak of this and that. I would play and sing for him at sundry parties, and find occasion to show him my sketches or my embroidery, or perhaps let it be known that I speak both German and French. I would not share my knowledge of Hungarian though, as that would mark me out as an oddity. As the summer progressed, we might go for walks together with Eliza and the Colonel in tow, or perhaps with Alice as a token chaperone. We would dance together at various gatherings, the dowagers and matrons throwing us together as often as possible. By the end of summer he would write to Sir Gerald or even to my own father to make his intentions known, and Eliza would help him to select a 'Toi et Moi' diamond ring for my finger. Then he would come to the door with his handsome face blushing red, mopping his brow. Eliza would whisk herself away and leave us alone, and he would drop to one knee and present me with the ring, his heart, and a respectable role in society as a vicar's wife. And there in Eliza's garden as summer drew to a close, I would sell my body and my soul and no longer be my own self.

I cut Eliza off with a curt 'No, thank you' and moved away, leaving her standing gaping like one of the recently netted fish whose odour so offended my nose. She rushed to catch up with me, and we walked up through the town in an uneasy silence as the wind blew harder and harder. I withdrew so far into my hood that I resembled one of Mr Darwin's tortoises. As we turned away from the main thoroughfares and up towards the West Cliff, we took a shortcut up through what Alice had told me was locally called a 'ginnel', and what I would call a dank alleyway. Eliza unexpectedly took my arm as we walked. Possibly she intended to prevent any further attempt to escape.

'Is it that you dislike Reverend Baker?'

'Well . . .'

'Or is it that you do not wish to marry?'

I decided to honour my friend with the truth.

'No, I do not wish to marry.'

The ginnel sloped upwards and turned abruptly to the left, and we were almost home. Eliza lowered her voice and leaned in closer.

'Is it because of Mafalda?'

I could not speak, rendered mute with the fear of such an admission, but Eliza saw the truth of it in my face.

'I thought as much. I—'

Without warning a great gust of wind came barrelling down the street and almost ripped my hat from my head. I cried aloud, and the heavens opened and rain poured down upon us. Eliza shrieked and began to run towards her house, dragging me along with her. We were soaked in very short order, arriving breathless and sodden on her doorstep.

I was afraid to meet her eye. I fussed with my skirts, shaking them out and rearranging them; anything to avoid acknowledging what had passed between us. Silly goose! This was *Eliza* for goodness' sake. Eliza with a kind word for anyone, Eliza my first true friend, Eliza who met me as a frightened little schoolgirl and treated me like her own cherished sister. When the door opened and we tumbled inside, she caught sight of our bedraggled reflections in the grand looking-glass in the hallway and began to giggle, a girlish noise that sounded like my childhood. I caught it with the swiftness of a fever and soon we were both helpless with laughter, Eliza grasping at the hatstand and I doubled over leaning against the wall. One of the housemaids was attempting to take our wet cloaks without success; the poor thing was so bewildered by the unbecoming behaviour of her mistress that she was practically hopping from foot to foot. I am surprised she did not call for the doctor and have us taken away and committed as hysterics.

Eventually we were divested of our wet clothes. Eliza fussed as she does whenever illness threatens, so we were bundled up in blankets and sequestered together in Eliza's private sitting room before a hastily built fire, with our feet in basins of hot water. Beef tea was brought, maids dismissed, and we were alone again. The storm raged outside but inside all was calm.

'I will put the Reverend off,' Eliza said firmly. 'I will tell him you could not bear to leave London, or that you feel yourself unsuited to the life of a vicar's wife, or anything you like. Make sure to drink all your Bovril, you don't want to catch cold.'

I took a sip as ordered, feeling the warmth spread through me.

'Thank you.' I took in a deep breath. 'I do not . . . disgust you?'

'Disgust me? You're my oldest friend! How could I ever be disgusted by you? It may not be the usual course of things, but I take seriously our Lord's warning not to judge others.'

My eyes filled with tears of relief and gladness and I dropped my head, embarrassed.

'I do worry for you though,' she continued. 'What if Mafalda were to marry?'

'She will not,' I said with a certainty I did not feel.

'But if she did?'

'She will not.'

Eliza paused.

'Well, I'm sure you're right. You know her best. If you were ever to need it, though, you would always have a home here with me.'

As my family home has long been closed to me this offer caused further tears, which fell in alarming quantities onto my blanket. What did I ever do to deserve such a friend as Eliza?

Letter: Alice Smith to Mary and Sarah Smith
Wednesday, 14th May 1884
Whitby, Yorkshire, England

Dear Mam and Sarah,

I hope you are both keeping well, and haven't got the sneezing so badly as last year. I can't seem to shake it. Cook had me go to the grocer's yesterday because Annie was in bed poorly and no one else had the time, and I must have sneezed every step the whole walk back. At least the sun is shining cheerfully. We had a dreadful storm last week, but now the sea looks wonderfully blue and there's a smile on every face. Every face that isn't sneezing, that is. On Nanny Roberts' afternoon out, little Miss Beth insisted we play in the garden and got very worried that my red eyes meant that I was crying for sadness. Bless her sweet soul, she spent all of our play time trying to cheer me up and brought me every toy of hers she could think of and piled them all in my lap. I enjoy the time I spend with her. She is so loved you might think she'd be spoiled but her nature is far too gentle.

Mam, I am doing your bidding to stay as far from gossip as I can. Cook was asking me if it was true that the vicar had wanted to court Miss North, and even though Mrs Cartwright had spoken of it to me while I dressed her the other day, I just shrugged and said I had no idea. I have to say I can't think why a vicar should marry at all. Father Anthony at St Hilda's does perfectly well without a wife.

I send you both all my love, and always remember you in my prayers.

Your Alice

P.S. Sarah, I can feel something wanting to be seen, some awful thing wanting to break through. The pull is getting stronger. I can hear echoes of it already, such desperation, such despair, such shame. I can't block them out. I'm so afraid that one day I'll see something so horrific that I'll be driven out of my mind and be no use to anyone ever again. Something around my throat, tightening and tightening—

[Editor's Note: The letter ends here, then resumes below in a hurried scrawl.]

Morton, it's to be Morton, the butler. I'll do all I can to stop it, but it hardly ever makes any difference.

Lucy North's journal
Sunday, 18th May 1884
Whitby, Yorkshire, England

Yesterday Eliza and I went to visit a poor family living down in the town: a recently widowed mother with three children and another on the way at any moment. With no child quite old enough to work and the woman obviously unable to do so in her current condition, they have been forced to go on parish relief, such as it is. The father was a jet worker of some kind, and the others of his trade bring a collection every month. The family seem to manage, just about, but gifts of food and clothing from the charitable ladies of the town go a long way to assist.

Eliza was quiet when we got home. We took tea in the parlour and discussed what else could be done, though I quickly found I was discussing the matter all by myself. The eldest girl was almost ten – was she quick enough at her lessons to be a pupil-teacher? If not, did Eliza know of anyone who might take her into service? She was still a little young, but perhaps a respectable single lady with a small household might suit? I was voicing a half-formed thought about establishing whether the woman might be willing to take in mending after her confinement, when Eliza quite unexpectedly dissolved into tears.

'I can't bear it! All those children, and in such circumstances! I would take them all if I could, and love them and give them a home—'

'Eliza, you're doing all you can.'

'I envy her, Lucy. That's the truth of it! I envy a woman living on charity, in truly desperate times, because she has all those beautiful children whom she cannot even feed!'

In my heart of hearts I am sure that Eliza did not mean for her words to sound quite so . . . quite so . . . let's say unchristian.

'You have so many blessings,' I said haltingly, foolishly confused.

Eliza looked up, her eyes red and streaming.

'I know, I know. I am so ungrateful. Please, excuse me.'

She hurried out, leaving me speechless and useless.

Eliza did not come to St Mary's with the rest of the household today but stayed in, pleading illness. I wish I had remained at home with her. I found the entire experience very awkward, given my recent rejection of Reverend Baker's overtures. I endeavoured to keep my gaze firmly fixed on the wooden pulpit, that I might not accidentally catch the eye of the Reverend while my mind squirmed in its knowledge of wrongdoing. As the Colonel and I passed the gentleman in question at the church door, my 'Good morning' came out as a strangled squeak. He smiled in a most over-friendly fashion and I hurried away as fast as I could.

Once home, I went up to see Eliza. I found her on her chaise with her hair loose, dressed in an old-fashioned men's banyan which I assume was a souvenir from the Colonel's time in the East. This may be indelicate but in my own journal I might as well be honest – Eliza is afflicted with her monthly indisposition and has been quite low in her mood.

I rang for tea and asked after her state of health.

'I'm afraid I'm not in the best of spirits. You must forgive me for being unfit company.'

'Please don't apologize. It's to be expected that you're out of sorts.'

'It's more than that.' She gazed unhappily down into her teacup as if it might hold all the mysteries of life. 'I want so much to have a child, a child of my own, and I worry that it's a sin of greed when I already have such a sweet little girl to raise.'

What a dunce I am! Why did I not understand that this was at the root of her sadness?

'Surely it isn't greedy,' I said slowly, watching my words in case I sounded as foolish as I felt. 'Perhaps you feel it all the more strongly, now that you know from caring for Beth how much joy motherhood might bring?'

I had meant to comfort her but my words seemed to have the opposite effect.

'The doctor tells me I ought not to hope.' She sighed heavily. 'He tells me that it will likely never happen, and sometimes I think I cannot bear it. I think of my mother and how many children she had, and I wonder what sin I committed to be punished so.'

'Oh, Eliza! Don't say such things. Of course you aren't being punished.'

She did not seem to hear me.

'I would so love for Beth to grow up with some companionship. I enjoyed life in a large family. All of mine and Beth's brothers are grown men, embarking on careers and lives of their own. They adore her and dote upon her when they visit, but it's not the same.'

I thought of my own little half-brothers, utterly unknown to me. Would I dote upon them if I could?

'I feel like such a failure on these days. I spend them wondering if I have done something wrong, or damaged myself in some way. Perhaps I have walked too much, or rested too much, or eaten too much, or not eaten enough. I try to throw myself into charity and good works, so my life might have some purpose. I only ever wanted to be a good and useful wife, and now . . .'

I took her hand and squeezed it.

'You are, and so much more. I promise you. Your husband loves and respects you, and you do much for the good of your friends and your community. Your sister is a sweet, kind, intelligent, cheerful darling. One need only spend a minute with her to know that she is being excellently raised. She will lose none of her qualities whether she grows up with other children or not. I promise you, with such a disposition as hers she will always have friends around her and never know a lonely day in her life.'

Eliza's eyes began to water.

'That means a great deal. I always . . . I mean, I try to . . .'

The tears began to overtake her. 'I try to love her as much as our parents would have, if . . .' I fished a clean handkerchief out of my pocket and passed it over. She sniffed into it, hopelessly inelegantly, before putting her face in her hands and giving in to her emotion. I couldn't just watch her weep; I went to sit next to her on the chaise and I put my arms around her, just as she had done when I was a frightened little girl on my first night at school.

'There now,' I said as she leaned into my shoulder. 'There now.'

'I'm so sorry—' she said, her words choked out between sobs.

'You've nothing to be sorry for. There's no shame in tears.'

I sat with her, stroking her hair and whispering the sort of soothing nonsense that she used to whisper to me, for as long as it took her weeping to subside. Eventually, she pulled away and sat upright, her face puffy and her eyes red, but her expression a great deal calmer. I suspect she had bottled all her feelings up for quite some time, and was quite in need of the release.

'Do you feel better?' I asked.

She nodded. 'I think I do.'

'Good. That's what matters.'

Eliza raised one hand to her face to wipe away the remnants of tears, my sodden handkerchief being useless for the task.

'I must look a dreadful fright.'

I held her at arm's length and regarded her very seriously. 'Yes, you do. Quite terrifying.'

She smiled a tiny smile, the sunshine after the storm.

Just then the first luncheon bell rang and there was a knock at the door. It turned out to be Alice calling me to dress.

'I don't need to go downstairs. Why don't we have a tray brought up?'

Eliza shook her head. 'No, it's quite alright. I really do feel better, but I think I might like to rest.'

'I'll come and see you later, then.'

'That would be lovely, thank you.'

I kissed her on the brow and made my way back to the Blue Room to change, assisted by a yawning Alice. Apparently she has had her sleep disturbed by nightmares of late. Poor girl.

Lunch was a quiet affair in Eliza's absence, and afterwards I read in the garden while the Colonel took himself off to his study. The nanny appeared with her charge, and they set themselves to playing a game of peek-a-boo. Beth's shrieks of enjoyment led me to put down my book and to forget about the delightfully monstrous creation of Mrs Shelley. The nanny and I shared the conspiratorial smile of two women admiring a child and I thought to myself, would I like to be a mother? I will be Aunt Lucy to little Beth, and perhaps one day my brothers' children might know me too, though that is a forlorn hope. But do I want my own children? I hardly dare to even begin to answer that question.

Lucy North's journal
Tuesday, 20th May 1884
Whitby, Yorkshire, England

I received two letters from Mafalda this morning, postmarked several days apart. The speed of the post is very uneven. It seems that letters can take far more or far less time to traverse the Continent depending on the whims of the various national mail carriers. I hate it. If I knew when to expect to hear from her, our separation might be easier to bear.

The details she gives me of Aunt Réka's illness are most disturbing. Poor Aunt Réka has suffered a great deal, and her mind is clearly struggling under the weight of so many extreme emotions. Compassion must be the only course. I have been praying for her, and will redouble my efforts.

It is self-involved of me, I know, but I am relieved that in these letters Mafalda does not mention Joseph at all. Whenever Mafalda receives a proposal of marriage, I am always the first to know of it. If one such had come from Joseph, I am certain she would tell me. Perhaps she would even send a telegram that we might circumvent the slings and arrows of outrageous postal services. I hope that I am doing the right thing by keeping my exchange with Joseph a secret. He is, in some measure, still a friend, and I should not betray his confidence. Besides, I tell myself, what would be the point? Mafalda will break his heart in good time, and all will be as it has always been.

On the unhappy subject of unwanted male attentions, Reverend Baker came to visit today. I had spent the morning with that copy of *Frankenstein* I borrowed from Eliza's library, letting the drizzly morning hours drift by. At lunchtime the sun came out, burning hotly as if making up for lost time. Everything dried out very swiftly, so Eliza, now mostly recovered, scooped up little Beth and we went to have a picnic in the garden. She was cheerful, though her cheer had a determined quality to it. Well. It is better than nothing.

When the Reverend arrived, he found us comfortably ensconced on a picnic blanket with the Colonel not far away, reading the newspaper and keeping a weather eye on the proceedings. Eliza has informed the good Reverend that his attentions would be unwelcome, but it seems that he has so rarely had a 'no' given to his handsome face that he did not understand the concept. After our conversation today, however, I doubt he will be calling again with courtship on his mind.

Ostensibly the Reverend had come to discuss parish business with the Colonel, who has some part in the vestry committee. They sat apart from our little party for perhaps half an hour while we ate our scones, drank our tea, and encouraged Beth in her faltering steps. Eliza tried to teach her to make a daisy chain but her tiny fingers could not manage the task and she was near to tears. Instead, I made one for each of us and we wore them like crowns. Beth giggled and clapped for joy, and Eliza picked her up and kissed both her cheeks.

'I see Aunt Lucy is on her way to being a favourite for life,' Eliza joked.

A shadow fell across me, and across our festivities. Eliza greeted the Reverend as she shaded her eyes from the sun.

'Good afternoon, Mrs Cartwright,' he responded. 'And Miss North, how do you do? And young Miss Gregor, of course.'

Beth squinted suspiciously at the interloper from her position on Eliza's lap.

'Good afternoon, Reverend Baker,' I said, forced to crook my neck in order to see him.

'Would you care for tea?' Eliza nodded to a waiting maid who scuttled back into the house.

'Thank you, most kind.'

I sensed with a growing feeling of resignation that he sought some conversational opening, and in catching sight of my recent reading material lying abandoned on the picnic blanket, he found it.

'Miss North, surely you do not enjoy such books?'

'It is one from my own collection, Reverend,' Eliza told him. 'It's a good story.'

'And more than a good story,' I added, wanting to rile the man in punishment for interrupting our pleasant day. 'A meditation on what is good and what is evil, and the meaning of what it is to be human.'

'Is that so? Well, Miss North, I must hear more.'

He lowered himself onto the blanket, narrowly avoiding Beth's abandoned ham sandwich, and looked at me expectantly.

It occurred to me that in another world, this would be the climax of a novel. The handsome hero with his looks exactly as they ought to be and the not-quite-so-beautiful heroine, discussing literature as a proxy for declaring their innermost feelings. In my mind, I can hear Mafalda laughing as I write this.

'My argument would be that it is Victor Frankenstein himself who is the true villain of the piece. In crossing the ethical and moral boundaries to create this creature, then abandoning it for only its ugliness when he might have shaped its character, he is culpable. All its later sins can hardly be its own, having been born into this world to meet with such callousness.'

'Well *my* argument, Miss North, would be that such books are entirely unsuitable for ladies. Why must novelists make up monsters? Why do we need to look to anything other than the Bible to teach us what is good and what is evil? No, I must put you right on that.'

'I am sure the author means us to examine our own humanity by presenting a being that is both of and not of the same stuff as we are.'

Reverend Baker's expression reminded me of Beth's when she inadvertently sucked on a slice of lemon, thinking it a sweet.

'I fear that this is why it is a commonly held opinion that young ladies ought not to read novels.'

'Do you know, I believe we might sit more comfortably indoors,' Eliza cut in, saving Reverend Baker from being on the receiving end of quite a lot of opinions held by this young lady.

Once in the drawing room I took up a position in the corner, as far as I could get from Reverend Baker, who had seated himself perfectly central on the Chesterfield. In her role as gracious hostess, Eliza engaged him in conversation about the vicarage garden. I took Beth onto my lap to use as a living shield. The Colonel came in to join us and sat by me. I suspect he observes and considers more than he ever lets on. He quietly related the contents of his newspaper, and now I know that the Fenians are active again, Greenwich is in the running to become the fixed point of the prime meridian, and the Mahdist war rumbles on and on and on. The business of the world continues.

Eventually, Reverend Baker stood to take his leave. I set Beth down and she was taken away by her nanny, shrieking into exile.

'I look forward to seeing you on Sunday, Colonel Cartwright, Mrs Cartwright. And, Miss North,' he said, presenting me his hand, 'perhaps a book of sermons should replace your current reading material?'

I smiled widely. 'I fear I must disappoint you on that score. Mrs Shelley has in me far too adoring a disciple.'

He withdrew his hand, and with it his approval. I have never been more cheerful to lose someone's good opinion. Mafalda would be proud.

Night

There has been a very sad and shocking occurrence. My earlier levity feels almost indecent. The butler, Morton, has taken his own life. It looks so stark written in black and white, I can hardly believe it.

Alice brought a cup of tea to his room late this evening, where she found him hanging from the ceiling. Her screams woke the house and the Colonel, poor man, had to cut down the body. Morton was his batman during his time in India, and they saw action together in the Mutiny. I have heard the Colonel say that Morton saved his life on more than one occasion, so of course he is deeply affected. A note confessing to gambling debts only compounded the matter.

'Why didn't he tell me?' the Colonel asked over and over,

as he paced up and down the hallway while we waited for the doctor. 'Why in God's name didn't he tell me?'

As soon as the doctor arrived, the Colonel vanished into his study. He is not the sort of man who would permit himself to weep in front of women. Eliza took receipt of the death certificate and told the servants that the master was not to be disturbed. She gave everyone a tot of medicinal brandy, and sent us all to bed.

I would not be Alice tonight. I have no hope of sleep and I saw nothing of the thing, so how much more dreadful must it be for her? If I cannot sleep then I will pray. An exercise in futility, Mafalda would tell me, but there is precious little else I can do.

Note: Alice Smith to Sarah Smith
Wednesday, 21st May 1884
Whitby, Yorkshire, England

Sarah,
I tried, but it was no good. I was his shadow; I hardly let him out of my sight. He died anyway.
    Alice

Lucy North's journal
Wednesday, 28th May 1884
Whitby, Yorkshire, England

Picking up my pen has been too arduous a task for the last few days. The pall of waiting for the funeral settled over the house and left us all in a kind of sad lethargy. The Colonel, hide-bound by masculine pride, has suffered more than anyone. If he were a woman, he would have spent this time giving free rein to his emotions and finding some relief, but alas.

This morning, the entire household attended Morton's burial. The Colonel himself paid for the plot on the north side of the graveyard just beyond the church wall, looking out to sea. A peaceful spot. The service itself was rather threadbare, being for a suicide. Reverend Baker read a prayer through gritted teeth and seemed poised to make a fuss about Eliza laying flowers, though his better nature, if he has one, prevailed at the last.

The tiny reception afterwards, held here at the house at Eliza's insistence, did not go even half so well. Morton had only two relatives present, a niece and a sister. No amount of polite sympathy on Eliza's part could manage to overcome their self-consciousness. I'm not sure if this was due to the manner of poor Morton's passing, or if they would have been more comfortable downstairs in the servants' hall. Eliza did her best, but they were clearly out of their element.

Afternoon

Everyone has now left, and Eliza has gone to lie down. The afternoon post came some while ago, with a veritable stack for me. I settled at my bureau in the Blue Room to read. A thick packet was dated earliest. The stamps on its hide showed it had been delayed by Customs twice on its journey, and had been sent almost three weeks ago. Three weeks! Two other letters followed, of more recent dates but still overdue. Why? Are we at war in Europe and no one has thought to mention it?

I was still cursing these overzealous border guardians when I opened the packet, and pages and pages in Mafalda's handwriting poured forth. I have tucked them into the cover of this volume. When I finished reading, I found myself weeping. How could anyone not be moved by such a sad and frightening tale? I can only assume that Baroness Tolvay succumbed to some sort of madness after her nightmarish experience. I do not like to use the word 'hysterical' of another woman, as it is so often used to pathologize perfectly acceptable emotions in the female sex, but I fear that in this instance it may be correct. I hope she has since received the medical help that she clearly so badly needed.

Mafalda asks me why Aunt Réka would have had these letters to her husband in the first place. This almost disturbs me more than the tale of adultery and murder they contain. The only explanations that come to my mind are dark ones. My beloved also asks me what she should do with them, but I am at just as much of a loss as she is. What on earth ought I to tell her?

Night
As it turned out, help came from an unexpected source. This evening, I asked Alice to bring me a light supper in my room. I had paced and fretted for hours, and was not up to a formal dinner.

'It's not just you, miss,' Alice told me. 'T'master and mistress didn't dine either. It's been a bit of a day.'

'Yes, it has. How are you?'

'I'm . . . well enough, miss.'

'Are you quite certain? I'm sure Mrs Cartwright would let you have some time off. You could visit your family.' Alice made a non-committal noise as she set out my tray on the tea table. 'Is Mrs Cartwright available, do you know? I'd like to speak with her.'

'I can check, miss, but she took a tincture not long ago and I put her to bed.'

'Oh. Well then.'

'Do you need one yourself, miss? I've some in t'still room, or I can send out for Beecham's if you'd rather?'

'Goodness, there's no need to send anyone out at this time of night. Have you something calming, but not too heavy-handed?'

'How about some camomile and valerian tea? It'll help you sleep.'

I agreed and set about my tray while she fetched it, then sipped as she began the long and arduous task of undressing my hair.

'Are you really alright, after today? It must have been awful for you. Should you be working?'

'I'll be reet, miss. Don't worry about me.'

'If you're sure?'

'Quite sure, miss.'

'Did you know Morton well?' I asked, which I worry now might have sounded prying.

'Not very well, but he was a good sort. He'll be missed. Cook is very upset; they were great friends. She was quite beside herself earlier. I had to give her something for her nerves.'

'I hope she recovers soon,' I replied. 'You're quite well-versed in remedies, I take it?'

'Oh yes, miss. My nana was a herbalist, and my mam and sister keep up her shop. I used to help out, before I entered service.'

'You must have a wealth of useful knowledge.'

Alice picked up the brush and began to work. 'Aye, I'd like to think so, miss, though I was brought up to believe it's God as guides our hands.'

'Are your family quite devout, then? If you don't mind my asking.'

Alice paused. 'I . . . would say so, miss. My nana, certainly. She were always right keen on making sure we knew what was what.'

I thought for a moment. I was in dire need of a confidante, and Eliza was unavailable. Besides, Mafalda might be angry if I told Eliza without permission, and Mafalda's anger is fearsome. Surely the upstanding and devoutly raised Alice would be a safe harbour for a secret?

'Alice, may I ask for your advice?'

'Of course, miss, I'm happy to help. Tilt your head forward if you would.'

I tilted, and addressed the wood of the dressing table.

'A friend of mine has accidentally come into possession of some very personal correspondence, which does not belong to her. My friend has asked me what to do with it, and I've no idea. What would be the right thing to do?'

'Goodness, miss, I was thinking you were going to ask about hair rinses or suchlike. But . . . let me think.'

The swish of the brush and its gentle tug continued as Alice considered the matter.

'Well, miss, the letters belong to the person they were written to, so I'd say make sure that person gets them back.'

'That's very sound, Alice, but unfortunately the recipient is dead.'

'Oh.' Brush, brush, brush. 'Best to give them back to the person as sent them, then. If that person is still alive themselves, o' course.'

'Even if that person would be, let's say, embarrassed to know that my friend had read them?'

'If you'll pardon me, miss, the Bible tells us to be honest. Giving them back would be the honest thing to do.'

'Thank you, that's very sound indeed.'

'I hope it helps, miss. There now, let me plait your hair for overnight and we're all done.'

Alice had a bit of a funny turn after that and had to step out, but she was fine again given a minute or two. Poor thing, she works so hard and she's been through an awful ordeal. She's a good girl, and Eliza is lucky to have her. I will write to Mafalda tomorrow, and give her my counsel. Or rather, Alice's counsel.

Oh goodness, was it selfish of me to have asked it of her, when, whatever she says, she must be still quite upset? I must be kinder to her to make up for it.

Letter: Alice Smith to Mary and Sarah Smith
Wednesday, 28th May 1884
Whitby, Yorkshire, England

Dear Mam and Sarah,
I've got some sad news. Mr Morton the butler died suddenly last week, and today we all turned out to go to his funeral up at St Mary's. The mistress arranged everything personally, Mr Morton having served her husband so faithfully and for such a long time. I expected that women wouldn't be allowed to go, but when I said so in passing to Mrs Cartwright she told me that Mr Morton's only relatives were a sister and a niece and it would be cruel to let such old-fashioned notions stop them coming to say goodbye. These women, a Mrs and Miss Irby, came from out Darlington way just for the day. The mistress offered them to stay and Mrs Irby just about fell over and said they couldn't possibly. Neither of them seemed too cut up about Mr Morton's death, so I suppose they weren't close. If anything, the Colonel has been the most grief-stricken. He's so sad, it hurts my heart to see. Of course Mr Morton will be missed downstairs, but he and the Colonel had quite a history – apparently Mr Morton saved the master's life in India in the fifties, when they were young men soldiering together.

Don't worry about me; all things considered I'm quite well. Please pray for the family here as they grieve.

All my love,
    Alice

P.S. The funeral was a poor show, but don't tell Mam. Morton wasn't allowed a proper burial service, having taken his own way out, and I heard from Cook that Colonel Cartwright practically had to threaten Reverend Baker to get him to even read a prayer. The mistress laid flowers, though Reverend Baker didn't want her to. She gave him such a look, then he shut his foolish mouth and let her get on with it. Poor man. I did try, Sarah. I did try. Pray for his soul with me.

This evening while I was with Miss North, I could feel one of those waking dreams coming on. I thought I might be sick. I wobbled out into the hallway, where I sat down heavily on the floor until it passed. I've kept up with your lemon beebrush tea but I could still feel the vision wanting to slip through, pinching and prodding and poking at my mind, trying to worm its way in. I had this this nauseating feeling of – and you know I don't use this word lightly, Sarah – *evil*. And Miss North was right in the middle of it.

PART FOUR

Sir John Seward's personal diary
Friday, 16th January 1903
Littlemore Hospital, Oxfordshire

I have finally made my first examination of the mind of Lady Lowell. I wish I had been able to see her sooner but it's been an extremely busy week here, with more than one emergency admission.

This morning Dr Knight tapped on my door at a quarter to ten, and we walked to the women's wards together.

'I've been thinking about our patient,' Dr Knight said as we made our way through the corridors. 'We hypothesized that her condition is due to external trauma, and even though we believe we may have located it, we must also consider that she suffers some internal disorder of the brain, with no external cause.'

'Yes of course. We'll explore all possibilities.'

Dr Knight had arranged for her ladyship to have a private room, which was where our interview would take place.

Nurse Bridges met us briefly before we went in.

'Good morning, sir. The patient was a little agitated last night so we gave her a sedative. Otherwise, nothing unusual to report. I can confirm that she's currently lucid.'

'Excellent, thank you. Leave your notes on my desk and I'll put them in the file.'

'Yes, sir.'

Lady Lowell received us cordially. She had dressed, or had been dressed, in a collarless chemise and modest dressing gown with her hair simply braided. She is an elegant woman in her late thirties, though unlike her husband she looks rather younger. I would say she is above-average height for a woman, with a certain willowy grace. I found it hard to imagine her in such a fit as that of which we have photographic evidence.

After our introductions were made Lady Lowell asked us to please sit down, quite as if she were our hostess. Her voice is as refined as one would expect from a person of her social position, and she showed a remarkable level of self-awareness.

'Thank you for accepting me at your establishment, Sir John,' Lady Lowell began. 'My husband tells me you are a renowned expert, and that you may be able to help me where others have not.'

Her composure was somewhat surprising. I have found that after being transferred to a new institution, incoming patients are usually either more volatile or catatonic.

'I hope so, your ladyship. I apologize for not having been able to meet with you before now. I trust you are settling in well?'

'Well enough. Your staff have made me as comfortable as I am ever able to be. I was a little uneasy last night but a nurse gave me something to help. I was happy to have it. I often have nightmares.'

She had my every sympathy there.

'Would you like to tell us about them?' I asked.

'Not really as I find them very upsetting, but I imagine it's necessary.'

'Yes, I'm afraid so. There are quite a few questions we need to ask, some of which you may have been asked before. As I told your husband, we need to make our own assessments.'

'Very well. I understand.'

She took a deep breath, and appeared to be steeling herself for the task.

'There is always screaming. Always. Often I awake to find that I am the one screaming, but sometimes not.'

'What sort of screaming?' Dr Knight asked.

'Screaming as of violence.'

'Not of pain?'

'I'm not sure how I would tell the difference.'

'Indeed. Forgive my interruption, your ladyship, please continue.'

'My emotion is always terror, and the sound is always screaming. Sometimes there is also howling, and chanting of a religious nature. The twenty-third psalm to be precise.'

'"Though I walk through the valley of the shadow of death"?' I interjected.

Lady Lowell closed her eyes and swallowed hard.

'Yes. May I please have some water?'

Dr Knight went to the door and requested some be brought. I did not continue until the orderly had returned and the patient had drunk her fill.

'Thank you.'

'You are welcome to ask for whatever you need,' Dr Knight said kindly. Lady Lowell smiled at her, and my heart felt a twinge of pity. I might have to suppress it often but without that human feeling I could never be a good doctor.

'Could you describe the visual component of the nightmares?' I asked.

'Yes. Often it's complete darkness, with a feeling of a malevolent presence standing very close behind me. Close enough to touch.'

She twitched, as if she wished to turn around and look over her shoulder.

'At other times I see the night sky above me, a full-blown storm. More rarely I see the colour red. Blood red. Those dreams are silent but are the more horrifying for it, as if I were waiting for something terrible to happen that I cannot avoid. My nightmares do not much vary. It's a rare night when I do not dream. I love those nights. I have trouble sleeping too, though I confess I often don't try very hard to sleep, knowing what awaits me.'

'Many would feel the same, I'm sure.'

We had read all of these details in the patient's case notes, and I was glad to see that Lady Lowell's own account tallied with what her doctors had recorded.

'Are your hallucinations similar to the nightmares?'

I wanted to see if she acknowledged the hallucinations as such.

'No.'

'No?'

'When I hallucinate, I see people. Shapes, figures. They mean me great harm.'

'Like the presence in your nightmares?'

'I suppose so, yes. I can see them, though vaguely, rather than simply sensing them.'

'I see.'

Dr Knight was writing at speed. I could hear her pen scratching even as I maintained eye contact with the patient.

'And what of your more physical symptoms?'

'Those come and go, doctor. I get chills fairly often, and I seem to catch all manner of minor illnesses. I often feel nauseated, and have aches in my head and my neck.' She rubbed at her throat and I recognized it as a gesture intended to soothe herself, likely performed unconsciously.

'We can certainly manage those symptoms, which will give you some relief.'

'Thank you. I dislike feeling my own physical weakness.'

'Is that so?' Dr Knight said mildly.

'Yes, of course. I wish to be strong.'

'What do you mean by strong, precisely?'

I sat silently, giving Dr Knight space to follow her line of thought.

'Full of life.'

Lady Lowell's eyes were beginning to take on a slightly glassy look and I readied myself in case she became violent.

'Is that why you consumed the ants?'

'Yes. They're strong, are they not? I needed their strength.'

Those suffering delusions always reason well within their own scope, as I have seen so many times before.

'Why did you need their strength?'

'I have been so weak. Weakness is dangerous. The most dangerous thing.'

Lady Lowell began to sway, colour draining from her face.

'Why? Why is weakness so dangerous?'

It was too late. Lady Lowell fainted dead away and slumped onto the floor.

Later

'I don't know what to make of it all,' Dr Knight said, shaking her head. 'It seems our theory was wrong.'

It was just after five o'clock and already dark. We were seated in my parlour, the light of the lamps giving our surroundings a warm glow utterly unsuitable for the sombre tone of our conversation.

'The content of her nightmares and hallucinations could correspond to a traumatic mental disturbance of some sort,' I pointed out, 'just not to witnessing a fatal carriage accident.'

'It could be another trauma of which we are as yet unaware, but it could also be some disease of the brain. Maybe it's simply hysteria.'

I sighed rather heavily. 'I suppose I wanted it to be a trauma, because then we would have a much better chance of treating her and returning her to her family.'

'I feel much the same, but we must not lose sight of the fact that her symptoms could fit any number of diagnoses. Even though we have notes and records and papers galore, we simply don't yet have enough information.'

'You're quite right. Us sitting here feeling sorry for ourselves will hardly help.'

'I have some experience of hypnosis,' Dr Knight said. 'We could consider that?'

'We could. I have seen it performed, but have never performed it myself. I know it can be useful but I would hesitate to rely on it. Are you a Freudian, Dr Knight?'

'On occasion. As you've said, we must use all the tools at our disposal.'

As our talk turned to other patients and administrative matters, I continued to admire Dr Knight's sharp, sensible mind. Even though we seem to have fallen at the first hurdle, she is determined we dust ourselves off and forge onwards. I find myself thanking Providence that my predecessor had the foresight to hire her.

It was after seven when she left, intending to take her evening meal in her rooms while getting through some paperwork.

'May I take Lady Lowell's records?' she asked. 'I'd like to read them again, when I've finished my other tasks. Perhaps something will leap out at me.'

'Certainly. Would you mind leaving me the photographs?'

I wasn't sure why I asked but I had what I can only describe as a *feeling*, a sense of something flickering, scratching at my brain, as when a word is on the tip of one's tongue.

'Of course.'

She plucked them from the file, and handed them to me.

'Good evening, Sir John.'

'Good evening, Dr Knight.'

I rang for fresh tea, and began to think.

When the clock on the mantelpiece struck midnight, I awoke to find my head on the table and the tea quite cold in the pot. Goodness knows what the poor housekeeper must think of me. I have sat in thought for some while longer but nothing has come of it. I am for bed.

Early next morning

I must write this down as quickly as possible. My God, my God! It is a coincidence, but such a coincidence that it must be Fate at work!

At just after four o'clock I awoke with a start and shot out of bed. My brain had been working while I slept, and what work! I threw on my dressing gown and hurried down to my study. I opened every drawer in my desk before finding what I was looking for – a magnifying glass. I went back to the dining table where the photographs lay and feeling like a frenzied Sherlock Holmes, I sat down to see if this new notion so hot and fresh in my mind might be correct. I studied the early pictures and there! There on her throat! I took a deep breath, trying to caution myself against wild speculation and failing utterly. I needed the notes; I needed to see *where* on the Continent she had travelled, where *exactly* she had been on that ill-fated trip that ended in tragedy. I dashed upstairs and dressed so rapidly that it was mere good fortune I did so correctly. I ran out of the house and into the main building. I am not a young man, but the adrenaline spurred me onwards. It was not yet anywhere near dawn, and I am sure I caused great comment among the night staff as I ran through the corridors.

I had not had any reason to visit Dr Knight's rooms, and I realize now how my presence in the women's staff quarters was wildly inappropriate. At the time I had no thought for such things. I found the door which featured her nameplate and knocked loudly, calling her with such urgency in my voice that she appeared rapidly despite the late hour.

'Sir John! What is it?'

I saw her take in my agitation and my breathlessness. 'The notes! I need the notes!'

She opened the door fully and stepped back, allowing me through into her small sitting room. The file I sought so desperately sat open on a low table before a neat little sofa. I flung myself towards it, flicking desperately through the papers.

'What's happened? What are you looking for?'

'I know what's wrong with her; at least, I think I do. I'm not yet sure – oh, confound these doctors and their appalling handwriting!'

'What do you need? Sir John, what is the meaning of all this?'

That brought me up short a little. I looked at her and realized she must have been quite completely asleep when I arrived. Her long red hair was loose, her eyes were puffy with sleep like a child's, and she was wearing a nightgown with a robe thrown over the top. I became suddenly aware of how beautiful she was, and the sheer indecency of my presence.

'Dr Knight, I beg you to forgive me. I am embarrassed by my conduct. It is highly improper of me to be here. I will leave at once.'

'Don't be ridiculous,' she said sternly. 'There is clearly some emergency, which takes precedence over social niceties. Tell me at once.'

'I need to know where Lady Lowell was when she witnessed the carriage accident.'

'Where?'

'Yes, the exact location is of vital importance. Have you read it somewhere, in all of this?'

If Dr Knight was confused by this line of questioning, she did not say so. 'Yes, I have.'

My heart seemed to stop. 'You have? In the records?'

'Yes. Do you read German?'

'Not well, not these days.'

'Then it's fortunate that I do. It was in that letter from the hospital where she was treated for possible pneumonia, written to her own doctor in London. Let me find it for you.'

She rifled through the papers on the coffee table, and handed me the incomprehensible document.

'Can we make a translation?'

'I have already done so; it's on the next page.'

There – there amid the clean strokes of her precisely formed lettering, was the information I sought. Even though I had felt so strongly that it must be so, to see it confirmed in black and white was a dreadful shock. My knees buckled beneath me and I subsided onto the sofa. I tried to breathe, deliberately recalling how we put the hellish, monstrous Count to death and sent him to whatever Beyond awaited one such as he, reminding myself that all living things were now safe from him and all his kind. It is over, I said to myself with all the firmness I could muster. It is over.

'Sir John, are you quite well?'

A glass of brandy appeared in my hand and I beheld Dr Knight before me with a medicinal bottle.

'Yes. No. I'm not sure.' I drank, and the alcohol burned down my throat. 'Do you know the place?'

'No, I can't say I've ever heard of it. I looked it up in my atlas and it is quite remote. Do you?'

'Yes,' I said weakly, 'I know Transylvania. I know the Borgo Pass. I have been there.'

'You have?'

'Yes, ten years ago, I—'

The memories of that terrible time rose before my eyes – not just the vampire's final defeat, but all of it. The deaths of people I loved; the horror as we understood what was before us; the desperation; all that I had tried to bury and all that rose over and over as surely as the evil creature had done, until Jonathan Harker and Quincey Morris, may he rest in peace, ended the demon's reign of terror.

'Sir John, you're evidently in the grip of some intense emotion. You're shaking. Drink up and I'll see you're returned home. Let's discuss this at a more reasonable hour when you're yourself again.'

I wish I could say that the steadiness in her tone returned me to myself then and there. She rang the bell while I drank, and Burton came to take me home. I saw her hand him a banknote, I assume for his discretion. He walked beside me in silence all the way to my own front door. I made it to my bed but I am still awake, my mind whirling.

This is the truth of the matter, the stark unyielding truth as revealed by photography and confirmed by the letter from the Buda-Pesth hospital. Lady Lowell's throat once featured those same wounds as marred the throat of dear Mina Harker, and of her closest friend and my first love, poor Lucy Westenra. In the early photographs of Lady Lowell, these wounds, these bite marks, had scarred, suggesting what? Why, that her ladyship had escaped him, that monster that we put into the ground! She had been bitten, survived, and bitten no more! And where were the scars now? Healed, after the fiend's final death, just as Mina's were!

Lady Lowell's trauma and madness can only have come from her suffering at the hands of . . . even after so long I shudder to write the name . . . none other than Count Dracula.

Letter: Mafalda Lowell to Lucy North
Monday, 19th May 1884
Buda-Pesth, Austro-Hungarian Empire

[Editor's Note: This letter refers to another which is lost. Please note the date; I recall to the reader's mind that for the sake of comprehension, a precise chronological order has not been followed. Also note ML's English translation of RJ's formal title, rendered here and elsewhere as 'Madam'.]

Dear Lucy,
I was going to castigate you for your silence, but a short and delayed letter has just arrived bearing a plethora of stamps from those Customs and Excise people whom Papa hates so much. I imagine hundreds more missives from you piled high in some uniformed grunt's office, desperate to be delivered, full of the loving common sense I am dying to hear.

The Baroness's letters are burning a hole in the pocket of my dress. I don't dare leave them anywhere until I can contrive a suitable hiding place where even the maids will not find them. I have no one I can safely confide in, not even Mama.

I have been trying to distract myself by putting all my effort into the business of the estate. I have a small piece of news on that front, although the bearer of it has caused concern. Mr Török, the land agent, came to tell us in person that the sale of the old manor and its land to this Count Drago or Dracul or whoever he is has at last officially completed. Unfortunately Mr Török is not at all well and seemed most ill at ease, even more so than he usually is in Mama's presence. His face was as pale as milk and had a sweat-stained sheen, and he tugged continually at his collar as if it irritated his skin. I am quite sure I saw some sort of lesion peeking out from the fabric. I do hope that whatever he has is not contagious. The last thing we need in this house is some catching illness running riot.

It is a shame his visit did not cross over with that of Dr Arminius, who came this morning to examine Aunt Réka. Afterwards, Mama brought him into the study to make his report, ordering me to take down his instructions for her care. The doctor is a funny little man who talks all around the houses, but Aunt Réka will have no one else.

'Your ladyship,' he began as I took up a fresh sheet of paper and shunted aside the French property manifest I had been examining, 'I am glad to report that your sister is in better health than I had expected.'

'I am very surprised to hear you say so. To me she seems to be as weak as ever.'

Dr Arminius shook his head. 'It is not so. She is fully recovered from her . . .' Here he shot a glance at me, which I did not understand and pretended not to notice. '. . . from her previous indisposition, and the modified rest cure we have been practising has returned her to a state of physical equilibrium. In her mind, however, she has become convinced that she is too overcome to be anything other than an invalid in the future.'

My mother gasped.

'No, no, do not concern yourself, your ladyship, this is not correct.'

'Oh, thank goodness.'

'I strongly suggested to Madam Jacobinus that she take a

water cure but she refuses to do so here in the city where she is an object of, forgive me, some notoriety. Instead, I am prescribing a strengthening diet, gentle exercise, and daily coca wine. We will see how she progresses. I also advise plenty of fresh air, which your Florence Nightingale tells us is so beneficial. Keep the curtains and windows open and allow the air to circulate. It will do the patient a great deal of good.'

Mama found this to be sage advice. She has since spent a considerable time explaining to Cook how to make English beef tea, to the woman's extreme consternation, and opening every curtain and every window in Aunt Réka's vicinity. My aunt is not thrilled about either of these developments. When I sat with her this evening, she was at least well enough to be irritated. Still, when I brought her post up to read to her – a thinly disguised wooing from Major Oberleitner, well-wishing from this countess and that lady, carefully worded missives from her nationalist friends – none roused her much beyond a brief nod, and a 'Write back with my thanks, Mafalda, would you, dear?'

I forgot to say, the doctor has discontinued her morphia. She is more awake and more herself without it. I want her to be well, I do, but the mystery of the letters hangs over our every interaction. My aunt is at the very least a snoop and a thief, and I cannot forget it.

I must leave off. Mátyás requires me to come and look at some anomaly in the accounts from Paris. I hope a letter from you arrives soon, my darling. I will await your wisdom, and if it aligns with my own judgement then I will take it as a sign to proceed.

With all of my love,
    Mafalda

Letter: Mafalda Lowell to Lucy North
Wednesday, 28th May 1884
Buda-Pesth, Austro-Hungarian Empire

Dear Lucy,

Nothing and nothing and nothing from you! Are you well, my love? I would sooner believe it is the fault of the Customs men than you; surely you would never abandon me so! I swear this waiting drives me to distraction. If I do not hear from you soon I will send a telegram to Eliza's house, expense be damned.

We are shortly to depart for the basilica for the forty-day prayers for my uncle, and then to lay flowers at his mausoleum. Dr Arminius has worked a miracle on my aunt; his coca wine is nothing short of an alchemical elixir! Each day Aunt Réka has been a little better and a little better and a little better, until she is so much improved that I can hardly believe my eyes. She has taken to sitting in her boudoir rather than her bed, and yesterday she even came down for lunch and a little walk in the courtyard. Still, no amount of medicine will carry her through today unscathed. Mama tried to convince her to stay at home but she wouldn't have it.

'Nurse Weber will be there in case I become unwell.'

Have I mentioned Nurse Weber, late of Vienna? She is all that we had hoped her to be and more, a veritable ministering angel with a manner so terrifying that all ailments flee before her.

'But, Réka, please, consider your health.'

'I was his wife, Maria. It is my duty to attend, and attend I will.'

As Papa is wont to comment, the stubbornness of our family is legendary. The trait showed itself strongly in both Mama and Aunt Réka in the ensuing argument. Mama lost.

I will write of how it went when I return.

Later

Lucy, wait until you hear what I have to tell you! I said we had planned to lay flowers at Uncle Gabor's grave. In the end, I went alone with only Partridge for company as Aunt Réka fainted during the service and had to be carried out by Major Oberleitner. In the flesh, he is nothing more than an opportunistic cavalry moustache with a slab of body attached. Aunt Réka did not need to be held anything like so closely, and she would have slapped him for impertinence had she been conscious. Mama saw Aunt Réka home, firmly refusing the Major's offered escort, and then sent Partridge and I on to Kerepesi Cemetery by ourselves.

It began to rain the moment we arrived. Partridge being prone to complaining about her joints in any kind of bad weather, I left her in the carriage. A fine and gloomy drizzle seeped through my every layer of clothing and left my long veil hanging limp and heavy over my face. The cemetery is not even forty years old, and was planned to feel more like a park or a garden than a graveyard. Today, all sunlight hidden by thick grey clouds, it felt very much a place for the dead.

The Jacobinus family mausoleum is one of the oldest there. My uncle's father is here, as is his grandfather, who was interred the very day the cemetery was opened. It is a grand place, full of the great and the good. It is also vast, and I lost my way all too easily. I began to wish I had brought Partridge with me after all. It was eerie, and silent except for the patter of the rain. I felt as if I were the only living person for miles, as if it were only me and the dead.

I got the shock of my life when a gravedigger appeared from seemingly nowhere.

'Can I be of assistance, miss?' he asked, his voice somehow too refined for his working-man's attire, and his accent that of somewhere far away from Buda-Pesth.

'You startled me,' I said, perhaps rather accusingly.

He bowed, a formal sort of bow. 'I can only apologize. Are you lost?'

I did not want to admit it. I was, after all, alone here, but without guidance how long might I wander?

'I am . . . visiting the mausoleum of Jacobinus Gabor.' I indicated the now slightly wilting wreaths I held.

'I see. You must allow me to escort you.'

'Thank you, but that will not be necessary.'

'Please, I must insist. It is not far.'

Thinking about it, I can't say why he unsettled me so other than by having made me jump. He was an older man, I think, with grey or white hair and a moustache of the same colour. He was tall, more slender than one would expect for a man whose work is physical labour, and he had an odd sort of wolfish look, but other than that? I have no idea. I don't think I have described him well, and the more I try to recall his face the more it slips away from me.

I walked half a pace or so behind him, keeping him in sight as we walked through the endless tree-lined boulevards, past the resting places of the sundry worthies who sleep in that place. The gravedigger did not speak, but nor did he lead me wrong. At a turning from the main avenue, a carved angel prayed atop a stone marked simply 'Jacobinus'. Beyond this stood the mausoleum of my uncle's family.

'Thank you,' I said to my guide, wondering if I ought to give him a coin or two, or if that would invite trouble.

'You are welcome.'

I turned to him, not quite knowing what I did, and he extended his hand as if he wished me to shake it. This hand was broad with squat fingers and, I remember this most clearly, hairs in the centre of the palm. Isn't that odd? I have some idea he touched that strange hand lightly to my covered head in a sort of benediction, but that can't be right; I would never allow such a peculiar liberty. I blame the stress I have been under for such a garbled tale, and for straying so far from the original intent of this letter. I would be infuriated to receive such, but I know you will forgive me. Let me return to my purpose.

The Jacobinus mausoleum is very grand. Made of a white stone, it is raised above its surroundings and has wide shallow steps on one side leading up to the door. Above, a grand dome that mimics the basilica is topped by an angel with her wings spread, gazing upwards towards Heaven. I tell you all this so that you appreciate the full effect of the sight that greeted me. As I looked along the gravel path leading up to this edifice, I saw the figure of a woman dressed in darkest black flung face down upon the steps, on a carpet of dead and dying flowers.

The sound of the figure's weeping became audible as I drew nearer, deserting my strange companion. This was true abandonment to sorrow, a total and complete loss of control and lack of care of the fact. By some extra sense or through that ether that the spiritualists speak of, I felt the deep distress of this other human soul. It sickened me.

'Madam!' I called.

At the sound of my voice, she started. She stared wildly for long moments, then scrambled upright and fled as fast as she could into the trees.

Lucy, I am sure it can only have been Baroness Tolvay herself! There are, as far as I know, only two women who would lay on my uncle's tomb and give themselves over to weeping. One was at home being tended to by her nurse, so the Baroness must have been the other. She loved my uncle ten years ago, that much we know from her letters, but now I see how much she must love him still. Even dead, she cannot let him go.

I abandoned my wreath of flowers, crushed where I had gripped them. I did not care that Partridge was furious with my ruined dress. I did not care that Mama fussed around me like Eliza would, muttering about catching cold by being out in the rain. I have been wrapped in a blanket with my feet in scalding water and forced to drink hot toddy after hot toddy just to get my insistent nurses to leave me alone.

Lucy, I have been a fool. I have thought only of my aunt's part in things. What does it matter how Aunt Réka came by the letters? They must be returned to Baroness Tolvay.

With love,
    Your Mafalda

Letter: Mafalda Lowell to Lucy North
Tuesday, 3rd June 1884
Buda-Pesth, Austro-Hungarian Empire

My darling Lucy,
Finally! After so long, to see your beautiful script is balm to my soul! I was sure you would be of my mind. It is the only thing to do, to get the letters back to their sender.

I have been working out the how of it for almost a week. It must not become known, as my aunt's reputation would be entirely ruined. If I am to maintain the necessary secrecy there is only one way the thing can be done. I must go myself, and go alone.

Thursday, 5th June 1884
Early morning
It was not yet quite dark when I set out with Baroness Tolvay's letters tucked in my pocket. I wore a great black cloak with a vast hood, hoping against hope I would not be recognized. It is not

far from here to Andrássy Avenue, from where I planned to hail a hansom cab. It was not exactly quiet, with carriages carrying the great and the good home from the theatre and the opera and wherever else they might have been. All the way I feared some gentleman might see me and decide to be inconveniently chivalrous. A premonition, I suppose, but I will come to that. I confess I felt uneasy, as if I were being watched, but try as I might I could spot no unsavoury characters paying me particular interest. The great wide boulevards of respectable Pesth were free from both ruffians and over-zealous knights errant.

A hansom responded swiftly to my summons, the driver making no comment about ferrying a lone woman about at night. I know what he took me for, but what was that to me? The journey to the absconded Baron's Italianate mansion took no time at all. I had planned to leave the letters and be on my way, assuming that if I sent up my card the Baroness would have me thrown straight back out onto the street. It was with this in mind that I had the hansom wait while I handed the letters to a liveried servant at the door. Though I returned extremely slowly to the cab, we were about to move off when a breathless footman called me back. The Baroness had received my delivery and would like to see me.

I was relieved of my cloak before tracking the footman obediently through the grand yellow foyer with its urns and faux-classical statues, and up a marble staircase to the first floor. The Baron had evidently abandoned the traditional plan of a Hungarian city dwelling and allowed himself to be over-influenced by his travels. The effect was disconcerting, as I traipsed down a burnt-orange hallway with large picture windows on one side, and Greek gods in niches on the other.

At last the footman led me into a small and rather cramped salon before withdrawing promptly. No faux-classical nonsense was to be found in here. This room contained all the necessities of modern life, but the walls . . . Honestly, Lucy, just recalling this makes me shiver. The walls were hung all around with religious paintings and crucifixes and icons to the point that there was barely a square inch of the paper underneath left visible. Wood and gold and silver and oils all conspired together to make an environment that was doubtless artistically excellent, yet extremely disturbing when taken in all at once. The Baroness had collected images of the suffering of Christ in all possible artistic forms. Everywhere I looked there He was, writhing in torment, flagellated and bloodied. I have never before been disquieted by the image, but to see so many! Wherever one's eye might fall! At the time I wondered how anyone could elect to be surrounded by so much painted agony, though from what happened later I have some idea – but again I am ahead of myself.

In the very centre of this shrine to anguish, occupying a long sofa in the local style sat the woman caught in adultery herself. Her fashionable black gown was lit golden by the lamplight, and I thought how furious Aunt Réka would be to see this woman wearing mourning for a husband not her own.

I had seen Baroness Tolvay twice by now, but both times she had been veiled. I had thought that either she would be a painted Jezebel, glorious and tawdry in sin, or else a shamed and twitching wretch, barely able to lift her eyes from the floor. She was neither of these things. Her skin was marked by the sun to a colour I have never before seen on a noble lady, likely a legacy of following her husband on his travels in the East and in Africa. Her eyes shone all the more brilliantly blue for it, a fact I was able to note as she did not direct her gaze downwards but regarded me openly. Her long chestnut hair was loosely bound and her neat square hands lay tidily atop the packet of letters in her lap. She had the air neither of a harlot nor a cringe nor the madwoman I had also speculated that she might be.

Baroness Tolvay looked me up and down, her eyes lingering too long for comfort on my face. She left me standing on the Persian carpet before her as if she were the headmistress and I a miscreant schoolgirl. It was a studied rudeness, a wall between us after our encounter in the cemetery.

'To what do I owe the honour of this gift, Miss Lowell?'

To my surprise she spoke to me in fluent English. Her voice was deeper than a woman's usually is, her tone firm and her jaw set.

'This "gift" is rightfully yours. I found your letters, and could not in good conscience keep them from you.'

The Baroness narrowed her eyes.

'Well then, I suppose you want me to thank you.'

I attempted to take the high road. 'You are welcome.'

'Am I indeed? How lucky for me. You read them, of course?'

'Yes, though I hope you will forgive me for it. At the time I did not know—'

The Baroness waved away my explanations. 'It is no concern of mine. I hope your aunt is very proud of herself, to have brought me down for a crime so long ago committed. Does she know that you are here?'

I hesitated for too long.

'I thought not. She would not have permitted it.'

'I would not have distressed her by discussing it. My aunt has been very ill.'

'Oh, I know. One hears things.'

Lucy, did I not say that Aunt Réka's servants could not be trusted?

'I think I ought to leave. I apologize for having intruded on your grief.'

I turned to go, but the Baroness was not done with me.

'Your mother and I were friends, years ago. Tell me, are you more like your mother or your aunt?'

'Like my mother,' I said quickly.

The Baroness smiled a cold smile.

'Perhaps that's true, perhaps not. There is some little compassion in you, so I think I'll tell you the truth of it all and break your tender heart. You may tell Maria, from me, and break hers too.'

'I—'

'Hush. Listen. You have read my letters. I was true to my word, and I never ceased to love your uncle. Know that. Your uncle married your aunt, and still I loved him. We never corresponded, never even spoke except at public events. I travelled everywhere with my husband, never remaining at home. I was a paragon. For ten years, I was a devoted and faithful wife. I burned all the letters your uncle had sent to me during our affair, and I assumed he had done the same.'

'Perhaps he did, except for these few.'

'He could have kept them all, and the outcome would have been the same. I came to Buda-Pesth with my husband for only a few days this April. We visited friends, we went to receptions, we did all that was expected of us. One night I saw your uncle at a ball, alone, while your aunt was indisposed. We spoke a little, very little. The next morning, a note arrived for Baron Tolvay from your aunt. It contained a neat précis of the contents of these letters.'

She held up the battered little pile.

'Your aunt was quite prepared to provide them to my husband, or to send them to the scandal-sheets and tell the world that I was not only a whore but a mad one too. The Baron brandished the note before me, asking if its tale of adultery and a bastard child was true.

'What was I to do? What would any powerless wife do? I threw myself upon his mercy. It had been so long ago, I told him. We had built such a life together, and I had been faithful ever since. Our two little girls were his own. He turned cold eyes on me and said nothing. He left. He was gone for hours. When he finally returned, he was covered in blood. I knew as soon as I saw him what he had done. The look on his face . . .'

The Baroness took in a deep breath, steeling herself.

'My husband had been shot clean through the shoulder. I wanted to summon a doctor but he had me forcibly removed from his presence and locked in my chambers. He ordered the servants to leave me there until he was gone – yes gone, even with a hole in his flesh. I have no idea where he is now. Not in Hungary, certainly. I suspect he may have gone over the frontier and sought refuge with the Ottomans.'

I felt my gorge rising.

'So this . . . all this . . . my uncle's death . . . Aunt Réka caused it all?'

I wanted so desperately for it to be some mad lie, an invention of a diseased mind, but I knew in my heart that the Baroness was telling the truth.

'By her jealousy of an affair that had been over for years, long before she wed your uncle. Yes. She is an animal, that one. Capable of great sweetness until she is cornered, and then she is vicious as any wild beast. She will lash out again and again, clawing at what attacks her, mindless. Is it not so?'

'No! She didn't do as she threatened and send the letters to the press, did she?'

'Hah! No, but I would be only a little more ruined if she had. I doubt it was altruism. More likely she was too horrified by what she had wrought to follow the threat through. Enough of the tale came out to ruin everything.'

I thought of the mausoleum, the winged angel guarding the resting place of my uncle. My aunt, his own wife, had put him there for no better reason than vengeful jealousy. She sent the man she loved to his death. No wonder she had been so ill. It was not only grief that tormented her, but guilt.

I felt faint. I wanted to sit but still Baroness Tolvay offered me no chair. I thought I might weep, so I chose instead to bite down hard on my lip.

'You know your aunt would be destroyed if I were to make this public,' the Baroness said, as lightly as if she were commenting on the weather. 'We could make a bargain. An exchange, for my silence.'

'What sort of bargain?'

'A simple one, I promise. You will ensure that a particular payment continues to be made from your uncle's estate, and I will keep your aunt's evil a secret.'

'You want *money*?'

It seemed so strange, so material. I don't know what I had expected, but it wasn't this.

'Yes, but not for myself. I owe a debt which your uncle has, I believe, been paying for many years. I do not have the means to take it up myself. Not now.'

The Baroness plucked a notecard from the side table and wrote a line or two. She held it out to me. She had written a French name and an address in Paris in her looping hand. It seemed somehow familiar, but even now I cannot place it.

'How much is the debt?' I asked.

'More than I can ever repay.'

My uncle was a very wealthy man. What could I do in the circumstances but agree?

'Very well. I'll take care of it.' I hoped for all our sakes I could make that true. 'What will you do now?'

I don't know what I meant by asking. Curiosity perhaps, or merely pity. The Baroness shrugged, a delicate twitch of one shoulder.

'I can't stay here. My children are with relatives, so I will leave and go . . . somewhere. A convent, perhaps. The true religion is the only safety, after all.'

'Safety? You mean salvation?'

'No, child. Safety from the evil that walks the earth. I have seen it, I have felt it. I have stood in its very presence more than once and survived, and that can only have been by the protection of Our Lord. He deserves my full-hearted devotion now. He deserves yours too.'

What can one say to such a pronouncement? This must be why she surrounds herself with such morbid *objets d'art*. Lucy, she truly *believes* in the supernatural demon she wrote of in those letters. I had to remind myself, as you would have reminded me if you had been there, to have compassion for one who has experienced such earthly tragedy and been so painfully warped by it.

I left half-wishing I had simply abandoned the letters on the doorstep.

I warn you, things took a little turn after that. I walked out into the night to find that my cab was gone. Baroness Tolvay kept no carriage, the Baron having taken it in his flight, so I set out to seek another hansom to return me home. The Baroness had offered me no attendant and my mind was in such a state as I walked, turning over what I had heard, that I did not think to return and ask for one. I ought to have had more fear of being out alone at night. I should have paid more heed to my surroundings.

I was startled out of my agitation by a noise behind me, not quite a footstep, not quite the flapping of wings, but when I turned I saw nothing but shadows. I felt that prickling again, that sense of being watched, of some observer drawing nearer and nearer. The streetlamps were few and far between, and the lights of the grand houses had been extinguished as their occupants slept. I swear I have never experienced such gloom or such silence in a city. I was frozen to the spot, eyes staring into the darkness as I tried to make shapes out of the shadows. For achingly long moments I could hear only my breath and my racing heart.

Then all at once the shadows seemed to change, to move decisively towards me, and the spell broke. I ran, aiming for the next corner which would lead to a busier road with the possibility of other human beings. I can only blame the pressures I have been under, the time of night and the strangeness of the Baroness's tales for such ridiculous behaviour. The true danger came upon me when I gained the imagined safety of the glowing corner streetlamp.

As I tried to catch my breath, a carriage drew up next to me.

'Good evening,' came an Austrian-accented slurring which, sadly, I recognized. I turned and yes, it was my aunt's sometime-suitor, the ill-starred Major Oberleitner. He started a little as he saw my face, and a recalculation happened behind his eyes.

'Miss Lowell, I presume you are in some difficulty? Might I offer you assistance?'

I made some calculations of my own. How far I was from my destination, how late the hour had become, the likelihood of hansom cabs.

'Why, thank you, Major. How kind.' The door was opened, and in I hopped. 'Goodness, my aunt will be so grateful to you. I was visiting a friend, and there was a misunderstanding about my transportation. I was quite at a loss.'

I managed to smile prettily, but looking at his glassy-eyed stare I saw all my nonsense was lost on him. He was drunk.

Extremely drunk. Everything came into sharp focus, and in the face of clear and present danger I set all else aside. What, I wondered, was the likelihood of this *rescuer* being able to keep up with me should I need to hurl myself out of his coach and make a run for it, again?

We trotted through the streets in silence for a time. The Major stared at me, unblinking. I smiled vacantly, as one does, my cheeks aching in their rictus.

'I've been at the gaming tables,' he said, out of nowhere. 'Lost a damn fortune.'

'I'm sorry to hear it.'

'Ach, I'll win it all back tomorrow. Probably. You know what I'd like?'

I looked politely enquiring, even as I discreetly peered out to see if we were anywhere near home. Not long now, not far.

'I'd like a wife to spend it on. Dress her all up in fine jewels and gowns, hm? A pretty wife. She'd have to be pretty. My last wife was a sow.' He snorted at his own joke. 'Your aunt now, she's very pretty.' He leaned forward. 'You're just like her. Younger, though, and your eyes are green. They look better green.'

I invoked Aunt Réka, and hoped her implied presence might hold him.

'Yes, my aunt is held to be a beauty. By now she'll be frantic with worry about me. We must get me home as soon as possible.'

He goggled for a moment then lunged for me just as the carriage pulled up, sharp. Not a moment too soon. I hurled myself past the Major towards the door but he caught me and held me fast. Though intoxicated, he is a very large and very strong man.

'Now, aren't you going to show me a little appreciation for bringing you home? Rescuing a damsel in distress?'

It was his own fault for holding me back by my left arm. I

swung, and the heel of my right hand connected with his nose with a satisfying crack. Blood gushed everywhere, and his cry of pain filled the night. I was out and onto the doorstep in an instant, the carriage door slamming behind me.

'Drive on, for God's sake!' I called to the driver. 'Your master has injured himself!'

The driver shrugged, and moved off with no urgency whatsoever. There is no love for the master there, it seems.

I managed to put myself to bed unseen by all but the doorman, to whom I gave a substantial bribe. Do you know, it is quite some while since I have been forced to defend myself in such a manner. I expect my hand will feel rather sore in the morning. I find myself shaking with the shock of it all, though pleased that the skill has not left me.

What an evening I have had! I cannot rest, love, despite being crushed with exhaustion. This hasn't ended well, has it? That woman in her room surrounded by her Messiahs as if they were a fortress . . . Because it is late and my mind is swimming in sleep and yet unable to bring it fully about, I wonder, is it possible there was some fiend wandering free and wreaking havoc a decade ago in Transylvania? Not a supernatural being, but some man so deranged as to be capable of heinous acts? More heinous than the average attempted rough wooing of an unwilling woman, I mean. Did the Baroness really see something so awful, so cruel and dark and twisted, as to push her into this extreme religious fervour? There have been many, many wars in that part of the world. Might a man have had such a time of it in battle that his mind was left utterly sick and thirsting for blood?

Ah, I daresay in the morning this will all seem foolishness.

All my love,
Mafalda

*

Darling, I had to unseal this to tell you – I awoke late but with a certain knowledge of where I had seen that Parisian address before. Mátyás had shown it to me quite recently, as something strange in my uncle's French accounting. I went barefoot and in my nightclothes to the study to check the details. It is a regular payment, going back to 1874. It is made to a man by the name of Pierre-Henri Dupont. Dupont! Lucy, I believe this is the family of the Baroness's maid Giselle, who died so horribly in Transylvania. My uncle kept faith all these years, even after his beloved broke off their affair. Can Baroness Tolvay really want so small a thing for her silence? It is no great sum, roughly the salary of an upper servant. It must be meant to replace that which the family lost when they lost their daughter. I can hardly believe it. It feels like good fortune, and yet at the same time dreadful to see a silver lining in such a dark cloud.

Now, I must try to think of what to do next. Baroness Tolvay wanted me to tell Mama what Aunt Réka has done, but I don't see what good would come from it. What would Mama even do with the knowledge, except suffer? Send me more words of wisdom and comfort, my darling.

M.

Lucy North's journal
Wednesday, 11th June 1884
Whitby, Yorkshire, England

Has anyone ever been more useless than I am at this moment! I cannot help Mafalda, who is a thousand miles away embroiled in some strange and unsettling family horror, forced to run around the city at night and endanger herself. I cannot help Eliza, who is under the same roof as me and longs for something that, try as she might, nature will not give her. I cannot even help Alice, who seems to grow sadder and quieter with each day that passes since she found poor Morton's hanging body.

I wrote to Mafalda today, attempting to calm her and counselling that she speak to Lady Maria and lay everything before her. I am certain she will ignore me. If only I were there! If I were there, I could make her listen to me. I could hold her beautiful face in my hands and look into her eyes and *make* her. If I were there, I could share her burden. I could sit with Aunt Réka, distasteful as that might be. I could entertain her and read to her, I could write correspondence for her, I could be the space from her that Mafalda will need as the full vileness of her aunt's crimes comes home to her. I said as much, for all the good it does, but at this distance I am useless.

I have tried to support Eliza in practical matters, thinking that would at least be of some service. She had been interviewing replacements for Morton but the Colonel disliked all the prospective candidates and has decided to dress himself for the time being, so now Eliza is seeing prospective housekeepers instead. I have been sitting in and making notes, hoping that I am not looking into my own future as these sensible, tidy women parade in and out. I have been attempting to persuade Eliza that once a housekeeper is in place we should go on an excursion, ideally to Harrogate where we might take the healing waters and where she might find some peace. Eliza has been before, of course, and found much benefit in it. Those tale-telling old wives say, do they not, that a harried woman never finds herself in an interesting condition? But how am I to say such a thing to her?

For Alice, I can do nothing but be kind. I have suggested she visit her family for some home comfort, but she will not go. She had no fear of losing her place, she said, but would simply rather be at work. And so she stays.

I have gone round and round in my mind too long. I will go for a walk, in the hope that my mind will clear and solutions will present themselves.

Letter: Mafalda Lowell to Lucy North
Wednesday, 18th June 1884
Buda-Pesth, Austro-Hungarian Empire

My darling Lucy,
The world has never known such a generous soul as yours. You are better in every way than I could ever hope to be. Thank you, thank you for offering to be my shield. Mama is writing to Eliza to make the formal invitation, but you are to come here as soon as you are able!

I have been stuck since Baroness Tolvay's dreadful revelations, unable to speak of them but also unable to forget them. I pleaded my work on my uncle's estate as an excuse for avoiding Aunt Réka, but when your last arrived yesterday, I decided to put your plan into action that very evening. My simple asking would never work; my aunt would have to think it all her own idea.

I offered to take up Mama's usual after-dinner station in Aunt Réka's boudoir, so that Mama might go to bed early for once. I swallowed my considerable discomfort, and insisted we play écarté. It is the only card game for two of which my aunt is not fond. A useful foundation, I decided, boredom suiting the purpose perfectly.

'I could send for Mama, and we could play at loo?' I suggested, as Aunt Réka began to voice her dissatisfaction exactly as expected.

'Well, we could—' she began, though of course I cut her off.

'But we should not, I know. Mama needs to rest.'

'Yes, your mother never takes the time to rest. I've often thought that.'

I did not point out that it was she herself who was the cause of this.

'Aunt, don't you think it's time to invite a friend or two to visit?' I said, as I dealt.

'As charming as society would be, I couldn't possibly. No, stop that, darling, I can't face any more écarté.'

I set the cards aside.

'Are you set against receiving guests? Dr Arminius is so pleased with your progress.'

'The gossip, Mafalda, I couldn't bear it. Everyone is so enmeshed with everyone else, and tittle-tattle is a currency. Everything I said and did would be reported on. My looks, my attitude, everything.'

This prospect seemed to genuinely disturb her and she pulled her wrap closer about her shoulders.

'Of course, just as you wish. A good friend is hard to find here, it seems.'

'Not only here, but everywhere.'

I shook my head vehemently. 'No, I must stand up for my Lucy. I have always been able to trust her, and to rely on her.'

'I'll allow you to make an exception for her then, since you insist. How is dear Lucy? Is she well?'

'Well enough.' I sighed, a little theatrically. 'I do miss her. We've never been apart for so long.'

I fell silent, gazing into the middle distance.

'Hmmm . . .' Aunt Réka said to herself, tilting her head as she thought the thought that you and I had implanted in her mind. 'Do you know, I have the most delightful notion!'

I affected surprise.

'Yes, Aunt? What notion is that?'

'Why do we not invite Lucy to come and join us here?'

'Here? But you said—'

'Lucy is a delightful girl. I always enjoy her company, and she's not connected with the sniping rumourmongers that would thrill to rip me apart. Do you not think she'd like to come?'

'I'm sure she would! But she'd need a chaperone—'

'Isn't she staying with your friend? What's her name? Elizabeth?'

'Eliza, yes.'

'Any friend of yours and Lucy's is a friend of mine. I insist. They must both come as soon as possible.'

'What an excellent plan! You're so clever, Aunt.'

I felt like quite the ham actor.

'I wouldn't go so far,' she said, clearly pleased. 'Perhaps I have my moments.'

So there it is! It was the easiest thing in the world. I put it to Mama and to Dr Arminius together the next morning, in front of Aunt Réka. Dr Arminius was practically dancing with what he saw as evidence of her progress. Mama was a little hesitant, and she expressed concern about young ladies undertaking such a long journey without any assistance. I scotched this by suggesting that Mátyás meet you in Paris. This will serve a dual purpose as he also needs to meet with Uncle Gabor's French agent, as well as ensure the Dupont payments.

All you need to do is convince Eliza. Buda-Pesth has healing waters steeped in the magic of the ages, far better than Harrogate for assisting a would-be mother. Tell her so. Tell her she would not wish to let down a friend, would she?

But, darling, all that is by the by because we will be together again! Write to me at once as soon as you get this, and tell me I won't have to wait much longer!

    Love always,

        Your Mafalda

P.S. I forgot to mention, our household has heard nothing at all from Major Oberleitner. I don't know if he was so drunk as to forget our little contretemps, but I am extremely satisfied with the silence from that quarter.

PART FIVE

Sir John Seward's personal diary
Saturday, 24th January 1903
Littlemore Hospital, Oxfordshire

Since I became a doctor, I have always found it dreadfully embarrassing to be ill. I spent the last week in a fever brought on, I assume, by coming into contact with the influenza that is so common at this time of year, and then running around in the chill of a winter's night when not dressed for the elements. For several days, I am told, I was quite delirious.

My nightmares, my constant companions of these many years, were given new power by my illness. I saw the monster at the foot of my bed, grinning his hideous grin while his mouth dripped gore. I was paralysed, unable to move so much as an inch. I could only watch as his unnaturally jointed form climbed over the footboard and crawled up my petrified body until I could feel his rank breath on my exposed throat. I felt the graze of his teeth against my skin . . . By God, I hope and pray that I am never so ill again.

I awoke in full consciousness yesterday evening to find Nurse Bridges mopping my brow and Dr Knight standing at my bedside regarding me with professional interest. She informed me at length that it was my own actions that had brought me to such a state, and I was, of course, suitably contrite. Dr Knight ordered Nurse Bridges to see about getting me some broth, that well-known cure-all, before seating herself by the bed and continuing the business of the brow-mopping.

'You're my patient now, Sir John. What's the last thing you remember?'

'I don't know,' I told her. 'It's rather foggy. Something was urgent, something about Lady Lowell . . .'

And then I did remember. The long pale face, the pointed teeth and the gleaming red eyes which had haunted my delirium haunted our patient too. I sat bolt upright, and attempted to get out of bed. Dr Knight watched as I flopped right back down again, weak as a kitten.

'I suggest you stay horizontal just now. What was that about Lady Lowell?'

She turned to dip the cloth in a bowl of water on the bedside table, then gave it a thorough wringing-out. I realize now that this may have been meant to give me time to gather my thoughts, which was just as well as there were many to be gathered.

Where a woman's sanity lies in the balance, I thought, does my doctor's oath not demand that I do all I can to heal her? And that other oath, perhaps even more binding, which our unlikely band of holy warriors took to wipe the vampire from the face of the earth, is that not even more sacred? If there are those in the world who still suffer from his evil work, then am I not doubly bound?

I decided to tell Dr Knight a part of the truth, for now.

'I have an idea that the carriage accident may be a false memory covering something else. Something her ladyship's mind could not accept.'

'I agree. I examined her under hypnosis while you were ill, and I came to the same conclusion. Would you like to tell me why this had you running into my rooms in the small hours, shouting about geography?'

I paused. 'My idea may be . . . rather . . . unorthodox.'

'I see. In that case, let's wait to argue about it until you're recovered. As your doctor I strongly advise you to rest.'

'Then I will be a good patient and follow your orders. I should like to read your notes on the hypnosis sessions though, if you could have them brought over?'

Dr Knight frowned. 'I wouldn't call that resting.'

'Nonsense, reading is a very restful activity.'

There was a knock at the door and Nurse Bridges returned with the broth. Dr Knight gave up the chair to her, and the nurse arranged my pillows that I might be propped up to feed myself.

'Very well, Sir John. If you insist.'

'Thank you. I am sorry to be an inconvenience.'

'Rest and recover, and think no more about it. I'll check on you again when I can.'

She swept from the room, and I found myself gazing after her. Nurse Bridges coughed delicately, and I returned obediently to my repast.

I know that I must share the truth with Dr Knight for the sake of our patient yet I have no idea how to go about it. I have decided to write to those of our little band of brothers still in this world – Jonathan Harker, Lord Godalming and my mentor, Abraham Van Helsing. I hope they will provide some much-needed perspective.

It is after nine now. I have been left for the night, though a nurse is stationed outside the door within call. Dr Knight has not returned, but has sent over her account of Lady Lowell's hypnosis sessions as promised. I am not a devotee of the art, but the more information and insight we have, the more likely we are to be able to treat poor Lady Lowell.

It infuriates me still to think of the trail of suffering that fiend left behind him. How many lives did he blight during his centuries-long wandering of this earth? Hundreds? Thousands? More? How many are there out in the world who still contend with the aftermath of his evil? By any method I can, I swear, I will at least save this one.

Date: Monday, 19th January 1903
Notes of Attending Physician: Dr Knight
Patient: Lady Lowell
Nurse attending: Nurse Weldon
First session.

Consent sought & received from patient's husband, now returned to Berkshire, via telegram. Also sought & received from patient for the sake of form. Explained procedure to patient (N.B. performed according to the James Braid focused-attention method), & informed her Nurse Weldon would be present throughout. Consent for this also sought & received, to encourage both trust & compliance.

Patient began composed & lucid, seated unrestrained in a chair opposite. Transitioned well into hypnotic state. Eyes began open & unfocused, breathing slow & regular. Initial standard question-&-answers on name, birth date, & year were answered correctly. Standard continuation questions on recent memories (breakfast this morning, dinner last night &c.) were answered correctly & calmly.

I asked the patient if she had travelled to Buda-Pesth. She responded in the affirmative. I asked what sights she had seen there. She lifted her eyes & smiled as if a person she was happy to see stood before her. 'It is a beautiful city,' she responded, but her smile faded & her eyes lost their focus as she continued: 'except when I am chilled & I shake & I cannot breathe & it hurts to try. They tell me I am very ill, they tell me I almost died. I think I wish I had.'

I asked her why she had wished to die, & she responded: 'I have nothing left to live for.'

'Nothing at all?'

'Nothing.'

'Why not?'

'She is gone.'

'Who is gone?'

Here the patient's tone changed. It was no longer the vague & slow tones usual to the hypnotized patient. This next was delivered staccato as if the syllables had been learned separately & not properly stitched together.

'We got out of the carriage to lighten the load for the horses. A noise startled them & they bolted. The carriage went over the cliff & into the river. There was nothing we could do.'

'Who was in the carriage?'

'We got out of the carriage to lighten the load for the horses. A noise startled them & they bolted. The carriage went over the cliff & into the river. There was nothing we could do.'

Further questions on who got out of the carriage, where this was, & any surrounding circumstances met with the exact same response, word for word.

'What was your last memory before that?'

Here the patient recited the entirety of the twenty-third psalm, recorded here for the sake of completeness:

'The Lord is my shepherd; I shall not want. He maketh me to lie down in green pastures: he leadeth me beside the still waters. He restoreth my soul: he leadeth me in the paths of righteousness for his name's sake. Yea, though I walk through the valley of the shadow of death, I will fear no evil: for thou art with me; thy rod and thy staff they comfort me. Thou preparest a table before me in the presence of mine enemies: thou anointest my head with oil; my cup runneth over. Surely goodness and mercy shall follow me all the days of my life: and I will dwell in the house of the Lord for ever.'

No further response could be gained from the patient.

First session ends here.

Comment:
Therapeutically this may not have been as successful as hoped, but the recitation of this particular psalm tallies with what the patient has consciously said about its place in her nightmares. This could be a trigger, or a type of key which may prove useful in the future. Her buried grief at a death, perhaps the death of a friend in the accident, could be part of the problem, especially if this grief has been strongly suppressed. Her repetition of the description of what she saw is odd & this should also be further explored. The form of the delivery strongly suggests this could be a false memory.

Date: Wednesday, 21st January 1903
Notes of Attending Physician: Dr Knight
Patient: Lady Lowell
Nurse attending: Nurse Weldon
Second session.

Consents sought & received as per first session. Patient succumbed equally easily to hypnotic state using the James Braid method. Acting on the hypothesis that the carriage accident may be a false memory, I began the Joshee Process as follows:

Instructed the patient to imagine standing before a locked door, with the key in her hand. Encouraged the patient to describe both door & key in detail; patient described a door & key such as might be found in any modern house. Instructed the patient to take the key & unlock the door, describing that process. The patient did so. Informed the patient that she was now in a large white room, & would be able to view her own memories as images.

Proceeded through recent memories again (today's breakfast, luncheon, activities &c.), patient responded well, describing memories as pictures just as suggested. Moved to disputed memory. Asked if she could recall the carriage accident.

'Yes.'

'Can you describe that memory?'

The words came exactly as before, in the same staccato voice:

'We got out of the carriage to lighten the load for the horses. A noise startled them & they bolted. The carriage went over the cliff & into the river. There was nothing we could do.'

'Please describe the memory as an image, as a picture, as if you could view it in a frame.'

'We got out of the carriage to lighten the load for the horses. A noise startled them & they bolted. The carriage went over the cliff & into the river. There was nothing we could do.'

I proceeded more cautiously. 'What colour were the horses?'

The patient did not respond. Paused for a count of two minutes, asked again.

'Do you remember what colour the horses were?'

Paused again for two-minute count, whereupon patient responded very quietly: 'Brown.'

'Do you remember what time of day the accident occurred?'

Another pause, timed at almost one minute, & then a quiet 'No.'

'When you remember the accident, what picture do you see in the frame?'

'Nothing.'

'When you remember the accident, what do you hear?'

The patient began to shake, & beads of sweat were visible on her brow. Her breathing became rapid. I timed her response at thirty seconds. It was delivered slowly & with great effort.

'I hear screams . . . so many screams. I hear . . . howling, I hear rain, I hear . . . I hear . . .'

Here the patient's eyes snapped into focus, as if onto an object perhaps three feet in front of her. Her posture changed, losing the relaxed pose of the hypnotized subject & becoming deliberate, as if in an attempt to entice. Her voice lost all softness, assuming a harsher but sensual tone:

'Come here, my love, come to me and kiss me, and we will be together for ever.' Blood began to run from the patient's nose but she continued speaking even as it dripped down over her lips. 'Is that not what you have always wanted? Is that not what you have always yearned for? Come to me, and be mine for eternity.'

Here, the patient smiled briefly, horribly, & then began to scream. I broke the hypnotic trance, whereupon the patient ceased screaming but wept uncontrollably. Nurse Weldon attended her.

Comment:

I have visited the patient briefly since this session & found her as well & lucid as before the hypnosis, though distracted & low in mood. I believe the hypothesis of a false memory is correct. The patient's breakdown at the end of the second session is likely to be the real, suppressed memory attempting to assert itself when the mental barriers are brought down. I recommend that this be very slowly & carefully explored with the patient in a conscious state, & that hypnosis not be considered again unless that exploration proves unsuccessful.

Letter: Eliza Cartwright to Maria Lowell
Friday, 27th June 1884
Whitby, Yorkshire, England

Your ladyship,
I have just this morning received your letter. I thank you for your invitation, and it gives me great pleasure to accept. I would be honoured to accompany Lucy and to join you, your sister and dear Mafalda at your sister's home. If Lucy's and my society can provide even momentary relief from the dreadful sadness the poor lady must be experiencing at such a time, then I am happy to do all I am able.

You must not be concerned about my leaving my own sister, though you are very kind to be so thoughtful. I will miss her, but we have engaged a truly excellent nanny and my husband positively dotes upon little Elsbeth. I know that she will be as well cared for as my late mama and papa could wish. Besides, as my dear husband pointed out to me, I would never want to set her the example of turning down a friend in need. He recently lost a friend who was a reliable companion for many years, so I daresay the lesson is uppermost in his mind.

It is good of you to offer us the hospitality of your house in London for the night before we leave for Dover. I look forward to seeing Sir Gerald, and I am to convey to him my husband's very best regards. He speaks fondly of their time in India together and wishes that they may meet again soon when his health permits.

I hope you will feel easier knowing that Lucy will not need to make the trip with a hired chaperone. As you say, there are many reputable agencies that provide such services but I do think it is much better to have a friend instead of a stranger as a travelling companion. On our honeymoon, the Colonel and I visited the Continent on one of Mr Thomas Cook's Swiss tours, so I have some experience of long-distance trains and of caring for one's health during the vicissitudes of travel. I have sent to Stanfords bookshop for several relevant Baedeker guides so that I might be as fully prepared as possible. I am nevertheless grateful that your late brother-in-law's steward will meet us on the way, as I fear my German is not so fresh in my mind as it once was. I will be glad to have a native speaker with us for that portion of the journey.

After studying her Bradshaw, Lucy has made us an itinerary which I have enclosed. Please do let me know if our arrival date is convenient, and also if there is anything I can bring you from London.

Yours sincerely,
Eliza Cartwright

Letter: Alice Smith to Mary and Sarah Smith
Friday, 27th June 1884
Whitby, Yorkshire, England

Dear Mam and Sarah,
I've got such exciting news! Mrs Cartwright is chaperoning Miss North on a trip to the Continent, and I'm going too! First

we'll take the train to Dover, then a ferry across to Calais. There we'll connect with another train to Paris, and then we'll get on a sleeping train which Miss North tells me is called *l'Express d'Orient*, which means 'the Eastern Express'. It goes all the way to Buda-Pesth in one fell swoop! Can you imagine? Hundreds and hundreds of miles on just one train! It was all I could do to keep myself together when Mrs Cartwright told me!

Really I ought to be ashamed of myself because the reason for the trip is sad. In London, Miss North lives with the Lowell family, Miss Lowell being her best friend. The lady of the house, Lady Maria Lowell, is a Hungarian by birth and her sister still lives in that country. This sister has just been widowed, and is not at all well. Miss North has been invited to help give her some comfort and society as she convalesces, I think. Of course, a young lady can hardly go that far alone, which is why Mrs Cartwright is going to go with her. And I'll be maid for them both along the way!

I'll write to you as often as I can, and tell you about all the wonderful things I see. I plan on noting everything down in my commonplace book so I can be sure not to forget. And I thought the move to Whitby was exciting enough!

I have to stop now, because my evenings have to be spent trying to learn some German before we go. In the Austro-Hungarian Empire they speak a lot of different languages but German is the most important one. Miss North has been helping me. It isn't so tricky as I'd thought, and I'm quite enjoying myself. I don't know how long Mrs Cartwright will be staying, so I don't know how long I'll be gone. Maybe a month? I'll write to you when I know.

All my love,
Alice

*

P.S. Sarah, please can you send more lemon beebrush before I go away? A whole stack of it? I don't want to dream while I'm gone, waking or asleep. I can't shake the memory of Morton's strangled face, and his feet in their perfectly shined shoes swinging back and forth, back and forth, above the floorboards.

Sorry, I don't mean to distress you. It's why I'm so keen to leave here. I'm all of a twitch, I can't sit still. It isn't only excitement, but also the nerves of going to places I've barely even heard of, the feeling of everything that could go wrong, that something *will* go wrong and I won't be able to do anything about it . . . Goodness, now I'm just getting myself wound up. I'm sure everything will be just fine.

Pray for me, and for poor Morton's soul.

Lucy North's journal
Saturday, 28th June 1884
Whitby, Yorkshire, England

When Mafalda's latest letter arrived, I was shocked at just how underhanded the whole thing seemed. Ever since I've known her, she has always been good at taking control of situations and ensuring that what she thinks should happen actually happens, but I had not meant for Mafalda to manipulate Aunt Réka quite so brazenly. I suppose I must have misunderstood, or perhaps Mafalda expressed it badly when rendering the conversation into English.

While my offer to play lady's companion was genuine, now that it has been accepted I find myself recoiling from the task. I want to believe that Aunt Réka was not of sound mind when she shared what she knew with Baron Tolvay. I want to have sympathy for her now, in her grief and her guilt. I want to feel Christian pity. And yet. The Baroness said Aunt Réka was like an animal, and when an animal is cornered, we expect that it will be all teeth and claws. It would have been no great leap to imagine that a man of high rank, in a society bound by rules of honour, would seek satisfaction over the adultery of his wife. In her rage and her humiliation, it may well be that Aunt Réka knew exactly what she was doing and decided she did not care about the consequences.

Thank goodness Eliza, who knows nothing of all this, will be coming with me to Buda-Pesth. I did not even have to do the convincing myself, as Lady Maria and the Colonel did that work for me. It will be to Eliza's good to be removed from her materfamilias role for a while, and now that a new housekeeper is installed there could not be a better time.

Alice seems happy to be accompanying her mistress on the journey. Eliza has lent her her old German schoolbooks so that Alice might be able to make herself understood, and therefore useful. She already has some French, of course, and seems to be picking up German remarkably quickly. I quizzed her while she dressed me for dinner yesterday, and she's come on in leaps and bounds.

I mentioned this to Eliza earlier while we took chilled lemonade in the garden under our parasols.

'I'm so glad. I was worried we would have to engage a new attendant for the journey. It would have upset her so, and been a dreadful hassle to boot.'

'Indeed.'

'I'll have to raise her salary sooner than I expected,' Eliza said, chuckling a little to herself. 'I was told she might have certain talents, though I wasn't anticipating those would be linguistic.'

'Oh?' I said, idly fanning myself with a discarded fashion magazine. 'What sort of talents?'

'It's stuff and nonsense really. Do you remember I mentioned a Mrs Saunders, who trained Alice up for service? She said that Alice's grandmother was once fined for what they used to call hag-riding, and that her mother tells fortunes even though she's long since lost her eyesight.'

'Goodness!' I dropped the magazine and gave Eliza my full attention. 'I thought Alice's mother kept a shop? No, not a shop, a—'

'An apothecary, yes. I thought having a maid with such knowledge would be useful for the household's good health.'

'She does make wonderful tisanes and things.'

'You know I don't agree with gossip,' Eliza said, 'but if you promise not to breathe a word? Especially to Alice – she's a true gem and I'd hate for her to take it into her head to leave.'

'I wouldn't dream of it.'

'Well, Mrs Saunders said she sometimes suspected that Alice knew things ahead of time. I'm afraid I laughed, and said that would be a useful quality to have in a servant.'

'What sort of things?'

'I don't know, she didn't say.'

'Do you think it's true?'

'Goodness, who knows? But this gives me a delightful idea. Why don't we walk down to the pier and have your palm read by a charming charlatan? It will be completely wrong, but it's the most wonderful fun.'

And so it was. According to the faux fortune-teller, complete with headscarf and crystal ball, I am to marry above my station, have two children, and live to a ripe old age. Lucky me!

Letter: Mafalda Lowell to Lucy North
Wednesday, 9th July 1884
Buda-Pesth, Austro-Hungarian Empire

Dear Lucy,

I am sending this post-haste to London, as I'm not sure it will reach you in Whitby before you set off. I am overjoyed that this is my last letter to you before I get to see you again. For one thing, I am desperate to have my hair back in your tender care. I swear Partridge has made it her mission to rip it out in clumps, and every time she comes near me with a hairbrush I begin by feeling apprehensive and end by feeling tenderized.

I have been working to prepare for your arrival. You are to take the room next to mine, which adjoins. The view is not spectacular, but I don't think we'll care too much, do you? Eliza will take a suite near Mama's, and the little polyglot maid with whom you seem so taken will have a single upstairs.

Mátyás has not long ago left for Paris, and he will take excellent care of you all on the journey from there. I promise that he is well-mannered and capable, as well as being very clever. Secretly, I hope that he will eventually use that cleverness to find a better position. Papa could do with a brain like Mátyás's at his office. Perhaps I should raise it with him.

I risk rambling on for hours if I do not put my pen down this instant. Know that I think of you constantly, and I am counting the days and minutes and hours until I see you.

    Your ever-loving
    Mafalda

Letter: Alice Smith to Mary and Sarah Smith
Wednesday, 9th July 1884
Whitby, Yorkshire, England

Dear Mam and Sarah,
This is just a quick note before we leave in the morning. I'm

scribbling it at the kitchen table, and Annie will take it down for the last post any minute. Sorry for the ink blots.

Please, please don't trouble yourself to worry about me. I borrowed a few of Annie's old copies of *The Lady* to make sure I know what's expected of a travelling-maid, and I'll be right careful to watch out for pickpockets. I can tell them off in English, French, and now German if I have to! I'll always have a spare coin or two in my shoe sole and my hem, just like you taught me, for if it comes to the worst.

I really must go, I've not yet packed my things. It seems so long since I was at home with you both, putting my clothes in Nana's old trunk to start my new life here in Whitby. I'll write to you when I next get a chance. I'm sending a list of the addresses where we'll be staying, so if you time it right I can still get your letters while I'm gone. Remember to collect all the foreign stamps when you get mine! Take care of yourselves, and pray for me and for Mrs Cartwright and Miss North as we go.

All my love,
    Alice

P.S. Sarah, you don't know what you're asking of me. If I were to stop the lemon beebrush . . . No, if Our Lord needs me to hear the message badly enough, He can get it to me some other way.

Lucy North's journal
Thursday, 10th July 1884
Lowell House, Kensington, London, England

It's very strange to be back at home without Mafalda, and stranger still that it's only for one night. My trunk remains packed and stowed safely away and only my carpet bag has accompanied me, so I feel as if I am camping in my own bedroom.

We left Whitby early this morning. Alice took firm charge of all our tickets and ensured both our luggage and ourselves were properly stowed. We were made quite comfortable thanks to her foresighted provision of seat cushions, flasks of tea and savoury biscuits. Her tasks thus discharged, Alice took a seat by the door and began to study her hand-me-down German grammar. Eliza had insisted that Alice could not possibly travel alone in third class, and the pair of rotund widows who took seats in our compartment an hour into the journey harrumphed a great deal at sharing with a domestic servant. I gave them a Mafalda-like hard stare, which seemed to quiet them down. They then fell asleep and snored like sows all the way to York where, praise the Lord, they left us. Alice, of course, maintained her dignity throughout.

From then on, Eliza and I read and slept and ate of our train picnic, and in between times I passed the hours gazing out of the window. The countryside slid past, all green fields and rolling hills. There is little drama in the landscape of England, only sheep.

At King's Cross station, Alice enlisted porters to assist us and in short order we were in a hansom, weaving through familiar streets to Kensington. As we were ushered into the hall at Lowell House, servants dashing around us to bring in our things, Sir Gerald appeared from his study. He looked rather tired, but my attention was ripped away almost immediately, for who should be following him, close as a shadow?

'Lucy!' Joseph greeted me, while Sir Gerald kissed Eliza's hand in a courtly fashion. 'How are you?' He grasped my hand and shook it, rather too firmly.

'Joseph, how nice,' I said weakly.

'Isn't it? I timed my visit so I might speak with you.'

'Please excuse me, I must greet Sir Gerald.'

'Certainly, certainly, but I have to insist.' He lowered his voice. 'It's a matter of great importance.'

'Well—'

Sir Gerald swooped in and gave me a moment's reprieve.

'Lucy, dear girl, it does these old eyes good to see you.'

'I'm glad to see you too, Sir Gerald,' I said as I kissed his grey-bearded cheek, shoving my fears aside as best I could. 'Are you well?'

'Quite well, thank you, quite well.' He coughed into his fist, giving the lie to his words. 'Such a pleasure to have you and Mrs Cartwright break your journey here.'

'Thank you for your hospitality, Sir Gerald,' Eliza said graciously. 'My husband is only sorry he could not join us.'

'Oh, no bother. Another time. I'll write to him and we'll fix it all up. Now, you ladies must go and, er, rest before dinner. Mrs Chappell will show you up.'

'Sir Gerald,' Joseph cut in, 'might I whisk Lucy away ever so briefly? The cherry tree we planted as children is giving fruit at last, and I must show her before I go.'

'Of course, dear boy, of course!' Sir Gerald boomed, whereupon Joseph took my arm in his giant's paw and steered me firmly down the hall.

'Joseph, what are you talking about?' I hissed. 'We planted a cherry tree at Beechwood, not here.'

'I have to speak to you,' he said in hushed tones. 'It's too serious to wait and I don't want us to be overheard.'

He propelled me outside into the walled garden behind the house, and down towards the orchard. I was indignant at being manhandled so, and made my feelings quite plain.

'Forgive me, Lucy, please, but I have to leave soon and we must speak alone.'

Joseph's expression was solemn, bordering on severe. I had never seen him in such a mood. I was seized by a strangling fear, as physical as if it had grabbed me by the neck, that he'd told Mafalda of our conversation on the train to Whitby. If she knew I had kept such a secret from her . . . I could not even finish the thought. Her fury at such a betrayal would be terrifying.

'Well, what is it that's so secret?' I demanded, as we reached the privacy of the trees. 'Is it about Mafalda?'

Joseph frowned, confused.

'Mafalda? No, this is about Sir Gerald. I'm deeply concerned about his state of health. He is ill, but he won't see Dr Williamson and he won't have a hired nurse. I've done all I can to persuade him to do either or both, but I've failed. I need your help.'

I felt the fear of future loss rise up and clog my throat.

'Are you quite sure it's as serious as that?'

'I am. He does his best to hide it, but it's easy to spot when you look for the signs. His lungs pain him more and more. He coughs a great deal, and the heat seems to make it worse. His breath wheezes with any exertion, and yet he refuses to limit his daily activities in any real way. I have tried, Lucy, I have tried over and over to help him but he is obstinate beyond belief.'

Joseph leaned back against the nearest tree, the strain painfully visible on his face.

'I doubt I would succeed where you have failed, if that's what you're hoping,' I told him. 'Mafalda can sometimes get him to change his mind on a matter, but Lady Maria is the only one who can reliably break through that Lowell obstinacy.'

Joseph conceded my point with a rueful twitch of an eyebrow.

'Well, that's as may be. But her ladyship . . . would she come, do you think? Would she return home if you told her all?'

'Return home! Would a letter or a telegram not suffice? What about Aunt Réka?'

'She's recovering, isn't she? Perhaps her ladyship could be freed from that obligation, especially if you and Mrs Cartwright are there to replace her.'

'Could she, though? So soon? Perhaps if—' I stopped short, as my brain caught up with my ears. 'Has Lady Maria told you the particulars of Aunt Réka's illness?'

'No, I heard from Mafalda. I've not told her about Sir Gerald's state of health, though. I don't wish to distress her.' My faint 'oh' went unregarded. 'You must see for yourself how things stand,' Joseph continued. 'Write and let me know, or send a telegram. Please, if you think there's even the slightest chance she might, do your best to persuade her ladyship to come home.'

'I will,' I said in my most reassuring tone, pushing my true emotions down and packing them tightly away.

'As for Mafalda, it would be easier to hear the truth of her father's state of health in person, from her most beloved friend. You will take care when you break it to her?'

'Of course.' I bit down hard on my lip.

'Lucy, I owe Sir Gerald so much. Everything I have, I have because of him. By accident of birth I might be his heir, but he was under no obligation to hand Beechwood over to me during his lifetime, or to take me into his family when I had no other left to me. You know me; I am not dynamic as he is, nor as bold. I don't know what I would have done without his guidance, and his example.'

Joseph's words wrung my unwilling heart.

'I suppose I . . . I feel much the same. If the Lowells had not taken me in, I don't know where I would have found myself.'

'Come now, you would have landed on your feet. I'm sure of it.'

I narrowed my eyes. 'You flatter me. I'd have expected better of you.'

'No, no, I do not mean to flatter. I speak as I believe to be true.'

'Even worse flattery!' He smiled at this, and the melancholy mood lifted a little. 'We will take the actions we can. I will tell Lady Maria all, and she can decide what to do next. Perhaps you could invite Dr Williamson to see *you* about some ailment, at a time when Sir Gerald is also at home?'

'I can't say I like the deception but it might serve. I'll come to town as often as I can. Perhaps I can persuade Sir Gerald to go to Beechwood for the change of air. It might help to be away from the city and its dirt and smog.'

'That's probably wise.'

Joseph took a deep breath, stood straight and squared his shoulders.

'Thank you, Lucy. You have lightened my burdens. You're a good and true friend.'

I cricked my neck to look up at him. For just a moment I felt a silly feminine desire to have a strong and steadfast man stand between me and all the ills of the world. Do not worry for my sanity, my imagined reader, the moment passed in the blink of an eye.

'Anyone would do the same, I'm sure.'

He shook my hand, almost managing not to crush it. 'I'm sorry but I really must go, or I'll miss my train.'

'Of course. Travel safely.'

'I should say the same to you. Take good care of yourself, and of the others.'

It is not Joseph's fault he has chosen Mafalda, I thought as I watched him walk away. He does not know better. I have not always written kindly of him in these pages, but even through all my jealousy I know how much we have in common.

I returned to the house deep in thought. My conversation with Joseph had unsettled me on more than only Sir Gerald's account. Mafalda has not mentioned that she and Joseph have continued to write to each other. I have been watching her letters for just such a thing. She must regard them as a non-event, not worth reporting. It's also strange that Joseph would not let Mafalda know about his fears for her father's health. Does he think her so delicate? I thought he had the measure of her, but if he believes her to be a fragile china doll then they are an even more poorly suited couple than I had imagined.

Alice will be coming to dress me soon so I must leave off. I will resume when I can.

Later
At dinner Sir Gerald and Eliza shared stories of India – Sir Gerald his own, and Eliza her husband's. Tales of elephants and red-veiled brides and statues of gods the colour of lapis bounced around the dinner table, and in any other state of mind I would have listened with rapt attention.

'What a marvellous place it must be!' Eliza was enthusing to Sir Gerald. 'I hope I have the chance to go one day, to see such wonderful sights and to meet people so different from myself.'

'Oh, you must go, Mrs Cartwright, you must! The transportation is so very much improved in recent years that it is no hardship to get about, even for a lady.' He launched into a tale about the Bombay to Delhi railway project but was taken by a coughing fit that lasted so long Eliza had to ring for water.

'Please excuse me. It's the smogs, you know. Not good for an old man. I'll be right as rain in short order.'

Eliza made soothing noises, before claiming the extreme fatigue of travel and suggesting that she and I ought to retire to bed. Outside my room, Eliza stopped me as I began saying my goodnights.

'Lucy, Sir Gerald needs a doctor.'

'Joseph said he already tried, and Sir Gerald refuses to see one. Joseph thinks Lady Maria should come home and persuade him.'

Eliza nodded sagely, doubtless familiar with the power of wives over husbands in matters of health. 'If that's so, then we must exert ourselves to be of use to Madam Jacobinus, so she might do without her sister.'

Eliza kissed me on the cheek and left me with that. I retreated to mine and Mafalda's salon. I owe Sir Gerald so much, to think of him deathly ill or worse pains my soul. Mafalda brought me here, but it was Sir Gerald and Lady Maria who allowed me to stay and make my home with them. I hope upon hope that even if Mafalda were to spurn me and marry Joseph, they would still be my family.

Night

Why did I not ask Joseph when and how he plans to propose? How much agony I might have saved myself!

Lucy North's journal
Friday, 11th July 1884
L'Express d'Orient

Like Nellie Bly, I now seem to be in the habit of reporting my location. To that end, I'll begin by putting down that I am writing from my bed aboard *l'Express d'Orient* as we are whisked through eastern France and into the German Empire.

We left very early this morning, an exhausted-looking Sir Gerald waving us off. Poor dear man. I am resolved to convince Lady Maria to return home, even if that means we are all left motherless while away.

Eliza and I, and Alice of course, departed from Victoria

Station. At Dover we were herded onto the ferry by a liveried ferryman, in much the manner I imagine a harassed farmer's wife would herd her chickens. Our luggage has been labelled 'through to Gare du Nord' but Alice had the man go and check on it anyway. She managed the voyage quite well, though poor Eliza did not. She spent most of it white as a sheet with her mouth clamped tight shut, staring directly ahead.

In service of my own digestion, I abandoned our cramped cabin for a turn around the deck. At the last moment, Alice asked if she might join me for some fresh air. Eliza assented with a brief nod of her head, a movement it seemed she regretted after the fact.

On deck, I stood at the railing and watched England fade into the hazy distance. I felt myself begin to slip into a fresh round of worried thoughts, saved only by Alice's enthusiasm for travel.

'Goodness, miss, look at that! In't it beautiful? Is it true on a clear day, you can stand at Dover and see France?'

'I believe so, or at least I've heard it said. Not today though.' I turned to squint over my shoulder in our direction of travel. 'Today it's too clouded.'

'That's a right shame, miss. I'd have loved to write home and tell my mam I'd stood nearly in England and seen France.'

'I'm sure you'll have a great many things just as wonderful to tell her by the time we get back. You aren't at all nervous to be leaving England?'

'It's kind of you to ask, miss. A bit, but Mrs Cartwright has been so many places, I know she'll see us right as we go. I'll do my best to make sure you both want for nothing on t'way.'

'Thank you, Alice. I appreciate it. This is your first post, I think?'

Anxiety flashed across Alice's face.

'Yes, miss, but I beg you not to worry. I was well trained; I was with Mrs Saunders in Robin Hood's Bay for four years before I came to Mrs Cartwright.'

'Oh, no, I didn't mean to imply you seem inexperienced. I was merely curious.'

'Ah, right, I see. Well, miss.' Alice twisted her hands before consciously gripping onto the rail. 'Yes, it's my first live-in post. I didn't live in with Mrs Saunders, I stayed with my mam and sister. We've lived in my nana's cottage on the seafront since my da passed.'

I thought of the jet-worker's wife, and the struggles a family would likely face if the breadwinner were to die suddenly. For many of the poor of the parish, the path to destitution begins with a father or husband's demise.

'I'm very sorry for your loss.'

'Thank you, miss, that's right good of you. It were, I mean, it was a long time ago. Da was a fisherman on Mr Saunders's boat, and after the big storm Mr Saunders made sure to take care of us. He paid our day-school fees, mine and my sister Sarah's, and then Mrs Saunders took me in to train for service.'

'Mr Saunders sounds like a good man.'

'He is that, miss, we were lucky. After Da died, he helped Mam get up my nana's old apothecary shop. Sarah helps her out now, and they're never short of customers. I can shift well enough at herbals, but I found I was suited to service. Mam was a housemaid before she married Da, so it must be in my blood.'

A chance to ask about Alice's female antecedents and their witchery! It was on the tip of my tongue, but I listened to my better angels. It would be cruel to embarrass Alice just because I wanted to pry.

'Yes, it must be. Although, by that logic you could just as well have put on a striped woollen jersey and taken to fishing.'

Alice laughed.

'I suppose I could, miss. I can't say as the smell is over-pleasant though.'

After that, Alice excused herself to attend to Eliza. I stayed out, letting the wind coax my hair from its moorings, and wondering idly how long it would take for the French coast to appear from the haze. If I were a man I think I'd have liked to be a sailor. What could I not do with such freedom?

Our transfer to the Paris train went smoothly. Mafalda would, I'm sure, mock me for it, but having finished *Frankenstein* I continued on the Villa Diodati theme and embarked on a re-reading of Dr Polidori's famous novella. I filled my mind with devilish rakes and kidnapped ladies and other such entertaining horrors until we reached Paris.

Our escort, the famous 'young Mátyás', met us off the boat train to shepherd us from Gare du Nord around the corner to Gare de l'Est. For some reason I had expected a skinny, scruffy-looking clerk scarcely old enough to shave. Instead, I found him to be a well-turned-out and tidily bearded man of middle build and middle height. His hands showed no sign of ink stains, his attire was entirely appropriate and not at all dishevelled, and he managed to be properly groomed without being a dandy. Despite myself, I found him rather handsome. Not as handsome as Reverend Baker, but certainly capable of turning a young lady's head.

He showed us to the Gare de l'Est station café, which was a glittering establishment, full to the brim of keyed-up ladies and gentlemen whose heads turned continually to check the large clock on the far wall. Alice, who I think was a little uncomfortable at sitting down with her mistress, offered to check that our trunks were properly stowed, again.

'Please rest assured, Miss Alice,' Mátyás said, 'the Compagnie Internationale des Wagon-Lits knows its trade. They say it has not lost a single item of luggage since the Express began running last year.'

I do believe 'Miss Alice' blushed! She thanked him, and then proceeded to stare intently at her coffee cup for the rest of our brief respite.

At seven o'clock precisely we made our way to the platform, ready for our departure on the famous *Express d'Orient*. Is the ingenuity of man not marvellous? How wonderful that one can now whip across a vast swath of Europe in a mere thirty-odd hours!

A man in a smart blue uniform helped us aboard and showed us to our wood-panelled compartments, already set up for sleeping. Eliza and I have compartments that connect, with one bed apiece fixed low down onto the wall. I found the apparatus for washing tucked most ingeniously into a cupboard in the corner, and in the morning our beds will be put away and turned into seats.

As the train slipped out of the city and into the countryside, the conductor knocked on the door and announced that the first sitting for dinner was to take place, for 'ladies and gentlemen', with 'attendants' to be called later. When I read about this train's first journey last year, I thought the opulence must have been exaggerated. It was not so. Bright-white tablecloths and napkins, glittering glasses and crystal-clear water decanters abounded just as the writer promised, and the food was as good as or better than anything I have ever eaten. Eliza's company added to my enjoyment of the evening. Dining alone with her was a great deal of fun.

'Did you know,' she said as she delicately speared a stalk of asparagus, 'they say spies use this train to dash across Europe with secret documents?'

'Is that so?' I replied, the intrigue making me prick up my ears. 'Who says that?'

'I have no idea. Do you think it could be true?'

I glanced around the dining car.

'Perhaps. That rotund little man with the moustaches could be an undercover police officer.'

'On a secret mission from Paris to the Ottomans?'

'Absolutely!'

Respectable matron Eliza might be, but away from her duties I have found she is not yet too matronly for games and silliness.

The delicious food left me pleasantly sated, and rather drowsy. We will not be awoken at the frontier as we have entrusted our papers to the guard, who will perform the necessary formalities. I am glad of it, being so very full of wine and French delicacies and wanting only my bed.

I wonder where we are now? I can see nothing from the window, and at this time of year it means the hour must be very late indeed. I will set down my pen, and let the motion of the train rock me to sleep.

Letter: Alice Smith to Mary and Sarah Smith
Saturday, 12th July 1884
L'Express d'Orient

Dear Mam and Sarah,

I'm writing to you from *L'Express d'Orient*! Can you imagine? I'm having a wonderful time, even though it does take a while to get used to walking, dressing and even sleeping on a moving train. The compartments are small, and it's right clever how they get all the fixtures and fittings in. I'm sharing with another maid, Karolina. She doesn't know English, so we've been speaking German together. I'm glad to have the chance to practise, and Karolina is patient and corrects my many mistakes. She's a Hungarian, and is trying to teach me some of that language. It sounds odd to my ears but I'm doing my best. I've been trying to teach her a bit of English in return.

We set out from Paris this evening – wait, no, I suppose it's yesterday evening by now as it must be past midnight. Miss Lowell's aunt sent her steward to escort us, and last night I went to dinner with him and Karolina at the servants' dinner sitting. Eating on the train was a bit tricky, especially given the stew they served. Karolina said it's called goulash, and while it tasted delicious it did want to slop about all over the place. Karolina had to finish in a hurry as her mistress wanted her but there were lots and lots of people about, Mam, so it wasn't like I was left alone with Mátyás, the steward, in a way that wouldn't be proper. I didn't talk much, being too concerned with not making a show of myself trying to eat, so I let him tell me all about Buda-Pesth. It sounds like a magical place, full of beautiful buildings and all sorts of people from all over the Empire. I had to keep reminding myself that when Mátyás said 'the Empire' he meant the Austro-Hungarian Empire, not the British Empire. Apparently Buda-Pesth is the joint capital city with Vienna, though I can't see how that works, and is itself somehow two cities with the river Danube in the middle. They only built a bridge to connect the two some forty years ago, and it was designed by an Englishman and built by a Scotsman. I felt so proud! I'll try to find a postcard of it to send to you.

Apart from that, I've mostly been occupied with attending Mrs Cartwright and Miss North. Dressing and undressing and keeping their hair in proper order and such are all much harder duties to carry out in the small compartments, especially when we're always rocking to and fro. Mrs Cartwright likes me to play cards with her, so that takes up my time too. Miss North has been helping me with my German, and between her and Karolina my brain feels so full of German words that if I turn my head too fast they might fly out of my ears.

I must try to get some sleep now. We arrive in Buda-Pesth very early on Sunday morning, and I will post you this letter from there.

All my love, and all my prayers,
    Alice

P.S. Sarah, I swear I can hear you rolling your eyes at me. You have to stop thinking I'm going to make a fool of myself over every pleasant man I meet! I've spent a goodly few hours in his company now, and Mátyás has been nothing but polite. Having said that, if he tried anything, I'd not stand for it however much I might like him. I've always got my hairpins.

Sunday 13th July
P.P.S. I had to unseal this letter because – I don't know. I saw someone who seemed . . . wrong? I don't know what I mean. I'll tell you what happened, and you can tell me if you think I'm losing my mind.

We arrived at Buda-Pesth right on time. The ladies of the Lowell family met us on the platform even though it was so early, and a Sunday too. Miss Lowell and her mother look like the same person but at different ages. It's very strange.

The whole party was just about to leave when Miss North realized she couldn't find her gloves. I hurried down the length of the train, telling each and every porter or guard who tried to stop me that I must fetch my lady's *Handschuhe*. I bless Karolina for teaching me names for clothing in German! In the compartment Miss North had just left, her gloves were lying on the table by the window. How she missed them I don't know. I scooped them up, and walked at a more respectable speed back out onto the platform and down to where the ladies waited. Having to dodge newspaper-sellers and luggage-porters and cabmen and lost tourists slowed me down to a crawl.

Then, from the corner of my eye, I saw an older man dressed all in black. He was standing completely still in the middle of the moving crowd. His face was very white, at odds with his deep red lips and dark iron-grey hair. His gaze was fixed on my group of ladies, in total concentration. Maybe I mean 'fascination'? It was a look of such intensity as it moved from one to the next it was almost a glare. I realized I'd come to a complete stop as I stared, watching him.

A large American passed in front of me shouting loudly, and when my view was clear again the strange pale man had vanished. I shook myself, and found a cold dampness had stuck my shift to my back. It seems so silly now, but at the time . . . It's been a hard few weeks so maybe it's my tired mind playing tricks on me. Perhaps you'd best ignore this as just my exhausted ramblings.

I'll write again soon.

PART SIX

Sir John Seward's personal diary
Tuesday, 27th January 1903
Littlemore Hospital, Oxfordshire

Today I have been allowed out of bed. It reassures me that my staff are so careful with their patients' health, but I have been chafing at the bit. I spent the last two days fixating on how I could take Dr Knight into my confidence without her immediately summoning Burton to bring the strait waistcoat. I do not doubt that I must tell Dr Knight all I know, but *how* can I? I myself was only convinced of the truth when the physical evidence of vampirism was before my eyes and in this case the evidence is not physical but mental. Dr Knight's sessions of hypnosis prove it. Whatever Lady Lowell has seen, whatever has been done to her, is buried so deeply in her mind that she cannot access it without extreme pain, and therefore she cannot begin to heal. Some years ago in these pages I detailed a particular case of a soldier who had returned from the Boxer Rebellion with no memory of the conflict at all but with a host of symptoms similar to Lady Lowell's. Only when a former comrade came to see him and recounted tales from their time together did the memories begin to return. The man had seen truly terrible things, but as he slowly confronted those experiences, under medical supervision, his symptoms retreated. Lady Lowell sadly has no one living who knows of her experiences and can recount them back to her. I can make educated guesses based on my own knowledge of the vampire, but will that be of use?

A note has just arrived from Dr Knight. I will include it here as it is potentially highly relevant.

Note: Dr Beatrice Knight to Sir John Seward
27th Jan.

In an attempt to learn more about the origin of Lady Lowell's mental illness I contacted a friend at the British Library, who has access to the newspaper archives there. I was hoping, though not truly expecting, to find some clue as to what really happened to our patient in Transylvania.

To my surprise, there were two pieces which seem to confirm the original story or, at least, do not disprove it. The first is a brief article from *The Times*, barely a paragraph in length. It states that a carriage carrying several English ladies went over a cliff and into a river, and that no remains have been recovered. The second, published on the very same day in the very same newspaper, is a death notice for one of the ladies in question. A copy is enclosed.

DEATH NOTICE
THE TIMES OF LONDON
TUESDAY, 9TH SEPTEMBER 1884

Word has been received that Eliza, wife of Colonel Edward Cartwright late of the British Indian Army, has died unexpectedly during a touring holiday on the Continent. Her gentle kindness will be missed by all who knew her, and her many friends will unite in their bereavement. A memorial is to be held on Saturday at 10 o'clock at St Mary's Church, Whitby, presided over by Reverend Jonathan Baker.

I have also asked a friend in Vienna to check at the Austrian National Library, in case there is further information there.

Lucy North's journal
Monday, 14th July 1884
Buda-Pesth, Austro-Hungarian Empire

Early morning
I awoke far too early, but have given up trying to get back to sleep. Instead I have propped myself up in bed to write, though I must take care not to move too much for fear of disturbing Mafalda. She is still sleeping deeply. Grey circles under her eyes show against her pale skin, her hair lies loose and black against the white of the pillow, and were it not for the deep pink of her lips she would be only shades of light and dark. I could look at her forever.

When we arrived yesterday, Aunt Réka showed us all over her home, slowly, carefully, leaning on her nurse's arm. The house is the shape of a square, four sides around a courtyard, and is truly vast. Of course, we were required to admire every inch. Up and down tall arched corridors we went, tired feet trampling the expensive imported Ottoman rugs in beautiful room after beautiful room. I took in none of it. A well-stocked library, a fashionable pink drawing room, a flower garden, even a ballroom – what could such glories matter when I had been reunited with my beloved? A ladylike rest after lunch, prompted by Eliza's genteel wilting, was extremely welcome. I have never been more thrilled to hear the click of a door locking behind me as when entering Mafalda's bedroom, with only ourselves tucked away inside.

Late morning

I spoke to Lady Maria about Sir Gerald. I repeated what Joseph had told me, and added my own observations. Her ladyship nodded grimly, and decided to send a telegram at once to Dr Williamson. I'm sure all will be well now that she knows the truth of the situation. Lady Maria told Mafalda herself, and she was quite sanguine about it. I suppose that is a good thing. Mafalda has always been very clear-headed.

I'd also thought I might need to drum up some courage to ask about her correspondence with Joseph, but in the end the question answered itself. Mafalda and I had just finished breakfast, when the morning post arrived. We were alone in the enormous wood-panelled dining room, unmarried women being denied the privilege of the breakfast tray here just as in England. Mafalda sorted through the letters, groaning as she reached the last.

'What is it?' I asked, pouring myself a third cup of rich Austrian coffee.

'Another letter from Beechwood.'

'From Joseph?' I said, as innocently as I could manage. 'What does he have to say?'

Mafalda tore open the envelope and scanned the contents.

'More of the same. Listen to this, darling.' My beloved read the missive with a smirk playing on her lips. '"The shearing is finally over, and we have an even greater quantity of wool this year than last." Why does Joseph think I want to know about sheep shearing? Have I ever expressed the slightest interest in sheep?'

She tucked it away, disregarded, and continued with her breakfast. How did I ever doubt her? Did I really think that she would have been writing cooing love poems and planning her future as a country squire's wife?

'Lucy,' Mafalda said as she pushed her empty plate away, 'let's go out into the city today. We can't leave without you having seen the castle at the very least.'

'Do you think your mother will mind?'

'I doubt it. Mátyás and I have an interview with a new land agent this morning, but after that?'

'A new land agent? What happened to Mr Török?'

'Oh, he passed away. I thought he was ill the last time I saw him, and it seems I was right.'

'How sad. I'm sorry.'

Mafalda shrugged. 'A great shame, and something of a nuisance, but these things happen. So, are we decided on visiting the castle?'

I thought she was being a little callous, but I couldn't bear to argue after so long apart. Instead, I took her hand and kissed it.

'I'd be delighted.'

'Wonderful. Go and tell Eliza, she loves anything ancient. Like her husband.'

'Mafalda! You're a disgrace.'

'Yes I am, and you adore me for it.'

I found Eliza in her room, with Alice putting the final touches to her hair.

'I thought we were resting at home today?' she said when I told her Mafalda's idea.

'You're welcome to, if that's what you'd prefer.'

'No, I'd love to see the sights, but we should see Madam Jacobinus before we go. We wouldn't wish to be rude.'

Aunt Réka spends much of the day resting in her small private sitting room. Small by the standards of the rest of the rooms in this house, that is. I had expected Lady Maria to be with her but when Eliza and I were admitted she was alone, lying reading on a chaise.

'Mrs Cartwright, what a charming dress!' Aunt Réka cried delightedly as she threw her book aside. 'Is it from London?'

Aunt Réka was visibly cheered by Eliza's presence. The two of them seem to get on well, which I did not anticipate, given that they are so different in character. If Eliza knew what I know . . . Well. I imagine it would be quite different.

'Yes, it was a gift from my husband.'

'He must be a man of excellent taste, though that's evident from his choice of wife. And dear Lucy! Please do come and sit by me.'

We made ourselves comfortable on low padded chairs of the same powder blue as just about everything else in the room. Aunt Réka began to talk of the fashions of London and how they might compare to those here; not a topic of deep interest for Eliza but her natural grace prevailed. When the subject was exhausted, Aunt Réka had me read aloud from *The Peril of Sziget* to practise my Hungarian. I butchered it dreadfully. Rather than taking pleasure in the poem Aunt Réka instead found amusement in my pronunciation.

'Thank you for your efforts, dearest,' she said, laughing, 'but why don't we try some Keats instead?'

'Could you not help me learn? I'm sure I can do better.'

'Perhaps later. For now, let's say you are helping me to practise my English.'

'Your English needs no practice, you're quite fluent.'

Aunt Réka tutted and tossed her hair a little, a gesture I have seen before on Mafalda when she responds to flattery she considers to be true.

'Well, I can't say I agree with you but it would be rude to refuse a compliment. Tell me, dear, who is your favourite poet in all the world?'

As we talked of literature, I found myself in something like awe. I had forgotten how cultured a lady Aunt Réka is. I can easily imagine her dazzling in salons and ballrooms. She looks almost well now, though the lines around her eyes tell of the turmoil she has survived. I am not supposed to know the dark truth of her melancholia and so I treat her as I always have, just as I promised Mafalda. I find it easy. I wonder if that ought to concern me?

Aunt Réka dismissed us only when the time came for her to change, so her nurse could accompany her to church. Eliza and I have chosen to sit in the shaded area of the courtyard while we wait for Mafalda. It is a beautiful spot, with fruit trees all around and a fountain playing in the centre. I do like it here. I'm so glad we came.

Evening

Our visit to the castle was certainly educational. Eliza produced a guidebook from about her person, making our magical journey on the new Castle Hill funicular not only a glorious adventure but also a history lesson. I did not have the heart to shush her, and after a while her excited pronouncements became so much background noise.

The view as we journeyed upwards was spectacular. As we passed the height of the Chain Bridge, I marvelled at the vista over the garden pavilion, the winding Danube, and across to Pesth where the domed towers of St Stephen's Basilica were visible in the distance. I glanced at Mafalda, concerned she might be reminded of her last visit there for her uncle's funeral.

I need not have worried. She turned to me, grinning, and squeezed my hand. If we had been alone, I would have taken her in my arms and kissed her. I fear that our fellow tour-takers – a party of chattering schoolboys and their harassed master, a tall pale man in mourning-black, and a pair of aged German spinsters – would not have reacted well to such a spectacle.

Eliza and her guidebook led us around the areas of the castle that are open to visitors. From her continued and continual reading aloud, we learned that in the course of recent building work, a chapel had been uncovered after having lain forgotten for several centuries.

'It was still being used until the Ottomans took the city in 1541. They let the castle rot. How ghastly. Eventually, they turned it into an armoury and powder magazine. Can you imagine? Letting all this crumble?'

Mafalda gasped dramatically. 'How dreadful. Tell us more.'

I made a face at her, not wanting her to tease our friend.

'In 1686, in another siege, much of the castle was blown up and this chapel was lost until the renovations began. The restoration was completed last year, and in the original Gothic style too. How marvellous. Shall we go and see?'

We followed Eliza like ducklings following their mother, in the direction the others of our impromptu party had already taken. Down stone passages and winding staircases we went. We saw carvings of this and paintings of that, and all the time I was conscious of nothing but Mafalda. Her arm about my waist, the perfume of her hair, the swish of her dress against mine in a sad proxy for skin. I did not mean to exclude Eliza; I swear I did not. The joy of reunion was still upon me, upon us, and I was weak in the face of it.

The much-vaunted lost chapel turned out to feel somewhat cramped, what with the number of tourists whose interest had been sparked by the tale of its rediscovery. It is difficult to be impressed by the historical significance of a place when it is overrun with schoolboys. As Eliza admired the ceiling with delighted cries of 'Rib-vaulting! How elegant!', Mafalda took my arm and steered me back the way we had come, to a small alcove half-hidden by a tapestry of a maiden and a unicorn. She stopped before it, and looked critically about her.

'Based on the height of that window and the angle of the wall . . . yes, let's see what's hiding here.'

Mafalda shoved the tapestry aside and disappeared into the alcove.

'What are you doing? You can't touch that!'

'Why not? Now let me see . . .'

Her voice was muted by the thick cloth of the tapestry. I stepped forwards uncertainly, seeing nothing ahead of me but the dim outline of Mafalda's crouching form. Then there came a hideous grinding noise, and a sudden rush of fresh air and light.

'Yes, I thought so! Come and look!'

I was almost blinded by the sunlight streaming through the now-open half-size wooden door. Mafalda had gone through so I could do nothing but follow. I found myself on some kind of battlement, not overlooked and yet looking out over the entire city. The Danube shone silver, the green of the surrounding countryside standing out against it, and the city itself seeming to glitter in the sunlight. Mafalda stood with her arms stretched wide, her dress billowing in the fresh breeze.

'How did you know?'

'I came here as a child once, when I ran away from my nursemaid.' She sighed deeply, contentedly. 'Oh, Lucy, I feel I've not felt the sun, really felt it, in such a long time. I've been shut up in that house with all those ghosts.' She turned to me, her face alive and joyful. 'Come here, my love.'

There . . . Well. I find myself unable to put words onto paper without blushing and catching myself. I aim, though I do not always succeed, to write factually of events, but now I fear I am on the edge of overheated romance. I will remain silent on such matters but suffice it to say we were gone so long that we began to worry for Eliza, whom we had after all simply abandoned.

'We'd best go,' my beloved said reluctantly through kiss-swollen lips, 'or Eliza will think the Ottomans have carried us off.'

'Mafalda! Don't joke.'

'They probably did carry off some ancestress or other of mine, and whisked her away to a seraglio. All those steaming baths, and lying around entirely unclothed—'

I giggled. 'Stop it! You demon.'

We made our way back, and allowed ourselves to be found admiring the tapestry.

'Do you think the unicorn looks sad?'

'I don't think the unicorn looks anything, not even very much like a unicorn. Ah, Eliza, there you are. Where have you been?'

Eliza seemed confused.

'Why, in the chapel of course.'

Mafalda's face was the very picture of innocence. 'For so long? We thought we'd lost you.'

'No, well, I met the most fascinating man. A historian of some sort, I think. He was very knowledgeable about all the invasions and such things—'

Mafalda cut across her, foreseeing a lengthy speech. 'Fascinating indeed, but I couldn't possibly appreciate all that on an empty stomach. Why don't we see about lunch?'

At a respectable establishment on the Pesth side of the river, Mafalda managed to mostly steer the conversation away from Eliza's recent historical learnings and on to other things. We ate pastries and drank tiny glasses of Tokay, and let the afternoon take on a pleasant, dreamy quality.

A beautiful day, in a beautiful city, with my beautiful Mafalda.

THE BRIDES

Letter: Eliza Cartwright to Edward Cartwright
Monday, 14th July 1884
Buda-Pesth, Austro-Hungarian Empire

[Editor's Note: EC wrote to her husband frequently during the trip, but few of her letters were relevant to the matter at hand.]

My dear husband,
I am glad to let you know that I continue in good health, as does Lucy. We arrived safely in Buda-Pesth to a wonderfully warm welcome. Lucy and Mafalda are thrilled to see each other, and Lady Maria was kind enough to let me know, discreetly, that she is glad to have another married woman in the household. Lady Maria's younger sister, Réka Jacobinus, has been most gracious and hospitable though her tired face shows all the pain of the newly bereaved. I have been doing my best to ensure my society is pleasant to her.

Today I accompanied Lucy and Mafalda on an outing to the Royal Castle, across the Danube on the Buda side. We took the funicular railway, which is a true marvel of engineering. It is only the second funicular railway built in Europe, and it rises to a great height of almost 170 feet. There has been a fortress on the current site of the castle for some 600 years, but most of the palace dates only from the middle of the last century. A great deal of building work is going on at the present time, and a long-lost chapel has recently been uncovered and restored to its former glory. You would have been enthralled, my love.

I was fortunate enough to meet an expert, who provided far more detail than my guidebook on the subject. A sort of unofficial tour group had formed, filling the newly opened chapel to bursting. Despite the high ceilings, done in the most wonderful Gothic rib-vaulting, it felt altogether too close. I had managed to lose my friends, and found myself squashed into a corner near the window. There was a group of animated schoolchildren taking up much of the space and while their enthusiasm was adorable, it was *loud*. I felt quite overwhelmed. I was taking a moment to breathe deeply and gaze out of the window when I noticed that lower down on the wall there were names and dates carefully carved into particular stones. I have read of this practice, common in our own country in times of hardship and plague, so I knew these to be rudimentary memorials. There were a great many of them, with death dates following hard on the heels of birth dates. These melancholy carvings stretched back centuries, with an abrupt halt at the point where the chapel was partially destroyed in an Ottoman siege. I confess it moved me deeply to think of the parents whose lost little ones were remembered here. I thought of Beth, and it was all just too much. I fumbled for my handkerchief but true to form I found none, and to my embarrassment tears began to fall freely down my face. I thought that no one had seen, but then a plain white cotton gentleman's handkerchief appeared before my eyes.

'May I be of assistance, *meine Dame*?'

I turned to find a gentleman, for such he certainly was by his dress and manner, standing to my left just out of the sunlight. I find I cannot quite recall his face, only a vague impression of his noble attitude and strangely penetrating gaze.

'Thank you, sir,' I replied, in my best school-German as I took the proffered square and dabbed at my eyes. 'You are very kind.'

'It is my pleasure.' His voice was deep, and he spoke with an accent that I had never heard before, old-fashioned and curious. I suppose that within this other empire, the lingua franca is spoken with various accents which would all sound peculiar to those of us only schooled in the standard variety of the language.

Despite his assurances, I could feel a humiliating blush rising to my cheeks.

'Please forgive me, I am ashamed to have made such a show of myself.'

'They are a sad sight, these monuments. You must not chastise yourself, *meine Dame*. It is no shame to be so moved. You are an Englishwoman, I think?'

'Yes, sir, though a Scot by birth.'

'Noble races indeed.' Here he paused, and began to speak in English. 'I have studied your language though as yet I only know it from books. You will forgive my intonation, I hope. Perhaps by our conversation I may better it.'

I reassured him that he spoke English perfectly well.

'Thank you, you are most kind. Let me tell you, madam, the people here are more free with the expression of what is in their hearts than in your island home. No one will think badly of you for your tears when confronted with such a sight as this.'

He gestured to the wall carvings.

'That's good of you to say. Looking at these names, I couldn't help but think of my own infant ward, my sister. I was quite overcome.'

He nodded gravely. 'It is a most affecting sight. I myself have lost three of my children to foreign wars.'

Words cannot express my mortification to have spoken of my fears for Beth when she is safe under your care, and will never face death by violence far from those who love her.

'I'm terribly sorry. To lose a child – sir, I cannot imagine such grief. Please accept my condolences.'

'Thank you, madam.' He looked at me rather searchingly before continuing. 'It was a long time ago, and they died with honour in the defence of their homeland. I would have expected nothing less. In times gone by my family guarded the frontier to the land of the Turks. My children had the spirit of warfare in their blood.'

Such a masculine attitude would have been familiar to you, husband, but is alien to my own sensibility. I said as much, and the gentleman nodded.

'Then you must permit me to explain something of the country in which you find yourself. This land has been fought over for generations, placed as it is in the heart of this continent. Any peoples that would expand their territory must pass through it, be they Ugric, Hun, Magyar, Lombard, Avar, Bulgar or Turk. And so, the very soil comes to be soaked again and again in the blood of both invader and noble defender. This city where we stand has been besieged many times throughout the centuries. Since its founding by my own forefather, the great Attila, it has been taken by Árpád, by the Mongol Khan, and by the so-called Suleiman the Lawgiver. Here, we are made by both nature and circumstance a warlike people. You will find no man who does not have something of the lion about him, ever ready to defend what is his and guard it against any foe.'

'You know your history well, sir.'

Here he paused, and smiled a faintly unsettling smile.

'It is something of a passion of mine.'

I became aware that the noise around us had ceased, and that the schoolchildren were nowhere to be seen. Nor was anyone else. I was suddenly conscious of being alone with an unknown man, even one so excellently mannered. I sought to extricate myself as politely as possible.

'A worthwhile pastime, certainly, and I thank you for sharing your knowledge with me. Now I must go and re-join my companions.'

'I hope I did not bore you with my talk of ages past.'

'Not at all, it was most interesting. May I—' I held out his handkerchief, dirtied though it was.

'I have no need of it, please do not trouble yourself.'

'Thank you, sir. Good day.'

'Good day.'

I left the way I had come, my head rather spinning with all this talk of blood and battles. I seemed to hear the cries of the combatants around me, and the tumble of stone as Ottoman forces wrought their dreadful work upon the castle. I half expected to turn and see the chapel behind me crumbled to rubble, but of course it was only my strange fancy.

I found Lucy and Mafalda admiring a tapestry, and as we were all feeling rather tired from our wanderings we returned over the Danube for a leisurely luncheon. I did my best to appear in good spirits, but I still find my ears ringing with the terrible history that the gentleman spoke of. It certainly puts this grand city in a different light, and I appreciate the peace and serenity that now reigns here all the more.

Kiss Beth for me, and tell her that I love her very much.

Your wife,

Eliza

Letter: Alice Smith to Sarah Smith
Tuesday, 15th July 1884
Buda-Pesth, Austro-Hungarian Empire

Dear Sarah,

For goodness' sake don't read this letter to Mam. I don't want her to think I've lost my head. Yesterday and today have been quiet, as Mrs Cartwright and Miss North have been out and about with Miss Lowell. I don't know how they're managing it, it's far too hot. Lady Maria sent a telegram this morning and the footman who took it to the telegraph office came back bright red and sweating and had to have a lie-down in the cold cupboard. Even so, in such a large household there's not nearly as much for me to do as at home. I've been using my extra leisure time to get to grips with the Hungarian language. Mátyás has been helping me. The other servants aren't very welcoming, so apart from him and Miss Partridge I've not made any friends. I can't say as I mind though. Excepting Nurse Weber and Cook, a woman twice the size of any I've ever seen, they're an unpleasant lot.

Have I mentioned Miss Partridge before? She's lady's maid to Lady Maria, and I'm learning a lot from her about everything from tending linens to hairdressing to cleaning jewellery. I've been trading with her for my herbal know-how. Last night she got to talking about the family she serves. I'd met Mátyás on my way down to get my bit of dinner, late, as the ladies had been up for longer than usual. Mátyás had been hard at work in the late master's study and was finally headed to the kitchen, so we chummed along together. Normally we'd eat in the servants' hall, but of course it was too late in the evening for that. The kitchen was empty but for Cook and Miss Partridge, sharing a glass of something medicinal at the long kitchen table. Miss Partridge greeted me like an old friend, which had me thinking she might not be on her first helping. I don't mean to judge; she works very hard and if she wants to relax with a tipple then that's her business.

While Mátyás settled down to some cold cuts, Miss Partridge bid me come and sit by her.

'How are you, Miss Smith? How are you managing in this heat?'

'I'm coping, Miss Partridge, thank you for asking.'

'It's not Yorkshire, that's for sure.'

Cook brandished the bottle at me, and I shook my head.

'Teetotal?' Miss Partridge asked. I nodded. 'Quite right too, good girl.'

Miss Partridge held out her glass to Cook, who filled it right to the top.

'And something *kalt* for Fraulein Smith here,' she said, in a mix of bad German and loud English.

'*Ja*,' the large woman replied. She vanished into the cold cupboard for a moment and brought out something that smelled of blackcurrants. It was very refreshing, though it didn't go well with my ham and cheese supper.

'It's a wet heat here, isn't it?' I said, by way of making conversation.

'An unhealthy heat is what I'd call it. It certainly can't be doing Madam Jacobinus any good.'

'Oh dear, I thought she was getting better. Is she very poorly still?'

'I don't think that fool of a foreign doctor has the first idea how poorly she is or isn't. She's been up and down and up and down. And now with the master back home not well, who knows what's going to happen? Her ladyship and Miss Lowell have been having quite the discussion about what to do.'

Now, I'm not right proud of myself and maybe Miss Partridge's tongue wouldn't have been so loose if she hadn't imbibed, but I led her on to talk. Mátyás's eyes were firmly fixed on his plate, though I could tell his ears were practically flapping.

'Is that so?'

'Oh, yes. Very friendly they are of late. Her ladyship has been relying a great deal on Miss Mafalda's judgement – she's got her pa's head, that one. Always has had. Smart as a tack. I've been with her ladyship since before Miss Mafalda was born, and she's always known she was a clever girl. Having said that, Miss

Mafalda didn't have an ounce of compassion or humility until she met Miss Lucy. Miss Lucy's a good influence. She's a sweet girl, a very sweet girl. Bright too, in her way. Calm. Miss Mafalda would have run wild without her.'

'Miss North has been very kind to me.'

'Oh, she would be, she would be. Doesn't have much, bless her; I think she worries she's going to end up as a lady's companion one day, and being gentle with the servants pays the goodwill forward that she'd hope for for herself. Not that she'd think in those terms, I don't mean to say that. No, Cook, no more, thanks all the same.'

Cook begrudgingly put the bottle away, and poured herself off to bed. Mátyás and I watched her a bit warily, in case she took a tumble on the kitchen stairs. They're stone, and it wouldn't do anyone good to slip on them.

'I will say, Miss Mafalda isn't suited to tending the sick at all. You can tell she hates every minute, but needs must. Madam Jacobinus looked awful even when we got here; it was enough to move a statue to pity. Poor woman. She's had quite a time of it. Lost a baby, you know.' Miss Partridge looked sideways at Mátyás and I think she'd have said more if it'd been only us women present. 'Well, I really ought to be getting to bed. Make sure you get one of those yellow candles from the upper store cupboard and burn it for a bit before you go to sleep. It keeps the flying devils away.'

'Thank you, I will.'

'Don't you two stay up too late now.'

'No, Miss Partridge. Sleep well.'

Mátyás merely nodded, his mouth full. Miss Partridge held her drink rather better than Cook, and made it out and up the stairs with barely a wobble.

'You're very quiet,' I said to Mátyás as he finished his plate.

'I would not dare to interrupt Miss Partridge. I think she could be quite fierce.'

'You're probably right.'

He tugged at his collar, loosening it. Even at this time of night it was still over-warm. 'I will be pleased to leave the city and get some fresh air.'

My heart sank. 'Are you going somewhere?'

'Some of my late master's tenants in the countryside are in difficulties because of an argument about . . . what is the word . . . borders? Between farmers' lands?'

'Boundaries, do you mean?'

'Yes, boundaries. I must go and see what I can do. It's no great hardship to go, except . . . except that I may not get to see you for some time.'

A blush began to peek out from his collar, and made a swift way up his neck. I pretended not to notice.

'No, I suppose not.' Honestly, Sarah, I could barely get the words out.

'I will look forward to seeing you again. Very much. Will you . . . will you look forward to seeing me?'

His breath was catching in his throat, and his nervousness was the sweetest thing. A huge unladylike smile took over my face.

'Yes. Yes, I think I will.'

He grinned back at me, and we sat there all smiles until the kitchen clock clanged loudly and interrupted us. I bid him a very chaste goodnight, and I floated upstairs on wings of air. Oh, Sarah! I feel guilty to be happy in a house that has known so much sorrow of late, but I wouldn't wish it away for anything. It makes a nice change.

Mrs Cartwright has called for me, so I've got to end here. I'll write again as soon as I can. I know you're worried about me, and I bless you for it. I promise I won't go doing anything silly.

All my love,
    Alice

P.S. I know what you're going to say, Sarah, not everything in Nana's books exists in the nowadays world. Just because there's stories in there about wights and other cursed creatures doesn't mean I saw one at the train station. I'm sure he was just another traveller, and my tired and hurting mind was playing tricks.

Letter: Eliza Cartwright to Colonel Edward Cartwright
[Unsent; discovered later with Mrs Cartwright's personal effects]
Tuesday, 15th July 1884
Buda-Pesth, Austro-Hungarian Empire

My dear husband,
I continue to enjoy the company of our hostess a great deal. Madam Jacobinus is a charming woman with a refreshing directness to her, even though her bereavement and subsequent ill health have left her weakened. It turns out that she and I have some particular things in common. I can only beg your forgiveness for sharing our struggles with a near-stranger but she has given me such a glimmer of hope!

I sat up with her in her salon late this evening. The damp summer heat had made me restless, and it seems Madam Jacobinus sometimes suffers from insomnia. As the other ladies retired to bed one by one, we eventually found ourselves talking alone. I showed her a picture of Beth, and when she made some casual comment about my providing her with a playmate or two, I was unable to keep my emotions from my face.

'Ah,' she said to me, nodding sagely, 'you have been hoping for a child of your own, and he or she has not yet arrived.'

My eyes began to fill with tears. I weep so much lately! I blame the lateness of the hour, the intimacy of sitting together in a pool of lamplight and the hope of camaraderie for taking her into my confidence without first consulting you.

'Yes, yes exactly so. The desperation . . . Sometimes it overwhelms me.'

'I understand. It has been some time, and you wonder if you should give up?'

'It's hard to keep hoping and having those hopes dashed. My mother had three children by the time she was my age, yet I continue to fail.'

'Dear Mrs Cartwright, you must not pain yourself with such thoughts.' Madam Jacobinus reached over and laid her slender, elegant hand atop my wringing and cringing ones. 'We are our own people. You are not your mother and I am not mine, and let us thank the good Lord for that. Now, have you a doctor, in England?'

'Yes, but so far he has not been entirely helpful.'

'Then I must make a recommendation to you. While you are here, you must see my own doctor. All the fine ladies in Buda-Pesth go to him. Dr Arminius is his name. He is an expert on life in all its forms.' She took in a deep breath. 'I will be frank with you, Mrs Cartwright, woman to woman. Becoming with child was not my particular struggle, it was that those lives never took proper root within me. It is only thanks to Dr Arminius that none dragged me with them when they left for the next world. In time I did have a little girl, thanks to Dr Arminius's medical witchery. I called her Maria, after my sister. A fever took her mere weeks after her birth. I had some hope again a few months past, but I lost that when my husband . . . my husband . . .'

A sob caught in her throat. I took her hand and held it, and we sat together in our shared pain.

It seems that lately all the world would tell me of its lost children. Such grief is a tragedy for men, of course, but for women we must bear loss and emptiness in our own selves. We feel we are at fault, and if only we had done or not done this or that, then all would have been well.

Husband, I think I will not send you this letter. Although you would do your best, you would not, could not, comprehend this extreme emotion of which I write.

I love you always,
Eliza

Letter: Alice Smith to Sarah Smith
Wednesday, 16th July 1884, early morning
Buda-Pesth, Austro-Hungarian Empire

Sarah, I forgot. I am a fool, a silly little fool. One night, one smile from a handsome face, and I forgot the lemon beebrush tisane. The dreams came swirling out of the black at me, for hours and hours and hours. I couldn't wake up, even though I tried.

In my dreams, I was someone else. I was walking through the night to a woodland, to a white stone building that looked like a chapel. An evil thing followed me, or this other woman I seemed to be. She knew this monster was stalking her, but she never looked back. It didn't matter, she'd decided, and that decision was resistance, power. She reached the white chapel, and knelt down in front of it. The monster came towards her but she still wouldn't turn. She wouldn't let it win. She lifted her eyes to Heaven and filled her mind with memories of love, raised a gun to her head, and fired.

Then everything went dark and all I could hear was that voice, that voice I knew but couldn't place, saying a psalm over and over. The twenty-third, that one about 'though I walk through the valley of the shadow of death'. On and on, over and over. In my dream I screamed to be told why, why I had to see and hear these things, but there was no answer.

All I know is that as much as I wanted to run away, it hasn't worked. Pray for me.

Alice

Lucy North's journal
Wednesday, 16th July 1884
Buda-Pesth, Austro-Hungarian Empire

This morning I kissed my noon-bird and left her half-asleep, taking myself to the breakfast room alone. I finished my book as I ate, so I had the Hungarian-language morning paper brought to tide me over while I drank my coffee. As I unfolded it, still warm from the iron, I caught sight of the headline. It would have been hard to miss, splashed across the front page in wording so simple even I could read it at a glance.

I rose at once, and went back upstairs to wake Mafalda.

'What?' she grumbled, as I shook her by the shoulder.

Wordlessly, I handed over the newspaper.

'What on earth – oh, oh no. Did you read all this?'

'Only the headline.'

Mafalda heaved herself upright, her eyes not leaving the text.

'"Baroness Tolvay Piroska has been found dead in Kerepesi Cemetery, at the tomb of Jacobinus Gabor. It appears that the Baroness took her own life. This savage act will only add to the scandal that currently afflicts both the Tolvay and Jacobinus families, after the shocking death of Jacobinus Gabor at the hand of Baron Tolvay earlier this year."'

Mafalda read on, growing angrier with each sentence. A photograph underneath the headline showed a mausoleum with a domed roof and Greek portico, just as Mafalda had described it to me in her letter. The Baroness had shot herself, and there was a lurid description worthy only of the most scurrilous tabloid – all stained white marble and splashes of dark blood. Vile.

Mafalda ground to a halt.

'Lucy, we must speak to Mama.'

She hurried into a dressing gown and strode out towards her mother's rooms as I trailed along behind.

Partridge ushered us into Lady Maria's sitting room. If I had been there under different circumstances I would have appreciated the fine French furniture and the beautiful view of the castle, but as it was, all that was left in my mind was an impression of dark blue damask and full-length windows. Lady Maria was breakfasting, wearing an unexpectedly fashionable peignoir with her hair already impeccably dressed. Before she had time to even wish us good morning, Mafalda was brandishing the newspaper and announcing the grim news.

'Baroness Tolvay is dead.'

'What?'

'Look. She killed herself.'

Lady Maria took up the paper.

'Good God. In the cemetery! Does your aunt know of this?'

'I don't think so. She doesn't read the news these days.'

Lady Maria nodded, her lips pressed together. 'Good. Is she still in her room?'

'I don't know.'

'If I may, your ladyship?'

'Yes, Partridge?'

'Madam Jacobinus went out to hear a private Mass not long ago, with one of the maids attending.'

Lady Maria and Mafalda exchanged the same worried glance.

'Mama, we have to keep it from her. Her constitution wouldn't stand it, not yet.'

'I don't see how. We can burn the paper today, but after that? Letters will arrive, her friends will call, the servants will talk.'

They fell silent, each chewing on the inside of her cheek, an identical expression of fierce concentration on their faces.

'What if—' Mafalda began, but her words were cut brutally short by the slam of a door, the smash of china, and a loud screeching wail. Lady Maria leapt to her feet at once.

'Réka!'

She darted away, Mafalda hot on her heels, leaving me open-mouthed. How dreadful must things have been if Lady Maria could recognize such a hideous noise as emanating from her sister? I followed the sounds of distress through the house to find a scene of great disorder in the entrance hall. A burly moustachioed gentleman had Aunt Réka taken up in his arms, even as she screamed and sobbed and struggled. Aunt Réka's maid stood by, silently weeping. A decorative vase had been swept from its place of display and lay shattered on the floor. Lady Maria was attempting to speak calmly to her sister, though how she expected to be heard above the racket I have no idea.

I watched as Mafalda surveyed the situation as a general might a battlefield, and took unquestioned charge. She snapped her fingers at the maid, her other native tongue coming harshly from the back of her throat as she raised her voice. I think I have her words right, or the sense of them at any rate.

'You, send for Dr Arminius at once. Go! Now! Major Oberleitner, bring my aunt upstairs. Mama, make way.' Mafalda caught sight of me hovering on the edge, and switched to English. 'Lucy, run up and get the nurse to make ready.'

'What's happened?'

'Just go, now.'

I did as I was told, though the nurse had heard the animal howls of her mistress and was already preparing a treatment. Led by Mafalda, the Major carried Aunt Réka in and deposited her on the bed before beating a hasty retreat, mumbling apologies.

Lady Maria knelt by her sister's bedside, attempting alternately to soothe and distract her as she screeched. The only words I could make out were 'profaned', 'unholy', and, unfortunately, 'whore'. Lady Maria held her sister down as Nurse Weber administered the sedative.

'Mafalda,' she called over her shoulder, her eyes flashing with a ferocity I had only ever seen in her daughter, 'get rid of that man and make sure he doesn't come back.'

'Yes, Mama.' Mafalda took hold of my arm and propelled me out of the door. 'Lucy, come with me. We must outnumber the enemy.'

'Do you think Aunt Réka has heard about the Baroness?'

'Yes.'

'Do you think it was the Major who—'

Mafalda's lips set into a grim line. 'Yes.'

Major Oberleitner had been put in the Rose drawing room where he sat uncomfortably on the blush-pink settee, under the watchful eyes of the twin portraits of Aunt Réka and Uncle Gabor either side of the ceramic stove. Mafalda had made him wait while we dressed. He stood as we entered. I noted with some pleasure the fading remains of two black eyes still visible on his reddened face, and that his nose was healing rather crookedly.

'Miss Lowell.' He snapped his heels together and nodded sharply.

'Major Oberleitner,' Mafalda responded with an Arctic grace. 'Please allow me to present Fraulein North, of London.'

'Fraulein North.' That same heel snap.

'I am pleased to make your acquaintance,' I replied. I must have done so badly, because the Major switched smoothly to English.

'Likewise, Miss North.'

Mafalda did not ask him to sit again, nor did she order refreshments. We stood on opposite sides of the room, battle lines drawn.

'Let us get to the point, Major. This morning, my aunt was relatively well. Now she is not. My mother and I would know your account of the cause of this episode.'

The Major marshalled his forces.

'I was on my way to pay a call here, in the hope I might at last be admitted. I met Madam Jacobinus as she came from Mass.' His face twisted in the way men's faces do when they must admit to some emotionality. 'I have a great regard for your aunt. I thought I might be of use or perhaps some comfort to her, if she had found the shocking news about Baroness Tolvay at all . . . difficult. I assume you know that the Baroness has . . . has . . .' He groped for wording appropriate to use before ladies.

Mafalda cut him off. 'Yes, we are aware. We had intended to keep it from my aunt for as long as possible, due to her delicate state of health.'

Major Oberleitner swallowed hard. 'In my desire to be of service it seems that I myself was the one to tell her. She became quite hysterical, and I brought her home with all haste.'

Mafalda regarded him for a long moment. Then she sighed deeply, a sigh of utter disappointment. 'Major Oberleitner, would I be right in supposing that you hope to court my aunt once she comes out of mourning?'

'I . . . That is . . . Yes, Miss Lowell,' he answered, like a schoolboy awaiting punishment. It came, swiftly.

'In that case, it is my duty to inform you that your suit would not be accepted by the family.' Mafalda's eyes bored into his, and this old soldier seasoned by war after war quailed before the twin horrors of his own shame and a beautiful woman's contempt. 'You will leave this house. You will not be admitted again, ever. Your time would be best spent praying for my aunt's recovery.'

As two of the burlier footmen escorted the Major out, she hissed, *sotto voce*, right into his quivering, loose-jowled face, 'Your eyes look better black.'

The Major's face was a picture of suddenly retrieved memories, and he blanched as the door slammed behind him.

Mafalda turned to me, her lips contorted in a snarl of fury.

'Why is it that men cannot keep their mouths shut? They say we are the ones who are so emotional and so irrational and yet they spray their innermost feelings all over the place and force us to attend to them, all the while pretending these fools are stoic Romans and not incontinent children!'

She swept up an ornamental shepherdess and flung it against the stove, where it exploded into fragments.

'They have no idea how to deal with any emotion that is not anger, so they treat a sensibility like a deep universal truth rather the nonsense it is. A man having an emotion is the most important occurrence in the history of the world, and everyone else be damned! The Major has a *feeling* that he wishes to be useful to my aunt in a time of trial, but has no idea how to go about actually answering to her needs – no, he wants to be a dragon-slayer and have her faint damsel-like in his arms in overwhelming gratitude, whilst doing nothing to truly help. Men have all the power and we have so little; we must fight and scrap for every ounce with our capability ignored and demeaned and declared impossible, and theirs assumed even against all evidence to the contrary! And as for—'

Mafalda stopped abruptly, teeth gritted.

'Darling—' I began.

'Not now, my love, I must go upstairs and see what else needs to be done.'

She swept past, rage blinking out like a candle without air, and left me standing there, alone.

Evening

Eliza and I dined *à deux*, early, and saw nothing of the family until afterwards. Not knowing quite what else to do we settled ourselves in the drawing room. The remains of Mafalda's earlier anger had been cleared away, save for a chip in one of the swirling pink patterned tiles of the stove. Eliza sat down at an escritoire in the corner and began a letter to her husband while I tried my best to read, but *Wuthering Heights* could not hold my attention, and I found myself instead gazing morosely out of the grand arched windows at the courtyard.

Just after the clock struck eight, Alice appeared.

'Good evening, madam, Miss North. Miss North, I'm to tell you that Miss Lowell asks you up to her bedchamber. Madam, Dr Arminius says that he got your note and can see you while he's here, if you like.'

'Thank you. That would be most convenient.' I must have looked quizzical, because Eliza answered my question as if I'd spoken. 'Madam Jacobinus says he has been a great help to her and other ladies with . . . well, you know.'

'Oh, I see. I hope he has useful advice.'

Alice led our little procession upstairs. When I entered Mafalda's bedroom I found her fully dressed on her old-fashioned four-poster bed, propped up and sipping some flower-scented concoction. I went to sit by her, the soft mattress giving beneath me.

'How are you, my love?' I asked as I leaned over to kiss her.

'Utterly drained. I could sleep for a week.'

'Is Aunt Réka any better?'

Mafalda took a gulp from her cup before she answered me.

'Nurse Weber says so but I don't know how she can tell. My aunt was nigh on inconsolable. The doctor said her pulse was incredibly erratic. He put it down to the shock but also the heat. He left some sort of cooling salve, which smells terrible, as well as some laudanum. Darling, my head hurts, will you fetch the lavender oil?'

I found the familiar stoppered bottle on her dressing table. Mafalda turned sideways across the bed while I moved a chair that I might sit by her head. I started to rub her temples with the sweet-smelling oil and wondered to myself, how many times have I performed this act for her? I know how she needs it done to soothe her headaches – slowly, walking that slender line between firm and gentle, never stopping until she gives me leave.

Eventually her brow began to uncrease, as it always does when the oil performs its work.

'You can press a little harder.'

I did so, and she sighed in pleasure.

'How does that feel?'

'Better, don't stop.'

I rubbed until the pads of my fingers tingled, and they will probably smell of lavender for days. Eventually Mafalda wanted to rest and decided she was too overheated for my company, so now I am kissed and banished to my own room next door. I know she does not mean for me to feel so . . . dismissed. She has always been to-the-point, how can I begin complaining now? Besides, I must remind myself that in such a time of high stress she needs

THE BRIDES

my support, and not my condemnation for something so unimportant as a little unthinking rudeness.

I too find I am far too hot for sleep but I suppose I must try. I will have Alice bring yet more cool cloths and I will lie layered in them like a mummified pharaoh.

I am trying not to think of the poor Baroness. I reread those terrible tragic letters of hers, and though her mind must have been wounded to write such things they seem so hideously real. The poor woman deeply believed herself to be pursued by evil. Perhaps this imagined persecution became too much for her to bear and she sought the only way out she could see, as close to the man she loved as she could manage. It is a great sin, we are told, but I will pray for her all the same.

Letter: Eliza Cartwright to Colonel Edward Cartwright
Wednesday, 16th July 1884
Buda-Pesth, Austro-Hungarian Empire

My dear husband,
Thank you for your last letter. I am glad your brother's visit passed off so well. I hope his presence was a comfort to you. I'm delighted to hear that Beth was so taken with her new little – what would he be? Her nephew-in-law?

On that same subject, I have some news myself. By now you will have received my telegram, and I am glad to tell you that I have met with the doctor in question. His name is Arminius, which makes me think of my classical history lessons at school, and he is the doctor of choice of the Buda-Pesth gentry.

He happened to come to the house today because Madam Jacobinus returned from church having been seriously affected by both the heat and some distressing news. Her condition is now stable, but it caused a great deal of worry as she has lately been so unwell. Once Dr Arminius had attended to her and left her in the hands of her nurse, he sent to ask if he might see me.

The good doctor turned out to be a diminutive man with a prematurely bald head and a complete lack of affinity with his famous name. He questioned me on all the usual subjects in a most kind and understanding fashion, so that whilst it was of course awkward to speak so intimately, it was not as excruciating as it might have been. He speaks decent enough English, which is fortunate as I certainly lack the necessary German vocabulary. After taking a case history, he said he believed he would be able to assist me. I am to visit his consulting rooms on Saturday at eleven o'clock. Fortunately he has had a cancellation, which was made because the lady patient found herself *enceinte* and no longer had need of his help! I take this as an excellent sign.

Please kiss Beth for me.
Your ever-loving wife,
Eliza

Letter: Mátyás Lakatos to Alice Smith
Thursday, 17th July 1884
Debrecen, Austro-Hungarian Empire

Dear Alice,
I have been thinking of you often. I hope you do not mind my taking the liberty of writing to you.

The lands of my late master that we spoke of are in quite some turmoil, as the problems with the neighbouring landowner are more serious than expected. I hope that it may be complete before the end of the month, though it may be longer depending on how things progress.

If it is not an imposition, I would like to tell you that if you cared to write to me in return I can be reached at the Empress Hotel in Debrecen. It would make me very happy to hear from you. If you feel that it is fitting, please tell me if I should apply to your family or to Mrs Cartwright for permission to correspond with you.

Please accept the expression of my most affectionate regards,
Mátyás

Lucy North's journal
Friday, 18th July 1884
Buda-Pesth, Austro-Hungarian Empire

Sometimes, Eliza is quite brilliant. This morning, she came to Aunt Réka's boudoir where I sat reading from Byron's *Childe Harold's Pilgrimage*. It has become clear that while Aunt Réka is physically returning once more to good health, the shock of the Baroness's suicide has plunged her into a dark self-pity. Eliza could not allow this to stand.

'Madam Jacobinus, I have come to ask a favour of you,' she said as took a seat next to Aunt Réka on her powder-blue chaise.

Aunt Réka looked up with eyes that were doing their best to be haunted.

'I'm sure I would do anything you asked of me, only—'

'Excellent! Thank you, I'm so glad. You know how much I miss my infant sister, even though our stay here has been so lovely. Hasn't it, Lucy?'

'Yes, lovely,' I agreed, wondering where this was heading.

'I had a notion to send Elsbeth a photograph, that she might see her sister and her sister's dear friends. I hoped you might know of a professional whom we could entrust with such a task?'

'I'm sure I could find a name for you.'

'Thank you, I knew you would know. We can go today!'

'But, Mrs Cartwright, I'm not at all sure that I feel strong enough to go out.'

'Of course, I wouldn't dream of asking you without medical approval. Lucy, would you ring for Nurse Weber?'

Nurse Weber examined the patient, dispensed medicine, and agreed that such a trip would be perfectly safe, especially if she herself attended and if we took another servant along to be sent for the doctor in case of emergency.

'And we must go soon, before the day is too hot for Madam,' the nurse said, blunt as always.

'Then it's settled. You must let me make a gift of the picture to you all.'

In the end, Alice was the lucky maidservant selected to attend us, on the grounds that Eliza was performing the selection. As an aside, I've noticed Alice has seemed rather tired for the last few days. When she was helping me on with my going-out dress, I asked her if she was well. She said something about nasty dreams of being chased.

'I hate those nightmares,' I said. 'They're so unpleasant. What chases you? A wolf? When I was a child it was always a wolf. I blame "Little Red Riding Hood".'

'I don't know, miss. A shadow, in some kind of little wood. Then we get to a white chapel, like the kind they have here, and . . . well then the dream ends. It's very sad.'

But I digress. Alice came along as ordered, yawning discreetly as all six of us piled into the carriage. Aunt Réka fussed less than expected. Mafalda told me later how impressed she was with

Eliza's skills at manipulation. I think Eliza would be horrified to hear her efforts described as such.

Fortunately, the photographic establishment seemed not to be doing much trade when we arrived. A stout and somewhat rotund man, who turned out to be the photographer himself, received us with something close to alarm. He showed us into the studio room at the back of the building, filled with props and settings of gardens, fireplaces, salons and all sorts. I felt sorry for him as he apologized for the dusty state of the room.

'Ladies tend to prefer a photographer to attend them in the comfort of their own home,' he informed us, in rather sad German.

'Oh, but that would be no fun at all!' Eliza reassured him with a smile, the effect of which was slightly spoiled by Nurse Weber experiencing a violent sneezing fit. Aunt Réka sent her to wait outside and off she went, sneezing all the way.

I had not been photographed since my debut when Lady Maria organized for Mafalda and I to have pictures taken for our cartes de visite. I did not enjoy the experience, even though the eventual product was quite charming and presented my face in a far better light than any mirror ever has. On that anxiety-inducing occasion I had been photographed alone, and had felt like a specimen being studied. I found that being among others made the experience much more pleasant.

This photographer, a Mr Hrovat according to the block printing on the back of the finished product, certainly knew his trade. Aunt Réka chose the background, a faux-salon, and in all else we were guided by him. He placed Mafalda and I together in the centre, sitting on armless chairs turned slightly in towards each other. As we were seated she caught my hand and held it, bold as brass. No one seemed to notice and there it is now, caught forever. Aunt Réka he placed behind Mafalda with one hand on her shoulder, and Eliza behind me just the same. She even managed to hold a slight smile for the entire exposure. Alice hung back, assuming she was not to be included, but Mr Hrovat placed her anyway and no one objected. There she is, preserved for posterity, on an ottoman at my feet.

With several of us in various forms of mourning dress, the photograph ought to make for a grim scene. Yet, somehow, there is a lightness to it. Eliza's gentle Mona Lisa smile, Mafalda's clasp on my hand, Aunt Réka's slightly Amazonian pose – they all speak to the character of the subject quite aside from how they are presented. Alice looks faintly startled and leans in towards me, as if shying away from the camera. My own expression is dreamy, vague, and a little vacant, which is the best I can hope for. My hair, at least, is dressed well. Brava, Alice.

By the time we returned home, to weather the heat of the day as best we could, even Aunt Réka was cheered. Whether or not she deserves cheer I cannot say. Eliza ordered a copy for each of us, and paid extra so that the finished product would be delivered this evening. They came just after dinner, and I have pored over mine ever since. Truly, a thing to treasure.

Letter: Alice Smith to Sarah Smith
Saturday, 19th July 1884
Buda-Pesth, Austro-Hungarian Empire

Dear Sarah,
I've started this letter over and over because I hardly know how to tell you what I must. I'm enclosing a copy of a picture my mistress had taken so you know that I've not run mad, that these are real people who these things are happening to, and real people who suffer as a result.

It started this morning when I went in to wake Mrs Cartwright and open the curtains. Her room has a view out over a side street, and on the opposite side was a man dressed in rough-looking clothes. I could've sworn he was staring up at the window until he saw me, when he lowered his head and sloped off. I never saw his face. I convinced myself I was imagining things and that it was just some idle workman, but now I think he was watching. Waiting.

Mrs Cartwright had made an appointment to see Madam Jacobinus's doctor at his office, so I dressed her to go out. She wanted her linens sorted for mending and a new pomade mixed up, so I was to stay behind. I tried to persuade her to borrow a maid from the household, but she said she'd have a carriage driver and a footman and that was quite enough people put out for her sake. If I'd tried harder, maybe it would have made a difference?

Time passed and I got on with this and that. I was mending in her room when there were sounds of a commotion from the corridor. Two footmen burst in, bearing my mistress between them, followed by the ladies of the house in various states of distress. Mrs Cartwright's skin was deathly grey and she was only just conscious. As the men laid her on the bed I saw a red smudge on her cheek and two red wounds on her throat, which had bled freely into the collar of her dress. I dropped my armfuls of linen and rushed to her side.

Nurse Weber, God bless her, was there with a nerve tonic ready-made. I lifted Mrs Cartwright's head that she might drink. That's when it happened. A vision took me and I saw everything that she'd seen, heard everything she'd heard, felt everything she'd felt.

Mrs Cartwright had left the doctor's consulting rooms disheartened and disappointed. She'd been hoping for so much, and he'd been able to give her so little. Other women were blessed with more children than they could manage, she thought – why was she not to be permitted even one? All she wanted was to be alone so she could cry.

Madam Jacobinus's carriage was waiting outside, and as Mrs Cartwright went to it a gentleman appeared next to her, as if from thin air. I recognized him at once – the strange man with the staring, preying eyes I saw at the train station. Mrs Cartwright recognized him too but felt none of the threat of him. She raised a hand in a reluctant greeting but before she could speak a weakness came over her, like a faint but more so. Without a word, the man swept her up in his arms and held her in an iron grip.

'*Achtung!*' he called to the coachman. 'Come and help! Your lady is taken ill!'

Mrs Cartwright was barely aware of the coachman and footman as she was lifted into the carriage and laid across the seat.

'You must take her home at once!' the gentleman ordered, in such a tone as would brook no argument. Not that there was any from either servant, even as the gentleman got into the carriage and seated himself. They didn't question him even once, as he so obviously fell into that class we in service think of as being our betters.

'Madam,' he said to Mrs Cartwright, 'I will accompany you. You should not be left alone.'

My mistress could do nothing, say nothing, her head thick with fog. I felt my own dread but Mrs Cartwright was impassive. The footman slammed the door, and the carriage drove off as swiftly as it could through the traffic.

'Well now. Sit up, my dear,' the gentleman instructed, and my mistress's body obeyed. 'I have been looking forward to meeting you again after our enjoyable discussion at Buda Castle. If I may say, it is a pleasure to once more be in the presence of such beauty.'

Reaching out, he took her hand and kissed it. Mrs Cartwright, moving like a sleepwalker, didn't or couldn't resist. Inside her mind, I howled with revulsion at his touch. I felt his wrongness, his twisted nature. He smiled, a smile that spread slowly across his pale face and split his red lips wide, showing his pointed eye-teeth. Then, faster than a mortal man could move, he sprang across to take my mistress in his arms, and drive those sharp white teeth into her throat.

The memory will haunt me forever. For my mistress, the daze of this thing's mesmerism saved her from the hurt of it. Even as Mrs Cartwright felt no fear or pain, *I* felt it all. I felt the mortal body's loathing of such an evil being, its agony, its growing weakness as my mistress was fed on. I felt all the terror, and all the disgust of it. I tell you, Sarah, I'd rather die than experience it again.

When he'd quenched his thirst he still held her tight, brushing her lovely golden hair back from her face with a ghastly tenderness.

'Delightful. Quite delightful.' He kissed her cheek, and the stickiness of her own blood marked my mistress's face. Tenderly, so tenderly, he whispered into her ear. 'Do not be downhearted. I will make you mother of multitudes.'

[Editor's Note: The original document has a large stain here, for which I apologize.]

Sorry for the ink spill. I had to rush away to be sick. I know Nana always told us about the dark things in this world but I thought they were stories, fairy tales, monsters from long ago. To see them up close, to know they're real . . .

Anyway, I can't bear to write all that out again on a new page. I hope you'll understand if I just carry on.

As the vision drained away, I found Nurse Weber shaking me by the shoulder.

'Miss Smith? Miss Smith? You are shocked, drink this.'

Another swooning woman, another tonic. It tasted bitter, and peppery. I sneezed.

'Good, good. Sneeze is good. Go and rest, yes? Madam is fine here. *Herr Doktor* is coming.'

I refused. I couldn't leave my poor mistress as she lay so deathlike, whimpering in pain as she breathed. Carefully, I dabbed her dirtied face with a damp hanky, wanting to cleanse her in the small way I could. I was scared to touch her again in case I had another awful vision, but I just couldn't let that cruel mark stay on her lovely face.

The other ladies were in and out, praying, watching, crying. Miss North wept and wept to see her friend so ill, Miss Lowell tried to comfort her, and Madam Jacobinus sat unsteadily reciting rosary after rosary.

Dr Arminius arrived in short order, all of a lather. He had obviously hurried, and was sweating and dishevelled when Lady Maria showed him in.

'The coachman tells me that Mrs Cartwright fell into a faint,' she was saying, 'but as you can see, this is much more serious than a mere faint.'

The doctor took one look at Mrs Cartwright and almost keeled over himself. He swore, not quite under his breath.

'You are right, your ladyship, it is indeed more than a faint. You ladies should please clear the room.'

I wasn't sure if I should leave or not, not being a lady. The doctor had the nurse stand by as he took off his jacket and rolled up his sleeves. She cleaned his hands with some fluid or other and he sent her to prepare a syringe and wait to be called for. I made to move away but the doctor ordered me back.

'Miss, stay if you would. You are a strong girl, I think?'

'Yes, sir,' I answered, and stayed where I was.

The doctor took Mrs Cartwright's pulse and pulled up her eyelids to look in her eyes. As he did so, he prayed the Our Father. He turned her head gently to examine the holes the creature had left in her neck, and I saw him shudder. He *knew*. He'd seen this before. I was as sure as if he'd said it out loud. I must have gasped or made some noise because he looked at me sharply, his gaze piercing. I couldn't hide my horror. The doctor glanced at the nurse, far away on the other side of the room laying out the necessary instruments.

'You are her maid?'

'Yes, sir.'

'Good. Will you please take your mistress by her shoulders, and hold her down? Quickly, thank you.'

As I did so, I couldn't avoid looking at her face, so grey-white against her pillow, with her lips now drawing back and exposing her teeth.

'You have a good hold? You must be prepared. This will not be pleasant.'

I made my grip firmer. Sarah, I was so scared that I was shaking, but I held on as tight as I could, bracing myself in case I had another vision and praying desperately that I would not.

'Yes, sir.'

'Now we need . . . Ah, yes. This will do very well.'

The doctor took up the rosary where Madam Jacobinus had abandoned it on my mistress's night stand. Gently, very gently, he let the wooden beads slip through his fingers, dropping the crucifix closer and closer to the sweat-beaded pallor of my mistress's forehead. Slowly, it came to rest just between her eyebrows. Mrs Cartwright drew in a breath with an unnatural hiss, but didn't move.

'Thank God, it is not too late. You may let go.'

I straightened up, and the doctor put the rosary back in its place. He called the nurse forward with a syringe full of some cloudy liquid, which he injected into Mrs Cartwright's arm with the ease of long practice.

'What is that, sir?' I asked. 'Lady Maria will want to know what's been done.'

'Rightly so, though I must ask that you be wise in what you tell her. Yes?'

'Yes, doctor.'

'Good. This is a strong sedative, an opiate, so the patient will sleep. She must, absolutely must, sleep and then rest quietly when awake. She has lost a great deal of blood.'

He returned the syringe to the nurse, and sent her away.

'What is your name, miss?'

'Alice, sir. Alice Smith.'

'Miss Smith, you know of the *vampyr*.'

I started, and if he had not been sure before that would certainly have given me away.

'The . . . the what?'

'Do not be coy with me. You are not merely upset, or worried for your mistress. I see you, Miss Smith. You are afraid, terrified. I have seen others like you just so. You know of what I speak.'

I screwed up all the courage I had left. I thought of what I'd seen and of Nana's book, and the stories that weren't stories after all.

'I do know, yes, sir. How do you?'

'I have made him my study for many years. I had thought him long gone until lately. His strength, his vitality, it grows as he feeds, and your mistress has not been his only victim in recent days, though she is by far the luckiest. Our concern now must be entirely for her. Will you be my assistant in this?'

'Me? But Nurse Weber—'

'We cannot trust another. Those who do not know, who have not seen, they do not believe. It must be you. You must follow my directions and ensure all is carried out just as I say. Will you do that for me? For your mistress?'

'Yes, sir.'

'Good, I am glad to hear it.'

'Will she . . . will she become—'

'Like him? No. He has drunk from her, but she would need to drink from him in turn. We would know if that had happened as she would not have been able to bear Our Lord.' Dr Arminius nodded to the rosary. 'She would then have to die a human death, and rise again to take in human blood. Then, and only then, would she become a true and lasting *vampyr* in her turn. But remember, this is not science. It is a strange and dark thing, and as far as I know, different in some measure for each victim.'

I shuddered, an awful chill settling into my bones.

'By my experience, she will be well again in a few days if we can keep her safe. No stranger must enter the house. The *vampyr*, he cannot enter unless he is invited. Still, I recommend that the windows in this room be barred, and we will wreath it all about with garlic flowers. She must not be left alone. Hang that rosary from the head of her bed too.'

'Yes, sir.'

'Very good, Miss Smith. I will be back in the morning. Remember, she must *not* be left alone. He is circling, even now. Once he has identified his prey . . .'

The doctor shook his head.

'Do you mean he'll come after her even once she's well?'

'It is possible, yes, though if your mistress is removed far from here, he may forget all about her.'

I looked at poor Mrs Cartwright, who still appeared to be at death's very door despite the doctor's ministrations.

'But how can I possibly get her home to England as she is now?'

'Not home, I am sorry to say, but somewhere safer where she might recover fully from his attack. I will speak with Lady Maria and see what can be done.'

The clock is striking two now, and soon Miss North will come to relieve me from my post. I'm sitting here with only one candle for light, gripping Mam's crucifix in my hand so tight it hurts. I have written down everything that Dr Arminius said in my commonplace book, which I will keep closer by me than ever. The smell of the garlic flowers is overpowering. Dr Arminius has given out that they have healing vapours, and that's why the windows mustn't be opened. He's told Lady Maria that Mrs Cartwright was bitten by a poisonous insect, which made her ill. Of course, no one would believe the truth who hadn't seen it. He has persuaded her ladyship that fresh air and hot-spring bathing will speed my mistress's recovery, so the minute she can walk again we're all to remove to the family's ancestral home in the mountains.

Please pray for me, and for my poor mistress. Thank the Lord that we'll soon be beyond the monster's reach! Write back as soon as you can. You can reach me either here, or in the countryside at Székely Ház in Sárkányerdő, Transylvania.

Alice

PART SEVEN

Sir John Seward's personal diary
Monday, 16th February 1903
Littlemore Hospital, Oxfordshire

The last few weeks have seen us all rushed off our feet. Not only has Oxfordshire experienced severe snowstorms causing fluctuations in our receipt of supplies, but the hospital has been battling an outbreak of influenza in the male wards. This is likely the same influenza that previously laid me low. We instituted quarantine protocols to avoid a wider spread, and now at long last the tide seems to be turning. Fortunately there has been relatively little loss of life, though every letter I must write to the family of a patient who has passed away grieves me deeply.

Jonathan Harker was supposed to visit earlier in the month, following my communications regarding Lady Lowell, but obviously he has had to be put off. We are endeavouring to rearrange the visit for as soon as reasonably possible, and for me it cannot come soon enough. The waiting is quite a trial to the nerves.

Dr Knight has been a rock during this difficult time. I do not know what I would have done without her. She is indefatigable, and in some dark moments her energy and devotion to duty is all that has borne me onwards. Imagine my shock, then, to call in to her office on Friday morning to find her sitting in her desk chair with a burgeoning black eye and a split eyebrow, being stitched up by Nurse Taylor.

'Good God! Beatrice, are you alright?'

'Good morning, Sir John. Yes, I am quite well. Thank you, nurse. Please leave the ice and the iodine; I can manage.'

Nurse Taylor grumbled but did as she was bid. Against Dr Knight's protestations, I perched on the edge of her desk and took up the iodine myself. She winced as I began to apply it but bore the pain bravely.

'It was Mrs French, on the second floor. She didn't respond to a sedative quite as quickly as I would have liked. It will all be in my notes.'

I laid down the iodine and examined the damage, taking Dr Knight's chin in my hand and turning her face to the light. Her undamaged eye fluttered closed and I saw that her bruised one was almost fully sealed already. The gash cutting across her eyebrow was neatly stitched, but the plum of the surrounding contusion seemed to grow darker even as I watched. It filled me with emotion to see her injured, and gulping it down took more effort than I would like to admit.

'You should take the rest of the day off, just in case.'

'Don't be ridiculous. I'll ice it for a few minutes, and then I'll be back to my duties.'

I realized all at once that I had been holding her in place for far longer than a medical examination required. I sat back, hemming and hawing, and passed her the waxed ice pack. Dr Knight applied it to her eye socket, sighing in relief.

'I could order you to rest,' I told her, as firmly as I could manage.

'Yes, but you won't.'

'At least let me take care of your duties for the next few hours.'

'I've already set Dr Benjamin to finishing my round, but given my current appearance I'll allow you to take our next meeting alone.'

'Very well.' I hesitated, still too concerned by her injury to remember who we were meeting. I was forced to ask to be reminded.

'Lady Lowell's companion, Mrs Lakatos. She wants some sort of briefing. Were it not for the influenza and the quarantine requirements, we would have met with her before now.'

'Has Mrs Lakatos been in Oxford for the duration?'

'In Iffley village, just outside the city. According to the visiting records, she came regularly before the outbreak.'

'That shows admirable devotion. I'm happy to meet with her while you rest, if you promise that you will indeed rest.'

Dr Knight raised her uninjured eyebrow, and her one visible grey eye gave me a hard stare. 'You need to work on your bedside manner.'

'I'm sure you're right. I'll come and visit you later, and you can tell me how I might improve myself.'

'I certainly will. Now you'd best go, or you'll be late.'

I found it hard to leave her. It is not usual for a doctor to be attacked in the course of their work, though I suppose it must be rather more common in our branch of medicine than in others, and it is a thing that leaves one rather shaken. I did not want Dr Knight to be alone, so when I found Nurse Taylor hovering in the corridor I sent her in with strict instructions to take good care of our deputy director. I daresay Dr Knight will be irritated but one cannot be too careful.

I was informed by the nurse on duty that Mrs Lakatos was in the gardens. Lady Lowell had been given permission by Dr Benjamin to walk with her guest just outside the women's wing, where the paths have been freshly swept and cleared of ice. An orderly in a thick coat stamped his feet to stay warm while he watched the two bundled-up ladies make circuit after circuit of the garden.

I know this because I stood and looked down from the floor above, in case there was something to learn from the interaction. My findings are as follows. Mrs Lakatos cut a small but robust-looking figure, with mid-brown hair that frizzed out enthusiastically from under her sensible winter hat. Lady Lowell was much the taller of the two, by a head or more. As they walked she leaned heavily on Mrs Lakatos's arm, bending down in a listening attitude. At one point she seemed to grow somewhat agitated, to a pitch where I was almost minded to lean out of the window and call down to the orderly to step in. Then something rather strange occurred. Mrs Lakatos removed her glove and laid a hand across her ladyship's cheek. My patient calmed almost immediately. I recalled Sir Joseph telling me that Mrs Lakatos had a gift of soothing his wife, and it appears he may have been correct. An odd method, but apparently an effective one.

Downstairs I waited with the orderly, a dour Scot by the name of MacIntyre, until the ladies completed their circuit.

'Good morning, Sir John,' the patient greeted me in her customary manner, as if we were at a diplomatic function.

'Good morning, your ladyship.'

'Have you met Mrs Lakatos?'

'No, I have not had the pleasure. I am glad to make your acquaintance, Mrs Lakatos.'

I had spoken slowly and carefully, assuming by her name that the stout, flat-faced, rather tired-looking woman before me was not a native English-speaker. I did my best to hide my surprise when she answered me in a soft Yorkshire accent.

'And I yours, Sir John. I am grateful for the opportunity to meet with you.'

'I wondered if we might speak in my office, Mrs Lakatos? I'm afraid my colleague Dr Knight will not be able to join us, as she is indisposed at present.'

'Of course. Nothing serious, I hope?'

'No, nothing serious,' I replied, thinking of her black eye and split brow.

Mrs Lakatos looked me full in the face and for a moment I had the uncanny feeling that she knew I was not being truthful.

'Are you ready to go back to your room?' she said to my patient.

Lady Lowell bit her lip, and tightened her grip on her companion.

'If I must, I suppose. Will I see you tomorrow?'

'If Sir John allows it,' Mrs Lakatos replied, with a slight smile which implied that I would absolutely be required to allow it.

Lady Lowell relinquished her grasp with some disinclination but no refusal, and consented to be led away by MacIntyre. Mrs Lakatos watched him carefully as he guided Lady Lowell gently back into the building. I recalled Sir Joseph's account of the unpleasant and ineffective treatments to which his wife had been subjected, and saw reason for such scrutiny. I often cannot but reflect on how my predecessors in this branch of medicine have often done more harm than good.

Upstairs in my office, Mrs Lakatos got straight to the point.

'I'll be frank with you, doctor. While her ladyship's husband is very devoted, he's kept extremely occupied with his children, his businesses and his estate. It's long been my job to help him with . . . let's say . . .' She squinted a little as she searched for the word. '*Superintending* her care. When her ladyship first became so ill as to need to be in an institution, Sir Joseph was too trusting of the opinions of certain medical men who saw those poor souls in their care as little more than animals. He's never forgiven himself. I'm sure you can understand how important it is that Sir Joseph is sure of her ladyship's doctors. She's been through enough as it is.'

So she *is* checking up on us, I thought. Fair enough. Would I behave any differently if it were my own loved one in Lady Lowell's place?

'As I told Sir Joseph, here at Littlemore we are committed to using only the most modern and humane methods of care and treatment. We do nothing that is in contradiction to human dignity – no unnecessary restraints, no unnecessary medication, no physical chastisement. Where it is needed to maintain the safety of staff and other patients we do what we must, but only what we absolutely must.' I thought of Mrs French, most likely already in a strait waistcoat, though that comes under the heading of 'necessary'. 'We follow the dictates of science here, Mrs Lakatos. Not fear or superstition.'

Mrs Lakatos looked directly into my eyes in an unsettlingly searching manner.

'I believe you mean what you say. From this and what I've seen, and from what I already knew of you, of your deputy, and of this hospital, I'm satisfied. I'll tell Sir Joseph the same.'

'Thank you, I'm glad of it. I will always be happy to answer any questions or submit our methods to any inspection.' While we were on such excellent footing, I decided to give myself over to my curiosity. 'I understand you are not employed to care for Lady Lowell, so how is it that you came to be connected to her?'

'She's my dearest friend,' Mrs Lakatos answered simply. 'She saved my life, and I saved hers.'

I was left rather stunned by this statement, delivered entirely matter-of-factly. I now berate myself for letting it go so easily.

'On a different matter, doctor, Sir Joseph told me you asked him what set her ladyship to eating ants when she'd never done such a thing before.'

I would say my interest was piqued, if that were not far too mild a way of putting it.

'Do you know what happened to trigger it?'

'I think so. An old friend of her ladyship visited her, after many years. It did *not* go well.'

'I see. What happened?'

'There's not a right lot; I mean, there isn't much to tell. I went in and said to her ladyship there was someone come to visit. She seemed pleased. I brought in the young lady, and as soon as Lady Lowell set eyes on her she screamed and screamed and ran to the furthest corner of the room. She had to be sedated. After this, she started up with the ants.'

'Did her ladyship know this young lady well?'

'No, she'd not seen her since she was a child, not much more than a babe in arms.'

'I see. Would you be able to give me her name and correspondence address? I'd very much like to ask her about the incident.'

'She's a Miss Gregor, of Whitby. I'll look up the address and send it over.'

I recalled Dr Knight's newspaper clipping, the death notice.

'I don't suppose this Miss Gregor would be any connection to Colonel and Mrs Cartwright, also of Whitby?'

'Miss Gregor is the late Mrs Cartwright's sister.'

Before I could ask any of the hundred questions that flooded my mind, the tower clock began to strike, phenomenally loud.

'I must be going,' Mrs Lakatos said as she stood. 'I ordered a hansom to take me back to Iffley and it'll be waiting, if it's not got stuck in the snow.'

'Very well. Thank you for your candour today, Mrs Lakatos.'

'I find it always best to be right candid – excuse me, very candid.'

This self-correction provided me with a selfish opportunity.

'Mrs Lakatos, if you'll forgive me, I must ask how a Yorkshirewoman comes to bear such a name as yours.'

'My husband is a Hungarian by birth.' It sounds odd, but she seemed to squint at me a little before continuing. 'His family come from Transylvania.'

I started. 'Transylvania, you say?'

'Yes. Do you know it? There's not too many who are familiar with the place.'

'I . . . I travelled in my youth.'

'Well now.' Slowly, she put out her hand. 'It's been good to meet you properly, Sir John. I'm sure we'll speak again.'

We shook, and it seemed to me that she flinched. I let go at once, thinking I must have gripped too tightly.

'Likewise, Mrs Lakatos.'

I watched her go, pulling on her gloves as she left.

In my profession one gets a sense when one has not heard the entire truth, and that sense tells me that Mrs Lakatos is hiding something. I wonder what?

Evening

I visited Dr Knight this afternoon. She progresses well, though her bruise is turning a very ugly shade. She did not allow me to stay long, instead sending me away most decisively and telling me that there were others who had far more need of my care than she. I offered to take on some of her paperwork but she pointed out that one working eye was quite sufficient to see well enough to read and that her ability to write was likewise unimpaired. Well then.

I made my rounds and returned to find a parcel awaiting me, sent by courier. It was from Mina Harker, another most excellent woman. She has sent me our record, God bless her! Typed and elegant, this is the history of our dealings with the vampire Count. Mina points out very rightly in her covering letter that there may be something of help in the tale of our defeat of the evil scourge, who tormented so many in his life and even more in his death.

I must brace myself and read it through, though my heart shrinks from the task. A stiff drink is in order, and then I will begin.

Evening continued

This time, I have not marked my eureka moment by going screaming about the corridors, waking my colleagues and making myself ill. I will write my revelation down, quietly, calmly, and entirely faithfully. Here it is then. As I read through our record, when I reached the month of September in the year 1893, a passage from Mina Harker's own journal made me gasp aloud. According to Mina, Jonathan Harker had seen the Count on Piccadilly outside Giuliano's boutique, had seen him spot a woman in a Victoria carriage, and had then seen him follow her away, intent on some harm. The truth was obvious: Lady Lowell had been that woman!

I took out my notes from my conversation with Sir Joseph, and laid them beside the neat typewritten pages of our record. The accounts tallied exactly. Sir Joseph told me that his wife first became ill after a shopping trip on Piccadilly in September of 1893. She had waited outside in a carriage, and when Sir Joseph returned his wife had been so afraid of something or someone she saw on the street that she fainted. The monster had followed her, and wrought all that came after.

How did he reach her? One such as he cannot enter a home uninvited. Sir Joseph said he found his wife out on the terrace; perhaps she had been enjoying the view of her garden early one morning to soothe her nerves, or had sat out late caught up in a novel. One moment, one brief terrible moment, would be all it took. The demon followed her, he attacked her, and he fed upon her. This was why her symptoms began nine years after her original encounter with him! The false memory had been perfectly intact until she saw the monster again! Poor woman; she was confronted with the author of her suffering, and her battered mind broke from the strain.

My head spins as I write this, and I must resist the urge to once again fling myself out of bed and tell someone, anyone, what I have found. First thing in the morning I will send a telegram to Jonathan Harker bidding him to come at once, blizzards be damned.

Mafalda Lowell's notebook
Monday, 28th July 1884
Somewhere between Buda-Pesth and Kolozsvár or Klausenburgh, Austro-Hungarian Empire

Lucy is perpetually scribbling in her journal, so I have decided to start my own and see what all the fuss is about. I have stolen a notebook and safety pen from Uncle Gabor's study for the purpose.

I am writing while squashed into the window seat of a too-small compartment in a rickety train carriage, as the locomotive huffs its way from Buda-Pesth to Kolozsvár, on our way to Transylvania. My companions are all asleep, so it seems as good a time as any to begin my authorial musings.

It is a long time since I've been to our eventual destination of Sárkányerdő, or Drachenwald as the Germans have it. Mama's ancestral home is a short way outside the town itself, and can be cut off in winter if there's a deep enough snow. The last time we visited was before I went to school, and I ran wonderfully wild in the woodland and the hills. I used to keep the memory of that summer close during my first months at Medhurst, dreaming of climbing trees and paddling in streams as the schoolmistresses tried to forcibly impose some order on me.

Goodness, what strange paths writing leads one's mind to take!

Perhaps I should be recording things of interest visible from the window? No, I see only endless forest with the occasional ancient village perched on a hilltop, and the odd peasant wandering about in that strange garb they wear.

Papa never liked it here. I suspect it was because he was so poorly regarded by Mama's family, being a foreigner and a heretic and such. I do miss Papa. Mama is worried enough for his health that she plans to leave once we're settled. She took me aside yesterday during all of the preparation frenzy to tell me. At the time I barely took it in, though now I find I am filled with an irritation at the thought of having to manage everything out here without her. At least Mátyás will join us the moment he is able.

I've written to Joseph, berating him for not telling me the truth about Papa. Now that I know Mama is going to go and sort everything out I wonder if I ought to have been gentler? No, it must be absolutely clear that I will tolerate nothing less from him than total and complete transparency on all matters. I don't believe I have ever been so harsh with him, but he must know the standards I expect to be upheld in the future.

One hour later – only one! Time drags.
Eliza is awake and is doing her best to be cheerful. She is as pale as paper or paler, her gaunt face all eyes and teeth. For once her perpetual concern with her own and everyone else's health is justified. Yes, I know why she is as she is, and Lucy would have me give allowances for all the tragedies sickness has wrought around her, but I still find it irritating.

The insect bites on Eliza's neck are smothered in a calamine lotion, the stink of which covers even the odour of the coal and the smoke. Its reek is only mildly less offensive than the garlic flowers with which her room was festooned back in the city. We had to delay our journey until she was just about strong enough to manage it, and were it not for Dr Arminius insisting we go at the very earliest opportunity I would not have chosen to travel so soon. Ah well. I feel for Eliza, I do, or I tell myself I ought to. In truth I resent that just when we were so nearly past one round of playing nursemaid, another is suddenly required.

I must never let Lucy read this. She would be appalled to know that I could think such things. As for Aunt Réka, her recovery seems complete. Her appetite has returned along with colour in her cheeks, and even the lines in her face seem a little filled out. Her gaze can be somewhat glassy, though Dr Arminius says that is to be expected. The grey in her hair is the only remaining testament to her struggles that a stranger might notice. There is no justice in this world.

Enough. I think perhaps diary-keeping is not for me. I will sleep a little, and hope to arrive refreshed at our way station.

Letter: Joseph Lowell to Mafalda Lowell
Monday, 28th July 1884
Lowell House, Kensington, London, England

Dearest Mafalda,
Your last letter cut me to the quick. You are, as always, absolutely right. I can only apologize for not telling you the full and complete truth about your father's health. I beg your forgiveness, and I swear that from now I will only ever be completely honest with you.

I am at present in Kensington, and I am distressed to report that your father is changed for the worse. I continue to recommend that your mother returns as soon as possible, that she might bring her influence to bear. Sir Gerald is a strong-minded man, and, forgive me, he seems not to realize that this is a moment to bend to the opinion of others. I will let you know by telegram if there is significant deterioration but please do convey to Lady Maria how strongly I urge her to come back to London.

As much as I might wish that you would join her in returning, I know that you are too good-hearted to leave not only your poor aunt, but also your friend Mrs Cartwright. I was so sorry to hear that she has been taken ill, and am glad to know that she has been being attended by the best doctor available. When I met her, I found her a most kind and gracious lady. You have always been fortunate in your choice of friends. With that in mind, please pass on my greetings and best wishes to Lucy. It gladdens me to know that at this difficult time you have the support of a long-standing, loyal, caring companion.

On this same subject, it is my pleasure to agree to your conditions regarding Lucy's future living situation. After our marriage, it will be my honour to put the Beechwood dower house at her disposal for as long as she wishes. I have already taken the liberty of engaging a firm of builders to perform some renovations that will ensure her comfort.

Yours with all affection,
Joseph

Lucy North's journal
Tuesday, 29th July 1884
Klausenburgh, Austro-Hungarian Empire

Last night we arrived in Klausenburgh, or Kolozsvár if we are to be Magyar about it. Our lodgings for the night turned out to be a sort of inn rejoicing in the name of 'Hotel Royale', thereby showing quite some delusions of grandeur. The owner and his wife were kind enough to have waited dinner for us, which was a sort of spicy chicken stew with red pepper. It was delicious but left me rather thirsty.

We expected to continue our journey this morning but the promised connection to Bistritz did not materialize. Lady Maria took the matter in hand, and ordered those of us who wished it and were well enough to go sightseeing. The town is a mix of winding streets and the occasional grand square, as befits a long-ago now-forgotten capital city. Aunt Réka insisted on going to pray in St Michael's Church while Mafalda and I, being not of her faith, stood awkwardly by and pretended to admire the architecture. Alice slipped away to light a candle, which is her own business. The poor girl then had an altercation with a pushy street-seller outside and was not herself afterwards.

When we returned, Lady Maria met us in the hall and announced that we would be able to continue our journey tomorrow on the morning train. It will take longer than planned as the service is not an express, but given that there is no other option I'm just glad we will be on the move.

The evening passed quietly. Our party was given use of a small upstairs parlour, where we congregated after dinner. It was something of a crush, and I found myself relegated to a wooden stool by the window. I sat looking out across the red-tiled rooftops as the light left the sky, the streets slowly emptying and the resident bats coming out to wheel around the medieval buildings in their peculiarly erratic manner. This place has an odd feel about it, as if the deeper past could reach out and clutch at us. Even as I write I can hear a distant wolf howl, a sound which has surely echoed off these walls for centuries upon centuries. All the modern, civilized world is behind us, and ahead lies . . . what?

THE BRIDES

Goodness, how fanciful I am tonight! I must stop this nonsense and do my best to get to sleep. Tomorrow will be a long day.

Letter: Alice Smith to Sarah Smith
Tuesday, 29th July 1884
Klausenburgh, or Kolozsvár, Austro-Hungarian Empire

Dear Sarah,
We finally left Buda-Pesth yesterday, and I felt cheerier with every mile the train put between Mrs Cartwright and that monster. I've hardly let her out of my sight, sleeping on a pallet in her room, noting her symptoms in my commonplace book, and keeping by her side like a lapdog. She doesn't seem to remember the attack, for which mercy I thank Our Lord and his holy Mother.

Unfortunately, we're now stuck in a place called Klausenburgh until at least tomorrow because of a problem with the trains. Lady Maria said the ladies must go sight seeing to make the best of a bad situation. Mrs Cartwright was by no means well enough to go wandering about, so Madam Jacobinus ordered the nurse to stay with her. The nurse attempted to keep Madam Jacobinus behind, but she point-blank refused. She's had a shock recently, and is taking some medicine which seems to make her very hither-thither. I'd have gladly stayed too, but my mistress insisted on me attending Miss North. I couldn't very well refuse a direct instruction, so off I went.

We stopped at the town's great church, St Michael's. I nipped in to light a candle for you and Mam and for Mrs Cartwright, then stepped out thinking I'd enjoy the sunshine while I waited for the ladies. Two traveller women had set up a stall a little way from the church door, the sort of people we always used to see on the beach in summer selling things to the tourists. This pair were calling out to passers-by in much the same way, wanting them to come and buy flowers and ribbons and little bits and pieces. One of them was a girl of maybe nine or ten years old with wild dark hair caught back in a kerchief, occupied with selling a single rose to a young gentleman and his lady friend. The other, smothered in a black dress, was an extremely wrinkled old woman. It seemed her job was to drum up business. As I made to walk by, this old woman caught my eye and beckoned me over. I thought I'd like to have a little keepsake. There was a pretty carved wooden bird that would do nicely. As I paid the old woman for my new treasure, her crabbed hand brushed against mine.

Sarah, it was the strangest experience of my life. I could see my own self from the outside, my mouth frozen in jaw-dropped shock, all through the old woman's eyes. I felt her gentle amusement at my reaction, and her pleasure in meeting me. I felt calm and warm through and through, and it reminded me so much of being with Nana that I almost burst into tears.

'You see and you know,' she said, in . . . actually I don't know what language it was. Maybe it wasn't language at all. 'You must not fight it. It's a gift, child. Let it serve you, and others.'

'I don't understand. How?'

'Have faith. Even when it hurts. Especially when it hurts.'

I didn't get to ask anything else. The old woman glanced behind me, and her eyes flew open wide with fear. I wheeled about, expecting to see something terrible or violent, but saw only Miss North and Miss Lowell following Madam Jacobinus out of the church's door.

Suddenly the old woman leapt from her stool and grabbed my face in her hands, holding me fast.

'*You see and you know,*' she hissed. 'I tell you now, the Devil is searching for you!'

In her mind she showed me a young woman, hardly more than a girl, falling slowly and silently against a night sky. Then with a twisting lurch the vision shifted, and I heard a manic demon's laugh and saw a woman – where did I know her from? – writhing in overwhelming pain. I saw a man lying dead under the night sky, a lantern gripped in his hand. A dark shape loomed over him, feeding. I could hear the crack of its jaws, the gulping as it feasted. It raised its head and grinned an unnatural grin, flashing pointed teeth as it lunged towards me.

'Such a one took my daughter, her mother.' The old woman pointed a shaking finger at the dark-haired girl, now cowering behind their makeshift stall. 'You must not let the Devil and his kin take you too!'

All strength left my limbs and I sagged to the ground. The sense of evil coming took hold of me, strangling me. I heard the echoes of that psalm again, the valley of the shadow of death, in a voice I knew from somewhere and nowhere.

Dimly I was aware of the old woman leaving me be as she shrank back, making the sign of horns as the ladies approached. Madam Jacobinus clucked about while Miss North and Miss Lowell helped me to my feet, hustling me away most efficiently, checking I had my coin purse, asking if I felt faint, wanting to know what the old woman had said to me. They were so kind that I now feel terrible having lied to them, saying I couldn't understand the old woman because her accent was so strange and that it was just a funny turn from the surprise of being grabbed so.

Now I'm sitting up in bed looking at the carved little wooden bird, feeling so far from home and from you. What evil thing did the old woman show me? How could she control the Sight like that? Could I ever do it? Would I ever want to? I wish Nana were still here to tell me what to do. Please pray for me.

Alice

Night

Tonight's lemon beebrush did nothing. Nothing, Sarah. I dreamed of my mistress, my sweet and kind mistress. I dreamed of her standing in the light of the last sliver of a crescent moon, holding out her hand to a shadow. She doesn't deserve to die, not yet! She deserves to live a long and happy life and grow old with her husband, surrounded by many children and grandchildren. Please pray for her, and for me.

Lucy North's journal
Wednesday, 30th July 1884
Slow train to Bistritz, Transylvania, Austro-Hungarian Empire

The train lives up to its name. I swear it moves at no more than a walking pace. We have been aboard since morning, and now it is almost four o'clock. When the engine forces itself to chuff up these steep mountain inclines, we move so slowly that I worry we may roll all the way back down again. Each station stop lasts an age. We have at least been able to purchase food from the local vendors, who come right up to the windows of the train. Doubtless they have learned that those unlucky enough to be slow-train passengers will buy their body weight in pastries and breads.

We passed the morning in conversation and card games. Now, Lady Maria and Mafalda are reading and the recent invalids are asleep. I might risk a walk up and down the corridor to stretch my aching limbs. Thank goodness there *is* a corridor, although given the speed at which we have been moving I could simply get out and saunter alongside.

Later

I made only one length of the carriage because at the far end, as far from our party as possible, I found Alice. She was tucked into a shallow recess where a folding seat suggested that in this train car's better days a porter would have waited here, at permanent readiness to respond to the demands of the travellers. Alice was sitting on this seat, her head in her hands, weeping. A newspaper lay abandoned on her lap.

'Alice?' I said, raising my voice over the noise of the train. 'Are you quite well?'

She looked up at me, startled.

'Oh, miss, I'm sorry, I'm so sorry. Do you need owt? I mean, do you need anything?'

Her face was puffy with her crying. She was clearly mortified, and I felt ashamed for intruding.

'No, I was just walking. Is something the matter?'

'Nothing, miss,' she sniffed, wiping her eyes on a handkerchief. 'Please don't trouble yourself.'

'I'm sure we could get you some refreshments. Some water perhaps, or some tea?'

'Really, miss, I'll be alright in a minute.'

'If you've been sleeping badly,' I said, attempting to commiserate, 'that always makes things feel worse.'

Her head jerked up. 'Why do you say that, miss?'

'You've said something about nightmares, before. I thought you might still be suffering.'

'Oh, well, thank you, miss, but I'll be alright. I ought to pull myself together now.'

Her movement caused the newspaper on her lap to fall to the floor. I picked it up, glancing at it as I made to hand it to her. It was a German-language paper from the capital, over a week old. The lead item on the front page was the Baroness's suicide, and the accompanying photograph showed Uncle Gabor's mausoleum.

Alice stared at me as I looked at the paper and then at her face. She was trembling, more so than when I had found her, as if I might speak to her harshly or do her some harm. Why? I thought we'd been getting on rather well.

'Here you are,' I said, holding it out.

'Thank you, miss.' She took it from me carefully and with some reticence, as if she expected me to snatch it back.

'Are you sure I can't do anything to help you?'

'If you could just . . . not mention this to anyone, please?'

'Of course, I wouldn't dream of it. I'll go and leave you be.'

'Thank you, miss.'

Alice is usually so composed that to find her overcome in such a manner is very odd. I must remember to check on her later.

Evening

We arrived at our lodgings too late for dinner, and the innkeeper begrudgingly laid bread and cheese before us. It would have been a poor feast had I not been full of all the local food we'd eaten on the train. Neither the innkeeper nor his wife seemed very pleased with us, the opposite of our reception in Klausenburgh. Mafalda, now leaning over my shoulder and watching me write, even as she runs her fingers through my hair in an attempt to distract me, bids me put down that neither of them will meet her eye when she speaks. Earlier I could have sworn I saw the wife make a two-crossed-fingers sign behind Lady Maria's back, and consultation with Eliza's guidebook informs me that this is meant to ward off the evil eye. Mafalda says there is still some tension in this part of the world between the many races who live here, and suggests that we have chanced upon people who bear a dislike for those of her family's particular appearance and heritage. That must be it.

Ah, Mafalda has moved away so now I can write more freely. I did not have Alice in tonight to help me undress as Mafalda took on the task, so I've not spoken to her at any length. I did catch her briefly in the hallway, but she told me all was quite well and I need not bother myself. For now, I suppose I must take that at face value. I would not wish to intrude.

Mafalda is most insistent that I put away this journal and come at once to bed. I am sure no one can be quite so insistent as Mafalda, so I will do as I am commanded.

Letter: Eliza Cartwright to Colonel Edward Cartwright
Friday, 1st August 1884
Sárkányerdő, Transylvania, Austro-Hungarian Empire

My dearest husband,
I am sorry that you were made so concerned by Lady Maria's communication about my state of health. It's not quite so bad as all that. Dr Arminius not only agreed that I was well enough to travel but also that removing to the country would do me good, and he was absolutely right. We arrived at Sárkányerdő yesterday, and with each breath of clear hill-country air I feel myself improving. Last night I slept with the balcony doors of my allotted bedroom wide open, so that I might make the most of it.

The house itself is perhaps a mile or so from Sárkányerdő, a most convenient distance. On the drive from Bistritz station, Madam Jacobinus told me that her grandfather had won the house from an impoverished nobleman in a game of cards. Lady Maria tutted and said that that was nonsense, which is a shame. I would love to believe in such an entertaining story.

The building is three floors high, with a square tower topped by a pyramid-shaped roof at one corner, and a circular tower at the opposite. Both of these rise one floor higher. It produces a strangely lopsided effect to look at, though when her ladyship gave us a tour I found the view from the square tower to be quite spectacular. My balcony looks out onto it and to the mountains beyond. The grounds are charming, and from my window I can see the lawn sloping gently down to a little wilderness, which I look forward to exploring.

Madam Jacobinus tells me that as the terrace faces due west we will see some wonderful sunsets. So far we have been too fatigued from the journey to stay up long enough to take advantage of this promised show of natural splendour. Perhaps tonight when we are all properly rested we shall be more ready to sit and be awed.

This morning Mafalda was kind enough to accompany me down into the town for a visit to the baths. Don't worry, my love, we had a hired conveyance, and it is a very safe and easy path through the trees with picturesque cottages here and there along the way. Sárkányerdő is hardly a town at all, really more of a large village surrounded by the forest. The baths here are not among the most famous, though Lady Maria tells me they enjoy a quiet renown in this region for their healing properties.

Lucy was not able to join us, as Madam Jacobinus had specifically requested her company that they might read Keats together. Mafalda and I were alone, which is a rare thing. At the baths she took gentle charge, making sure I knew where to go and what to do. It is some while since I have bathed at a hot spring and I'm sure I would have made a dreadful show of myself without her guidance. As we relaxed in the swirling waters, Mafalda told me of their mythic origins, which I will share with you that you might add them to your collection of strange tales from far-away places.

Apparently, a great dragon sleeps under this particular ridge of hills. It guards a treasure hoard which is the property of its master, who is none other than Attila the Hun himself. He is considered to be the forefather of many people in this region and specifically of those from whom Mafalda is descended, a fact which she related to me with no small amount of delight. The breath of this sleeping dragon warms the water which bubbles to the surface imbued with the beast's powerful magic. Why a dragon should have healing magic is beyond me, but as the waters were extremely soothing I would be churlish indeed if I were to complain.

'Of course,' Mafalda continued as we sat side by side in the pool, with steam rising up and clouding our faces so we could hardly see, 'every superstition in the world is found here in some form. Aunt Réka adores folk tales, and when I was a girl she sent me a book of the folk stories of the Carpathians. It was completely unsuitable for a child, and naturally I absolutely devoured it. Apparently the legend of the werewolf first began here, as the spirit of a man who was violent in life and rose from the grave in wolf form to wreak havoc on the living.'

'And your aunt thought this was an appropriate gift for a little girl?'

Mafalda laughed. 'There were far worse tales than that! There was one story about a witch with flaming eyes, sharp nails a foot long and hair down to her ankles, who could curse a naughty child for life if she touched them. That was quite terrifying. Or perhaps you'll prefer the tale of the stick man who takes children away when they misbehave, and keeps them in his cave for an entire year?'

'I see a theme emerging. If a child is disobedient, then some manner of fantastical monster will come and punish them.'

'You'd think it would have had more of an effect on me, would you not? I ought to have been the best-behaved girl in all of Christendom.'

'A fine argument for why scaring children into good behaviour is ineffective,' I said, thinking of Beth and smiling a little to myself.

'I'm sure I'm very proud to embody such an agreeable argument as that.'

As we fell to sitting in companionable silence there in the healing waters, I thought of the howling of wolves that I heard in the forest last night. It is no wonder that the local people have invented such legends, and the mind certainly does play tricks on one out here. I'm sure it was that cacophony that led me to have peculiar dreams, though the first night in a new place is so frequently beset by such irritations that it hardly seems worthwhile my mentioning it.

I beg that you will not worry about me. I am perfectly safe here with my friends, and a nurse on hand to boot. Remember, I am following the advice of the best doctor in all of Hungary! Fresh air, plenty of rest and regular visits to the baths will see me right as rain in no time at all.

With all my love, your wife,
Eliza

Lucy North's journal
Saturday, 2nd August 1884
Sárkányerdő, Transylvania, Austro-Hungarian Empire

Lady Maria left for London this morning, after only two days here with us. We said our goodbyes before breakfast, lined up outside the house in the cool of the early morning. I was the last, watching as Lady Maria embraced her sister, her daughter and then, carefully, a fragile-looking Eliza.

'Mafalda will need you,' her ladyship whispered in my ear as she finally enfolded me in her arms. 'Take care of her.'

'I will,' I promised.

'Good girl.'

With that, the comforting presences of Lady Maria and the redoubtable Partridge got into the carriage and drove away. Her ladyship waved gracefully until they passed into the trees and out of sight. I waved back, a sour feeling in the pit of my stomach. I hope she will be able to persuade Sir Gerald to see sense about his health before it is too late, and of course she must go where she is most needed, but how are we to manage all that must be managed without her?

My unease was compounded later. Alice came to me as I sat reading on the terrace, trying and failing to bury my disquiet in Mafalda's copy of '*La Morte Amoureuse*'. Eliza was resting in her room, and Mafalda and Aunt Réka were in the salon arguing over some business of the house. I'd tried to intervene but Mafalda had shooed me away, telling me that at least one of us ought to be enjoying ourselves. The sound of bickering floated out through an open window, though thankfully I couldn't make out the words.

'Excuse me, miss,' Alice said as she approached. 'Can I speak to you?'

'Of course.' I laid the book down on the table, glad of the distraction from my own glum musings. 'Are you alright? Is it about the other day on the train?'

'No, miss. I just had a funny turn,' she said, resolute. 'It's about Mrs Cartwright. I think she's more ill than she lets on. I don't mean any disrespect in speaking to you of her personal business—'

'If you're afraid for her health, then it isn't disrespectful in the slightest,' I said with as much authority as I could muster.

'Thank you, miss. What I mean is, I think she's getting worse. I thought that the baths and the clean air would help, but today she can't stand the daylight. She hasn't been sleeping properly either, she just sits out on her balcony. I found her there this morning, and yesterday morning too. She always has such a care for her health, but now . . .' Alice trailed off, wringing her hands.

'Has Nurse Weber attended her?'

'Yes, miss, just now. Nurse says her pulse in't as strong as it ought to be. Mrs Cartwright told her she was fussing.'

Try as I might, I can't imagine Nurse Weber *fussing*. Is Eliza more ill than we all thought?

Evening

Aunt Réka decided we must all join her on the terrace to watch the sunset. Eliza declined the summons, retiring early. She'd eaten little at dinner, picking at her food and hardly speaking. The dark circles under her eyes were almost black, livid against the sad sallowness of her face.

After Aunt Réka had finished rhapsodizing about the golden reds and pinks and oranges and so on, I pulled Mafalda aside.

'We need a doctor to come. Eliza isn't getting better.'

'She does look like she's at death's door. I was worried she was going to drown in the baths yesterday.'

'Do you think the exhaustion of the journey made her worse?'

'What are you girls whispering about over there?' Aunt Réka called. 'Let's send for some wine and play cards in the parlour.'

'Thank you, but Lucy is very tired and I have letters to write. We'll say goodnight.'

'Don't be ridiculous! You young people have no idea how to have fun.'

'I can only apologize, Aunt.'

'Are you sure I can't persuade you?'

'Not tonight. Perhaps tomorrow.'

'Well, if you must you must, I suppose. Goodnight, my dears.'

Aunt Réka blew us a kiss, and wafted away down the hall.

'She seems . . . heightened?' I said, as we headed upstairs.

'Dr Arminius warned Mama that it might be an effect of the medicine. A slight mania. I suppose it's better than the alternative. If she could only stay out of the running of the household, I'd be much happier.'

'Not to mention the other matter.'

'Shh, not here.'

Mafalda hustled me down the corridor into her bedroom. She dismissed the tidying housemaid with her most gracious smile, which dropped from her face as soon as the girl shut the door.

'What do we do when Aunt Réka finds out that the letters are missing?' I asked.

Mafalda sat down on her bed. 'I think she would keep that to herself, unless she was sure I was the thief. She didn't bring the book with her; I checked.'

I went to sit beside her, taking her hand in mine.

'I still think we should tell your mother everything.'

'And what would she do? Mama is afraid that Aunt Réka will descend into a lasting madness. If she thought such a confrontation would end with her sister in an asylum, it wouldn't matter if Aunt Réka had murdered her husband with her bare hands.'

'Then what do you think we should do?'

'At the moment? Nothing at all.'

She closed her eyes and leaned heavily against my shoulder.

'You'll come up with something. I know you will,' I told her, more for my own reassurance than for my beloved's.

She squeezed my hand, and asked if she might sleep alone tonight. So, once again, I sit up in my bed by myself, scribbling and worrying, worrying and scribbling.

PART EIGHT

Sir John Seward's personal diary
Thursday, 19th February 1903
Littlemore Hospital, Oxfordshire

Morning

I have received a reply from the aforementioned Miss Gregor of Whitby. She must have sent it by return of post for it to have arrived so swiftly, which I must say I appreciate.

It does seem that Miss Gregor's visit could have triggered Lady Lowell's zoophagy, though as yet I do not know why. A shock, yes, but beyond that?

I have enclosed her letter with these notes as it may be of importance later.

From the pen of Elsbeth Gregor
Tuesday, 17th February 1903

Dear Sir John,

I am not sure how much help I can be to you, as I have only visited Lady Lowell on one unfortunate occasion, but if my account of it can be of some benefit to her then I am glad to give it.

In your letter, you shared with me Mrs Lakatos's description of the events of my visit. It is entirely accurate except in one particular, of which dear Mrs Lakatos may not be aware. When I first entered the room, her ladyship did in fact speak to me.

Almost too low to be heard, she hissed: 'You!' She then began to scream and back away, ending by cowering in the corner. I was overcome with emotion at this, and I fled.

I hope this information will be of use. Her ladyship was a close friend of my late sister Eliza Cartwright, and I am mortified and distressed in the extreme that seeing me may have exacerbated her condition. Please do write and let me know if there is anything else I can tell you, and also if you think it would be appropriate for me to visit Lady Lowell at any time in the future when her health allows. I would very much like to do so if at all possible.

Yours respectfully,
Elsbeth Gregor

Evening

My good friend Jonathan Harker arrived just before dinner, having begun the journey from Exeter as soon as he was able. He came bearing gifts of various foodstuffs from his wife, who, it seems, has a married woman's typical view of a widower's life and is endeavouring to keep me fed for the foreseeable future. Harker looks well, and his legal business is booming. He tells me that little Quincey, named for our heroic departed friend Quincey Morris, is in similarly good health and has reached that stage of childhood where he asks a hundred questions an hour of anyone who might be in the vicinity.

After dinner we removed to the snug to enjoy a glass of port by the fire. By mutual, if unspoken, agreement we'd not yet discussed the reason for his visit.

'Are we to expect Lord Godalming and Professor Van Helsing?' Harker asked, by way of broaching the subject.

'Sadly not, though both have communicated that they will support whatever action you and I see fit to take. The professor sent a telegram, saying he hopes to see the patient when the winter storms have passed. He claims he's too old to sail on anything other than a flat calm sea.'

'How like him.'

I smiled, thinking of my mentor's array of quirks and eccentricities. 'Indeed. He has also promised to contact this Dr Arminius of Buda-Pesth, whom it seems he used to know at one time.'

'That could certainly be useful.' He raised his glass. 'To absent friends, then.'

'To absent friends.'

We drank, honouring all those we had fought alongside, both living and dead.

'So, Jack,' Harker said after a brief moment of silence, 'let me make sure I have it right. You believe that your patient and her unfortunate friends somehow met with the Count in Transylvania, almost ten years before he blighted our own lives.'

'Yes.'

'Those friends were murdered by him, and Lady Lowell barely escaped with her life. She was terribly ill, and when she recovered she had no memory of any unnatural thing. Instead, she had and still has a false memory of witnessing their deaths when their carriage fell down a ravine.'

'Exactly so. Deputy Director Knight believes that she confirmed this under hypnosis. I must show you the notes.'

'Ah, the famous Dr Knight. She sounds most capable.'

'She certainly is.'

'Do you think she could be taken into our confidence?'

I paused. 'I hope so. I can say no more than that.'

'Well, we can consider that question later. To return to Lady Lowell, you say she came back to England suffering from the after-effects of illness and grief, but nothing worse. She married, she had children, and life was bliss until the vampire came to London in 1893.'

'Yes.'

We quieted once more. I remembered all those we lost to Count Dracula in that dreadful year. My first love, sweet Lucy Westenra. Her poor mother. Quincey Morris, our dear friend. And, so very nearly, Harker's own wife Mina. Perhaps there are still others in the world who by our actions we released from the Count's influence. I pray, as I have done for the last ten years, that all those who were touched by his evil might find peace.

Harker roused himself first.

'So then, in September of that year the Count accosted her ladyship and attempted to drain the life from her over the course of several days. Fortunately, her husband took her away and we kept the Count too busy to follow.'

'Do you think he came to London in search of her?'

'I imagine it was a part of his plan. We know he was vengeful. It would have pleased him that she had thought herself safe, only for him to prove that it was not so. By God we did good work in ridding the world of his kind!'

Harker's face grew dark and for his sake I am glad the housekeeper chose that moment to knock on the door.

'Forgive the interruption, sir. A note has just arrived for you from Iffley. The boy who brought it says he was told to wait for a reply.'

'Thank you, Mrs Stevens. Please take him to the kitchen and give him something to eat.'

I opened the note, thinking it must be of vital urgency to send a messenger out on such a cold and unforgiving night. As I read, my expression must have alarmed my friend.

'What is it? What's happened?'

'It's from Mrs Lakatos, Lady Lowell's companion. See for yourself.'

'"Dear Sir John,"' Harker read, '"I must see you as soon as possible. I have information which will help you in your care of her ladyship, and I must share it with you before my courage fades. Please let me know by return if you can see me first thing in the morning." How mysterious. I wonder if she knows about the Count? Do you think it's possible?'

'How could she? Lady Lowell couldn't tell anyone even if she wanted to. Unless—'

The realization dawned on both Harker and I at the same time.

'Unless she was there!'

Unable to sit still, I leapt to my feet and began to pace as I thought aloud.

'When I met Sir Joseph, he said that Mrs Lakatos had known his wife for twenty years, which covers the time of that trip to Hungary. When I last spoke to Mrs Lakatos herself, she told me that her husband's family came from Transylvania. She may well have met him on their travels there.'

'It would be quite a coincidence if it were not so. Yet isn't it rather unlikely that both women managed to escape the Count's clutches?'

'Perhaps. Mrs Lakatos did say that Lady Lowell had saved her life, which seemed extraordinary and yet I didn't manage to inquire further. What a fool I am! I need a pen and paper. We must see her as soon as possible!'

I responded as requested by return, and a meeting is fixed for tomorrow morning. Harker and I agreed not to tell Dr Knight anything until I can see a way of doing so that will not have her sedating me and putting me in restraints.

I hope against hope that we may finally solve the mystery that has surrounded Lady Lowell, and that in doing so we may yet restore her to herself.

Letter: Alice Smith to Sarah Smith
Monday, 4th August 1884
Sárkányerdő, Transylvania, Austro-Hungarian Empire

Sarah,
Yesterday morning I found Mrs Cartwright collapsed on her balcony, limp and chilled to the bone, her mouth ringed blackish red as if she had bitten deep into her tongue and filled her mouth with blood. I thought she was dead. I ran to her and felt for her pulse, and when it came, after long, long moments, it was hardly there at all. Nurse Weber and I sat with her most of yesterday, as she lay abed half-conscious. She flinched away from the daylight where it fell across her pillow, so I kept the curtains closed and burned candles instead. I did all I could to warm her up. I had the stove lit and Margit the upstairs girl brought an earthenware hot water bottle, which I wrapped in a blanket and tucked at my mistress's feet.

I've never prayed so hard in all my life. No poultice or tonic or any of Nurse Weber's medicines had any effect. Miss North sent the boot boy into the village for a doctor but the local man is away and apparently there's no other for miles. Miss Lowell has had a telegram sent to Dr Arminius asking for his advice, and I pray a reply will arrive in short order.

All day Nurse Weber and I stayed in with my mistress, watching and waiting. Finally, late in the evening as the sun set, she stirred.

'Alice? Is that you?'

'Yes, madam. I'm here.'

I took the liberty of taking her hand, still cold despite my best efforts.

'I'm thirsty.'

'Here's water, madam.'

Nurse Weber held up her head, and I helped her to drink. Mrs Cartwright gulped it down as if she were parched, and demanded more. Nurse Weber and I gave her another cup, and another.

'That is enough,' Nurse Weber told her. 'You will make yourself sick.'

'I'm hungry. Is there anything to eat?'

'I will permit you some broth. Alice, go to the kitchen.'

I went downstairs to see if the cook, a Polish woman named Bożena, could make some broth in a hurry.

'Worry not,' she told me in her sideways German. 'I already make something to help the sick *Frau*. My grandmother's recipe. I give to you.'

Bożena showed me a big pot full of heavy black liquid. Waving away the kitchen maid, she ladled the stuff into a bowl herself. It smelled like a butcher's.

'What do you call it?' I asked, commonplace book and yellow pencil at the ready.

'It is called czernina, black duck soup. Better than broth. From the blood of the duck.'

'Duck's . . . blood?'

Bożena nodded.

'Yes. The *Frau* will be strong again very quickly. You will see.'

I wasn't sure about this and neither was Nurse Weber, but just the smell of the soup seemed to be reviving Mrs Cartwright.

Nurse Weber fed it to her slowly, so slowly that it must have been cold by the time she reached the bottom of the bowl.

'Is there more?'

'You may have more later. Not too much at one time.'

My mistress scowled, a look I'd never before seen on her face.

'You should sleep, madam,' I said, hoping to soothe her.

'I don't feel tired. Just hungry.'

'You must try to sleep all the same,' Nurse Weber ordered. 'Then you may eat a little more.'

'I suppose I must, if you insist.'

'I do. If you cannot sleep, lie quietly. Perhaps you would like someone to read to you?'

'No, I can read to myself.'

'Just so. A maid will come in case you have any need during the night.'

'Can Alice not – Alice, have you been here all day?'

'Yes, madam, of course.'

'You look exhausted. And you too, nurse. I will be quite well by myself.'

Nurse Weber pressed her lips together. 'I could not possibly permit it.'

Nurse Weber wouldn't budge and neither would Mrs Cartwright, so I suggested Margit sit outside and look in twice an hour, and fetch help at the first sign of any difficulty. She promised to come for both me and the nurse at dawn in any case. Hopefully nothing will go wrong in the meantime.

Tuesday, 5th August 1884

I was woken up at dawn, but not by Margit. The sunlight hitting my face roused me from where I'd collapsed fully dressed on my bed the night before. I dashed downstairs at once, practically bursting into Mrs Cartwright's room.

It was chaos. Furniture was scattered about all knocked over and askew, the great mirror from the wall lay face down in pieces, and one of the shutters was half off its hinges. Mrs Cartwright, dressed only in her shift and leaning her full weight on the bedpost, stood over the senseless form of Madam Jacobinus.

'Alice! Thank goodness you're here,' she said, sitting down heavily on the bed as if her legs were too weak to hold her any longer.

I knelt by Madam Jacobinus, rolling her carefully onto her side like Nana taught us to do when someone's fainted.

'Madam, what happened here?'

'She said she couldn't sleep, so she came to check on me,' my mistress told me as I listened for the poor lady's breathing. 'We talked for a while, and I must have dozed. The next thing I knew, it was light and she was shrieking and flailing about the room. I think she was hallucinating. She was saying the strangest things.'

I felt for Madam Jacobinus's heartbeat, carefully shifting her collar. It was sluggish and weak, but there was worse than that. On her neck, bold as brass, were the same two red marks the monster had left on my mistress. Madam Jacobinus had been drunk from by the *vampyr*.

I gasped despite myself, feeling my hands start to shake. No vision came, thank the Lord and all his angels, but I still sat trembling like a leaf.

'Alice? Alice?' Mrs Cartwright's voice broke through my horrified haze. 'You look unwell yourself. I'll ring; we must have Nurse Weber in at once.'

'Did Madam Jacobinus go out onto the balcony?' I demanded of her, forgetting my place in my distress.

'I don't know. Perhaps? She said something about the moon,

the poetry of the crescent moon. Yes. I remember now. It must have been just as I was going to sleep. Why?'

I didn't reply, occupying myself with covering Madam Jacobinus with a blanket. Why didn't I understand it sooner? Mrs Cartwright wasn't just exhausted from her ordeal. The *vampyr* has found us.

Nurse Weber arrived at great speed and I told her the only thing I could, Dr Arminius's own lie. I said that Madam Jacobinus had been bitten by a poisonous insect.

'We ought to see about getting some garlic flowers,' I said after the nurse had cleaned and dressed the wounds. 'Like Dr Arminius did for Mrs Cartwright.'

'If you can find some in such a backwater as this. How did this happen? Why was I not summoned? Where is Margit?'

Margit was found in the servants' quarters, cringing and apologizing for having left her post. She'd only been gone long enough to get some food from the kitchen, she said, and she was so hungry from having been up all night. Besides, Madam had gone in to see the sick *Frau* so where was the harm? Nurse Weber was furious, and Margit is banished to the scullery until Madam Jacobinus can decide what to do with her. I'm cross too, I am, but by wandering off Margit may have saved her own life.

God must have been with me on my hunt for garlic flowers. Even though it's late in the season, I knew I'd seen some in the garden. I fetched as many armfuls as I could carry, as fast as I could. Some say the creatures of darkness can't walk in the sun, but this one was out and about in broad daylight in Buda-Pesth without a care in the world. My head was practically swivelling, trying to keep watch while I worked.

When I got back, safely thank God, Madam Jacobinus had been moved to her own bedroom. All the morning Miss Lowell didn't leave her aunt and Miss North didn't leave my mistress, so their compassion kept them both safe indoors. I hung the garlic all around Madam Jacobinus's bedroom, where she lay breathing that familiar harsh, rasping breath. Miss Lowell helped me a bit. She might have raised an eyebrow when I hung her aunt's rosary from the bedpost, but she didn't stop me.

At least my mistress is a bit better after her long rest of yesterday, and the strengthening diet of duck-blood soup. Nurse Weber ordered her to stay in bed for another day, and I really ought to have waited on her but then I'd have had to send someone else out for the garlic and that wouldn't have been fair. I wanted to put some in her room too, but she wouldn't let me. She said it made her head swim and reminded her so much of being ill back in Buda-Pesth that she felt sick. What could I do? I'll have to satisfy myself with locking her hastily mended shutters and taking the key away with me.

The young ladies swapped over their sitting-in duties partway through the day before going off about their own business, but still kept inside for fear of the biting insects. I've been stoking that fear all I can. I hope the other staff, who are mostly locals, don't say anything contrary.

It's well past sunset now. I've closed and barred or locked every window or its shutters, and I've used the tiny bit of authority I've got to make the maids check all the doors are not just locked but bolted too.

Dr Arminius must be told about what's happened. I'll tell Mátyás as well, or what parts of it I can. Tomorrow I'll have to send the boot boy out again to wherever the nearest telegraph office is, and then I'll bribe him to stay safely away.

Tell Mam I love her. Pray I'll have the strength to do whatever I must.

Alice

Lucy North's journal
Tuesday, 5th August 1884
Sárkányerdő, Transylvania, Austro-Hungarian Empire

Early morning

Eliza is ill, perhaps desperately so. I am beside myself. I cannot sleep, I can barely eat. Once again, I am useless. I tried to write to Colonel Cartwright, but could not find the words to tell him what had happened. Mafalda took over, and the screwed-up results of her various attempts are littered all over the house.

If it were not for me, Eliza would be at home in Whitby. Eliza, to whom I owe so much. She comforted me when I cried on my first night at Medhurst, she helped me with my schoolwork when I struggled, she taught me that I had human worth despite my father's lack of regard for me. After my late mother, Eliza was only the second person in my life to show me what it meant to be loved. And this is how I have repaid her! Badly done, Lucy! Badly done!

Sunrise

It is a strangely chill morning. There is a mist rolling across the valley, leaving this house a lonely island adrift in a silent grey sea. Or, it is simply an unseasonable fog and my own strange mood, my exhausted unravelling, is making it seem more than it is.

My lonely night was disturbed several times by the noise of a window banging somewhere, or perhaps it was a bat colliding with the shutters. I took up this very journal to distract me from my self-flagellations, having no book to read that I have not already devoured and not wanting to go down to the library in the dark. I thought I might look through my writings and see if they could be transformed into some travel article, and perhaps, back in London, sold.

This next will sound very strange. In the time I spent reading over my own scratchings, I wondered more and more about Alice. I know that many of the most learned people believe in mental or etheric or spiritual phenomena these days, and much scientific research is done into how such things work. With that in mind, I believe that Alice has twice complained of nightmares which have been followed in short order by tragic and unexpected deaths. I'm convinced she dreamed of the Baroness's suicide, which was why she was so distraught when reading about it on the train. It is quite possible that that was the moment she learned of it having actually happened. The true reason for Aunt Réka's distress was kept from all but the nurse, and I don't think she was close enough to the other servants to hear the news as gossip. I also believe she knew beforehand about Colonel Cartwright's manservant, and may have even tried to stop him from doing what he did. Could her 'nightmares' be something much, much more? I do not pretend to understand the science of it, but it seems reasonable to assume there may be a hereditary component. Eliza told me of Alice's abilities, though in jest, and that Alice's grandmother had been punished for witchcraft. Could it be that it was simply some psychic phenomena misunderstood by the people of the time? I am hoping to find the right moment to ask Alice about it, though I can't yet fathom how I will phrase the question. I—

Later

Alice herself came in and cut off my strange musings. Eliza is awake and much improved, but Aunt Réka was felled in the night by one of these terrifying biting insects.

'I'm just coming to you from her rooms now, miss. Mrs Cartwright says she had some kind of fit.'

'No! Is she in any imminent danger?'

'That would be a question for the nurse, miss, but it doesn't seem so. Might you be able to talk to Miss Lowell and see about removing somewhere else? Before anyone else is taken ill?'

'Do you think other people will become unwell?'

'I do miss, yes.'

'Would you say you have a foreboding? A presentiment?'

Alice looked at me strangely, hesitantly.

'I . . . I suppose I would, miss.'

I'd have asked more but a maid came in with a breakfast tray – yes, a tray, in defiance of all tradition. In the circumstances Alice had ordered it for me, God bless her.

After my hasty breakfast and hastier dressing I went in to see Eliza, finding her sitting propped up in bed and looking less deathly than she has in days.

'You have a little colour back at last,' I said as I entered.

'That's kind of you to say. I suppose the local air is finally doing its good work.'

'Not a moment too soon. Do—'

I stopped as something crunched under my step, and I felt a sharp jab against the sole of my slipper. I lifted my foot carefully. A sliver of glass was stuck in the fabric. I wiggled it out, careful not to cut myself.

'Eliza, look what got caught in my shoe.'

'Oh no! Are you injured?'

'No, but we should get someone in here to sweep. Did something break?'

I sat down in an old-fashioned high-backed chair set up next to the bed, placing the piece of glass on Eliza's bedside table.

'It must be from the mirror. The truth is, Madam Jacobinus

got quite . . . quite violent. She smashed it and glass went absolutely everywhere. The maid must have missed a bit when she tidied up.'

'Violent? Were you hurt?'

'No! Nothing like that, thank goodness.'

'Alice said something about taking ourselves somewhere where the insects won't be a problem any more, though I don't know where we would go.'

Eliza looked thoughtful. 'We ought to go further up into the mountains. The family must have friends in the region who could take us in.'

'I almost want to say we should just go back to London. I know Aunt Réka and Sir Gerald aren't the best of friends, but surely in the circumstances . . . ?'

'Lucy, have you seen Madam Jacobinus today?'

'No, I came to you first.'

She squeezed my hand. 'That's sweet of you, but only a fool would think that Madam Jacobinus was in a fit state for a journey of such a duration.'

It was strongly worded, for Eliza.

'I'm sorry for suggesting it.'

'Don't be, you only want to keep us all safe. It's laudable. Now, please do entertain me or I'll be bored stiff by the time I'm fully mended.' She handed me a pack of cards from a drawer in her bedside table. 'Would you like to deal?'

The morning passed in playing every two-player card game we could think of. Alice came and went, fetching and carrying and tidying with admirable thoroughness. Certainly no slivers of glass were left on the floor to cause anyone any damage. Nurse Weber threw me out just before luncheon, ordering her patient to rest. I ate alone in the dining room, gazing absent-mindedly out of the window. I'd had some idea that I would return to my favourite spot on the terrace but I dithered, considering Alice's pronouncements about everyone being in danger from the poisonous – or should it be venomous? – insects. I was in the hallway, reduced to a statue by the indecision of it, when Mafalda appeared from I know not where.

'Lucy! There you are.'

Her eyes were tired beyond belief. I checked over my shoulder to make sure we were alone before taking her in my arms.

'Darling. Are you alright?'

'I – no. I don't think so.' She buried her face in my neck. 'What am I to do? I cannot fix things as they ought to be fixed.'

'I'm here, my love. We will manage together.'

'I'm so tired. I'm so tired of cajoling and persuading and asking nicely and keeping track and running everything.'

'Let me help you. Eat something, then go and lie down.'

'I ought to stay with Aunt Réka.'

'I will take your place, if you promise to do as I said.'

'Thank you.' She laid a warm hand against my cheek. 'I don't deserve you.'

Upstairs, pungent garlic flowers hung all about Aunt Réka's bedroom. I suspected Alice's handiwork. The indefatigable Nurse Weber fluttered around in the background. I wondered if the woman ever slept.

In contrast to well-mending Eliza, Aunt Réka was barely sensible. It was as if she were in that state of just having awoken, but perpetually.

'Lucy,' she greeted me sleepily. 'I'm so glad you're here. You have such a calming presence.'

This was the first I'd ever heard of it.

'Thank you, Aunt. How do you feel?'

'Oh, fine, fine. A little tired. I had the strangest dreams.'

Dreams, again!

'Dreams are often strange,' I said in my most soothing tones.

'I was with Mrs Cartwright. We were looking at the stars, I think, and then someone came and she fell down and was so quiet, and so still, and so cold. I thought she was dead. Is she dead, Lucy?'

'No, she's not dead. She's much better today.'

'I thought she was dead. I went to find help, and then she wasn't there.'

Aunt Réka began to grow agitated, shaking her head from side to side.

'Shhh, now, shhh. Don't upset yourself. Nurse?'

'No, she wasn't there! She wasn't in the mirror and then I turned and she was behind me and her *eyes* . . . So red . . .'

'Enough of this rambling now, Madam,' Nurse Weber said sternly. 'Back to sleep, I think.'

The nurse administered a sedative. Once again she sent me away, telling me to stop exciting her patients. I drifted for the rest of the afternoon, floating aimlessly about the house. An oppressive lethargy seemed to have settled over everything. In the end I returned to my room and began to read this diary again from the beginning. I suppose it must not have held my attention, as I fell sound asleep until Alice came in to dress me for dinner.

Later when seeing me to bed, Alice made very sure the windows and the shutters were shut and firmly locked, testing and shaking them before deeming them secure. I certainly don't want to be the next victim of the vile little creatures, so I let her go to it. I wonder what breed of insect it is exactly that causes such infirmity in its victims? I will go down to the library tomorrow and see if there might be any information there, hopefully in a language I can read. I must do all I can to be useful. That's the ticket, as Sir Gerald would say.

Lucy North's journal
Wednesday, 6th August 1884
Sárkányerdő, Transylvania, Austro-Hungarian Empire

I am a fool. I am a silly, trusting fool. I thought, when this grim spectre first arose so long ago, that we would never come to this point. And yet, here we are! I, racked and writhing in agony. My beloved skipping through life giving orders, making demands, making choices for others, and believing that all will fall in line!

In the grip of emotion, I have committed the cardinal sin of all writing and hidden the true matter of the story. I must work harder, since now my need for a career has become pressing. Here it is then. Mafalda has agreed to marry Joseph, and she did not even have the common decency to tell me.

Today, I breakfasted alone. Nurse Weber had forbidden visitors to either invalid until later on in the day, and Mafalda was, I was told by the parlourmaid, hard at work writing letters in the library. When I had eaten I made my way there, thinking I would spend time on my entomological research while she wrote.

I found the room empty but only recently so. My beloved's perfume still hung in the air, the writing desk temporarily abandoned. It may have been wrong of me to look at her half-written letter, but why should I have suspected any secret to be contained in something left so casually out in the open? Why should I have expected her to have any secret from me at all? Yet there it lay as if it were nothing, a heart-breaking, soul-rending secret. Mafalda's elegant hand loped away across the page, the ink not yet quite dry.

Dear Joseph,
I thank you for your kindness. You know I could not possibly abandon Lucy, and I am grateful that you are already making the dower

house ready for her. I will therefore accept both your apology and the offer of your hand.

I found the letter that this answered beneath, sent from London a week ago. I read it through, beginning to shake as understanding dawned. Mafalda had kept this from me. She had lied to me and deceived me in equal measure. Mafalda was not the person I had believed her to be. Forthright, yes. Demanding, yes, she has ever been so, but fundamentally dishonest?

At that moment, that very moment, I heard her calling.

'Lucy? Lucy?'

She appeared in the doorway, framed by the dark wood. Her black curls were caught only half pinned back, leaving the rest long and wild, spilling down over her shoulders. Her freckles, brought out by the sunshine and unhidden by any artifice, spread brazenly across her nose and cheekbones. I will never forget her expression as she looked questioningly at my stricken face. Then, as she saw that I held Joseph's letter, her green eyes grew wide beneath her thick brows.

'Lucy, my darling.' She came towards me with her arms outstretched. 'Please, let me explain.'

'Liar.'

I could hear the coldness in my own voice. It seemed to unsettle her. Of course, she had known this revelation would come; she had had time to envision my response. She would have rehearsed my tears and recriminations. Perhaps she even thought I would beg.

'No, darling. I never lied to you.'

'You prefer "deceiver", then.'

'Don't be angry. All will be well! Nothing needs to change. Joseph will spend his days occupied with the estate, and you and I will stay in London. We can live as we always have!'

'I'll be living in the dower house, apparently.'

She took my limp hand and held it tightly, her expression painfully earnest.

'Whatever you want, my love! Whatever you want.'

'Why?'

'Why? So we can be secure, of course. Joseph is a good man but not an intelligent one. With such a pliable husband, such a known quantity—'

'You would use him so?' I spat. 'You would give him only half a wife? You would vow fidelity, knowing it meant nothing? How can you be so cold, so selfish?'

'You call me selfish? This is all for you, Lucy, for *us*.'

This was such a blatant untruth that I ignored it.

'Joseph is not an idiot. Eventually, he would put two and two together.'

'Would he?' She smirked. 'I doubt it.'

I thought I might scream, or choke her.

'And what of me? Did you think of me at all?'

'We would still belong to each other in all the ways that matter.'

'Do *I* deserve only half a wife? That is what you offer me, or not even that. You would make me your mistress, tucked away in the dower house, taking crumbs from your husband's table while living on his charity.'

Mafalda tilted her head to one side.

'You live on my father's charity, so why not on my husband's?'

It was as if she had struck me. I pulled my hand free of hers and I ran. I did not care where to. Out of the library and through the entrance hall, wrenching open the vast front door and thence out into the grounds. I could hear her calling but I did not falter. I passed a startled Alice picking flowers in the garden, almost knocking her out of the way. I stopped only when I was hidden among the trees in the half-wild woodland where I collapsed onto a stump, my tears finally permitted to fall.

Mafalda did not follow me. I wept and wept until my eyes burned and my head ached. I do not know how long I remained there, Joseph's letter still clutched painfully tight in my fist. Since I first knew her she had been high-handed, and I had accepted it as part of her personality. I even believed that I had tempered it as time went by, but now? Was this what she had always truly thought of me? A charity case whose only emotion ought to be gratitude, with no right to refuse her commands? How dare she! How dare she insult me, how dare she betray me, how dare she take my choices from me, how dare she decide on the direction of my life? How could she not understand that to see her being Joseph's wife would be the cruellest possible torment? Does she imagine I would willingly resign myself to dark corners and stolen moments for the rest of my miserable existence? We have always been forced to hide, it's true, but as long as I have known her I have held out the hope that one glorious day we would be able to live and love alone together. She has murdered that hope, and all that went with it.

Throughout this rambling rage, I felt myself in a strange sympathy with Joseph. As my anger cooled and turned to grief, I found that I could not hate him as my rival. Instead I felt an affinity with him, as another who would be injured by Mafalda's obnoxious plan. Then a worse thought dawned. If it were not Joseph, might it have been someone else? Might we always have come to this point? Had Mafalda anticipated this all along? This notion shocked me more than anything that had come before, stunning my internal monologue into a bleak silence.

My rescue from this dark place came in the form of dear Alice. I ought to have heard her approach but I was so lost in my own wretchedness that I was not aware of her until she was greeting me with a 'There you are, miss,' which managed to be both relieved and empathetic at once.

'What are you doing here? Shouldn't you be with Eliza?'

'Mrs Cartwright is sleeping. You seemed upset so I thought I'd best see if I could be of service. We really ought to get back inside.'

'How did you find me?'

'Well, it weren't that difficult, miss. I've brought you something that'll help. Here.'

She carried a leather pouch, from which she handed me a small stoppered bottle.

'Thank you. What is it?'

'A herbal remedy, miss, for nerves. My sister's recipe. You'll need to drink it all.'

I did so, swigging from the bottle like a pirate. I tasted camomile, rosemary, and something sweet that I couldn't identify.

'Thank you. You're very kind.'

'I've a few other things waiting for you indoors, miss, if you'll come with me?'

We made a slow way back to the house, my unwillingness making my feet leaden despite Alice's herding. She brought me in through the servants' entrance, 'so you needn't see a soul, miss', whisking me past the kitchens and storerooms and pantries and I know not what other quarters of the below-stairs. Up a dark and narrow staircase we went, the dust getting into my nose and causing me to sneeze over and over into my bedraggled handkerchief. Eventually, Alice opened a hidden door onto a familiar corridor, and brought me into my own chamber without anyone any the wiser.

She laid out the 'other things', these being a flask of lemonade, some biscuits, a cloth and a basin, and small face towel fresh from my linens. After I shoved Joseph's letter into my pocket, the unfolding of my hand revealed a multitude of paper cuts which Alice cleaned without comment. I washed and dried my red and swollen face, and felt the better for it. I claimed I was neither hungry nor thirsty but Alice knew my needs better than I did, and insisted I partake of both lemonade and biscuits at once.

'I feel I ought to apologize,' I said, when I had done as I was told.

'No need, miss.'

'I mean, when you must be so concerned for Eliza—'

'There's not much more I can do, miss. I've been praying for her. Now, if you want to be alone, I can give out you've a headache?'

I did feel a dull throbbing in my temples, so it wasn't even untrue.

I thought I might sleep, so Alice helped me to change. It was a false hope. I lay here in the half-dark, re-reading Joseph's letter and wondering if I am to follow Aunt Réka's pattern of destructive anger, melancholia and hysteria. An age passed in this way. The lunch gong sounded and Alice knocked to ask if I would like a tray but I refused. No one else has come up so I can only assume Alice has done as she said. I ought to go and do my duty by Eliza, and I will, I swear I will. Not yet, though. I would not be able to contain my emotions, and that would doubtless do more harm than good.

I must work out a plan for my future. I must think of all the things to do to manage my life so that I can support myself. I must consider every option, and every obstacle. I must put a life together, so I have something worth going home to.

Letter: Mafalda Lowell to Lucy North
Wednesday, 6th August 1884
Sárkányerdő, Transylvania, Austro-Hungarian Empire

[Editor's Note: This can only have been delivered by hand.]

My darling,

I hear you are not well, so I am reduced to this note-passing as if we were still schoolgirls.

My love, my heart, do you think I want to marry Joseph? A glorified farmer, lumpen and dull as ditch-water? I have chosen this course for you, so that we might be together with nothing to divide us. The subterfuge was necessary or you would have talked me out of it, and because of my affection for you I might have been swayed. It will help us to have a protector, a man who can stand between us and the world, and who would never try to take my father's business and our source of income from me.

This is the right decision for us. Joseph cares deeply for you as his lifelong friend, and I can manage him well enough to ensure that he will take care of us both. I cannot bear to think of what might happen to you without me – some poor rooms with but one servant, a quiet bookish life, you frowned upon and vilified by the world as an old maid. This way you will always be with me and will want for nothing. I am more than willing to make the sacrifices that I must for you and for our love.

Say you understand. Give me even one word, one look, one brief touch of your hand to let me know that I am forgiven!

All my love, always,
    Mafalda

Letter: Réka Jacobinus to Maria Lowell
Saturday, 9th August 1884
Sárkányerdő, Transylvania, Austro-Hungarian Empire

[Editor's Note: Translated from the Hungarian.]

My dearest Maria,
By the time you read this, I daresay some very panicky communications will have made their way to you. I beg you not to be too alarmed. Everyone is making the most dreadful fuss about nothing. I had the misfortune to be attacked by one of the vexatious insects that seem to plague this part of the world, and that is all. Apart from a bout of light-headedness and some unsightly bruising, I am perfectly well. Mrs Cartwright's little maid sourced some garlic flowers from somewhere and put them all round about, as they did so well for Mrs Cartwright when she had a run-in with the little biting creatures. The flowers smell vile but as their vapours have such healing properties, I'm sure I will forbear. Dear Mrs Cartwright has had to excuse herself from attending me as the odour of the garlic flowers reminds her of her own illness and she cannot stand it. Apart from that, she seems to have returned mostly to health, though I'm told she still sleeps into the day and her colour hasn't yet come back. It is quite miraculous, and apparently our Polish cook's culinary skills are the cause. Personally, I doubt it. That woman barely knows how to cook any meal that isn't dumpling-based.

Mafalda and Lucy have been charming and have sat with me in turns. I think they have had some little falling out but I cannot tell who is the sinner and who is the sinned-against. Doubtless all will soon be mended, as it always is with girls.

The weather has turned cool for the time of year, and if one did not know better one would think it was almost autumn. We have been having dramatic thunderstorms of late, which set all the windows to rattling. Last night I was awoken when some poor bird or other crashed into my own casement repeatedly, doubtless driven to confused desperation in the high winds. Mrs Cartwright's attendant had had the foresight to close and lock the shutters, thank goodness.

I have left the best news until last. We have received an invitation from my nationalist friend and yours, Count Dracula, to visit him at his ancestral home. It is higher up in the mountains, on the other side of the Borgo Pass, where we will be quite safe from the insect problem. As soon as I am recovered enough to travel, we shall sally forth!

I close by entreating you not to feel you must turn around and return to wait on me. We are staying indoors as much as possible, and the servants are lighting yellow candles all about the place. All will be perfectly well.

Your most loving sister,
Jacobinus Gáborné Székely Réka

PART NINE

Sir John Seward's personal diary
Friday, 20th February 1903
Littlemore Hospital, Oxfordshire

Mrs Lakatos came to my office for our meeting. She brought with her a large carpet bag, carrying it with an ease which demonstrated surprising strength for so small a woman.

'Mrs Lakatos,' I said, moving forwards to greet her and holding out my hand. 'Welcome.'

'I'm not sure you'll be welcoming me when you hear what I have to say.'

I wasn't quite sure how to respond to that, so I continued with the formalities.

'May I present my good friend Mr Jonathan Harker. He is a lawyer.' Harker left his position by the window, and the two shook hands. 'Mr Harker has a perspective which may prove useful. He will be bound by the same rules of confidentiality as I myself.'

Mrs Lakatos squinted a little, looking intently at his face.

'Have we met before, Mr Harker?'

'I don't believe we have, but I may be mistaken.'

'Hm, no, I'm sure the mistake is mine.'

After this strange introduction we were seated, and Mrs Lakatos got straight to the point. Her jaw was set, and I had the strong impression that she had decided upon a course of action and was determined to see it through, come hell or high water.

'I've brought you some information which will help your understanding of Lady Lowell's condition. I've sworn to myself every year she's been ill that I'd tell the truth if it might be of service, and every year my courage has failed me, which means I've failed *her*. Until now. Until our discussion of t'other day.'

She patted the carpet bag, held close on her lap.

'These papers, which I've collected over many years, will tell you the full story of what happened to make her as she is.'

I felt my heart begin to race as Mrs Lakatos opened the bag and took out several large leather document holders. These she placed on the table in front of me with something approaching reverence.

'I'll leave these with you. When you've read the contents, if you still want to help her ladyship, please contact me. If not, then I'll speak to her husband about having her moved elsewhere.'

Her voice cracked as she spoke, and she began to rise as if to escape.

'Wait just a moment,' Harker interjected. 'Mrs Lakatos, I once had an ordeal so terrifying, so beyond any experience of my normal life, that afterwards I was seriously ill for some time. In my body, certainly, but also in my mind. I doubted that anyone would believe me if I spoke of what happened. I had a written record of it all in my journal and though it read like wild ramblings, there were those who did believe it. John Seward was one such. You do not know me, madam, and so my word will not mean much, but I will give it nonetheless. You can trust this man.'

Harker's words moved me, for had he not suffered most at the monster's hands?

'Mrs Lakatos,' my friend continued, choosing his words with great care, 'if I were to say to you the name of Dracula . . .'

Mrs Lakatos's reaction spoke for itself. She gasped a hideous rattling gasp, and her hands clamped themselves over her mouth. She shook from head to foot, and lost all her colour in an instant.

'Jack – smelling salts,' Harker ordered. I produced them from a drawer and handed them over at once. I have made it my custom to always have them available given how often they are necessary, and not only for ladies. Harker held the vial under Mrs Lakatos's nose, and she inhaled deeply. Slowly, slowly, she ceased to shake. I poured her a drink from the decanter, and she took a small sip before making a face of disgust.

'You have had a shock,' I told her firmly. 'Drink it all.'

My concern for her wellbeing managed to override all else. After a minute or two Mrs Lakatos returned to, if not a state of calm, then to a state of tension which was within the bounds of normal under the circumstances.

'What did he do to *you*?'

There was a definite stress on that final word.

'Ten years ago, he held me captive in his castle. I escaped. Eventually, we – that is, myself, Sir John and several of our friends – we hunted him, and we ended him.'

'You ended him?'

'Yes, madam. He is finally and truly dead.'

'Are you certain?'

'I am.'

Mrs Lakatos crossed herself. 'I'd hoped and prayed it might be so when the scars were gone,' she choked out, through the tears that had begun to stream down her cheeks, 'but I could never be sure. Dead! Thank God, thank God, now we are safe.'

'I promise you, it is over,' I told her, in my best calm bedside manner. 'You have no more to fear from him or his kind.'

'His kind? What do you mean "his kind"?'

'The others like him,' said Harker. 'The females, his vile brides, they are all ended. They have gone to whatever hereafter awaited them.'

'They're dead.'

Harker answered her as if she had asked a question, though I realize now that it was not one. 'Yes. Truly dead.'

'What happened?'

'Mr Harker slew the Count,' I told her, 'together with our friend Quincey Morris, may he rest in peace.'

'No, no, I mean the ladies. What happened to them?'

'My mentor, Professor Van Helsing, was the one who killed them.'

The quality of Mrs Lakatos's emotion changed. I could not understand it. Still she wept, but not with relief.

'That's good. Yes, that's good. They're at peace.'

'If those monsters deserve peace,' Harker said bitterly.

'Oh no, sir! No! Don't say such things! You don't understand.'

That brought us both up short.

'What do you mean, madam?'

'They were her friends, doctor. Her friends!'

Harker and I were none the wiser. Two such educated men, so oblivious to the obvious right before us, and I with Miss Gregor's letter in my own pocket at that very moment!

Mrs Lakatos opened one of the document holders and pulled out a photograph.

'It was taken at a studio in Buda-Pesth. It was meant to be a souvenir. Look.'

It was a typical arrangement of ladies, with flowered pillars and suchlike in the background. Seated on a footstool slightly off to one side was the younger version of the stout lady before me. Two young women, one dark and one fair, occupied the very centre, seated turned slightly inwards and so near as to be almost touching. No, they *were* touching, discreetly holding hands. Behind the dark girl stood an older woman who was her spitting image but dressed in widow's garb. On the other side, behind her fair companion, stood a young matron. In contrast to her fellow subjects, she wore a hint of a smile.

'Do you see? This is Lady Lowell.'

Mrs Lakatos pointed to one of the seated girls, and indeed it was her. Young, unworn by cares, but it was without a doubt my patient.

'And these—'

'These are they!' Harker had come closer, and was staring at the photograph with his face a mask of familiar horror I had thought never to see again. 'These are the demon women in his service! These are the ones who tried to take my life, to make me like themselves! These two, and this one standing here.' He turned his wide eyes on Mrs Lakatos. 'You knew them? We thought they were centuries old, but you knew them when they were human?'

'Yes. I managed to save her ladyship, but the *vampyr* had already made the others like himself. There was nothing I could do. I've prayed for them every day since I carried Lady Lowell from that place.'

Of course! I bit down on my lip to keep from shouting out.

'Can you tell me if one of these . . . ladies . . . is Eliza Cartwright?'

'Yes, this one here. You mentioned her name to me once before; how did you come to know it?'

'From my own research into my patient's history. Do you know if her sister, Miss Gregor, has grown to look very like her?'

'Yes, she is her very image.' Her face fell as the implication dawned on her. 'No! That's why her visit got Lady Lowell started on the ants!'

Mrs Lakatos buried her head in her hands. I glanced at Harker, still staring at the photograph.

'Tell me their names, Mrs Lakatos,' he asked. 'Please. For my own sake.'

I cannot go on. I cannot. How is it that those demons of Harker's night terrors were women of our own modern age? All I can think is that they were not the first to be turned, in the monster's centuries-long campaign of terror.

Now my poor friend is in the snug, drinking and smoking and staring at nothing. I am hidden in my study, pouring this onto paper as if I would empty out the unhappy contents of my brain. I have all Mrs Lakatos's papers laid out on the dining room table, but neither of us can face them yet. Perhaps tomorrow we will be able to begin.

Lucy North's journal
Wednesday, 20th August 1884
Traveller's Rest, Transylvania, Austro-Hungarian Empire

After nearly a fortnight of being shut up in the house, both in fear of the biting insects and in waiting for Aunt Réka to recover well enough to travel, we are finally gone. Our party is in the process of removing higher into the mountains on the strong recommendation of Dr Arminius, received by telegram from Buda-Pesth. Apparently the risk was too severe to brook any greater delay, so we packed up and left as swiftly as we were able.

Today, therefore, we are on our way to stay at the country home of a friend of Aunt Réka's, one Count Dracula. He is Aunt Réka's nationalist compatriot, who some months ago purchased a parcel of land from Uncle Gabor's estate. It is very kind of him to take in several ladies he has never met, but he seems a generous sort. I suppose all the nationalists must stick together. His letter to Aunt Réka formally issuing his invitation was so courteous that I suspect she is half in love with him already.

The journey was planned to take most of the day. A hired coach and driver would take us as far as some little village whose name I cannot even hope to spell, and there, at the last inn on this side of the Borgo Pass, we would meet the Count's conveyance. It is from this rustic hostelry that I am writing. Barely more than a large room in the innkeeper's house, it has the feeling of a medieval tavern, with low ceilings and straw on the floor. A slight though fluffy ginger cat, with impressive whiskers and a grubby pink nose, has made itself at home on my lap. I am grateful for its warmth. I knew it would be cooler up here in the mountains, but it feels as if we have left summer far, far behind.

Unfortunately, we arrived to find no sign of the promised conveyance. We have been here for hours while the rain pours down outside, waiting to be collected like so many parcels. And this is not our only trouble. The redoubtable Alice has been taken ill. We were served some kind of local tea when we arrived, and it seems it did not agree with her. She and I were talking, and she was telling me loudly and earnestly that we ought to turn back. Then she drank, as did we all, whereupon she grew extremely flushed and fainted dead away on the floor. The innkeeper, accompanied by Eliza and by Nurse Weber, who is certainly earning her pay, have put her upstairs. I attempted to join them but the attic room was so tiny that my presence meant there was simply not enough space for Nurse Weber to work. It does not seem that Alice has been attacked by the insects, but is overcome by some other malady. I'm truly worried for her, given that we are so very far from civilization. I find myself hoping it is only exhaustion, the strain of the events of recent weeks beginning to tell on her, but what do I know? I will trust to Nurse Weber.

Though the innkeeper and his wife have been most solicitous of Alice, overall their conduct bears a strong resemblance to those hostelers in Bistritz who would neither speak to nor meet the eyes of any member of Lady Maria's family. These here also seem nervous of Eliza, and even my feline companion refused her caresses, hissing and taking refuge under a chair. It is all quite unsettling, not to mention that this leaves me the only lady deemed inoffensive.

On that subject, I must report something rather odd. Some little while ago, with frequent glances over her shoulder to where Aunt Réka sat chattering away like a mad coca bird, the innkeeper's wife came and joined me on this bench seat where I sit by the door. I chose this spot because from here I can look out of the window and see the road, for all the good that has done.

'Miss, may I talk?' she asked me, in Hungarian accented so strongly and oddly that I had to concentrate hard to understand. I nodded, and assumed my most attentive attitude.

'I overheard where you are going. I beg you, please reconsider. It is not a good place.'

'What do you mean?'

'You will not be safe there. You should turn around and go home.'

'Why?'

'It is not good there. Not good for you.'

I assumed that this had to do with the aforementioned tensions in this land, though as I write I wonder if she meant that the Count has a particular reputation as a corrupter of local virtue. If that's the case, then surely we have safety in numbers. Wait, no, it can't be – Lady Maria spoke of him as an older gentleman, so would he not have lost interest in such pursuits?

'Thank you,' I told the woman, 'but I must go with my friends.'

'Your friends! No, miss, your friends—'

A great creaking overhead interrupted us, the cause of which turned out to be Eliza coming down the stairs. The innkeeper's wife hustled away, and the cat leapt off my lap and hurried after her in the same fashion.

'She's none too friendly,' Eliza remarked as she sat down in the spot the woman had vacated. 'Is there any sign of Count Dracula's carriage?'

'No, not yet. How is Alice?'

'Rather confused, and not herself at all.'

'Perhaps it's all been too much for her.'

'Perhaps.'

Eliza seemed rather less worried than I would have expected, but of course she trusts, as we all do, in Nurse Weber's competence.

'Alice is so capable that I often forget how young she is.'

'Indeed. Nurse Weber seems to think it's some sort of mild apoplexy.'

I thought of my convictions about Alice's particular set of skills, and wondered how much of a toll such a thing might take upon a mind. How useful Sir Gerald's library would be to me now, in exploring the science of it!

'Shall I go and see about some dinner?' I asked, thinking privately to myself that Eliza still looked rather gaunt. 'I'm sure I could persuade them to feed us. At least, I hope so.'

Eliza shook her head. 'No, thank you, I'm not hungry.'

'Are you sure you didn't ought to eat?'

The strangest change came over her face, her blue eyes almost seeming red for a flash of an instant. I feel uneasy to recall it. Goodness, I must be very tired to be so affected by a trick of the light.

'No, I'll manage quite well until we reach our destination. I do feel dreadful about Alice. I wonder if I did right to bring her from Whitby at all.'

'It's not your fault. She was so keen, and it made so much sense at the time.'

'I suppose. Send up to tell me if anyone arrives, won't you?'

'Yes, of course.'

She patted my arm in a friendly enough manner, yet the unexpected touch made me recoil. My own state of mind is not particularly robust at present and I worried in case I'd given offence but she seemed not to notice. So here I am, warmed by the return of my friend the ginger cat, waiting, reflecting. It is all very well the innkeeper's wife telling me to go home, but even if I could, where on earth would home be?

Letter: Mafalda Lowell to Lady Maria Lowell
Wednesday, 20th August 1884
Traveller's Rest, Transylvania, Austro-Hungarian Empire

[Editor's Note: During this time period ML sent several letters to her mother which have been lost. This last was kept separately by her ladyship in her dressing-table drawer.]

Dear Mama,

Please forgive the hastiness of this note. At present we are on our way to Castle Dracula, and now await Aunt Réka's friend the Count at a rural coaching stop. I will prevail upon the innkeeper to post this on.

I'm glad to know that Papa has at long last consented to see Dr Williamson. I'm not sure he will enjoy the recommended sea-bathing cure but I hope that with you to guide him he will see the necessity of doing as he is told, for once. Please tell him I send my most respectful filial regards, which is sure to make him laugh.

Let's not go into the question of Joseph. I must ask for your patience on that score. I promise to write more, though out here in the wilds I'm not sure when I will have the opportunity to send a letter.

I remain, as ever, your affectionate daughter,
Mafalda

Lucy North's journal
Thursday, 21st August 1884
Traveller's Rest, Transylvania, Austro-Hungarian Empire

No carriage came for the rest of the day, nor even passed by the place. Eventually night fell, and the innkeeper grudgingly offered to make up beds for us. The sleeping quarters were rudimentary. One tiny room under the eaves held two low cots, just across the stairway from where Alice lay. Mafalda (there, I wrote her name!) manipulated the situation so that she and I would take this room. Eliza, Aunt Réka and Nurse Weber had pallets on the floor in the main room downstairs. The innkeeper's wife, wringing her hands all the while, apologized over and over that this was unsuitable for ladies. It grew quite wearing.

Not, of course, as wearing as Mafalda using this stolen privacy to bend my ears with her sorrow, her pleading, her justifications and her fury in turn. After a fortnight of carefully avoiding her, I was irritated to be coerced into such close proximity. Knowing as I do that she has no patience, I simply lay down and turned my face to the wall. She kept up her flow of talk for perhaps half an hour, and then gave up. I will not repeat what she said to me. It is hardly worth it.

I did not expect to sleep, and yet I did so, deeply. I woke to Mafalda shaking me by the shoulder and calling my name in increasingly incensed tones.

'Lucy! Lucy, wake up! Lucy!'

'What?' I mumbled, my mouth dry and my tongue unwieldy.

'Finally! You must get up!'

'Why? What's happening?'

I blinked heavily, dragging my eyes open.

'The carriage is here! We have to leave!'

I followed her down the stairs, stumbling, to find we were alone. My luggage sat shabbily by the door. The innkeeper was engaged in hefting Mafalda's trunk out into the rain where a calèche waited, its hood up.

'Where is everyone?'

'Our host there said they left in the night. That sad excuse for transportation wouldn't fit us all, so Eliza decided they'd go on ahead and send it back for us.'

'Didn't they leave a note?'

'The man said not.'

I peered out through the nearest window. The hood was deep, but it was by no means an appropriate vehicle to drive several women in varying states of ill health around in on a wet night. What could Eliza have been thinking? How could Nurse Weber have allowed it?

After a hasty breakfast Mafalda has now gone to settle the bill, finding money from wherever it is she has stashed her secret hoard. I wait by the door, cloaked and ready, my feline friend waiting with me. A moment ago, the weeping innkeeper's wife pressed a rosary upon me and would not take no for an answer.

'I am not a Catholic,' I told her, attempting to hand it back.
'It matters not. Please. I beg you.'

It was no less than an entreaty, so I took this offering and tucked it into my capacious pocket. It is a rough-hewn wooden thing, a peasant's devotional object. It must have cost her a great deal to give it to me, and that realization makes me strangely fearful. I—

Later
Castle Dracula, Transylvania, Austro-Hungarian Empire

It is late and I am extremely tired, yet sleep will not come. I tremble at every strange noise in this place, and jump at every shadow. I hope that if I set everything down on paper, I will be left clear and empty and will at last find some rest.

To continue where I left off, the cat sat bolt upright and hissed violently at the door before taking to its heels. In the doorway stood a giant of a man who wore a great thick scarf and a large black hat, a combination which conspired to hide his face.

'*Guten Morgen*,' I greeted him, relying on manners in my discomfort. 'Thank you for waiting. I'm sure we'll be ready soon.'

He inclined his head briefly. I thought perhaps he did not understand me, but before I had time to try a different language Mafalda returned with the innkeeper. Our driver turned and stalked away, leaving us to follow.

I looked back as I stepped out into the rain, and saw the old man and his wife fork their fingers at our driver's retreating back. A thrill of fear ran through me, but what could I do but go?

This final part of our journey was also the most challenging, though even the sunniest and most charming day would not have soothed my queasy soul. The roads were not good, and we made a slow way. The Count had thought to provide travelling rugs, at least, but as we went on the sky grew darker, the rain came down harder, and the wind blew with ever increasing vigour. Water dripped down the back of my neck, chilling me even more.

I wish I could describe more of the country we passed through but I could see almost nothing from my seat. I have only an impression of an endless upwards road through a sodden forest, which at once stretched away for miles and yet confined us. Mafalda did not attempt to make conversation. I lunched on a leftover piece of bread, there seeming to be no question of stopping. The miserable conditions encouraged me to huddle down as best I was able, and to see if I couldn't find relief in slumber.

I must have slept, because one moment we were surrounded by trees and the next we were drawing up into the courtyard of our final destination. The storm clouds rendered the sky almost as dark as night. I twisted around as best I could, peering out from under the hood to see the castle looming before us. Its broken blackness was outlined dimly against the sky. The battlements showed jagged in many places, and parts of the building were clearly ruined. It looked like something out of a nightmare. What kind of place had we come to? Even as I yearned for a warm fire and the solace of a hot meal, for two pins I would have stayed in the carriage in my damp dress and ridden all the way back to Sárkányerdő.

The driver handed me out, his grip like steel and just as cold. Through the gloom I could make out the far side of the large courtyard, with three or four dark round archways leading off it to who knows where. The driver unloaded our luggage, tossing our heavy trunks as if each weighed no more than a pillow. Once all our boxes sat on the flagstones, he seated himself once more and drove the calèche away across the courtyard and under one of the archways. We were left entirely alone.

Mafalda stood apart, her hands on her hips, head tilted

upwards, turning to take in the great lonely fastness before us. She squared her shoulders in a gesture I knew as well as if it were my own, and strode across the flagstones to the Medieval iron-studded wooden door. She moved as if there were no rain, no howling gale, no chill seeking her bones. To my own frustration, I marvelled at her as I hunkered along in her wake.

There was no knocker or bell so she hammered on the door with her fist. Then she waited, listening intently. As she lost patience and raised her hand once more there came the clanking sound of bolts being drawn back, and the door creaked slowly open.

In the doorway stood a squat man dressed in the unassuming garb of a lower servant, who neither spoke nor reacted to the sight before him.

'Please alert your master that the remainder of Jacobinus Réka's party has arrived,' Mafalda began, giving her aunt's name in the local fashion. 'We are in need of assistance at once, as you can see.'

The man said nothing, but instead looked back over his shoulder and stepped aside, responding to some signal I did not hear. Behind him, approaching the doorway and apparently filled with concern, was the master of the castle. He was younger than I had expected from Lady Maria's description. His hair was dark rather than white-grey, and he was clean-shaven, not moustachioed. His pale and slender face was somehow familiar, with an aquiline nose and thick brows which almost met above it. He was clad entirely in black with no trace of any colour about him, making him seem even taller than his actual six-and-then-some feet.

'Welcome to my home! Miss Lowell, I presume? Please forgive the wait; I apologize most sincerely.'

His voice was deep and resonant, and he spoke English in a formal, almost literary style. I have done my best to render it accurately.

'Count Dracula?'

By her expression I could tell that Mafalda was also surprised by the age of our host.

'Yes, I have that honour. Please, enter freely. You are most welcome to my house. The day is unpleasant and you must be in need of rest.'

He gestured broadly, revealing a coarse clutch of hairs strangely situated on the palm of his hand, which would have drawn more of my notice if I had not been in such a damp and sad stupor. Mafalda responded politely to his welcome, and stepped across the threshold. Abandoning our luggage to the ministrations of the squat manservant, I followed her inside.

'I am afraid many of my people are with their families. It is a holy day here, so I will show you to your rooms myself,' the Count was telling Mafalda.

'I apologize. If we had known we would have chosen a more convenient day to travel.'

'Please, it is no matter.'

He turned to me, and I had to suppress a tremor which was not the result of the temperature. I must have been thinking of the innkeeper's wife, and the Count's questionable reputation.

'My friend, Miss Lucy North,' Mafalda said, by way of introduction. I smiled a tight smile and made a small curtsey, hoping for some reason that the Count would not try to kiss my hand.

'You are welcome to my home, Miss North. I am delighted to have you here.'

'Thank you. May I ask if our friends arrived safely?'

'Ah! Of course, you must have been dreadfully concerned. Madam Jacobinus has been put carefully to rest, with Mrs Cartwright and her nurse to wait on her. Now, if you would follow me?'

I found myself cringing back from the Count as he moved past, as if assaulted by an unpleasant rankness though there was none. The dark clouds outside rendered the inside so dim that as we wound our way up the grand staircase I wondered at how our host could see at all. The very air was dusty, and my concern about the decayed state of the place where we were to stay only grew. How would Aunt Réka be able to recover if she had been put to bed in damp and mouldering accommodation? And what of poor Alice, too far beneath a nobleman's notice to even be mentioned? I resolved to ask Eliza at the first opportunity.

On and on we walked, through the castle's grey and sombre stone-built passages. So ancient were they that the crumbling medieval walls held brackets for flaming torches. I almost protested as he led us up a staircase with no balustrade of any kind, but my fear of being left behind propelled me on. Eventually, the Count stopped outside a solid oak door which gave a grinding crack as he pushed it open. I have to say, I was pleasantly surprised to find a bright and charming suite of rooms, laid out along a corridor on the southern side of the castle.

The Count showed us to the main salon where a female attendant of the same build and appearance as her brother-servant awaited us. Tall windows looked out to the east and south, and the walls seemed to grow from the great mountainous precipice on which the whole edifice stood. The views stretched away to a horizon where mountain peaks met wide-open skies with roiling storm clouds, and for a moment the dramatic beauty of the sight burned away all else.

'I hope you will be most comfortable,' Count Dracula said with a grand, sweeping gesture. 'I will leave you to settle yourselves.'

I thanked him politely, and tried not to show my relief as he left.

The attendant served coffee from an elegant coffee pot in the Ottoman design. I sat and sipped quietly, relishing the warmth.

Mafalda demanded of the servant that a fire be made and lit as soon as possible. Summer in the Carpathians feels to me a lot like autumn anywhere else.

By and by we were warmed. Mafalda did not speak to me, doubtless vexed by my ignoring her last night. And if our silence seemed odd to the servant I can't say I cared. When our cups were empty, the woman showed us to our own rooms. All of these branched off one side of the main passage and therefore all looked out onto the same spectacular vista. Our belongings were already present, so I suppose there must be some other access point to this suite than the one by which we entered. I imagine antediluvian places such as this are filled with secret passages. My bedroom, or rather, my chamber, was warm and comfortable. A great four-poster bed with thick curtains to keep out the cold was a welcome sight, and everything a lady might need for her toilette was already laid out. With no Alice and certainly no Mafalda to undress me, I suffered the attentions of the stoic attendant. I attempted to speak to her in every language at my disposal but none drew a verbal response, though I believe she understood my German. I would have liked a bath but I suspect it would have taken hours to prepare. At least I was able to dry off and put on fresh clothing.

I asked the woman for a mirror, thinking I would try to manage my own hair, but she shook her head and scurried out as if I had said something terrible. I did the best I could, then sat down on the bed, not knowing quite what to do with myself. I leaned against the carved bedpost, and I believe I must have slept again.

I awoke to a knock at the door. My neck and shoulder ached from my awkward position, suggesting that I'd been there for some time.

'Come in!' I called, instantly regretting it in case my visitor was Mafalda.

'Lucy! You look worn out. Are you quite well? Would you rather not dine?'

It was Eliza, cheerful and full of solicitude.

'Yes, yes, I'm perfectly well. I fell asleep.' I rubbed my aching neck as I hauled myself to my feet. 'How are you? It must have been a hard journey to make in the dark.'

'I'm absolutely fine. I feel very refreshed by the change of air.'

'How is Aunt Réka? And Alice?'

'Both resting, and being well cared for by the nurse. I've been helping in what little ways I can.'

I sighed with relief. I hadn't realized just how worried I'd been until that moment. All of a sudden Eliza twitched, turning as if in response to a summons.

'Ah! Lucy, I think I hear our host.'

I had heard nothing, but in the interests of being a good guest I pulled myself together and followed her out into the corridor.

Eliza had been correct. Count Dracula smiled a warm and amiable smile as we approached, though it didn't quite reach his eyes. He gave a small formal bow.

'Miss North, how charming you look.'

'Thank you, that's very kind.'

I made my best attempt at a gracious and ladylike nod of acknowledgement before turning to Eliza.

'I wonder if I might go and sit with Alice for a while? She's worked so hard for us all, I feel as if I ought to.'

'Not just now, she's fast asleep. Tomorrow, I daresay. I was just making my excuses to Count Dracula, as I won't be joining you for dinner. I promised Nurse Weber some relief.'

'You have a good heart, madam.'

The Count bent over her hand and kissed it. It was a gentle

and chivalrous exchange but I felt that same strange distaste as before, and had to fight the urge to back away. I shook the feeling off as a clean and tidy Mafalda appeared, and we processed to dinner after our host.

I had expected to be taken to some kind of great baronial hall, but in fact dinner was served in the salon where we had taken our coffee. A fire roared in the grate, and all was well-lit comfort.

Dinner itself was a marvel. A fantastic array of dishes was laid out before us, each more delicious than the last. The Count had dined earlier, he said, but he sat with us anyway and made conversation on the subject of our travels. Well, he made conversation with Mafalda. I may as well have been a wood carving for all I added to the discussion.

As the meal finally came to a close, the conversation turned to England.

'I have always wanted to visit your country, Miss Lowell. I have often thought that the people of a nation that covers just half an island yet which came to rule a third of the world must be remarkable indeed.'

'I'm not sure the English are remarkable, exactly,' Mafalda replied. 'I might say they are determined.'

'The way you speak, it sounds as if you do not count yourself among their number.'

'I am half English,' Mafalda said, shrugging, 'but we are a long way from England.'

'Indeed, a man need only to look at you to know the rest of your origins. The shape of your face, your colouring – blood will out, as I believe the English say.' Where another woman would have dropped her gaze and blushed, Mafalda met his eyes without false modesty. The Count nodded as he appraised her, briefly enough not to be rude and yet still slightly too long for my own jealous comfort.

'Miss Lowell, if you would do me the honour of accompanying me, there is something I would show you.'

I trailed behind, though both seemed to have forgotten my existence. Count Dracula led us from the well-appointed suite and out into the cold walkways of the rest of the castle. The chill of centuries had sunk into the stone, and I shivered to think of all that might have happened here over the years. The Count carried a lamp of an antique design, and this was the only light. Mafalda followed him closely and I hurried to keep up, afraid to be lost or left behind. We went down one staircase and up another, even passing through something like that great hall where I had imagined we would dine. I could see nothing of it in the gloom, and was left only with the impression of a vast echoing space. I wondered where the Count had his quarters, as these grand rooms were clearly unused.

After more staircases, we entered a long passageway with windows on one side which, as far as I could tell, looked out over the courtyard from a great height. I glanced over my shoulder, and saw that our footsteps had left marks in the undisturbed dust of long years. The thought made me long for the warmth of the salon.

This passage ended in an iron-banded wooden door of the same style as every door in this place. The Count drew out a large key and fitted it into the rusted lock. The key turned with a hideous screeching noise, and I flinched. Our host pushed open the door with some effort, and stood back. Mafalda passed through into the obscurity beyond. When it came my turn to approach the threshold, I looked up into Count Dracula's face as I went by, wearing my best polite and smiling mask. The lamplight threw strange shadows across his visage, turning his eyes a gleaming crimson. He returned my smile, revealing teeth that were bright white and strangely pointed. My heart rose into my throat. The world slowed, and shrank to nothing but my human fear of darkness and oblivion. I might as well have been a mouse cornered by a cat, trapped under that red stare, that grim smile.

'Could you bring the lamp nearer so I might see a little better?' Mafalda called from inside. The spell was broken, and the demon-visage turned into a pleasant expression of generous hospitality.

'Of course, Miss Lowell. Miss North, if you please.'

I moved forwards, doing my utmost to rid myself of my superstitious dread. The Count held the lamp high, allowing it to cast its light far enough that I could see we stood in a long gallery which vanished into distant murk.

The walls were lined with portraits of varying antiquity, stretching away and back down the years. As far as I could tell the most recent was several hundred years old. I regarded the one nearest me, stepping closer to squint at it. A knight in armour practically scowled out of his frame, a thick moustache and stern gaze combining to give his face a furious appearance. I was glad not to have met such a man in life.

Mafalda wandered here and there within the circle of the light, before calling that she would like to see more and might we not go a little further?

'Indeed,' the Count replied. 'If you will allow me, I would like to show you that which I brought you here to see.'

Mafalda and I followed him in silence. I could not help glancing right and left at the long-dead men who adorned the ancient walls. I studiously avoided Mafalda's gaze in case my resolve shattered and I turned to her for comfort in my mammalian fear.

'Does your own portrait hang here?' Mafalda asked as we moved so far away from the door that it vanished into the black.

'Sadly, I have found my likeness is never captured to my satisfaction. Here we are, Miss Lowell, if you would care to look?'

There she was, gazing haughtily out at us. Her black hair flowed down over her shoulders, her head adorned with a circlet of blazing green emeralds chosen to match the rich fabric of her attire. That aquiline nose, those thick dark brows, that pale skin with the lightest and faintest touch of golden freckles – all were present. She was Mafalda in every respect but for the colour of her eyes.

My beloved, for such she still is, God help me, gasped as she took in her doppelgänger.

'Who is she?'

'This lady was my near ancestress, and I suspect was yours too.'

I shuddered as I realized why the Count had looked familiar. In this man who so unsettled me, I had seen the echoes of the face I loved the most.

'I hardly know what to say. What was her name?'

'She was called Anna. Her father ruled this land, for a while. She married a distant cousin, a Dracula, and held this castle while he was away at war. When the Turks came, many of her men fled but she stood firm. When it was at last clear that all was lost she hurled herself from the battlements rather than be taken away into bondage. She was a great and noble lady, sprung from our rich earth and enriching it still further by the blood of her sacrifice.'

It unsettled me to hear suicide spoken of in such terms, but Mafalda was not of my mind. She nodded slowly, thoughtfully.

'What else could she have done? A life of slavery is no life at all.'

'You are barely English,' the Count told Mafalda with great satisfaction. 'You see things as I do.'

There was something in the cast of his face that once again put me in mind of a great cat, licking its lips in anticipation of an excellent meal. Mafalda did not appear to feel the same, meeting his eyes with no trace of fear.

'Thank you. I appreciate the honour you do me in sharing the tales of your family. I must set myself to tracing my own lineage, to find where our lines converge.'

'My library here is extensive, and contains a great deal of the history of the Draculas. It is entirely at your disposal whenever you please.'

'Tomorrow morning, perhaps?'

'Just as you wish.'

He bowed courteously, deeply.

The return to our chambers through the dark and the dust was just as long, and was made all the more disturbing by the howling of wolves outside. I realize now that for me to have heard them at all they must have come extremely close, or the noise of the storm would have drowned them out. What manner of beasts would come so near to human habitation?

No, no, I blame the wife of the innkeeper for putting ideas in my head, which the strangeness of our surroundings has only exacerbated. What happened today, really? I had a long and tiring journey. I slept at odd times, leading to a feeling of disorientation. I was a guest at a pleasant dinner, our host took us to view his portrait gallery, the way was rather dark, and the weather was particularly stormy. Nothing else!

My hand aches from holding my pen, and my candle is burning low. Despite what I tell myself, I don't yet want to extinguish its comforting light. I could go and crawl into Mafalda's bed and put her between myself and my fears, but I will sleep cold and alone for the rest of my life and what's tonight in the face of that?

Lucy North's journal
Friday, 22nd August 1884
Castle Dracula, Transylvania, Austro-Hungarian Empire

A night of nightmares has not helped my mood. The storm outside continues to rage unabated. Surely it ought to have blown itself out by now?

Count Dracula has had to absent himself, leaving a note in the salon pleading matters of business and with directions to the library included for Mafalda. He seems not to be terribly bothered that his other servants have not returned from their day's holiday, though I suppose the weather is to blame for that. In the absence of poor Alice I was attended well enough by the silent maid who dressed me, served me at breakfast, and then vanished.

Having nothing else to do, I have taken up a station in the library. I would rather be of some use in the sickrooms, wherever they might be, but Eliza conveyed orders from Nurse Weber that neither Aunt Réka nor Alice are to be disturbed. She left, yawning, after delivering said orders, saying she would rest while she had the opportunity.

I find that I do not want to be alone any more than I must be, so here I am, even Mafalda's company being preferable to my own. I have perched myself on some sort of medieval recamier. It is not padded, so I have liberated some aged tapestry cushions to give me a little comfort. The room itself is smaller than I had imagined, situated in a wing of the castle further to the left than our guest suite, and one storey higher. It is accessed only via one central octagonal chamber, perhaps arranged so years ago to keep precious and ancient books safe in the event of an attack on the castle.

The walls are lined with bookshelves reaching almost to the ceiling. Tall, pointed windows are set at intervals along one thick wall. Mafalda sits at a great table in the centre of the room, working methodically through a pile of leather-bound volumes, attempting to find her familial link with the Dracula lineage. There are books in many languages, and if I could settle to it I might find one I could read. Instead, I sit and write and flick my gaze up as often as I dare. I ought not to be watching her and yet I find I can't help myself. We will never again be together for so long, so what can I do?

I should use this time to plan what I will do when I return to England, how I will survive, what explanation I will give to Sir Gerald and Lady Maria for leaving their home. I will need to speak to Sir Gerald in any case, to get a full and current picture of my investments. I am glad he has been so kind as to manage them for me, as I wouldn't have had the slightest idea where to begin. I wonder what—

Later
The maidservant came and whispered to Mafalda, leaving her grinning from ear to ear.

'Apparently "the Master" has a gift for me,' she announced as she stood. 'Please excuse me.'

When she returned, I could not have dragged my eyes away from her if I had cared to try. She looked for all the world as if she had stepped out of the portrait in the gallery. The dress, in the same dark green as her eyes, was trimmed around the neck and waist with fine gold knotwork, and gripped her hips in a manner that our modern era would find scandalous. The sleeves were snug to the elbow then dropped to a long and elegant point. Mafalda might have been the queen of this wild land, centuries ago.

'Do I look quite ridiculous?' she asked, in the full knowledge that she did not. Mafalda spun, the dress swirling as it followed her movements.

'Do you think it's a gift?' I asked, ignoring her question. 'Or did the Count merely mean to lend it?'

'I don't know. He left no note. I wish there were a looking-glass somewhere, but apparently he won't have them.'

Her beauty broke my heart. If she had asked me again in that moment, I'd have abandoned every principle and every hope and agreed to any plan she pleased, just so I might never be apart from her ever again. She twirled, laughing, hair spilling out behind her, delighted and delighting.

I am hollow, full of nothing but lasts. Our last night together, our last kiss, our last moments of loving and being loved. I was not sensible of their finality, but now every tiny thing might be its own last. The last time she speaks to me, the last time she smiles at me, the last time she laughs in my presence. I see these moments as the memories they will be when I return to them over and over in whatever future awaits me.

'I'm sure we're all vain enough,' I said flatly, turning away.

Alice Smith's commonplace book
Friday, 22nd August 1884
Castle Dracula, Transylvania, Austro-Hungarian Empire

The Lord is my shepherd; I shall not want. He maketh me to lie down in green pastures: he leadeth me beside the still waters. He restoreth my soul: he leadeth me in the paths of righteousness for his name's sake. Yea, though I walk through the valley of the shadow of death, I will fear no evil: for thou art with me. Art thou with me? My crucifix is gone, I think ripped off my neck. Lord, hast thou forsaken me?

I don't know where my visions end and this hell begins. I've got to remember, I've got to confess and die shriven. I remember the inn, I remember a horrible dark foreboding and saying we ought to turn back, I remember my mistress staring at me horribly close and a pinching at the edge of my mind, I remember a tisane that tasted bad, I remember my mistress's grinning face as I fainted away.

Then this room, cold and dark, held tight. A stink of death and decay and the earth of the grave, choking me. My head forced back, my throat bared to the demon that used to be my good and kind lady.

In the *vampyr*'s grip, I saw and I saw and I saw. I saw men in foreign clothes, nails hammered into their heads. I saw howling people boiled alive. I saw a forest made from tall wooden stakes, skewered human being after skewered human being dying slowly and in agony. I saw, I felt, all the pleasure he took in their pain, their writhings stretching away as far as the eye could see. I saw the woman I now know was Baroness Tolvay, and I realized with fresh terror that this was the monster who'd chased her to her death. *Sancta Maria, Mater Dei, ora pro nobis peccatoribus, nunc et in hora mortis nostrae.*

I saw Madam Jacobinus through his eyes, at a gathering where people waved banners and spoke of revolution. She was animated in a way I'd never seen her; passionate, full of life and nationalist fervour. The monster saw his own family in her face and knew he had found something he could use. In stalking her he found Miss Lowell and delighted in her determination, her calculation, her attitude of command. She was perfect, though she might have run from him when she did not understand. Yes, yes, he would have them both and they would serve him and his great purpose!

As I shook in his grip, tears streaming down my face, I saw my mistress as she was when he first noticed her at the railway station in Buda-Pesth. He wanted her for her beauty; he saw her purity and her goodness and thrilled at destroying both and making her like himself. He took her longing for children, her generosity, her selflessness and turned those qualities to his own ends, choosing her to mother his unholy spawn.

I tried to pray, as she sank her teeth into my throat. I tried to think of Our Lord and Saviour and to prepare myself to meet Him.

'Foul!' My mistress turned away, gagging, mouth red with my lifeblood. 'It tastes vile.'

'Humanity has an infinite variety. There are others you will like.'

'Thank goodness, because I refuse to take another sip of this one.'

'Leave her here. She might be of use later. Not everyone is so particular.'

Then they were gone. Vanished, in a haze of dust that swooped towards and around the door.

Blackness and nothing, then cold and fear and this bare prison cell. A drip drip drip comes from somewhere, and that's all there is to wet my lips.

God forgive me for what I've done, what I've left undone, and above all what I've failed to do. It's my fault, my fault, my most grievous fault. Help me keep my sanity, Lord, so I might hold you near me at the end.

Lucy North's journal
Saturday, 23rd August 1884, morning
Castle Dracula, Transylvania, Austro-Hungarian Empire

I have awoken tucked into my comfortable bed, in a fresh nightdress with my hair neatly braided, and with no recollection of how I got here. I did drink wine at dinner, but only two glasses so an excess of alcohol is no explanation. I am trying and trying to fix on the last thing I can remember, but it slips away each time. I think the Count was there, and Eliza, but . . . Perhaps I am going about it wrong, and ought to begin earlier.

I remember that Mafalda and I dined alone in the salon, the squat maid having summoned us from the library to dress and then shepherded us along to eat as if we were her chickens. It was a good dinner, hearty and warming, and not in keeping with the frosty atmosphere I was desperately endeavouring to maintain. It was not until coffee was poured that Mafalda attempted to speak to me, leaning back in her chair and looking at me over the rim of the silver cup.

'Lucy, do you like it here?'

'What do you mean, here?'

'I mean Hungary. Would you live here, if you could?'

'I don't think so. I'd rather go home.'

'It has everything that pleases you. Beautiful countryside, a little money going a long way. Rural children in need of a schoolmistress, even. Do you not think?'

I frowned, not liking where this line of questioning might lead. Fortunately, I was saved from having to answer by Eliza's happy arrival.

'I have good news,' she beamed, her grin toothy. 'Mafalda, your aunt is awake and asking for you.'

'That *is* good news,' Mafalda replied, rising at once from the table.

'What about Alice?' I interjected, rather rudely I now recognize. 'Can I see her?'

'Perhaps in the morning.'

It discomfits me to think how dismissive Eliza has become

of Alice, a young girl so far from home. I might speak with her about it when things are easier.

Eliza led us up to a large chamber somewhere above the salon, where Aunt Réka lay abed alone. In the soft candlelight she looked almost well, though not even the kindness of the gentle flickering glow could hide the deep hollows in her cheeks or the withdrawing of her gums, making her teeth seem peculiarly prominent.

'Girls, my dear girls,' she said, holding out both of her hands. 'How sweet you are to see me.'

'Of course, Aunt. I'm sorry not to have come sooner, but the nurse wouldn't allow it.'

'The nurse?' Aunt Réka blinked, screwing up her eyes as if trying to recall.

'Yes, Nurse Weber, who has been caring for you,' Eliza said gently. 'Her memory struggles,' she murmured. 'You must not think anything of it. She has had to take a great deal of medicine. Nurse Weber warned this could happen.'

'Will she recover?' I asked. 'Tell me, honestly.'

Eliza glanced at Mafalda, leaning over the bedside and speaking softly.

'Nurse Weber couldn't say,' she whispered. Her breath tickled my ear, and I took a step back from the uncomfortable closeness. 'Well,' she continued, loudly enough for Mafalda to hear, 'I will leave you for the moment. I must rest.'

I bid her goodnight then hovered uncertainly, unsure if I ought to leave Mafalda and Aunt Réka alone. Mafalda saw my wavering, and motioned me to a chair by her side.

'Now, Aunt,' she said in the most kindly tone I have ever heard her use, 'would you like me to read to you?'

'No, no. Not now. I have something I must tell you.' Aunt

Réka's breath came laboured, the worst I have heard it during all her illnesses. 'You are good girls, innocent, do you see?'

Mafalda shot me the quickest of glances.

'What do you mean, Aunt?'

'If you were to forgive me, it would be almost as good as a priest.'

'Goodness, what do you want a priest for?'

'To confess. I must confess. I have done such a thing, such a terrible thing . . .'

'I'm no priest, Aunt, and you mustn't exert yourself by talking about sad things long past.' Not so long past, I thought, if she meant the deaths of her husband and the Baroness. 'We could pray with you, couldn't we, Lucy? We could pray with you.'

'But my rosary, I have no rosary . . .' Aunt Réka's fingers clutched at Mafalda's strong hands, seeking the beads that must have been left behind somewhere, abandoned.

'Here,' I said, reaching into my pocket for the innkeeper's wife's parting gift. 'I will count for you.'

The unfamiliar Latin words snaked around me, each rough bead dropping through my fingers. I did not know my faithless Mafalda knew the prayer so well, reciting in a clear voice while Aunt Réka whispered. Time passed as it does here, a fluid thing. I might have fallen into some sort of trance, perhaps the very same as saints of old who thought it a holy blessing. I suppose that is in part its intention.

Aunt Réka slipped into sleep as Mafalda chanted on, the candlelight haloing her head and giving her black hair a golden sheen. Gently, slowly, she let her voice die quiet. Not looking up, she reached for my hand. God help me I took it, the rosary entwining around our entwined fingers.

'I must find a way forward,' she said, at last turning her green eyes on me. 'I must find a way forward for us. I cannot be without you. Will you not bend? Even a little?'

The trance still on me, her sainted face lit with pain, I answered truthfully.

'I cannot share you with another.'

She nodded, deliberately, thoughtfully.

'Well, then.'

Here it is, the last thing I recollect with any clarity. I must not have seen the Count after all. I must have dreamed it. If I puzzle on the mystery, I can shunt the pain aside a little longer. Whatever Mafalda might try to do, she is promised elsewhere, and so? All she can do is convince and cajole me to turn against myself, and I never, ever will.

Alice Smith's commonplace book
Saturday, 23rd August 1884, early morning
Castle Dracula, Transylvania, Austro-Hungarian Empire

I pray for the soul of Nurse Weber, ashes to ashes, dust to dust, whose earthly form lies broken over there. She was still alive when the demon threw her in here. Her breaths left and left and left. Throat all but torn open, chunks of flesh missing from her arms and legs and one of each broken. She whimpered as she died. My God, my God, why has thou forsaken me?

'Will it always be so?' My mistress's voice. 'Did I do it wrong, when I turned her? Did I make her so frenzied as to break a body like this?'

'She will calm enough, in time,' the *vampyr* said. 'The frenzy serves my purpose.'

'Ought we not to keep her chained, for now?'

Then the voices faded, and now only the dead are here.

Lucy North's journal
Saturday, 23rd August 1884, afternoon
Castle Dracula, Transylvania, Austro-Hungarian Empire

I do not understand why I am so tired. All my limbs feel leaden. Eliza has been behaving strangely but I am too dense to say how, or even why I think so. She came to the library where I was sitting alone on the recamier, staring out at the rain-soaked countryside. She was looking for Mafalda. I told her the truth, that I have not seen Mafalda since last night, not even at meals.

'Are you quite sure?'

'Yes, I am. I . . .' I attempted to order my thoughts. 'I suppose she must be with Aunt Réka?'

'She is not.' Eliza's tone was clipped, short.

'Perhaps I should go and visit her, then.' I made to rise, but Eliza was suddenly before me, pushing me back down into my seat.

'No. Madam Jacobinus is resting.'

'Alice, then? How is Alice? It has been days, I—'

'No.' Eliza's grip was iron. 'Nurse Weber is with her. Visitors are not permitted.'

'I could write to her family, then? To tell them she is not well?'

Eliza leaned down, putting her face close to mine. I have felt so distant from her that it is as if another has taken on my friend's form, her skin stretched over some new facsimile. This uncanny set of features gazed at me unblinking, and smiled an unfamiliar familiar smile.

'You're sweet to think of it. Are you not too tired for such a task, though? You look exhausted, perhaps it's better you rest.'

It was all I could do to nod, and lay down upon my uncomfortable couch. Hours have passed, I think, judging by the light or what there is left of it. Should I go to my room? No, I will stay here a little longer until I shake off this lethargy.

Later, night

Did I dream? I must have dreamed, I must have. In my dream I was here in the library, asleep but somehow seeing. Mafalda came in, lantern aloft, dressed in the green dress gifted to her by the Count. Her expression was determined, resolute. The Count himself followed her, moving with inhuman grace.

'You are certain?' he asked her as they approached me where I lay.

'I am. It is my price.'

She knelt and kissed me lightly on the lips, a promise I didn't understand.

I must leave this place. It plays tricks on my mind, and exhausts my soul. Come morning, I will speak to the Count about returning home.

PART TEN

Sir John Seward's personal diary
Saturday, 21st February 1903
Littlemore Hospital, Oxfordshire

It is just before midnight. My clothing is rumpled and stinks of pipe smoke. My eyes are swollen, and I am tired and heartsick. Together and separately, Harker and I have been making our slow way through the documents provided by Mrs Lakatos. It is painful work, and it has forced me to revisit the worst and most horrifying moments of my own life.

Mrs Lakatos must have worked diligently and for a long time to collect this material. She thought to provide a typescript of the most salient parts of this tragic narrative, and has even made translations where necessary. She is a rare calibre of person, to whom many owe much.

My heart breaks for Lady Lowell. Her deep affection for another woman may be officially regarded by the medical profession as a species of illness, but having read her own words I cannot believe it is the case. I too have loved deeply in my life, and I know true love when I see it. I suspect Sir Joseph is unaware of his wife's former attachment and it is certainly not my business to inform him. It seems he knows nothing of the truth of this entire matter, and both Harker and I judge it best that he is kept in the dark.

I have wept for all these women as I have come to know them. To read of their human lives, filled with human joy and human sadness, human goodness and human cruelty, breaks open all the old wounds I had thought healed within myself. My own griefs are exposed and raw once more, and now I also weep for myself.

Sir John Seward's personal diary
Sunday, 22nd February 1903
Littlemore Hospital, Oxfordshire

The day proper began when Dr Knight came to the door. Mrs Stevens the housekeeper showed her in, telling her in a very stagey and easily overheard whisper:

'Something is amiss, madam. Try not to be alarmed.'

I think it's safe to say that when Dr Knight saw Harker and I, unslept and unshaved, looking grim as death and surrounded by papers, she was indeed quite alarmed. We rose when she entered, and I found that I was swaying slightly. Dr Knight stood in the doorway, beautiful and modest in her Sunday best. Her radiant hair was pinned up under her hat. I noticed that her eye was healing well, even while her face twisted in shock and concern.

'What on earth—?'

'I did warn you, madam.'

'Mrs Stevens,' Dr Knight said, removing her gloves, 'I think you should bring coffee immediately, and tell the cook to put a good breakfast together.'

'Yes, madam, at once.'

She closed the door behind her, tutting as she left.

'I'm so sorry, Beatrice. Things are in a dreadful state.'

'Not just "things" by the look of it. What's happened? Have you had bad news?'

'No, or rather, yes, but—'

Harker interrupted me with a politeness I'd quite forgotten.

'Dr Knight, I presume? Please forgive Jack for not making the proper introductions. Jonathan Harker.'

He stuck out his hand. Doubtless Dr Knight wished she had remained gloved.

'I'm pleased to make your acquaintance, Mr Harker.'

'Likewise. Now that we are introduced, I must ask you to excuse me. My wife would be furious to hear that I'd been seen in such disarray by a lady. Jack, I'll order breakfast in my room and leave you to it.'

He left, and I could not think of a thing to say. I knew I had to take Dr Knight into our confidence but how to begin?

'I was going to ask if you wanted to walk to church with me this morning,' she said, breaking the silence. 'Looking at you, I suspect not. It would be wise if you were to sit, you're pitching from side to side quite alarmingly.'

Obediently, I sat. Dr Knight went to the window and threw it open wide. I gulped down the influx of fresh air as if it were a tonic.

'John, I'm worried. This is all very unlike you.'

Her use of my Christian name warmed my heart.

'I want to tell you everything, but I warn you it's going to seem very far-fetched. It has to do with Lady Lowell.'

'Lady Lowell? I thought you'd had some personal disaster.'

'I . . . We . . . Let's say that it seems Lady Lowell and I have a sort of shared history, a similar event which dramatically affected us both. In learning the truth of her experience, I have been forced to confront my own. It has been . . . challenging.'

Dr Knight frowned. 'I'm not sure I understand.'

'I apologize. I'm not explaining myself at all well. Perhaps it would be best if you could read the history of which I speak.'

'Is that what all this is?' She gestured to the room at large, papers and notebooks piled on every surface.

'Partly. Mrs Lakatos has collated a record of all that pertains to Lady Lowell's illness. The rest is the report that Mr Harker's wife put together and typed out, detailing my own, well, *our* own dealings with . . . with . . .'

In the face of her curious and concerned gaze, I faltered. I could not speak the dread name to her, not yet.

'You must excuse me. I'm not in a fit state. I think it best if you just read.'

I hung my head. Gently, she laid her hand on my arm.

'Alright, I will. Go and rest. We'll talk again later.'

I did as I was told. Mrs Stevens brought me breakfast on a tray, and after eating I slept, dreamlessly, for several hours. I bathed and I changed, and at least my physical form feels much improved. As for my mental state, that is another matter.

It is now almost evening and I must go and face both Dr Knight and my fear of her disbelief. I hope against hope that I have not lost her respect or her good opinion, because without those I do not know what I would do.

Sir John Seward's personal diary
Monday, 23rd February 1903
Littlemore Hospital, Oxfordshire

I will resume where I left off, with the events of yesterday evening. When I was suitably refreshed, I went downstairs and found Dr Knight in the dining room. Harker was seated opposite her, and it seemed I had interrupted some sort of interview.

'So you think that was why he chose Whitby?' Dr Knight was asking as I entered.

'It makes sense. There are other ports nearer to London, but because it was known to his . . . that is, to Mrs Cartwright, he landed there instead.'

'Not to mention the fact that a ship full of dead men landing at Dover would have attracted a great deal more notice.'

'Indeed. Ah, there you are, Jack. Dr Knight has been interrogating me.'

'So I see.' I took a seat at the head of the table. 'Have you read it? All of it?'

She nodded. 'I have.'

'And what are your conclusions?'

Dr Knight took a deep, measured breath.

'If I read as a woman of science, then on the face of it this is a completely fantastical tale.'

Harker and I glanced at each other. Had I made an error in judgement in sharing all this with her? Had I been blinded by my feelings?

'However, if two men such as yourselves claim it as truth, then it deserves to be taken seriously and subjected to the proper methods as far as possible. Looking at what we know of Lady Lowell's case, everything does indeed hang together. But then again, if I read as a human being, as a Christian, it horrifies me. The idea that such dark things, such unnatural things, have existed in the world, well, I don't want to believe it.'

'But you do believe it?' I found myself holding my breath as I awaited her answer.

'What I have read in both accounts fits in with the facts as I know them. So yes, I believe it.'

'I'm glad to hear you say so. As glad as I am sorry that I had to share it with you.'

Our eyes met, and I saw that behind her composure she was struggling to hold herself together. There was some quality to her expression which gave her away, a sense of deep emotion being barely controlled.

Harker, may all gods bless him, is a perceptive man. Marriage will do that to a person. 'Do you know, I might see about a plate of sandwiches.'

As soon as he had left the room Dr Knight dropped her pen and put her face in her hands. I moved to sit beside her, letting her lean into my shoulder as she wept. I spoke to her as soothingly as I could. I am aware of the shock and the fear that follows the revelation of the world being not as we had always supposed. It is not so ordered or so ruled by reason, and we are not so safe as we would like ourselves to be.

Dr Knight managed to collect herself after an admirably short time, though this sort of grief is a long and drawn-out thing and will take a fair while to truly resolve. Harker tactfully stayed away for a good half hour or so, returning bearing sandwiches only when all was well. Thus fuelled, Harker spoke of his own healing after being imprisoned at Castle Dracula, the hope being that this will help Dr Knight and I plan a path forward for Lady Lowell's treatment. Dr Knight's specialist knowledge of treating female sufferers of trauma will inform us further. Armed with all this, plus my own painfully won expertise, I am very hopeful for the future.

But first, we all agreed, we must meet with Mrs Lakatos once more.

Alice Smith's commonplace book
Sunday, 24th August 1884
Castle Dracula, Transylvania, Austro-Hungarian Empire

[Editor's Note: The following material is deeply distressing, more so than what you've already read. Please be prepared.]

Knowledge is better than memory. That's what they say, isn't it? Written down I'll know what's real. Not a vision, not a nightmare – real. Write it down, Alice, write it down.

Nurse Weber is over there in the corner. I covered her with an old sack. I tried to give her some dignity. Then screams, from somewhere not far away. Miss North, crying out, over and over.

'Mafalda! Mafalda!' High-pitched keening, grief-struck.

The demon that used to be my mistress answered her, but too low for me to hear.

'We were supposed to be safe!' Sobbing, howling. 'Where is the nurse? Can a doctor not be got, for God's sake?'

Miss Lowell must have been bitten, God save her. Miss North doesn't know the nature of this place. She doesn't know she's in Hell.

I thought this was a cellar, but if I'm close enough to hear Miss North then it can't be. A storeroom, then, or an old servant's chamber? Escape. Could I escape? The door is heavy, and locked, and bolted. There's no escape. I shouldn't lie to myself. I should face what is.

Weeping, my own, for myself and for Miss North, and Miss Lowell, and Nurse Weber. It must be Madam Jacobinus who is the frenzied one, who tore Nurse Weber nearly limb from limb. I'd throw up from fear if there was anything left in my stomach.

That keening, on and on. What use is your cursed gift to me now, Lord?

Later

Write it down, write it all down. Make it solid, remember, remember it's real.

The creature that was Mrs Cartwright came for me. She dragged me from my makeshift cell, out across a spiral staircase's landing, and through a hidden door on the other side. She hauled me down a stone passageway, pulling my arm almost out of its socket, then pushed me ahead of her through the only open doorway.

On a tapestry-covered bed, in a room full of grand old furniture, Miss Lowell was laid out like a corpse. Her skin was ashen, and two bleeding bites marked her throat. I cried out when I saw her. Quick as the Devil, the *vampyr* stood before me, gripping my body close with one arm and holding my chin in his free hand, staring hard into my eyes.

'She does not wake-sleep,' he hissed. 'Woman, why is this?'

'I don't know, my lord,' Mrs Cartwright told him. 'I can't make her. I had to use milk of the poppy to stop her mouth on the way here.'

As the Count's gaze bored into mine, I saw more and worse than before. Innocent people torn from their loved ones and put to his purpose, made into his children and marching out into the world, my mistress smiling and smiling as their army of offspring covered all Creation in darkness.

I felt the Count's mind, sharp and stark and *wrong*, pinching at mine, poking, searching for a way in. When he couldn't find one he looked at me with his head tilted, red eyes unblinking like a lizard.

'Hm.'

With no warning, he threw me aside as if I weighed no more than a feather. I fell on the stone floor, hard. The pain and the shock of it knocked the breath out of me. I stayed there, curled up in a ball, feeling my eyeballs all but bulging out of my skull.

Through all this, Miss North was sat by the bed in what Count Dracula called the wake-sleep, staring straight ahead. Her face was puffy with crying, but tears were drying fast on her cheeks. She was completely blank.

'Is this one all there is?' the Count asked, pointing at Miss North.

'Yes, though we can still use the other.' She flicked her head towards me. 'Madam Jacobinus got to the servants.'

'Unfortunate. She is contained now?'

'She is. We won't be disturbed.' Mrs Cartwright gestured to Miss Lowell where she lay, unmoving. 'Will it be . . . easy, my lord?'

The *vampyr* seemed to think about the question.

'It is always easy for me. You mean to ask if the turning will be for her as it was for you. It will not. You did not choose; I chose for you. She chose for herself.' He looked down at Miss Lowell with an expression of such pride, such twisted love. 'She is flesh of my flesh and blood of my blood like the other, but her choice makes a difference.' He stroked Miss Lowell's unconscious face. 'Wise, wise daughter of my House.'

Count Dracula pulled open his shirt, and with one long, sharp nail he tore the skin across his chest. As the blood began to ooze, he lifted Miss Lowell and pressed her mouth to the open wound. To my shame I just lay there, a coward shivering in my own fear, as he performed the unholy baptism. I don't know if Miss Lowell woke or slept or was held in the same trance as Miss North, but I saw her throat work as she swallowed the thick black-red liquid. My mistress wept for joy, holding her hands clasped before her face, every inch a proud mother. She rushed forward when the thing was done, as the Count set Miss Lowell down on her bloodied bed.

Mrs Cartwright mopped her brow, as if Miss Lowell were her very own child.

'How long will it take, my lord?'

'For her, not long.'

In a disgusting celebration, the *vampyr* took my lady in his arms and kissed her with his red-stained mouth. It was lustful, wanton, the sort of kiss that would have been an insult in her human life. His hands with their long fingernails grasped at her, clawing and grabbing. I think he'd have taken her then and there like the beast he is if it weren't for a sudden sound from the bed.

Miss Lowell had woken up, coughing and retching, turning onto her side and spitting oily liquid out onto the floor as if she was drowning. I saw her eyes, mad with fear or pain or both, all their tiny veins broken, turning the whites bright red. I don't know if the horror of it dawned on her then as she spluttered and scratched at her ruined throat, her body convulsing as it tried to reject the evil inside it. The Count looked on, waiting, until she couldn't fight any more. He knelt by the bed and tenderly, so tenderly, he pushed back her wild black hair. He took her face gently in his hands and smiled a broad and bloody smile. Then he broke her neck with a snap.

Lucy North's journal
Monday, 25th August 1884
Castle Dracula, Transylvania, Austro-Hungarian Empire

Some unfortunate souls, I have read, have a condition whereby they awaken in the night unable to move. Paralysed, they see all manner of ghoulish shapes and evil beings that are not truly there. I wish and will, with all my might, that this is such a thing.

I am asleep in my bed somewhere in England, Mafalda lying next to me. I have not spent long hours scratching desperately at my locked bedroom door, breaking my nails and splintering my palms, screaming myself raw for help. My throat does not ache with two deep puncture wounds, which ooze and drip down onto the collar of my nightdress. I do not now sit on an ancient creaking bed wrapped in a coverlet older than my grandmother, shaking with fear. No, Mafalda lies next to me, warm and safe, not somewhere in the castle, bitten and poisoned as I have been. Alive, she is alive, she must be alive. She cannot be dead, because how could she be dead and I yet living?

No one has come, not even the servant. Why is my door locked? Why does no one come when I scream? Where is everyone?

I don't remember falling asleep but I must have, because I awoke with Eliza leaning over me.

'Oh, Lucy, you poor dear. Here, have some water.'

I raised my leaden head and sipped a little, before collapsing back among my pillows.

'Where were you?' I demanded, my voice coming out as a rasping whisper. 'Why was I locked in?'

'I'm sorry. You must have been so distressed. So many sick, and so few attendants to go around. I was with Mafalda.'

'Mafalda!' I grasped for Eliza's wrist, memories coming back to me in a flood. Mafalda lying on the floor of her room, Mafalda bleeding from her neck. 'I must see her!'

'You will. Don't fret, she will be perfectly well very soon. And you too, sweetheart. All will be as it should be.'

'What about Aunt Réka, and Alice?'

'Réka is . . .' Eliza paused, the dim light falling across her face in such a way as to make her seem not herself, stark and inhuman. I blame my illness, and my current state of mind. 'Réka is still in bed as she was already so very weak, but the doctor has every confidence she will improve.'

'A doctor? A doctor came? But the storm—'

It was only then that I noticed how quiet it was.

'Poor thing,' Eliza crooned, stroking my hair. 'The storm has been over for some time now. The doctor came from a town nearby, I forget the name. He examined you, do you not recall?'

I frowned, searching my memory. I had a vague recollection of a man in black, and said as much to Eliza.

'Do not over exert yourself to think of it. You were quite unwell.'

'Should we not leave, as soon as possible? Should we not try to go home? This pestilence, these biting devils, surely it's a terrible risk to stay here?'

'Shh, dear girl. Of course we cannot leave, you are not well enough to travel. Besides, it is almost the time when we will no longer need to concern ourselves with such things.'

I blinked stupidly, my brain full of fog.

'The time of year, do you mean?'

'Oh, yes. The time of year. Exactly so.'

'Eliza, please, I do so want to go home. Perhaps the Count could make some arrangements?'

'I will let him know you have asked,' Eliza said softly, tucking an escaped twirl of hair behind my ear. 'I promise. You should sleep now.'

I suppose I did sleep, because I dreamed. Horrible, evil dreams, which have left me with a sense of discomfort, almost defilement. A tray of food was left for me, soup and a warm golden bread. The bite marks on my throat ache terribly and make it painful to swallow, but even so I feel better for having eaten. I will set my tray aside and perhaps settle to some reading. It is that or destroy myself with worry, although I can no more silence my fears for Mafalda than I can float weightless out into the evening sky.

Later

Is that what fate awaits me? Is that the sickness inside me?

I was trying to read, trying to stifle my gnawing anxiety, when from outside there came peculiar, muffled sounds. As I listened the source grew nearer, and the noise resolved itself into a fearful slavering and snarling. I realized then in a burst of terror that this noise was not coming from outside the castle, but from outside the door to my chamber! I ran to it and thankfully found it locked again, separating me from whatever prowled along the corridor. My first thought was of the wolves that we had heard in the forest, but as my curiosity overwhelmed my cowardice and I set my eye to the keyhole, I saw much, much worse than a wolf.

Eliza lied to me. Aunt Réka is not abed, tenderly cared for. Instead, she has been transformed into a mad thing, crawling and loping now on all fours and now crouched, sniffing the air like an animal. How could her nails have grown so quickly? Her hands and feet looked almost claw-like, her nightclothes ragged, perhaps torn by those same claws, her hair wild and pulled out in clumps. I looked on in an appalled mix of fear and pity, until, God help me, she turned and seemed to see me, or nosed me out with some heightened beastly sense. She was hunting, and hunting *me*. Her eyes flashed red and her mouth snarled open to reveal long pointed incisors as she advanced. I froze like a cornered creature, the oak door no more than a flimsy sheet of paper in my terrified mind. Aunt Réka, or what was once Aunt Réka, crouched to spring.

At that exact moment Eliza appeared, seemingly from thin air. I opened my mouth to cry out, to warn her, but she stepped smartly between the door and the mad beast-woman and then – what? My vision was blocked by her skirts. I heard a pointed silence, and then a whimper, and both were gone. Just, gone. I collapsed back onto the floor, the rush of aborted panic overtaking me.

Is this what can happen when a person is infected? Eliza recovered, didn't she? But she had expert professional care from the first. Aunt Réka had none. Nor does Mafalda and nor do I. Is it likely that some country doctor has the knowledge to halt this contagion?

There is nothing left to do but pray.

Lucy North's diary
Tuesday, 26th August 1884
Transylvania, Austro-Hungarian Empire

The last thing I knew, I had been quaking in my bed, touching the wounds in my throat and praying wordless weeping prayers. Then, I was returning to consciousness dressed and on my feet.

'With only my will?' I heard Mafalda say.

'Certainly.'

My eyes opened of their own accord. Mafalda stood before me, a cold hand on my cheek, smiling a bright smile.

'My love!'

I knew, though I do not know how. I knew she was wrong, fundamentally and horrifically wrong; uncanny, unholy. She was wrong in the same way that the creature I'd seen last night was wrong, the same way Eliza was wrong.

I tried to speak, but only a croak escaped my dry throat.

'All is well,' she said softly, stroking my shivering skin with her thumb as her hand rested against my face. 'All is well, and always will be. You will see I am not so selfish after all.'

I felt warmth begin to return to my body, a loosening, as of bonds. I turned my head this way and that, both wanting and not wanting her touch. The wounds on my neck ached horribly, and, though this disgusts me beyond measure to write, they made a vile sucking sound as I moved.

'My poor darling,' Mafalda whispered as I flinched, 'soon there will be no more pain. I swear it.'

It was as she pressed her lips together in a facsimile of sympathy that I saw it. Just below her lower lip, on the left-hand side. A brownish-red mark, a dot of dried blood. I jerked back, almost tripping on what I thought was a pile of rags at my feet. God save us, it was Alice. Bruised black and blue, but still alive and still human.

A girlish giggle came from far away, outside my limited field of vision. Mafalda's face changed, scowling as she turned away to find the source of this disturbance. I blinked and blinked and blinked, forcing my eyes to focus. We were in the great hall, now lit golden and red by the setting sun. Rough wooden floors, worn down by centuries, stretched across the vast space. Wooden panels covered the walls, giving way to stone fireplaces on which whole animals might once have been spitted and cooked. High up in the far wall was a minstrels' gallery, and it was from there that the incongruous noise had come.

Aunt Réka sat on the balustrade, wearing nothing but her bloodstained and ragged nightgown. She swung her bare legs like a child might, giggling that infernal giggle. Her mouth was stained red almost from ear to ear. As I watched, she launched herself from the wooden railing, falling in a tangle of limbs. She landed with a sickening thud on, dear God, the headless and torn-about corpse of the female castle servant.

Aunt Réka pulled herself upright in cracking unnatural bursts. She skittered across the floor towards me, snuffing at the air. I wanted to run, but succeeded only in stumbling backwards a pace or two. Mafalda placed herself firmly between me and the remnant of her aunt.

'Don't worry, Lucy dear,' called the voice of Eliza somewhere over to my left. 'She's perfectly well-behaved when she's sated.'

This being, this creature who was once my friend, glided smoothly across the floor to where Aunt Réka hunkered down, waiting. Eliza ran her hand through the older woman's tangled hair as one would pet an animal, then took hold of a great handful and pulled hard. Aunt Réka reared and howled, twisting in pain. Eliza let her hang for a moment and then dropped her, laughing as Aunt Réka whimpered.

'You see? Nothing to be concerned about, until she gets hungry.'

They laughed, oh, how they laughed! Mafalda, Eliza, and a deep male laugh that came from behind me.

'What is this?' It hurt to speak. My voice was barely more than a hiss.

'A gift. The fulfilment of all desires.'

Again I meant to flee, but even before the thought was formed Count Dracula was behind me, one arm tight about my waist and the other across my throat. His closeness revolted me, and I gagged.

'Desire is what drives a man,' he said, speaking low into my ear, 'or a woman, of course. It is a lock, to which I am the key. Look.' He turned my head to force my gaze on Eliza, her hands folded demurely, a sweet smile on her red lips. 'Here is my lady, my own queen, who will mother my children, tend them and teach them, and send them forth to create a new world. It is all her want, all her need. How happy she will be!'

Eliza made a deep curtsey. It was the truth and a hideous lie all at once. On she smiled, my poor dead friend, whom I now understand had been dying for weeks at his hand.

'And my enforcer, look! Look, girl!' He dragged my head to the right, the punctures in my neck gulping in protest. Aunt Réka crouched on the floor, blank-eyed. 'A true believer in our nation, and such a biting force within! In life she desired vengeance against those who wronged her, and wrought it. The animal, the beast in her nature, it has no home in the human world. She will snap at the heels of the laggards and the unwilling. What a gift to put in the service of my great cause!'

'Cause?' I don't know how I dared speak at all, let alone to ask a question. Perhaps I realized that every moment the Count talked on was a moment my human life was prolonged.

'Indeed. One day there will be many like me, as great a race as long ago, or greater. The nations of this modern world have devised such ways of travel, with such speed, that my children will soon be spread all across the face of the earth! Do you see, little one? How fondly Fate looks on my works?'

He is bragging, the small still-rational part of my mind realized. As men do, boasting of deeds not yet accomplished, to convince a female audience. But why? I thought. Why not kill me and have done with it?

'In one place, at one time, I found all that I needed. See, even of my own bloodline!'

He twisted my head again and held it, even as I squirmed from the pain. He had me look at Mafalda, her expression arrogant where once it was confident, ruthless where once it was merely decisive.

'A daughter of my own proud lineage to be my right hand, who both desired power and deserved it. She will lead my armies in the field, she will take my will and bring it into being, she will stand by me as I take this land in my fist, as is my right.'

The Count leaned down and with horrific slowness, ran his

tongue across my punctured, still-bleeding throat. My stomach roiled, my very skin trying to crawl off my bones.

'Unhand her. This woman is mine.'

The Count finished his slavering before deigning to look up.

'I had a price,' Mafalda said, her lengthened incisors showing as she spoke. 'I received your gift with gratitude, but I had a price. This woman is mine.'

I sensed rather than saw Count Dracula's almost-sneer. 'Indeed.'

He released me all at once. I staggered, and tripped over poor Alice. She reached out with a bruised and torn hand to steady me, and together we managed to stand. We clutched at each other, the only two living beings in that place.

'Holy Mary, Mother of God,' Alice whispered as we held each other. 'Pray for us sinners.'

'Now, and at the hour of our death,' I finished. Words of great power, even for one not of that faith.

Count Dracula and Mafalda faced each other, shockingly alike. Eliza glanced worriedly from one to the other, for all the world a mother who sees her child and its father about to come to blows.

'You must remember, young lady, that you do not command me.'

'What command? I remind you only of what you owe me for my sacrifice.'

'Sacrifice?' he spat, seeming to grow less and less human with every passing moment. 'Do you not have what you wanted?'

'Not all, not quite yet.'

She came to me, not moving, not walking and not floating, all at once she simply was before me. My God, her very image is burned into my brain. It was my beloved and yet not. It was some creature, wrong, twisted inside, made vile in a manner for which I do not have words. Her smile was not of warmth but of some species of malice, of cruelty, of hunger. The green dress she wore, made for a woman long dead in an era long past, fit her like snakeskin.

'Come here, my love,' she whispered in her siren's voice. 'Come to me and kiss me, and we will be together for ever.' She moved closer, holding out her cold white hand. 'Is this not what you have always wanted? Come to me, and be mine for eternity.'

I wanted to say yes. I wanted, deeply and truly, to say yes, more than I have ever wanted anything. I would have condemned myself to Hell, to turning the earth into a Hell all its own. I would have taken the side of the Devil. What have I ever wanted anyway, but her?

I didn't know I wept until I felt hot tears pouring down my face. Some still-sane, blessed and faithful part of me raised my hand, clutching the tavern wife's rough-cut rosary, forgotten in my pocket next to this diary until Alice had prayed out loud.

Mafalda reeled away from me, lips drawn back, eyes green no more but the blood red of the damned. I stumbled backwards, holding this piece of pure holy faith before me.

'A worthy general has no use for distractions,' the Count chided Mafalda. 'Let her die, and by her death she can nourish us all.'

'You need me, and without her you will not have me! We struck a bargain. This woman is mine!'

At these raised voices Aunt Réka sat up on her haunches, salivating. Her eyes darted from one combatant to the other, sensing the shift.

I was conscious of Alice by my side, pulling me backwards, dragging me from that place and all my worst desires.

'I have made my decision, girl. You will do as I say.'

Mafalda snarled and threw herself at the Count. I gasped

aloud but they paid me no heed. Mafalda had him by the neck, her clawed hands drawing oozing dark blood where they punctured his undead flesh. He laughed then, and that laugh will haunt my dreams until the day I die.

'There it is! There is the spirit of a Dracula! I did right when I chose you to serve me.'

He raised one arm and hurled her away from him. She hit the wall with a thud, sliding down and landing hard on her knees.

'No! Please, no!' Eliza cried out.

'I will not serve you!' Mafalda's defiance echoed around the cavernous space.

'You will! I have eternity to bend you, to break you if I must!'

Mafalda roared, and charged. Aunt Réka watched, her eyes twitching to one and then the other, and chose her side. She leapt, fangs long, at the man who would have been her master.

'No! You must stop this!' Eliza attempted to enter the fray and received a blow to the head for her pains. She howled in distress, lashing out.

My beloved was magnificent in her rage, laying into the creature that had lied to her and tried to enslave her until he clawed her face from hairline to chin, leaving great gashes, and flung her across the floor where she lay prone. As the monster fought Aunt Réka's frenzied attack, Mafalda lifted her head and our eyes met. I watched as her too-crimson lips whispered my name.

Alice gripped my arm, hard.

'Now we run.'

I left her there, the one I love more than all the world, in Hell.

PART ELEVEN

Sir John Seward's personal diary
Monday, 23rd February 1903, continued
Littlemore Hospital, Oxfordshire

Dr Knight has an appointment in the city today, and I must attend to my duties. However exhausted I am and however little those duties appeal to me, I will, of course, always care for my patients to the best of my ability. Last night I was treated to another round of ghastly dreams, which play around my brain even in daylight.

An interview with Mrs Lakatos has been fixed for tomorrow afternoon, and I have listed out the questions which yet need to be answered. In the meantime, Harker and I decided to send her the record of our dealings with Count Dracula. It felt morally right to do so, to trust her with our sad history as she has trusted us with Lady Lowell's, and indeed, much of her own.

Sir John Seward's personal diary
Tuesday, 24th February 1903
Littlemore Hospital, Oxfordshire

This morning's post contained a surprising letter from Professor Van Helsing. I enclose it here, because what it relates is both remarkable and relevant to the trials of Mrs Lakatos at the hands of the Count.

Professor Abraham Van Helsing
Amsterdam

My dear friend,
I have been visited by my old acquaintance Dr Arminius, now retired from his position at the university in Buda-Pesth. I hope you do not mind; I sent him a telegram when you told me of your patient, and he came up on the very next train. He lives in Paris these days, most convenient. He tells me that he remembers the young woman, then Miss Alice Smith, being possessed of the most remarkable mental strength, not to mention extreme common sense.

Dr Arminius brought with him his casebook from the relevant time, and together we examined its contents. I now suspect, and Dr Arminius agrees, that the secret to Miss Smith's survival, and by extension that of the then Miss North, to be a most mundane thing. If only we had known of it when we fought the creature!

Dr Arminius noted that when he knew her, Miss Smith habitually drank a great deal of a particular concoction intended to prevent nightmares. This she named 'lemon beebrush'. Well, my friend, what do you suppose? I looked this up in my library, and I find that this is the folk name for *Aloysia citrodora*, lemon verveine. This plant, most sacred to the Romans and other peoples in both the Old World and the New, has long been used to keep evil at bay. It seems that the *vampyr* cannot stomach it, and finds it to some small but significant extent a neutralizer. What gifts does Nature give to us!

I have many other thoughts on the matter, but I will wait until I read the documents you mention.

With the greatest and highest regard, I am yours sincerely,
Abraham Van Helsing

Had we but known! By God, had we but known!

Alice Smith's commonplace book
Events of Tuesday, 26th August 1884
Transylvania, Austro-Hungarian Empire

We made a path in the darkness, scurrying like rats down the freezing stone corridors. The screams and shrieks and howls of the *vampyrs* fighting each other echoed all around, sound coming from everywhere at once. I couldn't tell if any of them were chasing us, or how close behind they might be. I thought every step would be my last.

We came to a staircase leading down into the shadows, with no banister between us and a drop of who knows how far. I hurried downwards, as close to the wall as possible. My grip on Miss North's hand didn't let up for a moment, and thank God because I lost my footing and slipped. If not for her hauling me back, I'd have lost my balance and fallen into the abyss.

'I know where we are!' Miss North whispered hoarsely as we reached the bottom. 'This way!'

Hand clutching hand we went on, her leading and me following close behind. At last, at last we rounded a corner and there we were in what must have been the entrance hall, the centuries-old wooden door rising up in front of us. It was unlocked, because why would the *vampyr* Count need such a human thing as a locked door? I lifted the heavy latch, and then together Miss

North and I hauled on the metal ring of the door handle. The door ground loudly against the floor, in a deep groove worn over the long years. Any minute, I thought, any minute it's going to be the end. Holy Mary Mother of God, pray for us sinners, now and at the hour of our deaths.

As soon as there was a wide enough gap, Miss North pushed me ahead of her and all but forced me through. For just a moment I thought I felt her waver, but almost as soon as I thought it she was already squeezing herself through after me.

If any part of our escape could be called the most dangerous, this was it. The great hall looked out over the courtyard; I knew from when my late mistress had dragged me there. We'd be completely visible, but there was nothing for it. Hand once again in gripping hand, we ran as fast as we could across the flagstones and towards the archway between the two gate-towers. I expected to hear the grinding of the portcullis dropping, cutting off our exit, but there was only silence. My lungs ached with the running, heaving against my crushed and bruised ribs, but it didn't matter. We were out of the castle, and into the forest.

Miss North and I walked all night. Or rather, we ran for as long as we could, then we walked, and then we stumbled. It was the blackest and longest night of my life. Nothing stirred around us. We could hear only our own terrified breathing. A wolf howled, off in the trees to the left. Then another, this time to the right. I tried to drag Miss North, to get her to run again, but she was too weak. With grit beyond words she set her jaw, gripped her rosary, and marched onwards. I took her arm, and we leaned on each other. More wolves joined in the chorus.

'Talk, Alice,' she said to me. 'I can't bear it. Talk.'

'We ought to keep our breath, miss.'

'Please. I need . . . Please.'

'Alright, alright.' I said the rosary aloud, once, twice, three times. I lost count. I prayed the Latin prayers, then the English ones. Then I started on the psalm that kept me sane in that place, number twenty-three. You know the one.

'Yes. Yes, that's good,' she said, when I reached the end. 'Again.'

I did as I was told, and recited it over again. And again. And again. I now recognized the sound of my own voice, that voice I had known but couldn't place in nightmare after nightmare. But what did it matter knowing the meaning now, when no good came of it before?

On we stumbled, our way lit by nothing at all. Every second I expected to hear a wolf's tread behind us, every moment I expected to feel yellow teeth ripping into my flesh. Then it began to rain. It took hardly a minute to get soaked through, but there was no talk of stopping for shelter. I didn't know if we were pursued by worse animals than wolves, so to stop might be death and worse than death. On and on and on, we made our way. Only the downward slope of the path showed us where to go.

'The inn . . . Alice, we must find the inn. They will help us, I am certain.'

But there was no inn. We passed nothing and no one. I wondered if I'd died after all, and this was Purgatory. A never-ending path, mud and icy fear and dark, forever.

'I can't . . . stop . . . shivering,' Miss North said through chattering teeth.

'Don't worry, miss, shivering is good. My nana said it's when you stop that you're in trouble.'

'A . . . wise . . . woman . . . your nana.'

'Yes, miss. Exactly so.'

'Talk . . . Alice. Please. Say the . . . psalm again.'

So I did. She asked over and over. I kept going even until my throat was raw. The valley of the shadow of death, spoken into being.

I didn't dare to hope we'd live until dawn. More than once I was tempted to lie down and wait for nature to take its course. At least the wolves would give me a true death, with the reward of Heaven at the end, perhaps. But Miss North kept walking, and if she could, I could. One aching, frozen foot in front of the other. We must have stopped, must have rested, but I don't remember it. Maybe we didn't, the threat of the wolf pack always present even when we couldn't hear it. It doesn't seem possible, but then none of this seems possible.

Dawn, when it came at last, came suddenly. It felt like one moment it was dark, and the next there was daylight sneaking towards us.

'Miss North, look!' My voice was a shockingly harsh croak, but I was more shocked to look at my poor companion.

Her lips were blue, her skin brightest white, and she shook like a leaf. Somewhere along the way she'd lost her shoes, lady's slippers, and had only torn and bloody stockings on her feet.

'We are alive,' she said flatly, almost disappointed. Then she fainted, and fell into my arms.

I all but carried her the rest of the way. We never found the inn, only the rough hut of an elderly female charcoal burner. She didn't want to let us in, not after she saw the bite marks, but I held Miss North's rosary up in front of her face and begged without shame in every language I knew. She shook her grey head at me, but beckoned us into her one-room shelter just the same. There we huddled, wrapped in rough and scratchy woollen blankets, which were as welcome as the finest eiderdown.

The old woman shared her meal with us, some kind of thin

gruel. It was warm, and that's all that mattered. Miss North had already begun to cough, an unpleasant racking sound. After our sad meal she scribbled and scribbled in her battered diary with a sharpened end of charcoal, weeping, even when I begged her to lie down and rest.

'I will meet Death head-on if he's coming,' she told me, grimly. 'I'll stay awake or be damned.'

I didn't know where we were, or how far it might be to a proper town. I didn't know where we might even be safe. The only thing I was certain of was that we mustn't be out in the open when night came. Not for anything. Our enemy could hunt us in the daytime as well as at night, but if the old stories were true then at least he wouldn't be at his full power. I don't know why I thought he'd need all the evil at his command to hunt down two broken girls. I just wanted to hope. I wanted to hope I'd live to see my mam, and Sarah. I wanted to hope I'd see you again. I prayed for mercy, for any kind of good fortune, for some sign that there was a God in Heaven watching over me, but I was mortally afraid that my prayers went up to an empty sky.

Sometime around noon, a young man came to the hut with a cart. This was the charcoal burner's son, or maybe grandson. Through a mix of mime and grunted Hungarian he agreed to take us to, of all the places on the earth, Bistritz. Bistritz! I could have cried.

Miss North climbed aboard the cart slowly and painfully. In the daylight I could see how bloodied and ruined her feet were, and I took care to wrap them in one of the blankets while I settled her in the back of the cart with bag loads of charcoal. The other I wrapped around her shoulders. The old woman had forced us to take them, and I hoped it was from charity and not because she thought they'd become unlucky after having touched us. I sat in the front with the driver, there being no room behind.

'How long?' I asked. 'Few hours? Many hours?'

The young man, who was probably my own age come to think of it, shrugged. He wouldn't want to spend a night in the forest, would he, so we must be able to get to Bistritz before sunset. I had Hungarian florins worth about four shillings split between each of my shoe soles and the hem of my dress. Bless Mam forever for teaching me to keep a bit of money hidden on me at all times. There'd be enough to give some to the young man for himself and his grandmother, to buy us a little bit of food, and to send a telegram to Buda-Pesth. Dr Arminius would help us, surely. We could sleep in the station if we had to. If only we could make it to Bistritz before nightfall.

It was a long and jarring drive. Miss North slept at last, despite being jolted about like cargo. I gnawed at my nails as the sun sank lower and lower in the sky. I realized with a heavy heart that even when we did arrive, it would be long past the closing time of the telegraph office. We'd be stuck for two nights, not one, and that would be if Dr Arminius came straight away. Of course he would, I told myself. There couldn't be a question about it. We'd manage. Somehow. We'd wait in the station, we'd tell the stationmaster we'd been robbed. My little stock of coinage would go further here than in the city. They might remember us at the inn we'd stayed in on the way. They might let me work a bit for some food. They might even find a doctor for Miss North, for the sake of Christian charity.

All these sad little hopes died in me when we at last reached Bistritz. Our driver left us in the town square, such as it was. He shook his head when I offered him a coin torn discreetly from my hem, and made the sign of the cross over me before he drove away.

Everything was closed. There was no one on the street, and the station building was locked. Miss North stood on her bare feet, swaying, a sweat broken out on her brow but shivering in the charcoal burner's blanket.

'Come and take my arm, Miss North. We'll find where we stayed last time. We can stay there again.'

Miss North nodded, mute. We made our way through the deserted streets with her leaning on me heavily. We looked like beggars. With every step I was more and more sure the innkeeper would never let us in, but we couldn't stay out in the open. Even without the demon hunting us, I wasn't sure what state Miss North would be in come morning after a night on the street.

The inn was larger and more well-kept than I remembered. I felt my heart sink when I saw it. They'd never take us in, not even to work. I stood in the doorway with Miss North leaning on my shoulder, working up my courage to try anyway, when a shadow fell across me. My heart leapt into my mouth and I froze in fear.

'Alice? Alice!'

You know this next part, but you insist I keep going. You say it will help.

'Mátyás!' I cried, flooded with the deepest relief I've ever felt.

'My God! Alice!'

'Miss North needs a doctor, right away.'

You took one look at Miss North, and lifted her up in your arms.

'At once. Follow me.'

You sorted out a room for her, and for me, paying the innkeeper very liberally. The town's doctor was bribed from his bed, and his assessment was that Miss North should be moved to a hospital as soon as possible. He ordered her taken to Buda-Pesth on the train, under the care of a nurse. You gave him an astonishing amount of money to lend us his own nursing assistant, who arrived at great speed. Money really does solve a lot of problems, doesn't it?

When Miss North was settled down with proper medicine and proper medical attention, you took me into a parlour where a supper had been laid out. You rang for hot water and had me put my feet in a basin while I ate hot soup and slightly stale bread. You didn't ask me anything. Instead, you answered the questions I'd have asked if I'd had the sense to.

'I arrived in Sárkányerdő a week ago when my business with the tenants finally concluded. I found you and the ladies gone. The servants told me there was an outbreak of illness in the house, and the ladies had left to stay at the home of a friend of Madam Jacobinus, higher in the mountains. I planned to follow, as I have much to discuss with her regarding her properties and businesses, but no one seemed to know exactly where you all were. Those I asked were confused, disoriented. I sent out several of the servants in the directions you might have travelled, but learned nothing. Two of them didn't come back at all.'

I couldn't look at you. I could hardly breathe.

'There are stories about that forest. My grandmother lived not far away all her life and she told me such terrible tales, swearing they were true. I found myself half-believing them, when I never had before. I could not ask yet another to perhaps risk his life, so in the end I went out myself. I reached as far as an inn at the Borgo Pass. The innkeeper and his frightened wife, they said they had seen you. They said a demon had taken you all. The wife said she had begged a girl of Lucy's description not to go, to turn back. They said . . . Alice, they said you were deathly ill. So I left for the castle myself.'

'No!' I started, spilling soup and scalding my fingers.

You hurried for a cloth and wet it, cooling the pain. You kept hold of my hand.

THE BRIDES

'I couldn't find it. I felt I was going round in circles. There was nothing but forest, and a thick mist that seemed almost to follow me. I ended up back at the inn where I started, even though I could have sworn I was miles away. I tried the next day, and the next, and it happened again. In the end I came back to Bistritz, thinking I could report you all as missing. I thought the authorities would work hard to find missing noble ladies, and you with them. I came here to see if I could put a notice in the paper . . .' You trailed off, and hung your head.

I squeezed your hand, just a little bit, and then I told you everything.

Alice Smith's commonplace book
Events of Wednesday, 27th August 1884
Bistritz, Austro-Hungarian Empire

The express train to Buda-Pesth was due to leave at eleven o'clock the next morning. Miss North had to be carried down to the station in a moth-eaten sedan chair. The stationmaster held the train until the nurse had settled Miss North on a makeshift bed in one of the compartments. He'd grumbled about it until he saw her, looking so near death, and was moved to pity. I don't think you even had to bribe him, in the end.

I thought she was asleep as I sat myself down by her head, with the nurse at her feet and you hovering in the doorway. I jumped a mile when she reached out and grabbed hold of my sleeve.

'Listen,' she croaked, 'my diary, it's in my coat pocket.' She meant a shabby peasant coat you'd got for her from one of the tavern maids. 'Keep it for me. Read it, if you like, but I don't want it.'

'Are you sure, miss?'

She took a rasping breath, which turned into a bloody coughing fit. The nurse spooned some kind of thick green medicine into her mouth, which seemed to help.

'Yes. But don't ever, ever speak to me of it.'

'Alright. I promise.'

I rummaged around in the patched and mended coat and found the diary, still damp from the Carpathian rain. The nurse shooed me out, so I took it away with me. You and I moved down the corridor to an empty compartment, its plushness feeling callous in the circumstances. I found I was too full of nervous energy to sit still, so I paced up and down, watching the scenery fly past much faster than it had done on the way out. Miss North had been so kind to me on that awful journey, when I'd read in the paper about Baroness Tolvay. I said a prayer for her soul as we hurtled through the little towns and villages, and for Miss North's too. If she died after having been bitten, would she become like them? Would she become a *vampyr*? God save me, would I? I couldn't remember. Dr Arminius would know what to do, I told myself. Dr Arminius would be able to help. You'd already sent a telegram ahead, and with any luck the good doctor would be waiting for us.

I ought to write to Mam and Sarah, I thought, who must be right worried by not having heard from me in so long. What would I even do now, with no lady to serve? Maybe I could stay with Miss North. I'd serve her instead, as best I could, for as long as she'd have me. She'd saved my life in that place, she deserved nothing less. If she didn't want me, why then I'd go home to Robin Hood's Bay and try to start anew. Then I thought of leaving you behind, and my heart ached in my chest. I hadn't been honest with Mam and Sarah about how close we'd got, and probably not even with myself. How could I go home and never see you again?

You called my name, and broke in on my sad spiralling thoughts.

'Alice, please let me say again that I am so sorry. So very, very sorry. If I had come sooner—'

I cut you clean off, wanting to save you from yourself.

'You can't think like that. It'll drive you mad. We must deal with things as they are, not as we'd wish them to be.'

'That there are truly such things in this world, it horrifies me. We should tell the authorities. The Emperor could bring an army and destroy the fiend forever.'

'If you could get someone in power to believe you, who's to say the army wouldn't wander the forest for days like you did? I think that place can only be found when the Count wants it to be.'

'You are quite right. How foolish of me.' You rolled your shoulders and stood straight-backed, like a soldier ready to receive his orders. 'That is the last of such maudlin nonsense you will hear from me. There will be things to do when we reach Buda-Pesth. I ask you for the honour of managing them.'

I half-expected you to salute. 'Thank you.'

'I will write to Lady Maria, and to your late mistress's husband.'

'Nurse Weber, Madam Jacobinus's nurse – you must write to her people too.'

'Yes, of course.'

You began to pace, just as I'd been doing earlier.

'An accident. We will say there was an accident. You were all in a carriage, perhaps, and you and Miss North got out to lighten the load for the horses on a steep mountainside. The horses bolted, and the carriage came loose.'

I shivered.

'A ravine,' I added. 'It fell into a ravine, with a deep river at the bottom. Then Miss North and I walked all through the night to get help, but she was so ill from the cold and the rain . . . Mátyás, I feel sick to think of lying to people about their loved ones' deaths. Is it evil to deceive like this?'

'No,' you said sternly. 'It is a great kindness and a mercy.'

I thought of poor Nurse Weber, and wondered if she had a mother or father still alive. If I were them, how much worse would it be to know how my daughter had really died? I thought of the ladies, now not living but not given the peace of true death. It would be cruel to try to tell an unbelievable truth, and Nana used to say that being cruel to be kind was still a sin. I pray she was right, or my sin runs very deep indeed.

Alice Smith's commonplace book
Events of Sunday, 31st August 1884
Queen Elisabeth Hospital, Buda-Pesth,
Austro-Hungarian Empire

The hospital on the outskirts of the city was brand new, and had only been open a few months. Dr Arminius had some sort of advisor position there, although I didn't know that at the time. He met our unhappy band of travellers at the door, took one look at me, and prescribed immediate bed rest. I was led away to a little room on an upper floor, clean and bright, with a view of a courtyard garden. I slept, surrounded by Dr Arminius's garlic flowers. I slept and slept, a mercifully dreamless sleep. Kindly nurses woke me up for meals but apart from that, I slept.

On the Sunday morning after arriving, I awoke to church bells ringing and a beautiful ray of sunlight shining across my white coverlet. I'd forgotten where I was, and with it all that had happened. I smiled. It felt strange, unfamiliar. Then I remembered, and I turned my face into the pillow.

After breakfast a nurse ushered you in, hissing at you that you had thirty minutes and no more, she really shouldn't be allowing this at all, it was all most irregular. You'd brought flowers, bright yellow ones. You'd even thought to bring a vase from somewhere.

'Dr Arminius told me you might be awake today,' you said, carefully putting the vase down on the windowsill. 'He's been checking on you.'

'Has he? I don't remember.'

I know I ought to have been embarrassed to be seen in such a state, but the hospital bedspread covered my modest hospital nightgown and by the feel of it someone had been taking the time to brush my hair and wash my face.

'Well, you have been asleep. You needed to recover from your ordeal. Have you been' – you shot a glance towards the door, checking we were alone – 'dreaming?'

I'd already told you about my dreams, my visions, on that awful night when you rescued us. Why bother trying to hide what might be the more believable part of the story?

'No,' I said, surprised as I realized I hadn't.

'Good. I told Dr Arminius about your drink, your bees-brush. He made some himself for the nurses to give to you. Without you to ask, he was not sure exactly of the recipe, but if you have not dreamed . . .'

I felt such gratitude in my heart for you that I thought I might burst into tears. You forestalled it by bringing up the main reason for your visit.

'Do you feel well enough to talk about what is happening now?'

I pulled myself upright against the pillows, dragging the bedclothes with me.

'What do you mean? What's happening?'

'I sent a letter to Lady Maria, by a special messenger. She replied by telegram saying she and her husband would leave London at once. They will arrive tomorrow. I thought you would want to see Miss North beforehand, to decide what to say.'

'Oh. I see.'

'I have also written to Colonel Cartwright. I offered to have the, forgive me, the death notices made up and something sent to the papers, but he says he will arrange it. He has sent you your full wages, and more than enough money to return home, if you wish it. He has travelled to inform your family in person.'

My family! How worried they would be! But at least they had each other. I thought of the poor Colonel, sitting alone in the house, his wife and his oldest friend both dead and his children scattered far and wide. I hoped that little Miss Beth would be some comfort, and that he'd choose to keep her with him.

I opened my mouth to ask more questions but stopped, stuck on something. You tried to speak but I held up my hand, becoming bold in my concentration. It took full minutes for it to come to me. I'd seen it in a vision, so long ago, in the drawing room at the Cartwrights' house in Whitby. The Colonel, alone, weeping over a photograph. *Our* photograph, the one taken here in Buda-Pesth.

I said it out loud to you, falling over my words. What was the point of it? I demanded of you, of the world, of God, almost shouting. What was the point of this strange knowing if I didn't understand it or realize in time what it meant? All my anger and rage and pain poured out of me in choking sobs, incoherent. I got more and more agitated until you took my face in your hands and held it, stopping me in the middle of my outburst.

'Without you, Miss North would be one of the damned and the *vampyrs* would be poised to carry out Count Dracula's plan. Without you, we would all be in mortal peril. Your gift, it warned you over and over. You might not have understood completely, but you understood *enough*. You saved Miss North from a fate far worse than death. You saved her, and she saved you in turn. Together you caused the demon's creatures to turn on him. You are here, alive, and so is she. Alice, you are a hero.'

With your words, I allowed myself to break. Long past caring about any sort of propriety, I laid my head on your chest and wept. You held me in your arms and let me howl, just as you have many times since.

Alice Smith's commonplace book
Events of Monday, 1st September 1884
Queen Elisabeth Hospital, Buda-Pesth,
Austro-Hungarian Empire

Miss North wanted me to be with her when the Lowell family came. I still wasn't well and I wouldn't be for some time, but I wasn't as badly off as Miss North. Her fever had broken, but a painful cough racked her body every other minute. She was exhausted, and sometimes confused. Her skin had taken on a greyish tinge and according to a loose-lipped nurse, she was lucky to be alive.

Lady Maria and her husband were due on the first day of September. They were to come after breakfast, straight off the *Orient Express*, as we call it now. I'd managed to get myself up and dressed, and I'd done my best to look respectable. Bless you for having my one remaining dress washed and mended while I slept. A nurse helped Miss North to bathe, and I got her into a nice clean hospital nightdress. She wasn't quite all there, being so fatigued, but she was determined to keep hold of our carriage-accident story. She repeated it to herself under her breath while I brushed and braided her hair.

'You won't go, will you?' she said plaintively, when I was finished.

'No, not if you still want me to stay.'

'I do. I don't think I can speak with . . . with her parents alone.'

'I promise, I'll be right here.'

Miss North took a deep breath.

'"We got out of the carriage to lighten the load for the horses. A noise startled them and they bolted. The carriage went over the cliff and into the river. There was nothing we could do."'

'Exactly so, Miss North. Exactly so.'

She looked thoughtful for a moment. 'No, this won't do.'

'What won't do, miss?'

'Alice, after every terrible thing we have suffered together, I think you ought to call me Lucy.'

This kind sentiment was interrupted by a hacking coughing fit. A nurse came and gave her honey-syrup and a hot cloth for her back, and amid all the fuss I didn't get to tell her what it meant to me. Though in my mind I never quite manage it, I have called her Lucy to her lovely face from that day to this.

I got up when the Lowells entered, but given how quickly Lady Maria bid me sit back down I suppose I must have looked more frail than I felt. Seeing Lady Maria again was jarring. If her resemblance to both her sister and her daughter hurt and frightened me, how much worse it must have been for Miss North. She clenched the bedclothes in her fist as she accepted Lady Maria's embrace, her body rigid. Sir Gerald dropped a fatherly kiss on Miss North's head once his wife had let her go.

'Brave girl,' he said gruffly. 'Brave, brave girl.'

Tears began to flow down Miss North's poor sunken cheeks. She reached for my hand and clutched it, harder than I'd have thought she was capable of.

'We got out of the carriage to lighten the load for the horses. A noise startled them and they bolted. The carriage went over the cliff and into the river. There was nothing we could do.'

'It's alright, dear girl. Young Lakatos told us everything. Don't upset yourself.'

'I'm sorry. I'm so very sorry.'

He rested his great paw on her thin shoulder, while Lady Maria dabbed at her eyes with a handkerchief.

'Nothing to be sorry for.'

'No, Lucy, nothing at all. We're going to bring you home, and get you well again. Aren't we, Gerald?'

'Yes, of course we are.'

They fell silent, the void of grief filling the room. I caught your eye where you stood against the wall, hoping Miss North would let me go so I could be comforted by you. I closed my eyes, wishing myself away.

'May I come in?'

A sandy-haired man built on the same bear-like scale as Sir Gerald stood hesitantly in the doorway. He clearly hadn't slept, and if he'd had a shave it had been a haphazard one. His mourning clothes were fine but rumpled. No travelling valet for him, it seemed.

Miss North gasped. 'I didn't know you were coming.'

'No, well, yes, I mean, it was last minute. I was so . . . It was just . . . They said you could have died, and—'

'Joseph!' Lady Maria reprimanded. 'You mustn't say such things.'

'Sorry, your ladyship. You're quite right. Sorry, Lucy.'

'I forgive you,' Miss North said quietly, so quietly that now I wonder if she really meant for him to hear.

'You must excuse me, please,' you interrupted, feeling uncomfortable at intruding on this private family scene, as you told me later. 'Your ladyship, there are matters I must see to at your house. Forgive me.'

'My house? Oh. Yes. It is my house now, isn't it?' Lady Maria nodded. 'Thank you, Mátyás.'

You left with a brief look over your shoulder, just for me.

'Capable young man,' Sir Gerald remarked. 'Mafalda says I should offer him a job. She always knows what's what. Knew, I mean. Knew. My clever, clever girl.'

Unable to hold back his tears, Sir Gerald turned and fled.

'You should go with him,' Miss North told Lady Maria. 'I'll be quite alright.'

She took back her hand from mine, running it over her brow, pinching the bridge of her nose.

'Should I go too?' Joseph Lowell asked as her ladyship vanished in a flurry of skirts, calling after her husband. 'You look very tired.'

'I am, but I can manage a few minutes more. Please, sit.'

He lowered himself carefully into the spindly hospital chair on the other side of the bed. I wondered if I ought to go, but I'd not yet been dismissed and it's not done to just wander off and leave your lady without being told, not ever.

'May I ask you something?'

Miss North tensed. 'I told Sir Gerald and her ladyship how it happened. We got out of the carriage to lighten the load for the horses. A noise startled them and they bolted. The carriage went over the cliff and into the river. There was nothing we could do.'

'No, I mean, thank you, but I knew that. Mr Lakatos wrote it in his letter. You don't need to talk about it, it must be very distressing.'

'What did you want to ask?'

Joseph Lowell glanced at me.

'Could we speak privately?'

'Of course. Alice, would you be kind enough to step outside for a moment?'

'Yes, miss.'

I was relieved, certainly, but there wasn't a chance I was going to go anywhere. I stationed myself outside the door, just out of sight.

'Lucy, Mafalda must have told you that I asked her to marry me. Mafalda . . . God help me . . .' There was a long pause. 'Mafalda wanted so much for you to come and live with us at Beechwood, after we married. The dower house has been arranged just so, ready for you. I'd be honoured if you would consider making it your home. At least while you recover. I thought . . . I thought you might not like to be in Kensington. I went there and I . . . I saw her everywhere. It was more than I could bear. You were her best friend, and you're mine still. I cannot stand to think of you being tormented as I was. Lady Maria has offered to superintend your care if you wish it.'

There was another long pause, of a different quality.

'And Alice? If she'll consent to come.'

'Alice? Oh, your companion. Yes of course, please bring any attendants you like.'

'Thank you, Joseph. That is very kind. Now, if you wouldn't mind, I really must rest.'

'Should I fetch a nurse for you?'

'No, no need. Can you please ask Sir Gerald and Lady Maria to come back tomorrow?'

I didn't want to be found listening so I shuffled away, one hand on the wall, making slow progress down the corridor. The morning had left me drained, so I went back to my own room, helped by a kindly orderly who gave me a good telling-off for being up and about for so long.

I dreamed again, of course, just as I still dream, waking you in the night when I cry out. You hold me and rock me in your arms, much as you rock our son, and I love you all the more for your care and your pity.

I dreamed of them, the women who were now Count Dracula's conquests. The nurses had not yet brought my tisane, this day of all days, and so the dream was free to drag me back to the dark place I had escaped. I dreamed of them in the castle, kept captive in the suite of rooms they'd been guests in in life. Eliza Cartwright, Mafalda Lowell, and Réka Jacobinus. They swarmed together over the figure of a man, almost unconscious, in a dream himself. Unthinking, unheeding, his head was thrown back, his throat exposed to the *vampyr* women. They bared their white teeth, eager and hungry, and closed in.

PART TWELVE

Sir John Seward's personal diary
Tuesday, 24th February 1903, continued
Littlemore Hospital, Oxfordshire

Harker and I took a brief mid-morning constitutional around the village for the sake of exercise and refreshment. We spoke of nothing but architecture, flora and fauna, lapsing often into a tired silence. We returned to find a telegram waiting. Harker was recalled to Exeter with all due haste, some legal case having reached an unexpected crisis and needing his urgent attention. He did explain it to me, but at such speed and using such lawyer's language that I couldn't grasp a word of it. I walked with him to the station, doing my best to match his swift pace. By good fortune, the stationmaster informed us, there was a train due in short order following an earlier delay.

'I'll write and tell you everything I find out from Mrs Lakatos,' I assured him as we waited on the empty platform.

'Thank you, please do. By God, Jack,' he said, peering past me down the track, 'this business has aged me a decade. I don't know how you've coped alone these last two months, it all coming back like this.'

'"Be strong, saith my heart, I am a soldier. I have seen worse sights than this",' I quoted. 'Besides, I haven't been alone. I've had Dr Knight and all her expertise on my side.'

'Ah yes, Dr Knight.' Harker stopped his peering, instead fixing me with a rather probing gaze. 'Have you told her you're in love with her?'

I was stunned, and mildly horrified, to hear that my feelings had been quite so obvious.

'Dr Knight is a colleague,' I spluttered, when my voice allowed itself to be found.

'That would be a "no", then. Listen, Jack, don't waste time denying it to me when it's as plain as the nose on your face. I've seen you in love twice before, you can't fool me.'

He was right, of course.

'Fine, I admit it, but I don't see how I *can* tell her. She's a colleague and technically my employee. It wouldn't be appropriate.'

A puff of steam from the oncoming train appeared suddenly through the bare treetops, heralding Harker's departure.

'Your ethics are impeccable, of course,' he said as the engine hoved into view. 'I'm not suggesting you do anything incorrect, but a woman of such calibre doesn't come along every day.'

The train drew to a halt alongside us. Harker hefted his valise in one hand, and offered me the other. I shook it gladly, wishing we'd had longer together.

'Give my best to Mina,' I said as he boarded, 'and to little Quincey. I'll come down myself one of these days, and spoil him absolutely rotten.'

Harker laughed. 'I'll hold you to that, and so will Mina. Goodbye, Jack. Think about what I said. Mina's desperate to see you happy again.'

An embarrassing lump rose into my throat, cutting off any reply I might have made. I smiled and nodded instead, waving as the whistle hooted a warning and the train pulled away.

Afternoon

I tried to put my conversation with Harker out of my mind and focus only on the matter at hand. The material presented by Mrs Lakatos ended abruptly with Lady Lowell, as my patient would become, in a Buda-Pesth hospital. I already knew of the Count's attack on her in 1893 from Sir Joseph's recollections, but he was unaware of the full context. The focus needed to be on what Mrs Lakatos could tell me about that point in time specifically, and more generally of the period from Lady Lowell's return from Hungary until the present day.

I confess I also wanted to speak to Mrs Lakatos about her own abilities. The documents clearly report her having both prophetic dreams and clairvoyant visions, the scientific knowledge of which remains severely underdeveloped. As a student of the human brain, my interest could not help but be piqued.

Dr Knight and I took a hansom to Iffley. On a pleasant summer afternoon I might have wished to walk, but in grey February I was glad it wasn't necessary. The day had taken a chillier turn since I saw Harker off, and an orderly provided us with travel blankets for the journey. We moved along at a slow trot, the driver taking care on ground not entirely free of ice. I was conscious of Dr Knight's nearness, wrapped up in her winter coat and tucked under a tartan blanket though she might be. I found that I felt reassured by her presence, even as we were jolted and jounced along the country lanes like so much luggage.

Mrs Lakatos's lodgings turned out to be a neat and tidy cottage near the church, made of the same butter-coloured Cotswold stone as the hospital, and with an arch of would-be roses around the door. Dr Knight's knock was answered by a teenage housemaid, and we were shown into the front parlour where Mrs Lakatos sat waiting. I have a claustrophobic patient who would certainly have suffered in such a cluttered room, which boasted at least twice as much furniture as was strictly necessary.

Mrs Lakatos's host was a fussy woman who made a great to-do about not usually taking paying guests, but of course as a favour to dear Sir Joseph, her son the master of Christ Church's favourite former student, well, she was more than glad to. Tea things had been laid out, and the lady of the house seemed all set to remain with us for the duration. I had to gently remind her of the sanctity of medical confidentiality before she would leave. It occurs to me as I write that she might have listened at the door, though if she had indeed heard our conversation I suspect she would have thrown us out onto the street, favour to Sir Joseph or not.

I found I did not know where or how to begin. Mrs Lakatos poured the tea, and Dr Knight filled the silence with some light conversation on the house, the village, and the sort of thing any pair of ladies might discuss over their Assam. It was rather incongruous, given what we had come to talk about.

'Now then,' said Mrs Lakatos when the necessary rituals had been observed. 'I'm sure you'll have a lot you want to ask me.'

'Indeed. Might we begin by talking about your record?' Out of the corner of my eye, I saw Dr Knight get out her notepad and pen. 'The letters and diaries you provided are extremely extensive. It must have taken a great deal of time and effort to compile the information, and then to select what you thought most relevant for your typescript.'

'I did my best. I wasn't sure what would be helpful. I wasn't even sure if there would ever be a doctor who could be trusted with the whole truth.'

Mrs Lakatos met my eyes for a fraction of a second before continuing, silently acknowledging the string of tragedies that had made me so fit to help this particular patient.

'I started with the material that was easiest for me to get at. I still had my commonplace book, and my sister Sarah had my letters from back then. I also had her ladyship's diary still in my keeping. Lady Lowell herself had kept all the letters Miss Lowell had ever sent to her, and she'd had some of Miss Lowell's papers brought back from Sárkányerdő. Her ladyship gave those to me to look after in one of her more lucid moments. The rest took longer. Colonel Cartwright wasn't keen to part with any of his late wife's letters at all and it was only after he died, may he rest in peace, that I was able to add those to my record. Miss Gregor was very kind about it.'

'I've corresponded with her myself. She was very helpful.'

Mrs Lakatos nodded. 'She's a sweet girl, and a lot like Mrs Cartwright as she was in life. The Dowager Lady Lowell, Lady Maria, she helped with everything else. I explained to her what I was trying to do, and she helped me where she could.'

My eyebrows shot up. 'Did you—'

'I only told her as much as was necessary. I said that I was gathering correspondence from that time in the hope that some detail might prove useful in Lady Lowell's medical treatment. I couldn't hurt her with the truth. She'd lost her daughter and her sister, and then her husband too. You wouldn't know, but Sir Gerald died from a lung complaint a few months after . . . after we came back to England. Lady Maria devoted herself to Miss North, as Lady Lowell was then. She treats her as her own daughter, even now.'

Mrs Lakatos took a drink of tea, setting her cup back down in its saucer with exaggerated care.

'From your record,' I continued, 'it seems that the then Miss North knew quite well that the story of the carriage accident was just that – a story. At what point did you notice she had begun to believe it?'

'Not until *he* came to London, and did whatever it was he did to her.'

There was no need to ask who *he* might be.

'You didn't talk about what happened in Transylvania between yourselves?'

'Lady Lowell made it quite clear to me that she didn't want to.'

Mrs Lakatos's tone had become rather sharp, so I decided to leave this line of questioning for now.

'Thank you. Moving on—'

'What you really want to ask about is my dreams. Isn't it, doctor?'

'Did you read my thoughts?' I asked, quite seriously.

'No, only your face.'

I took the rebuke with a reasonable amount of grace.

'Yes,' I admitted. 'I know your own abilities might not have an awful lot to do with our case, but it's a new frontier in the study of the human brain and as a student of that science I'm afraid I'm extremely curious.'

'I thought as much.' Mrs Lakatos seemed to be steeling herself. 'My grandmother had the Sight, and it passed to my mother and to me. She thought it was a gift from God, although you'll already know I don't always feel so. I dream of death when someone near to me, or whose death will somehow affect me, is about to die. Sometimes it can be days before, or sometimes as long as months. I knew my da would be lost at sea a fortnight beforehand. That was the first time. I was still a young girl, far too young for such terrible knowledge.'

'Does it happen often?'

'No, thank the Lord.'

'And is it always of a death?'

'Yes.' Mrs Lakatos thought for a moment. 'No, wait. When I was in the hospital in Buda-Pesth, I dreamed of your friend, Mr Harker.

I saw him when they . . . when Mrs Cartwright and the others . . . when they meant to . . .'

I decided that to interrupt her would be a kindness. 'That was why you thought you had met Mr Harker before?'

She nodded. 'Yes, exactly so. But he lived.' Mrs Lakatos frowned a little. 'Are you a religious man, doctor?'

The question startled me, but on reflection it was a logical one.

'I suppose I am, yes, though I am a devotee of science first and foremost.'

'Then you might understand when I tell you that as much as I've struggled with my so-called "gift", I believe that God, or Fate, or some power greater than myself shows me what I need to see. I can only assume this power meant me to see what happened to Mr Harker, as part of bringing us here, now.'

I didn't quite know what to say, so I nodded deeply and made a note.

'That's an interesting perspective. Thank you. Might I move on, and ask about the other aspects of what you call the Sight?'

'If you mean the daytime visions, I didn't have those until I went to Mrs Cartwright's. Touch seems to be the trigger. I'll see times in a person's life of extreme emotion, either past or yet to come. That's more rare than the dreams, and I'm glad of it. As I've grown older I've found I can go looking of my own accord, as my late mother did when she told fortunes, though I can see more than she could. I don't go looking often, though. It's not a nice thing to do, unless someone's asking you to do it.'

I had a flash of realization. 'You saw something when we shook hands in my office, did you not? Did you look at my memories?'

Mrs Lakatos flinched guiltily.

'I'm sorry for intruding, but . . . Doctor, do you know what it is to hope? To hope so deeply for something and for so long that when it comes it feels overwhelming?'

I looked down at the floral carpet. 'I'm not unfamiliar with such an emotion.'

'Then you'll forgive me. It wasn't badly meant. You reacted so strongly to my mention of Transylvania, I had to know. I thought if you'd met the monster then I'd be able to see it, and I'd know you would believe what I had to tell you.'

'I suppose I understand, in the circumstances. Might I ask, what did you see? What, specifically?'

I wanted to know. I needed to know. Mrs Lakatos hesitated, glancing at Dr Knight.

'You may speak freely here,' I assured her, rashly.

'Very well.' Mrs Lakatos took a deep breath. 'I saw a young lady you loved, hopelessly, as she lay dying, murdered by the Count. I saw you give your own lifeblood in trying to save her, and I saw your part in freeing her soul from the vampire state.'

Immediately I wished I had not asked. Both ladies present had read the record, and both knew I had loved a woman, unrequitedly, whom the demon Count had turned into one of his kind. Knowing this did not help. Remembering that she had been freed and now rested peacefully helped a little more, but only a very little.

'After that, I knew you could be trusted. I'm sorry if my mentioning it causes you pain.'

My throat was too dry and choked to speak. I took a gulp of tea, and found it cold. Dr Knight took over the interview to give me time to collect myself.

'Mrs Lakatos, your letters mention you using a plant called "lemon beebrush" to try to reduce these dreams and visions. Sir John's mentor, Professor Van Helsing, has learned that this plant has historically been known for protecting against evil.'

Mrs Lakatos nodded. 'I know that now, but I didn't then. My nana swore by it to help her sleep – she had the dreams too, as you know. It worked well enough for me, most of the time. It might be a sin or it might not, but either way I still drink it. Her ladyship isn't the only one who has nightmares.'

Dr Knight leaned forward.

'If you ever wanted to consult a doctor on your own account, I would be glad to help you. Or I could refer you to a colleague, if you prefer. A person doesn't have to be as ill as Lady Lowell to benefit from medical advice in matters of the mind.'

'That's good of you to offer. I'll think about it.'

'Please do.' Dr Knight sat back, taking up her pen again. 'Now, are you aware that Sir Joseph believes you have some power to calm his wife?'

Mrs Lakatos smiled, just a little, a twitch of one side of her mouth.

'Yes, bless him. He's said such a thing once or twice. I might lay a hand on her arm, or her face, or take her hand, but it's nowt to do with the Sight. It's a matter of trust is all. Not that her ladyship doesn't trust her husband, they were always very attached, but what her ladyship and I endured together creates a bond. A sad one, but one that never goes away, whether we speak of what happened or not.'

I found myself nodding, thinking of Harker, Van Helsing, Lord Godalming and the late Quincey Morris. We were all bound in the same way, having fought the Count to the last.

'I see,' Dr Knight was saying. 'Yes, it did seem to be at variance with what we already knew. You mentioned earlier that both your mother and grandmother had this gift. Might I ask if your own children also possess it?'

'My grandmother had the dreams. My mother had the visions. My children have neither.'

Mrs Lakatos held Dr Knight's gaze, clear and open. She's rehearsed this, I thought to myself. She knew we would ask, and she has no intention of telling us.

Dr Knight seemed to sense this too.

'That's as well, then, I'm sure. It must have been difficult for you as a child, and then of course as a young woman, always wondering if the Count was going to return.'

Mrs Lakatos's hand went to her throat, the same gesture I'd seen when I first met Lady Lowell. She had been bitten too, I remembered, and she would also have borne the scars until Count Dracula's death.

'Yes. When he did, I was at a women's hospital in the countryside, about to have my second child. I'd not been well, and her ladyship insisted.' She looked down at her hands. 'I wasn't there to protect her.'

'Mrs Lakatos,' I said gently, 'if you had been, it would have been much the worse for you, and for your child.'

'That's what I tell myself in the dark hours, but you don't get over the guilt of such a thing. I'd spent years reading newspapers from all across Europe, constantly searching for hints that he was coming. I went nights without the lemon beebrush, welcoming all the terrible sights that Heaven could send so I might be ready. And when he did come, I was too far away and too ill to do a thing about it. I can't help but blame myself.'

'No!' My voice was shockingly loud in this hushed and ladylike den. 'No,' I said again, at a more reasonable volume. 'It is all *his* fault. The vampire is the author of all this suffering, and no one else bears any blame for it at all. Not you, not me, not any one of the other poor souls touched by his evil.'

'My husband has been telling me that for almost twenty years.'

'He's a wise man.'

'He is, and a good one too.' Mrs Lakatos looked down at her hands, clenched into fists. 'Now, Sir John, if you wouldn't mind, all this has been exhausting.'

'I quite understand. I would only say one last thing, if I may.' She nodded.

'I have a plan for how we might help Lady Lowell. It seems to me that a part of her mind is continuously reliving the moment at which she stood up against the vampires, in particular against the woman she loved. If we can move her unconscious past that moment and past the feelings of guilt and betrayal and grief that surround it, then we have a fighting chance. It will be a hundred times easier to break down the false memory when there is another person on hand who can validate the truth as it emerges. Will you do that, Mrs Lakatos?'

'We do understand that it may be quite difficult for you,' Dr Knight interjected. 'If you do not feel able, you are within your rights to refuse.'

'I'll do anything you need me to do,' Mrs Lakatos said, almost before Dr Knight had finished speaking. 'Anything at all.'

'I should warn you that her ladyship may get worse before she gets better. It is as if she has a wound that has festered and must be drained, which will not be pleasant.'

'If it's her best chance of being healed, doctor, then we should do it.'

I looked at this determined woman, who had already spent many years caring for her friend. I could see how much she meant what she said.

There was more I might have said, more I might have asked, but I could not in good conscience push further. Perhaps there would be other opportunities in the future. I thanked her and made my goodbyes, then went for the hansom while Dr Knight remained behind to wait in the stuffy warmth.

I found our driver at the cab stand by the market cross, warming his hands with a cup of soup and his heart with the flirting kitchen maid who had brought his repast from a nearby inn. I was loath to break up the scene. I resolved to tip the driver extra to take the girl dancing.

As the hansom drew up outside the cottage, Dr Knight was making her way down the path. Her cheeks were a surprisingly vivid pink in the cold.

'Don't forget what I said!' Mrs Lakatos called to her from the doorway.

'I hardly think I'm likely to,' Dr Knight answered, waving.

'What was that about?' I asked as I handed her in.

'Oh,' she said as she settled herself under the travelling rug. 'Just women's things.'

I wonder what she meant by that?

Sir John Seward's personal diary
Friday, 27th February 1903
Littlemore Hospital, Oxfordshire

The sun shone gloriously today. All afternoon I found myself ignoring the case notes in front of me in favour of gazing out of my window at the view of the fields. I was in the middle of one such reverie when Dr Knight knocked on my door.

'Do you have a moment?'

The early evening light caught her hair in just such a way as to make it look aflame. The grey outfit that is her professional uniform only emphasized the colour. I was so entranced that it took me an impolite amount of time to answer.

'Yes of course. Would you like to get some fresh air? It's a beautiful day, and I feel I need to stretch my legs.'

'Why not? Let me fetch my coat.'

Outside we made our way around the building, past the patients' garden and out into the walks frequented only by staff. At this hour, with the sun beginning to set, we were quite alone.

'You were right, this is refreshing,' Dr Knight said as we strolled along.

'Yes, it's a pleasant time of day for it.'

Inwardly I cursed myself for such an inane comment, the sort of thing one might say to a stranger, or a passing acquaintance. We had not been alone much without the distraction of a case since Harker had so pointedly commented on my feelings for my colleague.

'I've been thinking about Lady Lowell,' I said, in order to provide myself with that very distraction.

'As have I,' Dr Knight agreed. 'While I'm hesitant to suggest further hypnosis, given what happened last time, a very light hypnotic trance might help the patient to stay calm during each session.'

'Why Dr Knight, you *are* a Freudian!'

I meant my manner to be a joking one, but Dr Knight gave me quite a serious look.

'Professor Freud and I have corresponded on several occasions and whilst I do not always agree with him, some of his work on memory is highly relevant here.'

I had wondered briefly about Dr Knight's 'friend in Vienna', but I had never considered that it might be the illustrious professor himself. Goodness.

'It's something to consider,' I said, attempting to be conciliatory, 'especially if our proposed talking therapy proves more challenging than we hope. I'd prefer it to pharmaceutical—'

'Sir John, I have something to tell you.' Her serious expression caused my words to die on my tongue.

'What is it? Is it bad news? Are you not well?'

'Oh, no, nothing like that. I am quite well.' She stopped so sharply that I went on a step or two without her. I turned and found her biting her lip. 'I have decided to leave Littlemore. I have an offer of another position, and I must give you my resignation.'

'You're leaving?' I repeated, stupidly.

'Yes. I've taken up a teaching post.'

I was stunned.

'A teaching post? Beatrice, why? You're needed in clinical practice, you're brilliant! Your methods, your experimental ideas, your experience – they're irreplaceable! You're the most talented colleague I've ever had! I beg you to reconsider.'

It was all true, every word of it, but that doesn't excuse my base selfishness. The long, lonely days I had ahead of me without her seemed to stretch into infinity.

'I have to do this. I am so protected here, so respected, while the next generation of female physicians suffer with few in authority who truly believe them to be capable. These young women are crying out for teachers who will acknowledge that they possess the same capacity as their male peers, and who will allow them to study in a lecture hall free from prejudice.'

I looked away, afraid of what I might say if I met her eye.

'Oh, damn it all!' she said, clenching her fists in frustration. 'That was all very true and very important, but it isn't the only reason that I need to leave. I can't work for you any more, John, and if you don't know why then you're not the great student of the human mind that everyone believes you to be.'

If it were possible for a man to die of shame, then I would surely have done so in that instant. She knew, I thought, she knew and she felt she had no other way to escape my disgraceful clutches.

'Dr Knight, I can't apologize enough. I had no idea that you were aware of my feelings towards you. To think that I have driven you away with my unprofessional behaviour, even behaviour of which I was not consciously aware, mortifies me beyond words. I respect your decision, and I am deeply sorry about the reason for it. Please rest assured that I will give you the spectacular reference that you deserve, and will no longer presume upon you in any way. If you prefer, I will resign my post and leave at once.'

I finished my gabbling and turned to go, determined to march away, head held high, from the terrible situation I had created. If I could only reach my house I could lock myself in my study, pour myself a stiff drink, and get started on drowning this shame in a tide of whisky.

'That was a wonderful speech,' Dr Knight said, 'but you have quite the wrong end of the stick.'

I stood mute, nonplussed, still yearning quite forcefully for the ground to open up and swallow me.

'You have never, ever behaved incorrectly. How could you think such things of yourself? You're one of the most moral and upstanding people I have ever had the good fortune to know.'

'I . . . am?'

'John, I'm trying to tell you that it's for the sake of my *own* feelings that I must leave.'

'Your own feelings?' Slowly, embarrassingly slowly, I began to grasp her implication. 'Beatrice! Do you really mean it?'

She smiled broadly. 'I do.'

'But you're leaving, you'll be far away—'

'I never said that. The teaching post is at Somerville College.'

'In Oxford!'

'Unless you know of another Somerville College.'

My world had turned from the bleakest darkness to the most celestial illumination in the span of a handful of minutes. Beatrice would no longer be in my employ. There could be no impropriety in anything not in itself improper.

'Although,' she continued, 'I hope you'll still allow me to consult on cases of special interest. Lady Lowell's in particular. I would hate for Littlemore to lose all the glowing light of my brilliance.'

Her raised eyebrow and gently mocking tone made me laugh out loud.

'Of course, anything you like.'

'Really? Anything I like?'

'Anything, darling,' I said, with all the repressed feelings of the recent months finally given voice.

'Well,' she said as we began our return journey, tucking her hand in the crook of my arm, 'it seems that you and I are suffering from the same common kind of madness.'

I screwed my courage to the sticking place, and named it. 'Love has indeed long been considered so.'

'In which case, I would like to prescribe a sustained regimen of long walks, candlelit dinners, boating adventures, and the writing of heartfelt letters to the poor sufferers. What do you think?'

'I agree entirely,' I said, 'though how long did that course of treatment ought to be sustained? I'd rather ask the pertinent question now, this very minute.'

This was completely true. I'd have got down on one knee then and there if I thought her enough of a romantic to say yes at once.

'Now, John, we've only known each other a short time. I'd say we need at least a year for our therapeutic programme. We're too far past youth to be anything but sensible.'

'A year? Come now, I'm certain you will only improve upon further acquaintance.'

'How can you be so sure? I might be quite the harpy. No, it's only fair for you to discover all my terrible flaws and habits before making any lasting decisions.'

I kissed her then, as the setting sun shone obligingly gold, and the evening birdsong played from the treetops.

'I can hardly wait.'

EPILOGUE

It is twenty-one years since I last opened this journal. I am grateful to Alice for having kept it safe for so long. I have been reading over my writings from that time, and if I did not know them to be in my own hand I would hardly credit it that this young woman was once myself. Sir John has worked so tirelessly to make me whole again, and has returned such precious memories to me that I could not pay him back if I were to live a hundred lifetimes. And yet, I am so changed I hardly know the person who filled this book with her observations and her sensibilities.

My husband is the one who encouraged me to take up my pen, and he watches me now from across the wrought-iron patio table while pretending to read his newspaper. He insists that I must do it for my own benefit. Sir John has told him it will help to train my mind to remember things as it ought, and indeed my memories do sometimes have a habit of shifting like sands and hiding from me when I search for them. The good doctor tells me as time goes on this will improve, especially if I make sure to write as often as possible. Neither man wishes to read what I write, which gives me the freedom of glorious honesty. Nevertheless, I have chosen to write in a language which neither of them knows, just in case.

I suppose I ought to record this domestic scene, on this early summer day in our elegant walled garden, planted to dear Maria's taste. I will go and visit her later, at the dower house across the stream. I will take her some orchids from the hothouse or perhaps some garlic flowers, which I grow in their hundreds. Looking up, I see I have lost Joseph's attention as he gazes out across the lawn to where our daughter Maud walks here and there with the gardener, asking questions and making notes. She has a passion for all growing things, encouraged by Maria at every step, and has even begun to talk of studying at a university. I have a mother's natural concerns, of course, but also a mother's pride in my intelligent, determined child. If she wishes it, it will come to pass. Our son Gerald, our eldest, lives in Whitby at present. There he is learning all he must about the Lowell shipping enterprise which my husband founded, and which Mátyás Lakatos now oversees. Gerald has formed quite an attachment to Beth Gregor, dear Eliza's sister, who remained with the poor ailing Colonel until he passed away. She is a good girl, and I would love to see it settled between them.

I missed so much of my children's lives. When I first came home I feared that I would be a stranger to them, or worse, that they would be afraid of me. I thank God it was not so. They did not remember me well, but between their father and 'Aunt Alice', they had been raised to love such memories as they possessed, and so loved me with a greater fierceness than I had ever dared to dream was possible.

This is all my family, now. My half-brothers still live, but I do not know them. My husband contacted them on my behalf, years ago, but they have taken after my father and are not people whose company I choose to subject myself to. I can only assume I learned such self-assurance from my Mafalda, and it pleases me to think so.

The girl I was when I first began this journal would, I think, be confused or even displeased by the situation in which I find myself. A mother? And worse, a wife? It is true that I do not love my husband as I loved Mafalda. I am not capable of it. How could I love another, man or woman, after her? But I do care for Joseph. Truly, I do. I am no half-wife, turning my eyes elsewhere. In our shared grief at the loss of Mafalda we found solace in each other, compounded when Sir Gerald followed not long after. By that time, I was no longer the determined young woman I had been, with plans to earn my own crust and make my own path. I was exhausted. I was in pain. I was heartbroken. When Joseph offered me his hand, I felt the only thing I could do was take it. We are much alike, he and I, in that we were both to some degree abandoned, and the Lowells took us in when we had no other family who gave us much thought. I love my husband as the good and steadfast friend he has been almost all my life, even when I was too blind with jealousy to see it. I am hardly the first woman to accept a man on terms other than romantic love. Besides, I love my children, though that is in itself no virtue, and I cannot and will not regret the choices I made by which they were brought into this world.

I hope that Mafalda would understand. I see her everywhere, even now. I see her in the green eyes of my son and my daughter, in the turns of phrase that come unthinking to my lips, in the sometimes sideways glances of my husband. When I look heavenward, I picture her face. Her eyes sparkle, her smile tilts upwards on one side, her dark brows rise in affectionate mockery. She laughs, tosses her hair, blows me a kiss and calls me a fool, and I go on loving her, as I always will.

Yet, somehow, the business of life goes on. Alice and Mátyás are to come down from Yorkshire tomorrow. They are planning to arrive on the same train as Gerald. They will all stay the night here at Beechwood, and then we will travel to Oxford for the wedding on Saturday. Sir John and Dr Knight are to be married at the Church of St Mary and St Nicholas, and Alice is quite beside herself with excitement. To hear her tell it, she made the match herself with an opportune word to Dr Knight, though I believe it took Sir John some while before he formally asked for her hand. I see why. Dr Knight is quite the modern woman, and would make a lesser man quake in his boots. I know they will be very happy together, although I imagine dinner conversation in their house will revolve entirely around patients and treatments and case notes. Well, to each their own.

I admit, I do have some trepidation. Among the wedding guests will be the survivors of that band of brothers who finally ended Count Dracula, including one Professor Van Helsing who sent my friends and my beloved into the afterlife. I read his testimony, which Sir John so kindly shared with me when I was well enough, and I wept long over it. I understand that killing such undead creatures is by necessity a brutal act, and if the only path to salvation lies through the use of the wooden stake and the great carving knife then what else is there to be done? I choose not to think of the manner of their final deaths, only that thanks to this man, Eliza, Réka, and my Mafalda found that peace 'that passeth all understanding', and were released from their cursed state. Perhaps I will see this professor and hate him, but I hope not. I hope I can find it within me to feel only gratitude.

Unlike the others, Mafalda made a choice and, at the last, knew it to have been the wrong one. She made it, at least in part, for me, that we might continue together free from the constraints of the world. If only she had spoken to me of it, that I might have dissuaded her! No, no, Sir John says such thoughts are unhelpful to my recovery, and he is quite right. The truth is, this Professor Van Helsing freed my Mafalda from her undead existence, and thus helped to free my mind from the unconscious torment of supposing her still confined and still profaned. If only there were a hundred, or a thousand such men, to release those who are yet damned!

Sir John believes humanity preserved, that with the death of the sire the unholy offspring must surely follow him to dust. How, when he has no evidence for it, can he be sure that it is so? And he a man of science! Has he never seen the impossibly pale face in a crowd, or the flash of crimson in the eyes of a stranger? Has he never felt the pricking of the hairs on the back of the neck, the gift of that other sense that tells us when we are preyed upon?

I do not press the issue. Not now, not yet. I grow my garlic flowers, I drink Alice's beebrush tea, I sleep with my peasant rosary in my fist, and I pray. And I wait.

ACKNOWLEDGEMENTS

Humans love to embellish and reimagine our favourite stories. In the one hundred and twenty-nine years since Bram Stoker's *Dracula* was published an entire genre has grown up around its titular villain, but it wasn't the only popular vampire tale in the nineteenth century. To name a couple of big hitters, Sheridan Le Fanu's novella *Carmilla* had been published in 1872, and John Polidori's *The Vampyre*, which Lucy North enjoys on the train to Paris, came out to some acclaim in 1819 (mostly because Lord Byron was believed to be the author). Nevertheless, it's *Dracula* which became, and remained, a cultural touchstone. It's as foundational and recognizable as a Grimm's fairy tale or a Shakespeare play, and just as ripe for continued and continual reinterpretation.

Having said all that, when the idea for this book showed up in my brain on a Sunday afternoon in October 2019, I felt a little bit ashamed of my own arrogance. Who was I, who had never even managed to complete a novel let alone publish one, to think I had anything to add to the world that Stoker created? What on earth was I doing tapping away on my laptop, putting words into the mouth of the most famous fictional vampire, while the world fell to pieces? I'm still not sure I can answer that question; all I know is that once I started, I couldn't stop.

During the pandemic, which I spent with my partner in our flat in the village-turned-Oxford-suburb of Littlemore, I signed up for the Oxford University Department of Continuing Education's Advanced Creative Writing course. I owe course leader Elizabeth Garner a huge debt of gratitude for her wisdom, her well-thought-out classes, and her feedback which managed to be both challenging and uplifting at the same time. I'd also like to thank the rest of the class of 2021. It's hard as a novice writer to take yourself seriously, but we took *each other* seriously and that made all the difference.

I am fortunate to have a wonderful set of friends who volunteered to read *The Brides* in its earliest forms. To Rachel Moriarty and Drew Stanley, who read it as an old-fashioned serial when even I wasn't quite sure what was going to happen next, thank you for your comments, your encouragement, and most of all your patience. *The Brides* wouldn't exist without you. Rachel, your emotional support over the last six years while I've been completely losing my marbles over this book should get you some kind of award. To Bethan Richards, Natasha Harding, and Christine Velarde, who read it as a first (and second, and third) draft, thank you for giving me the feedback which helped turn *The Brides* into what it became, i.e. an awful lot better. Let's never speak of that first draft again.

After a great deal of editing and a few months in the query trenches, *The Brides* finally reached the wonderful Francesca Riccardi at the Kate Nash Literary Agency. I am deeply grateful for her belief in this book, and her quite literally tireless efforts to get it in front of the right people. Francesca, you are fantastic and all writers deserve an agent like you.

Speaking of the right people, I am truly fortunate to get to work with my editor, Sophie Robinson at Tor. From our very first Zoom call, she made it clear how much she loved *The Brides*. She has guided it through every stage of the publishing process with great care, and with a deep understanding of how to help it be all that it can be. Sophie, your consistent encouragement to give the book *more* – more dread, more intensity, more of everything I most love to write – made the notoriously challenging editing experience genuinely fun. Thank you so much.

I would also like to thank Grace Barber, Kate Tolley, and all the other staff at Tor who have put so much effort into bringing this book into the world, and who I've been so privileged to work with. Particular thanks are definitely due to copyeditor Hayley Shepherd, without whose fact-checking I would have publicly embarrassed myself in many and varied ways. Thank you, Hayley!

On a more personal note I have to thank my parents, Jo and Peter Cross. They did, after all, teach me how to read in the first place which has been a big help and, it turns out, something of a liability. They have also been recommending this book left, right, and centre to everyone they know, which I hope doesn't cost them any friends and get them cut off from the family without a Christmas pudding. Mum, Dad, when you read this, maybe skip the gory bits.

Without my partner, Trev Pack, *The Brides* would been no more than a random passing thought. Trev helped me with plotting when I repeatedly plotted myself into a corner, advised me on Yorkshire accents and dialect, and, above all, cheered me on when I needed it most. His continuing and unshakeable faith that this book would eventually become Something has meant the world to me. Trev, I love you. Thank you for keeping me moderately sane, and, most importantly, for making the vast majority of dinners I've eaten since I started work on this book.

I must also thank Hamish, my feline morale officer, who naps supportively in my vicinity while I write, and who sits on my laptop when he thinks I need to take a break. Good boy, Hamish. I even gave you a little cameo in Part Nine to show my appreciation. Now if you could please stop interrupting me while I write my acknowledgements, that would be very helpful.

Finally I would like to thank you, Reader. Thank you for taking a chance on a debut novel, and please forgive me all the artistic license I've taken with history, geography, and vampire lore. I hope that you enjoyed *The Brides*, and I hope that you remember its warning when you feel the pricking of the hairs on the back of your neck, or see the flash of crimson in the eyes of a stranger.

ABOUT THE AUTHOR

Charlotte Cross writes historical fiction, having been fascinated by stories of the past since she was a child. She grew up in southern England in a small town with a rich history, and spent many happy hours at the local museum where her grandmother was a volunteer. Charlotte now lives in central Scotland with her partner and their opinionated ginger cat. When not writing, she enjoys yoga, reading Victorian novels and exploring her adopted country. *The Brides* is her first novel.